Abou

Georgette Heyer novels
tastes as a teenager. But her writing life only started when
she was given a pile of Mills & Boons to read after she
had had her wisdom teeth extracted! Filled with strong
painkillers, she imagined that she could pen one, too.
Many drafts later, Sophia thinks she has the perfect job
writing for Mills & Boon Historical as well as taking art
tours to Europe with her husband, who is a painter.

Regency Rebels

Regency Rebels:

A Dangerous Engagement

SOPHIA JAMES

MILLS & BOON

First Published in Great Britain 2024
By Mills & Boon, an imprint of HarperCollins*Publishers* Ltd,
1 London Bridge Street, London, SE1 9GF

www.harpercollins.co.uk

HarperCollins*Publishers*
Macken House, 39/40 Mayor Street Upper,
Dublin 1, D01 C9W8, Ireland

ISBN: 978-0-263-32317-7

MIX
Paper | Supporting
responsible forestry
FSC™ C007454

MARRIAGE MADE IN REBELLION

Chapter One

The English declare they will no longer respect
neutrals on the sea; I will no longer recognise
them on land.

                    Napoleon Bonaparte

A Coruña, Spain—January 16th, 1809

Captain Lucien Howard, the Earl of Ross, thought
his nose was broken. His neck, too, probably, because
he couldn't move it at all. His horse lay upon him, her
head bent sideways and liquid-brown eyes empty of
life. A good mare she was, one that had brought him
up the hard road from Lisboa through the snows of
the Cantabrian Mountains and the slippery passways
of mud and sleet. He swore silently and looked away.

It hurt to breathe, a worrying thought that, given
the distance from any medical help. Another day and
Napoleon and his generals would be all over the harbour. It was finished and the British had lost, the

harsh winter eating into what was left of resistance and a mix-up with the ocean transports in from the southern port of Vigo.

God, if he wasn't so badly hurt, he might have laughed, but the movement would have most likely killed him. It was so damn cold, his breath fogging as he fought for what little air he could drag in, but a mist had come up from the sea to mingle with the smoke of battle hanging thick across the valley.

Lucien was not afraid of death. It was the dying that worried him, the length and the breadth of it and the helplessness.

Lying back, he looked up into the heavens, hoping that it would be quick. He couldn't pray; that sort of hope was long since past and had been for a while now. He could not even find the words to ask for forgiveness or penance. He had killed men, good and bad, in the name of king and country, but once one saw the whites of an enemy's eyes, the old troths and promises held less sway than they once had.

A man was a man whatever language he spoke and more often than not a family would be waiting at home for their return. As his was. That thought sent a shaft of pain through the greater ache, but, resolving not to die with tears in his eyes, Lucien willed it away.

It was late, that much he did know, the sun deep on the horizon and only a little left of the day. He could see the lights of resin torches further away along the lines of the olive trees and the aloe hedges, searching for those who still lived. He could not summon the strength to call out as he lay there, a rough stone wall to one side and an old garden of sorts on the other.

Lucien imagined he could smell orange blossoms and wild flowers, but that was surely wrong. He wondered about the warmth that he felt as the peace of a contrition he long since should have made came unexpectedly.

'Forgive me, Jesus, for I have sinned.' Not so hard now in the final moments of his life. He smiled. No, not so hard at all.

The English soldier was covered in the blood of his horse, the residual warmth left in the large animal's pelt saving him, allowing him life in the frigid cold dark dawn of a Galician January winter.

But not for long; his blond hair was pinked in a puddle of blood beneath his head and a wound at his neck wept more. The daybreak was sending its first light across the sky and as far as the eye could see there were bodies. English and French, she thought, entwined in death like friends. Only the generals could have imagined that such a sacrifice was worth it, the prime of each country gone before they had ever had the chance to live. She cursed out loud against the futility of war and removed the gold signet ring from the soldier's finger to give to her father.

When his eyes flicked open the pale in them was startling in the early-morning light, almost seethrough.

'Not...dead...yet?' There was disappointment and resignation in the broken question phrased in Spanish.

'What hurts?'

He smiled. 'What…does…not?'

The wide planes of his cheeks were bruised and his lip was badly cut, but even with the marks of war drawn from one end of him to the other he was beautiful; too beautiful to just die here unheralded and forgotten. Anger fortified resolve and she slashed at the gorse to one side of him, using the cleared ground to stand upon.

With space she pried a broken stake from a fence under his mount's neck and managed to lift it up enough, twisting the carcass so that it fell away from him, swirls of mud staining the air.

He groaned, the noise one makes involuntarily when great pain breaks through a consciousness that cannot quite contain it.

'Scream away, Ingles, if you will,' she told him. 'I most certainly would. Your friends have been evacuated by way of the sea and the French are in charge of the township itself, so nobody at all should hear you.'

My God, how tired she was of iron wills and masculine stoicism. Death was a for ever thing and if men taking their last breaths in a land far from their own could not weep for the sacrifice, then who else should?

Not her. Not her father. Not the officers safe with their horses on the transports home across a wild and stormy Biscay Bay. Other steeds roamed the streets of A Coruña, looking for succour, their more numerous and unluckier counterparts dead beneath the cliffs overhanging the beach, throats cut in clumsy acts of kindness.

Better dead than at the mercy of the enemy. Once she might have even believed that truism. Now she failed to trust in anything or anyone. The fury within alarmed her at times, but mostly she did not think on it. Adan and Bartolomeu had joined her now, their canvas stretcher pulled in.

'You want us to take him back?'

She nodded. 'Careful how you lift him.'

As Tomeu crouched down he scratched at a muddied epaulette. 'He's a *capitán*.' The tinged gold was undeniable and her heart sank. Her father had begun to be uncertain of a Spanish triumph and was distancing himself from the politics of the region. An officer would be less welcome than a simple soldier to Enrique. More complex. Harder to explain.

'Then we need to make sure he recovers to fight again for our cause.'

For some reason the man before her was beginning to mean something. A portent to victory or a prophecy of failure? She could not tell. All she did know was that the damaged fingers of his left hand had curled into her own, seeking comfort, and that despite all intentions to do otherwise she held them close, trying to bring warmth to his freezing skin.

He groaned again when they rolled him on to the canvas and she got the first glimpse of the wounds on his upper back, the fabric of his shirt shredded into slivers and the flesh hanging off him between it.

More than one sword had been used, she thought,

and there had been a good deal of hatred in the action. The blood loss was making him shake, so she shrugged off her woollen poncho and laid it across him, tucking it in beneath his chin.

Tomeu looked up with a frown. 'Why bother? He will die anyway.' The hard words of truth that she did not want, though there was anger in his tone, too. 'They come and they go. In the end it's all the same. Death eats them up.'

'*Padre Nuestro que estás en los cielos...*' She recited the Lord's Prayer beneath her breath and draped the ornate rosary across him in protection as they started for home.

The same lad on the fields was beside him again, sitting asleep on a chair, a hat pulled down over his face. Lucien shook his head against the chills that were consuming him and wondered where the hell he was. Not on the battlefields, not on the transports home, either, and this certainly was not hell given the crisp cotton sheets and warm woollen blanket.

Tipping his head, he tried to listen to the cadence of someone speaking far away outside. Spanish. He was certain of it. The heavy beams and whitewashed walls told him this house was also somewhere in the Iberian Peninsula and that whoever owned it was more than wealthy.

His eyes flicked back to the lad. Young. Thin. A working boy. Lucien could not quite understand what he would be doing here. Why was he not labouring somewhere or helping with one of the many things that would need attention on a large and busy hacienda? What master would allow him simply to sit in a sickroom whiling away the hours?

His glance caught the skin of an ankle above a weathered and scuffed boot, though at that very moment deep green eyes opened, a look of interest within them.

'You are awake?'

A dialect of León, but with an inflection that he didn't recognise.

'Where am I?' He answered in the same way and saw surprise on the lad's brow.

'Safe.' Uttered after a few seconds of thought.

'How long…here?'

'Three days. You were found on the battlefield above A Coruña the morning after the English had departed by way of the sea.'

'And the French?'

'Most assuredly are enjoying the spoils of war. Soult has come into the town with his army under Napoleon's orders, I suppose. There are many of them.'

'God.'

At that the lad crossed himself, the small movement caught by the candlelight a direct result of his profanity.

'Who are you?' This question was almost whispered.

'Captain Howard of the Eighteenth Light Dragoons. Do you have any news of the English general Sir John Moore?'

'They buried him at night on the high ground close

to the ramparts of the Citadel. It is told he died well with his officers around him. A cannon shot to the chest.'

Pain laced through Lucien. 'How do you know this?'

'This is our land, Capitán. The town is situated less than three miles from where we are and there is little that happens in the region that we are not aware of.'

'We.'

The silence was telling.

'You are part of the guerrilla movement? One of El Vengador's minions? This is his area of jurisdiction, is it not?'

The boy ignored that and gave a question of his own. 'Where did you learn your Spanish?'

'Five months in Spain brings its rewards.'

'But not such fluency.' The inflection of disbelief was audible.

'I listen well.'

In the shadows of a slender throat Lucien saw the pulse quicken and a hand curl to a fist. A broken nail and the remains of a wound across the thumb. Old injuries. Fragile fingers. Delicate. Tentative. Left-handed. There was always so much to learn from the small movements.

She was scared of him.

The pronoun leapt into a life of its own. It was the ankles, he was to think later, and the utter thinness of her arms.

'Who are you, *señorita*?'

She stood at that, widening one palm across the

skin on his neck and pressing down. 'If you say one word of these thoughts to anyone else, you will be dead, *desconocido*, before you have the chance to finish your sentence. Do you understand?'

He looked around. The door was closed and the walls were thick. 'You did not…save my life…to kill me…now.'

He hoped he was right, because there was no more breath left. When she let him go he hated the relief he felt as air filled his lungs. To care so much about living made him vulnerable.

'The others will not be so lenient of your conjectures were you to utter them carelessly and everybody here would protect me with their life.'

He nodded and looked away from the uneasy depths of green.

'I take it, then, that you are the daughter of this house.' He had changed his accent now into a courtly High Castilian and saw her stiffen, but she did not answer and was gone before he could say another word.

Who the hell was he, this stranger with the pale blue eyes that saw everything, his hair like spun gold silk and a body marked by war?

No simple soldier, that much was certain. The Light Dragoons had fought with Paget out of San Cristobel and yet he had been found east of Piedralonga, a good two miles away under Hope's jurisdiction. She frowned in uncertainty.

Captain Howard had spoken in the León dialect and then in the Castilian, easily switching. A changeling who could be dangerous to them all and it was she who had brought him here. She should say something of the worrying contradictions to her father and the others. She should order him removed and left far from the hacienda to fend for himself. But instead…

Instead she walked to the windows of her room and looked out across the darkness to the sea beyond. There was something about this *capitán* that she recognised in herself. An interloper isolated from others and surrounded by danger. He did not show fear, either, for when she had taken the air from his windpipe with her hands he had not fought her. But waited. As if he had known she would let go.

Cursing, she pulled the shutters in closed against the night.

Lucien lay awake and listened. To the gentle swish of a servant's skirt and then the harder steps of someone dousing the lights outside. A corridor by the sounds of it and open to the sea. When his rescuer passed without he had smelt the salt and heard the waves crashing against the shore. Three miles she had said to A Coruña and yet here the sea was closer, a mile at the most and less if the wind drew from the north as it had done three days ago. Now the breeze was lighter for there was no sound at all against the wood of the shutters. Heavy locks pulled the coverings together in three places and with a patina of age Lucien knew these to be old bindings. To one side of the thick lintels of double-sashed windows he saw scratches in the limewash over stone, lines carefully kept in groups. Days of the week? Hours of a day? Months of a year? He could not quite make them out from this distance.

Why had these been left there? A servant could have been ordered to cover them in the matter of a few moments; a quick swish of thick plaster and they would have been gone.

A Bible sat on a small wooden table next to his bed under an ornate golden cross and beside a bronze statue of Jesus with his crown of thorns.

Catholic and devout.

Lucien felt akin to the battered Christ, as his neck ached and sharp pains raked up his back. The sword wounds from the French as he had tried to ride in behind the ranks of General Hope. He was hot now, the pins and needles of fever in his hands, and his front tooth ached badly, but he was too tired to bring his arm up enough to touch the damage. He wished the thin girl would come back to give him some more water and sit near him, but only the silence held court.

She returned in the morning, before the silver dawn had changed to day, and this time she brought others.

The man beside her was nearing fifty, Lucien imagined, a big man wearing the flaring scarlet-and-light-blue jacket of an Estramaduran hussar. Two younger men accompanied him.

'I am Señor Enrique Fernandez y Castro, otherwise known as El Vengador, Capitán. It seems you have heard of me?'

Lucien sized up the hard dark eyes and the generous moustache of the guerrilla leader. A man of consequence in these parts and feared because of it. He looked nothing at all like his daughter.

'If the English soldiers do not return, there will be little hope for the Spanish cause, Capitán.' High Castilian. There was no undercurrent of any lesser dialect in his speech but the pure and arrogant notes of aristocracy.

Lucien was honest in his own appraisal of the situation. 'Well, the Spanish generals have done themselves no favour, *señor*, and it's lucky the French are in such disorder. If Napoleon himself had taken the trouble to be in the Iberian Peninsula, instead of leaving it to his brother, I doubt anything would be left.'

The older man swore. 'Spain has no use for men who usurp a crown and the royal Bourbons are powerless to fight back. It is only the likes of the partisans that will throw the French from España, for the army, too, is useless in its fractured purpose.'

Privately Lucien agreed, but he did not say so. The *juntas* were splintered and largely ineffective. John Moore and the British expeditionary force had found that out the hard way, the promise of a Spanish force of men never eventuating, but sliding away into quarrel.

The girl was listening intently, her eyes wary beneath the rim of the same cap she had worn each time he had seen her. Today the jacket was different, though. Something stolen from an English foot soldier, he guessed, the scarlet suiting her tone of skin. He flipped his glance from her as quickly as it settled. She had given him her warnings already and he owed her that much.

The older man moved back, the glint of metal in his leather belt. 'Soult and Ney are trampling over the north as we speak, but the south is still free.'

'Because the British expeditionary forces dragged any opposition up here with them as they came.'

'Perhaps,' the other man agreed, dark eyes thoughtful. 'How is it you know our language so well?'

'I was in Dominica for a number of years before coming to Madeira.'

'The dialects would be different.' The room was still, waiting, a sense of menace and distrust covering politeness.

For the first time in days Lucien smiled. 'Every tutor I had said I was gifted in hearing the cadence of words and I have been in Spain for a while.'

'Why were you found behind the English lines? The Eighteenth Dragoons were miles away. Why were you not there with them?'

'I was scouting the ocean for the British transports under the direction of General Moore. They were late coming into the harbour and he was worried.'

'A spy, then.'

'I myself prefer the title of intelligence officer.'

'Semantics.' The older man laughed, though, and the tension lessened.

When Lucien chanced a look at the girl he saw she watched him with a frown across her brow. Today there was a bruise on her left cheek that was darkening into purple. It had not been there yesterday.

Undercurrents.

The older man was not pleased by Lucien's presence in the house and the Catalan *escopeta* in his cartouche belt was close. One wrong word could decide Lucien's fate. He stayed silent whilst he tried to weigh up his options and he listened as the other man spoke.

'Every man and woman in Spain is armed with a flask of poison, a garrotting cord or a knife. Napoleon is not the liberator here and his troops will not triumph. The Treaty of Tilsit was his star as its zenith, but now the power and the glory have begun to fade. *C'est le commencement de la fin*, Capitán, and the French know it.'

'Something Talleyrand said, I think? Hopefully prophetic.' Lucien had heard rumours that the crafty French bishop was seeking to negotiate a secure peace behind his emperor's back so as to perpetuate and solidify the gains made during the French revolution.

El Vengador stepped forward. 'You are well informed. But our channels of intelligence are healthy, too, and one must watch what one utters to a stranger, would you not agree, Capitán? Best to hold your secrets close.'

And your enemies closer? A warning masked beneath the cloth of politics? Simple. Intimidating. Lucien resisted any urge to once again glance at his rescuer in the corner.

He nodded without candour and was relieved as the other man moved back.

'You will be sent by boat to England. Tomeu will take you. But I would ask something of you before you leave us. Your rank will allow you access to the higher echelons of the English military and we need to know the intentions of the British parliament's actions against the French here in Spain. Someone will contact you wearing this.' He brought a ruby brooch out of his pocket to show him, the gem substantial and the gold catching the light. 'Any information you can gather would be helpful. Sometimes it is the very smallest of facts that can make a difference.'

And with that he was gone, leaving his daughter behind as the others departed with him.

'He trusts you.' Her words came quietly. 'He would not have let this meeting run on for as long as it has if he did not.'

'He knows I know about...?' One hand gestured towards her.

'That I am a girl? Indeed. Did you not hear his warning?'

'Then why did he leave you here? Now?'

At that she laughed. 'You cannot guess, Capitán?' Her green eyes glittered with the look of one who knew her worth. To the cause. To her father. To the machinations of a guerrilla movement whose very lifeblood depended on good information and loyal carriers.

'Hell. It is you he will send?'

'A woman can move in many circles that a man cannot.' There was challenge in her words as she lifted her chin and the swollen mark on her cheek was easier to see.

'Who hit you?'

'In a place of war, emotions can run high.'

For the first time in his company she blushed and he caught her left hand. The softness of her skin wound around his warmth.

'How old are you?'

'Nearly twenty-three.'

'Old enough to know the dangers of subterfuge, then? Old enough to realise that men might not all be...kind?'

'You warn me of the masculine appetite?'

'That is one way of putting it, I suppose.'

'This is Spain, Capitán, and I am hardly a green girl.'

'You are married?'

She did not answer.

'You were married, but he is dead.'

Horror marked her face. 'How could you possibly know that?'

With care he extended her palm and pointed to her third finger. 'The skin is paler where you once wore a ring. Just here.'

She felt the lump at the back of her throat hitch up into fear. She felt other things, too, things she had no mandate to as she wrenched away from his touch and went to stand by the window, the blood that throbbed at her temples making her feel slightly sick.

'How are you called? By your friends?'

'Lucien.'

'My mother named me Anna-Maria, but my father never took to it. He changed it when I was five and I became Alejandra, the defender of mankind. He did not have another child, you see.'

'So the boy he had always wanted was lost to him and you would have to do?'

She was shocked by his insight. 'You can see such a truth in my father's face just by looking at him?'

The pale eyes narrowed as he shook his head. 'He allows you to dress as a boy and roam the dangerous killing fields of armies. He will have trained you, no doubt, in marksmanship and in the using of a knife, but you are small and thin and this is a perilous time and place for any woman.'

'What if I told you that such patronage works to my advantage, Capitán? What if I said you think like all the others and dismiss the mouse against the lion?'

His glance went to her cheek.

'I broke his wrist.' When he smiled the wound on his lip stretched and blood blossomed.

'Why did he hurt you?'

'He felt the English should be left to rot in the arms of the enemy because of the way they betrayed us by departing in such an unseemly haste.'

'A harsh sentiment.'

'My father believes it, too, but then every war comes with a cost that you of all people should know of. The doctor said your back will be marked for good.'

'Are you suggesting that I will survive?'

'You thought you wouldn't?'

'Without you I am certain of it.'

'There is still time to die, Capitán. The sea trip won't be comfortable and inflammation and fever are always possibilities with such deep lacerations.'

'Your bedside manner is lacking, *señorita*. One usually offers more hope when tending a helpless patient.'

'You do not seem vulnerable in any way to me, Capitán Howard.'

'With my back cut to ribbons…?'

'Even with that. And you have been hurt before. Madeira or Dominica were dangerous places, then?'

'Hardly. Our regiment was left to flounder and rot in the Indies because no politician ever thought to abandon the rich islands.'

'For who in power should be brave enough to risk money for justice?'

He laughed. 'Who indeed?'

Alejandra turned away from his smile. He surely must know how beautiful he was, even with his ruined lip and swollen eye. He should have been weeping with the pain from the wounds at his neck and back and yet here he lay, scanning the room and its every occupant for clues and for the answers to questions she could see in his pale blue eyes. What would a man like this be like when he was well?

As unbeatable and dangerous as her father.

The answer almost had her turning away, but she made herself stand still.

'My father believes that the war here in the Peninsula will drag on for enough years to kill many more good men. He says it is Spain that will determine the outcome of the emperor's greed and this is the reason he has fashioned himself into the man he has become. El Vengador. The Avenger. He no longer believes in the precise and polite assignations of armies. He is certain that triumph lies in darker things; things like the collation of gathered information and night-time raids.'

'And you believe this, too? It is why you would come to England wearing your ruby brooch?'

'Once upon a time I was another person, Capitán. Then the French murdered my mother and I joined my father's cause. Revenge is what shapes us all here now and you would be wise to keep that in mind.'

'When did she die?'

'Nearly two years ago, but it seems like a lifetime. My father adored her to the exclusion of all else.'

'Even you?'

Again that flash of anger, buried quickly.

He turned away, the ache of his own loss in his thoughts. Were his group of army guides safe or had they been left behind in the scramble for transports?

He had climbed the lighthouse called the Tower of Hercules a dozen times or more to watch for the squadron to appear across the grey and cold Atlantic Ocean. But the transports and their escorts had not come until the eleventh hour, all his intelligence suggesting that French general Soult was advancing and that the main body of their army was not far behind.

He thought of John and Philippe and Hans and Giuseppe and all the others in his ragtag bag of deserters and ne'er-do-wells; a group chosen for their skill in languages and for their intuition. He had trained them and honed them well, every small shred of intelligence placed into the fabric of a whole, to be deciphered and collated and acted upon.

Communication was the lifeblood of an army and it had been his job to see that each message was delivered and every order and report was followed up. Sometimes there was more. An intercepted cache from the French, a dispatch that had fallen into hands it should not have or a personal letter of inestimable value.

His band of guides was an exotic mix of nationalities only vaguely associated with the English army and he was afraid of what might happen to them if they had been left behind.

'Were there many dead on the field where you found me?'

'There were. French and English alike. But there would have been more if the boats had not come into the harbour. The inhabitants of A Coruña sheltered the British well as they scampered in ragged bands to the safety of the sea.'

Then that was that. Every man would have to take their chance at life or death because he could do nothing for any of them and his own future, as it was, was hanging in the balance.

He could feel the heat in him and the tightness, the sensation of nothingness across his shoulders and back worrying. His left hand was cursed again with a ferocious case of pins and needles and his stomach felt...hollow.

He smiled and the girl opposite frowned, seeing through him perhaps, understanding the pretence of it.

He hadn't been hungry, any slight thought of food making him want to throw up. He had been drinking, though, small sips of water that wet his mouth and burnt the sores he could feel stretched over his lips.

A sorry sight, probably. He only wished he could be sick and then, at least, the gall of loss might be dislodged. Or not.

'You have family?'

A different question, almost feminine.

'My mother and four siblings. There were eight of us before my father and youngest brother were drowned.'

'A big number, then. Sometimes I wish...' She stopped at that and Lucien could see a muscle under her jaw grinding from the echo of words.

Nothing personal. Nothing particular. It was how this aftermath of war and captivity worked, for anything could be used against anyone in the easy pickings of torture. His own voluntary admissions of family worked in another way, a shared communion, a bond of humanness. Encourage dialogue with a captor and foster friendship. The enemy was much less likely to kill you then.

Fortunes turned on an instant and any thinking man or woman in this corner of a volatile Spain would know that. Battles were won and then lost and won again. It was only time that counted and with three hundred thousand fighting men of France poised

at your borders and under the control of Napoleon
Bonaparte himself there was no doubt of the outcome.

Unless England and its forces returned and soon,
Spain would go the way of nearly every other free
land in Europe.

His head ached at the thought.

The girl came back to read to him the next afternoon and the one after that, her voice rising and
falling over the words of the first part of Miguel de
Cervantes's tale *Don Quixote*.

Lucien had perused this work a number of times
and he thought she had, too, for there were moments
when she looked up and read from memory.

He liked listening to her voice and he liked watching her, the exploits of the eccentric and hapless
Knight of La Mancha bringing deep dimples to both
of her cheeks. She used her free hand a lot, too, he
saw, in exclamation and in emphasis, and when the
edge of her jacket dipped he saw a number of white
scars drawn across the dark blue of her blood line at
her wrist.

As she finished the book she snapped the covers
together and leant back against the wide leather chair,
watching him. 'The pen is the language of the soul,
would you not agree, Capitán?'

He could not help but nod. 'Cervantes, as a soldier, was seized for five years. All good fodder for
his captive's tale, I suppose.'

'I did not know that.'

'Perhaps that is where he first conjured up the

madness of his hero. The uncertainty of captivity forces questions and makes one re-evaluate priorities.'

'Is it thus with you?'

'Indeed. A prisoner always wonders whether today is the day he holds no further use alive to those who keep him bound.'

'You are not a prisoner. You are here because you are sick. Too sick to move.'

'My door is locked, Alejandra. From the outside.'

That disconcerted her, a frown appearing on her brow as she glanced away. 'Things are not always as they seem,' she returned and stood. 'My father isn't a man who would kill you for no reason at all.'

'Is expedience enough of a reason? Or plain simple frustration? He wants me gone. I am a nuisance he wishes he did not have.' Lifting his hand, he watched it shake. Violently.

'Then get better, damn you.' Her words were threaded with the force of anger. 'If you can walk to the door, you can get to the porch. And if you can manage that, then you can go further and further again. Then you can leave.'

In answer he reached for the Bible by his bed and handed it to her. 'Like this man did?'

Puzzled, she opened the book to the page indicated by the plaited golden thread of a bookmark.

Help me. I forgive you.

Written shakily in charcoal, the dust of it blurred in time and use and mirrored on the opposite page.

When her eyes went to the lines etched in the white-wash beneath the window on the opposite wall Lucien knew exactly what the marks represented.

'He was a prisoner in this room, too?'

She crossed herself, her face frozen in pain and shock and deathly white.

'You know nothing, Capitán. Nothing at all. And if you ever mention this to my father even once, he will kill you and I won't be able to stop him.'

'You would try?'

The air about them stilled into silence, the dust motes from the old fabric on the Bible twirling in the light, a moment caught for ever. And he fell into the green of her unease without resistance, like a moth might to flame in the darkest of nights.

She was the most beautiful woman he had ever seen, but it was not that which drew him. It was her strength of emotion, the anger in her the same as that in him. She balanced books and a blade with an equal dexterity, the secrets in her eyes wound into both sadness and knowledge.

They were knights tilting at windmills in the greater pageant of a Continental war, the small hope of believing they might make a difference lost under the larger one of nationalistic madness.

Spain. France. England.

For the first time in his life Lucien questioned the wisdom of soldiering and the consequences of battle, for them all, and came up wanting.

Alejandra had known the man who had written this message, he was sure of it, and it had shocked her. The pulse in her throat was still heightened as she licked her lips against the dryness of fear.

He watched as she ripped the page from the Bible before giving the tome back to him, tearing the age-thin paper into small pieces and pocketing them.

The weight of the book in his fist was heavy as she turned and left the room.

God. In the ensuing silence he flicked through the pages and his eyes again found a further passage marked in charcoal amongst the teachings of the Old Testament. Matthew 6:14. *'For if you forgive men when they sin against you, your heavenly father will also forgive you.'*

Clearly Alejandra, daughter of El Vengador, sought neither forgiveness nor absolution. Lucien wondered why.

He woke much later, startled into consciousness by great pain, and she was there again, sitting on the chair near the bed and watching him. The Bible had been removed altogether now, he noted as he chanced a glance at the table by the bed.

'The doctor said you had to drink.'

He tried to smile. 'Brandy?'

Her lips pursed as she raised a glass of orange-and-mint syrup. 'This is sweetened and the honey will help you to heal.'

'Thank you.' Sipping at the liquid, he enjoyed the coolness as it slid down his throat.

'Don't take too much,' she admonished. 'You will not be used to much yet.'

He frowned as he lay back, the dizziness disconcerting. If he did lose the contents of his stomach, he was almost certain it would not be Alejandra who would be offering to clean it up. He swallowed heavily and counted to fifty.

After a few moments she spoke again. 'Are you a religious man, Capitán Howard?'

A different question from what he had expected. 'I was brought up in the Anglican faith, but it's been a while since I was in any church.'

'When faith is stretched the body suffers.' She gave him this as though she had read it somewhere, a sage piece of advice that she had never forgotten.

'I think it is the French who have more to do with my suffering, *señorita*.'

'Ignoring the power of God's healing in your position could be dangerous. A priest could give you absolution should you wish it.' There was anger in her words.

'No.' He had not meant it to sound so final. 'If I die, I die. If I don't, I don't.'

'Fate, you mean? You believe in such?'

'I do believe in a fate that falls on men unless they act. The prophet Buddha said something like that a very long time ago.'

She smiled. 'Your religion is eclectic, then? You take bits from this deity and then from that one? To suit your situation?'

He looked away from her because he could tell she thought his answer important and he didn't have the strength to explain that it had been a while since he had believed in anything at all.

The shutters hadn't been closed tonight at his request and the first light of a coming dawn was low on the horizon. He was gladdened to see the beginning of another day. 'Do you not sleep well? To be here at this time?'

'Once, I did. Once, it was hard to wake me from a night's slumber, but since...' She stopped. 'No. I do not sleep well any more.'

'Is there family in other places, safer places than here?'

'For my father to send me to, you mean?' She stood and blew out the candle near his bed. 'I need no looking after, *señor*. I am quite able to see to myself.'

Shadowed against the dying night she looked smaller than usual, as if in the finding of the words in the Bible earlier some part of her had been lost.

'Fate can also be a kind thing, *señor*. There is a certain grace in believing that nothing one does will in the end make any difference to what finally happens.'

'Responsibility, you mean?'

'Do not discount it completely, Capitán. Guilt can eat a soul up with barely a whisper.'

'So you are saying fate is like a pardon because all free will is gone?'

Even in the dim light he could see her frown.

'I am saying that every truth has shades of lies within and one would be indeed foolish to think it different.'

'Like the words you tore from the Bible? The ones written in charcoal?'

'Especially those ones,' she replied, a strength in the answer that had not been there a moment ago. 'Those words were a message he knew I would find.'

With that she was gone, out into the early coming dawn, the shawl at her shoulders tucked close around her chin.

Chapter Two

Alejandra watched Captain Lucien Howard out amongst the shadow of trees on the pathway behind the hacienda: one step and then falling, another and falling again. He had insisted on being brought outside each day, one of the servants carrying him to the grove so that he could practise walking.

She could see frustration, rage and pain in every line of his body from this distance and the will to try to stand unaided, even as the dust had barely settled from the previous unsuccessful attempt. His hands would be bleeding, she knew that without even looking, for the bark of the olive was rough and he had needed traction to pull his whole weight up in order to stand each time. Sickness and fever had left him wasted and thin. The man they had brought up from the battlefields of A Coruña had been twice the one he was now.

Another Englishman who had shed his blood on the fleshless bones of this land, a land made bare by war and hate and greed. She turned her rosary in

her palm, reciting the names of those who had died
already. Rosalie. Pedro. Even Juan with his cryptic
and unwanted whine of forgiveness written in a Bible
he knew she would find.

Each bead was smooth beneath her fingers, a hundred years of incantations ingrained in the shining
jet. Making the sign of the cross, she kept her voice
quiet as she prayed. 'I believe in God, the Father Almighty, Creator of Heaven and Earth and...'

Salvation came in many forms and this was one of
them, the memory of those gone kept for ever present
within the timeless words. After the Apostles' Creed
she started on the Our Father, following it with three
Hail Marys, a Glory Be and the Fatima Prayer.

She always used the Sorrowful Mysteries now as a
way to end her penance, the Joyful and the Glorious
ones sticking in her throat; the Agony in the Garden
and the Crowning of the Thorns were more relevant
to her life these days. Even the Scourging of the Pillars appealed.

When she had finished she placed the beads in her
left pocket, easily reached, and drew out a knife from
the leather pouch at her ankle, the edge of it honed so
that it gleamed almost blue.

A small branch of an aloe hedge lay beside her
and she lifted the wood against the blade, sliding the
knife so that shavings fell in a pile around her boots.

Her life was like this point of sharp, balanced on
a small edge of living. Turning the stick, she drew it
down against her forearm, where the skin held it at bay
for a moment in a fleeting concave show of resistance.

With only the smallest of pressure she allowed the wood to break through, taking the sudden pain inside her, not allowing even a piece of it to show.

Help me. I forgive you. A betrayal written in charcoal.

Blood welled and ran in a single small stream across her hands and on to her fingertips, where it fell marking the soil.

Sometimes pain was all she had left to feel with, numbness taking everything else. If she were honest, she welcomed the ache of life and the flow of blood because in such quickness she knew she was still here. Still living. Just.

Lucien Howard had almost fallen again and she removed the point from her arm, staunching the wound with pressure, setting blood.

He was like her in his stubbornness, this captain. Never quite giving up. Resheathing the blade, she simply leant back and shut her eyes, feeling the thin morning sun against her lids and the cold wind off the Atlantic across her hair.

Her land. For ever.

She would never leave it. The souls of those long departed walked beside her here. Already mud was reclaiming her blood. She liked to think it was her mother, Rosalie, there in the whorls of wind, drinking her in, caressing the little that was left, understanding her need for aloneness and hurt.

Her eyes caught a faster movement. Now the Englishman had gone down awkwardly and this time he stayed there. She counted the seconds under her breath. One. Two. Three. Four.

Then a quickening. A hand against the tree. The pull of muscle and the strain of flesh. Her fingers lifted to find the rosary, but she stopped them. Not again. She would not help.

He was as alone as she was in this part of a war. His back still oozed and the wounds on his neck had become reinfected. She would get Constanza to look at the damage again and then he would be gone. It was all she could do for him.

The daughter of El Vengador sat and observed him from a distance, propped against a warm ochre wall out of the breeze. Still. Silent. Barely moving.

He almost hated her for her easy insolence and her unnamed fury. She would not help him. He knew that. She would only watch him fall again and again until he could no longer pull himself up. Then she would go and another would come to lift him back to the kapok bed in the room with its gauzy curtains, half-light and sickness.

Almost six weeks since A Coruña. Almost forty-two days since he had last eaten well. His bones looked stark and drawn against thin skin and big feet. He'd seen himself in the mirror a few days before as the man designated to tend to his needs had lifted him, eyes too large in his face, cheeks sunken.

She had stopped visiting him in his room three weeks ago, when the priest had been called to give him the last rites. He remembered the man through a fog of fever, the holy water comforting even if the sentiment lay jumbled in his mind.

'Through this holy anointing may the Lord...'

Death came on soft words and cool water. It was a part of the life of a soldier, ever present and close.

But he had not died. He had pulled himself through the heat and come out into the chill. And when he had insisted on being brought to the pathway of trees, she had come, too. Watching. Always from a distance. She would leave soon, he knew. He had fallen too many times for her to stay. His hands bled and his knee, too, caught against a root, tearing. There was no resistance left in him any more and no strength.

He hoped Daniel Wylde had got home safely. He hoped the storms he had heard about had not flung the boat his friend travelled in to the murky bottom of the Bay of Biscay. 'Jesus, help him,' he murmured. 'And let me be remembered.'

A foolish prayer. A vain prayer. His family would miss him. His mother particularly and then life would move on. New babies. Other events until he would be like the memories he carried of his father and his youngest brother, gone before their time into the shifting mists of after.

'Hell,' he swore with the first beginnings of anger. A new feeling, this. All-encompassing. Strengthening. Only wrath in it. He reached out for the fortitude and with one last push grabbed the rough bark of the scrawny olive and pulled with all his fury, up this time into a standing position, up again into the world of the living.

He did not let go, did not allow his legs to buckle, did not think of falling or failing or yielding. Nay, he held on through sharp pain and a heartbeat that raked through his ears as a drum thumping in all the parts of his body, his breath hoarse and shaking.

And then she was there with her wide green knowing eyes and her hair stuffed under the hat.

'I knew that you could do it.'

He could not help but smile.

'Tomorrow you will take more steps and the next day more again and the day after that you will walk from this path to that one. And then you will go home.'

Her face was fierce and sharp. There was blood on her sleeve and on her fingers. New blood. Fresh blood. He wondered why. She saw where he looked and lifted her chin.

'The French have taken A Coruña and Ferrol. A resounding defeat with Soult now walking the streets of the towns unfettered. Soon the whole of the north will be theirs.'

'War…has its…losers.'

'And its cowards,' she tossed back. 'Better to have not come here at all if after the smallest of fights you turn tail and leave.'

He felt the anger and pushed it down. His back ached and his vision blurred and the cold that had hounded the British force through the passes of a Cantabrian winter still hovered close.

Cowards. The word seared into vehemence. So many soldiers lost in the retreat. So much bravery discovered as they had turned their backs against the sea and fought off the might of France. All he could remember was death, blood and courage.

'You need to sit down.' These new words were softer, more generous, and in one of the few times since she had found him on the fields above A Coruña, she touched him. A hand cupped beneath his elbow and another across his back. A chain lay around her neck, dipping into the collar of her un-buttoned shirt. He wondered what lay on the end of it; the thought swept away as she angled the garden chair beneath him and helped him to sit.

His breath shook as much as his hands did when he lifted them up across his knees.

'Thank…you.' And he meant it. If she had not been behind him seeing to his balance, he knew he would have fallen and the wooden seat felt good and steady and safe. Shutting his eyes against the glare of the morning, he allowed his mind to run across his body, accepting the injury, embracing the pain. The witch doctors in Jamaica had shown him this trick once when he had taken a sickness there. He had used such mesmerising faithfully ever since.

The Englishman had gone from here somehow, his body still and his heartbeat slowing to a fraction of what it had been only a moment before. Even his skin cooled.

Uneasiness crept in. She could not understand who he was, what he was. A soldier. A fighter. A spy. A man who spoke both the high and low dialects of Spain as well as any native and one who knew at every turn and at every moment exactly what was happening about him. Alejandra could see this in his stance as well as in his eyes now opened, the blue today paler than it had ever looked; alert and all-knowing.

She had never seen another like him. Even worn down to exhaustion she caught the quick glance he chanced behind to where a line of her father's men were coming in from the south. Gauging danger, measuring response.

'Where will I be sent…on from?' His gaze narrowed.

It was seldom she told anyone of plans that did not include the next hour, for it gave the asker too much room to wriggle free of any constraints. With him she was honest.

'Not from here. It is too dangerous in A Coruña now. You will leave from the west.'

'From one of the small ports in the Rias Altas, then?'

So Captain Lucien Howard knew his geography, but not his local politics.

'No, that area harbours too many enemies of my father. It shall not be there.' She turned and looked up at the sky, frowning. 'There is a storm coming in with the wind from the ocean.'

The clouds had amassed and darkened across the horizon, a thick band of leaden grey just above the waterline.

My father needs to find out who you are first before he lets you go. He needs to understand your people and your character and the danger you might pose to us should you not be the man you say you are. And if you are not...

These thoughts she kept to herself.

'I am not your enemy, Alejandra.' He seldom called her by her given name, but she liked it. Soft. Almost whispered. Her heart beat a little faster, surprising her, annoying her, and she looked away, making much of watching those who had come in from Betanzos. Tomeu was amongst them, shading his face and peering at them, the bandage on his wrist white in the light even at this distance.

'But neither are you my friend, Ingles, for all your sacrifice and devotion to the cause of Spain.'

He laughed, the edges of his eyes creasing, and she took in breath. What was it about him that made her more normal indifference shatter? She even imagined she might have blushed.

'I am here, *señorita*, because of a mistake.'

Now, this was new. A piece of personal information that he offered without asking.

'A mistake?'

'I spent too long in the Hercules Tower looking for the British transports. They had not arrived and the French were circling.'

'So they found you there?'

'Hardly.' This time there was nothing but cold ice in his glance. 'They had taken one of my men and I thought to save him.'

'And did you?'

'No.'

The wind could be heard above their silence.

Strengthening and changing direction. Soon the sun would be gone and it would rain. The beating pulse in a vein of his throat below his left ear was the only sign of great emotion and greater fury. So very easy to miss.

'He was a spy, like you?'

He nodded. 'There are weaknesses that are found out only under great duress. Jealousy. Greed. Fear. For Guy the weakness was cowardice, but he ran in the wrong direction.'

'So you left him there? As a punishment?'

'No. I tried to bring him safely through the lines of the French. I failed.'

For some men, Alejandra thought, the rigours of war brought forward cowardice. For others it highlighted a sheer and bloody-minded bravery. She imagined what it must have cost Captain Lucien Howard in pain to try to rescue his friend. She doubted anyone or anything could push him into doing that he did not wish to, but still, most men held a limit of what was sacred and worth dying for and a well-aimed hurt usually brought results.

Her father was the master of it.

But this Englishman's strength, even in the lines of his wasted and marked body, was obvious. Unbreakable and stalwart. She imagined, given the choice, that he would choose death over dishonour and pain across betrayal.

She wondered if she could manage the same.

The blood from his torn hands stained his white

shirt and the sweat from his exertions had darkened the linen.

But he was beautiful with his pale eyes and his gold hair, longer now after weeks of sickness and fallen from the leather tie he more normally sported. She wanted to run her fingers through the length of it just to see it against the dark of her own skin.

Contrasts.

Inside and out.

Lucien. The name suited him with its silky vowels. Almost the name of one of the three archangels in the Bible, the covering angel, the fallen one. Alejandra shook her head and cleared her thoughts.

'I will send Constanza to you again tonight with her herbs. She has a great prowess in the healing arts.'

When he brushed back his hair the sun flinted in the colour. 'If she leaves the ointment in my room, I can tend to it myself.'

'As you wish, then.'

Kicking at the mud beneath her feet, once and then another time, she left him to the coming rain and the wind and the rising tides of fortune, and when she reached the hacienda's stables she turned once to see the shadow of him watching her.

Chapter Three

Lucien woke in the night to a small and quiet noise. He had been trained well to know the difference in sounds and knew that the louder ones were those less likely to kill you.

This one was soft and muffled. He tensed into readiness.

The door opened and a candle flared as Alejandra's father came to sit on the small stool near the bed, stretching his long legs out before him and grimacing as though in pain.

'You sleep lightly, Capitán.'

'Years of practice, *señor*,' Lucien returned.

'Put the knife away. I am only here to talk.'

Lucien slipped the blade beneath his pillow, angling it so that it might be taken up quickly again if needed. He did not think the man opposite missed the inherent threat.

Alejandra had brought him the weapon on his second evening here, a quiet offering in the heat of his fever.

'For protection,' she had said in warning. 'I am presuming you know how to use it. If not, it is probably better...' He'd simply reached out and taken it from her, the insult smarting given the wounds on his back.

Tonight her father looked weary and he took his time in forming the message before he spoke.

'It has come to my notice that you are a peer of the English aristocracy, Capitán Howard.' The ring Lucien had been wearing lay in the older man's hand when he opened his fingers, the Ross family coat of arms shining in the candlelight. He thought it had been lost for ever. 'Lord Lucien Howard, the sixth Earl of Ross. The title sits on your shoulders as the head of your household and you wield a good deal of power in English society.'

Lucien remained silent for he was certain that there would be more to come.

'But your family seat is bankrupt by all accounts. Poor investments by your father and his father, it is said, and now there is very little in the Howard coffers. Soon there will be nothing.'

Well, that was not a secret, Lucien thought bitterly. The penury of the earldom of Ross was well known. Anyone could have told him of it.

But his attention was taken by a sheaf of papers the other man lifted into view. He saw his own face on the front cover of *The Times*, a black-and-white copy of a likeness his mother had once commissioned of him, smiling as if he meant it. My God, it seemed an age since he had done so with any sincerity.

'You have a good number of brothers and sisters and a mother who is heartbroken because you are presumed dead.'

Lucien imagined her grief. The Countess was neither a big woman nor a particularly robust one. If this killed her before he managed to get back…

'So I have a further proposition for you, my lord.' The last two words were coated with a violent dislike. 'I could slice your throat open here and now and no one would ever know what had happened to you, or…' He stopped.

El Vengador was a man who used theatrics to the full extent, Lucien thought and humoured him. 'Or…'

'Or as an earl you are well placed to offer us even more.'

Lucien closed his eyes momentarily. This guerrilla leader was a dangerous adversary and a man who would not make an easy ally. He was also holding all the cards as far as Lucien's life was concerned. Oh, granted, he knew that he might take a good handful of men with him if he were to fight his way out of here, but he was weak and he was also, to some extent, in debt to the man for his life.

But there were things that were not being said. Lucien was sure of it. He looked the other man straight on.

'Why me? Why not someone integrated into the fabric of English society, someone from here? It seems you have agents there already. Why not use them?' Lucien's eyes turned to the papers and the ring.

'But we could not access the places you do, my

lord. We could never hope to be within earshot of a king.'

'Society and the monarch do not write the law. England has a democracy and a parliament to do that.'

'And one of the Houses of Parliament consists of peers of the realm. Your name is included in that representation, is it not, Lord Ross?'

Finally he was gathering the sense of this assignment. If he had not been titled, he would probably have been disposed of by now and this conversation was a warning of it.

El Vengador held men in London, dangerous men, men with dreams of a Spanish free land in their hearts and the means to ensure it had the best chance of fruition.

England and Spain might be on the same side of the fight against Napoleon, but each had their own reasons for victory and the milksop version of democracy held by the Spanish army and the splintered *juntas* was a very different one from that offered by the guerrilla leaders. 'The little war' was the translation, but Lucien had heard tales of the French being killed in their hundreds by the partisan bands roaming the rough and isolated passes of the northern countryside, and many of those deaths had not been a pretty sight.

'The guerrilla movement might strike terror into the hearts of the French troops, but you also frighten much of the Spanish population with your forced conscription and looting.' He refrained from adding savagery and barbarousness to the list. 'What makes you think I would want to help you? I do not wish to be the person who facilitates the death of my country-men should a battle be badly lost and you have all the personal details of each commanding officer.'

A movement of the door had both of them turning. Alejandra came in. She had been asleep. He could see the remains of slumber in the flush on her cheeks and in the tangle of her hair.

God. She slept fully clothed and with a knife as close as his. The silver of her dagger glimmered in the candlelight. He was surprised she had not sheathed it when she saw her father in the room.

'I am not here to kill him, *hija.*'

An explanation of intention that underlined her presence. Lucien frowned. Did she sleep near? To protect him? Her eyes did not meet his own as they took in the papers and his ring sitting on the table to one side of the bed, giving him the notion that she had known of her father's quest. And of the danger.

'You will take him to the boat in a week, Alejan-dra. No later.'

'Very well.' Her answer held the same edge of hardness as her father's.

'Find another to travel with you. Tomeu, perhaps?'

She shook her head. 'No. I shall take Adan. He has people to the west and good contacts.'

'Then it is decided.' El Vengador's fingers drummed against his thigh as he stood. 'I do not expect you to do this work for Spain without reward, Lord Ross. A sum of money shall be deposited into a bank of your choice as soon as any business between us is conducted and I am satisfied with the intelligence.'

A *fait accompli*. Perhaps El Vengador was not used to having men turn down his offers of assistance. Still, he was in the lair of the tiger, so to speak, and it would be unwise to annoy him.

'I will think carefully on what you have proposed.'

A hand came forward, grasping his own in a surprisingly firm and warm way.

'For freedom,' the older man said as Lucien watched him. 'And victory.'

Then he was gone. Alejandra stood against the wall to the left of the window, one foot bent so that it rested against the peeling ochre. Ready to flee.

'You knew about this?' He gestured to the paper and the ring. 'You knew what your father might ask?'

'Or of what he might not,' she returned and crossed the room to stand beside him, lifting *The Times* in her hands.

'You look younger when you smile.'

'It's an old likeness.'

This time she laughed and the sound filled the room like warm honey, low and smooth.

'I think, Lord Lucien Howard, sixth Earl of Ross, that even my father could not kill you if he wanted to.'

'I hope, Alejandra, only daughter of El Vengador, that you are right.'

She placed the paper down with as much care as she had used to pick it up. No extra movements. No uncertain qualms. Death could have been in the room when she entered as easily as life and yet there was not one expression on her face that told him of either relief or disappointment.

But she had come and her knife was sheathed now, back in the soft leather at her left ankle. Would she have fought her father for him? The thought knocked the breath from his lungs.

'Thank you.' He offered the words, no sentiment in them but truth, and by the look on her face he knew she understood exactly what such gratitude was for.

She was gone as quietly as her father had left, one moment there and the next just the breeze of her going. He heard the door close with a scrape of the latch.

He dreamt of Linden Park, the Howard seat at Tunbridge Wells, with the sun on its windows and the banks of the River Teise lined with weeping willows, soft green in the coat of early spring. His father was there and his brother. The bridge had not collapsed yet and he had not had to try to save them as they turned over and over in the cold current, dragged down by heavy clothing, late rains and panic.

His mind found other happier moments—his sister, Christine, and he as they had ridden across the surrounding valleys, as fast as the wind, the sound of starlings and wrens and the first gambolling lambs in the fields.

He thought of Daniel Wylde, too, and of Francis St Cartmail, and them all as young boys constructing huts in the woods and hunting rabbits with his father's guns. Gabriel Hughes had come sometime later, on horseback, less talkative than the others, but interesting. Gabe had taught Lucien the trick of holding one's own counsel and understanding the hidden meaning of words that were not quite being said.

And then Alejandra was there in his thoughts, her long hair down her back and her skin lustrous in candlelight, full lips red and eyes dark. In his dream she wore a thin and flowing nightgown, the shape of her lithe body seen easily through it. He felt himself harden as the breath in him tightened. She came against him like molten fire, acquiescent and searching, her mouth across his own as her head tipped up, taking all that he offered; sweet heat and an unhidden desire before she plunged a knife deep through the naked and exposed gap in his ribs.

'Hell.' He came awake in a second, panting, shocked, his member rock solid and ready, the stupidity in him reeling. For the first time in all the weeks of pain and terror and exhaustion he felt like crying; for him and for her and for a war that held death as nothing more than a debt of sacrifice on its laboured way to victory.

Alejandra was her father's daughter. She had told him that again and again in every way that counted. In her distance and her disdain. In her sharpened blade held at the ready and the rosary she often played with, bead by bead of entreaty and Catholic confession.

Yet still the taste of her lingered in his mouth, and the feel of her flesh on his skin had him pushing back the sheets, a heat all-encompassing even in the cold of winter.

What would happen on the road west, he wondered, the thought of long nights in her company when the moon was high and shadow clothed the landscape? How many days was the journey? How many miles? If he was not to be taken out of Spain by way of the Rias Altas, was it the more southern Rias Baixas they meant to use? Or even the busy seaport of Vigo?

The dream had changed him somehow, made him both less certain and more foolish, the unreality of it sharpened by a hope he hated.

He wished there was brandy left at his bedside or some Spanish equivalent of a strong and alcoholic brew, but there was only the water infused with oranges, honey and mint. He took up the carafe and drank deeply, the quickened beat of his heart finally slowing.

Reaching over to the table, he slipped the signet ring on his finger where it had been for all of the years of his adult life and was glad to have it back. Then he lifted up the paper to see the date.

February the first. His mother's birthday. He could only guess how she had celebrated such a milestone with this news crammed on to the front page of the broadsheet.

He had always known it might come to this, lost behind the enemy lines and struggling to survive, but he had not imagined a thin and distant girl offering him protection even as she swore she did not. Taking his blade from beneath his pillow, he tucked it into the leather he had found in one of the drawers in this room before placing it back on the bedside table and glancing at the pendulum clock on the far wall.

Almost four, the heavy tick and tock of it filling silence. He would not sleep again.

He tried recalling the maps of Spain he had held in his saddlebag on the long road north to the sea. He and his group of guides had drawn many images, measuring the distances and topography, the ravines and the crossable passes, the rivers and the bridges and the levels of water. Much of what they transcribed he had determined himself as they had traversed across into the mountains, the margins of each impression filled with comments and personal observations.

When he had encountered the French soldiers the folder had been lost, for he had not seen it since lying wounded on the field above the town. He could probably redraw much of it from memory, but the loss of such intelligence was immense. Without knowledge of the local landscape the British army was caught in the out-of-date information that allowed only poor and dangerous passage.

A noise brought him around to the door once again and this time it was the one named Tomeu who stood watching him.

'May I speak with you, Ingles?'

Up close the man who had helped him from the battleground was younger than he remembered him to be. His right wrist was encased in a dirty bandage.

He closed the door carefully behind himself and stood there for a moment as if listening. 'I am sorry to come so late, Capitán, but I leave in an hour for the south and I wanted to catch you before I went.

I saw your candle still burnt in the gap beneath the door and took the chance to see if you were awake.'

Lucien nodded and the small upwards pull of the newcomer's lips changed a sullen lad into a more handsome one.

'My name is Bartolomeu Diego y Betancourt, *señor*, and I am a friend of Alejandra's.' He waited after delivering this piece of news, eyes alert.

'I recognise you. You are the one who got me on the canvas stretcher behind the horse the morning after I was hurt.'

'I did not wish to. I thought you would have been better off dead. It was Alejandra who insisted we bring you here. If it had been left to me, I would have plunged my blade straight through your heart and finished it.'

'I see.'

'Do you, *señor*? Do you really understand how unsafe it is for Alejandra at the hacienda now that you are here and what your rescue might have cost her? El Vengador has his own demons and he is ruthless if anyone at all gets in his way.'

'Even his daughter?'

That brought forth a torrent of swearing in Spanish, a bawdy long-winded curse. 'Enrique Fernandez will end his life here in bitterness and hate. And if Alejandra stays with him, so will she, for her stubbornness is as strong as his own. Fernandez has enemies who will pounce when he is least expecting it and a host of others who are jealous of his power.'

'Like you?'

The young man turned away.

'She said you were clever and that you could see into thoughts that should remain private. She said you were more dangerous than even her father and that if you stay here much longer, El Vengador would know it to be such and have you murdered.'

'Alejandra said this?'

'Yes. She wants you gone.'

'I know.'

'But she wants you safe, too.'

He stayed quiet as Tomeu went on.

'She is like a sister to me. If you ever hurt her...'

'I will not.'

'I believe you, Capitán, and that is one of the reasons I am here. You, too, are powerful in your own right, powerful enough to protect her, perhaps?'

'You think Alejandra would accept my protection?' He might have laughed out loud if the other man had not looked both so very serious and so very young.

'Her husband was killed less than one year ago, a matter of months after their marriage.'

'I see.' And Lucien did. It was the personal losses that made a man or a woman fervent and Alejandra was certainly that.

'Are there other relatives?'

'An uncle down south somewhere, but they are not close.'

'Friends, then, apart from you?'

'This is a fighting unit, ranging across this northern part of Spain with the express purpose of causing

chaos and mayhem. Most of the women are gone either
to safety or to God. It is a dangerous place to inhabit.'

'Here today and gone tomorrow?'

'Exactly.'

'Was it Alejandra who hurt your wrist?'

'It was. I asked her to be my wife and she refused.'

Lucien smiled. 'A comprehensive no, then.'

'The bruise on her face was an accident. I dragged
her down the stairs with me after losing my footing.
She said she would never marry anyone again and
even the asking of it was an insult. To her. She never
listens, you see, never takes the time to understand
her own and ever-present danger.'

'She loved her husband, then?'

The other man laughed. 'You will need to ask her
that, *señor.*'

'I will. So you think her father would harm her?'

'El Vengador? Not intentionally. But your presence here is difficult for them both. Alejandra wants
you well enough to travel, but Enrique only wants you
gone. The title you hold has swung opinion in your
favour a little, but with the slightest of pushes it could
go the other way and split us all asunder. Better not
to care too much about the health and welfare of others in this compound, I think. Better, too, to have you
bundled up and heading for home.'

A safer topic, this one. But every word that Tomeu
had spoken told Lucien something of his authority. A man like El Vengador would not be generous
in his fact sharing, yet this young man had a good
knowledge of the conversation he had just had with

Alejandra's father. Lucien had seen him glance at the signet ring back on his finger and in the slight flare of his eyes he had understood just what Tomeu did not say.

He was a lieutenant perhaps, or at least one who participated in the decision-making for the group. The young face full of smiles and politeness almost certainly masking danger, for the lifeblood of the guerrilla movement was brutality and menace.

Had Alejandra's father sent Tomeu to sound him out? Had Alejandra herself? Or was this simply a visit born from expediency and warning?

Thirty-two years of living had made Lucien question everything and in doing so he was still alive.

'What of her groom's family? Could she go there to safety?'

'My cousin, *señor*, and they want the blood of the Fernandez family more than anyone else in Spain. More than the French, even, and that is saying something.'

This was what war did.

It tore apart the fabric and bindings of society and replaced them with nothing. He thought of his own immediate family in England and then of his large extended one of aunts, uncles and cousins. Napoleon and the French had a lot to answer for the wreckage that was the new Europe. He suddenly wished he was home.

'I am sorry…' Lucien left the words dangling. Sorry for them all. It was no answer, he knew, but he could promise nothing else. As if the young man understood, he, too, turned for the door.

'Do not trust anyone on your trip to the west.'

'I won't.'

'And watch over Alejandra.'

With that he was gone, out into the fading night of a new-coming dawn, for already Lucien could hear the first chorus of birdsong in the misty air.

Chapter Four

The anger in Alejandra was a red stream of wrath, filling her body from head to foot, making her hot and cold and sick.

Tomeu had left, travelling south into more danger, and the Englishman was in his usual place on the pathway between the olive trees, struggling to walk.

Up and down. Slowly. He was not content with a small time of it, either, but had been there for most of the morning, sweat everywhere despite the cold of the day.

He was getting better, that much she could tell. He did not limp any more or lean over his injuries like a snail in a shell, cradling his hurt. No, straight as any soldier, he picked his way from this tree to that one and then back again, using the seat on every third foray now to stop and find breath.

Stubborn.

Like her.

She smiled at that thought and the tension released a little. She knew he must have his knife upon him for she had been into his room whilst he was out there and checked; a poor choice that, an act of thieves and sneaks. It was who she had become here, in this war of Spain. Her mother would have castigated her severely for such a lapse of decorum, but now no one cared. She had become part of the campaign to please her father, dressing as a boy and assembling intelligence because he was all she had left of family.

Lucien Howard suddenly saw her for he raised his hand in greeting. So very English. Someone like him, no doubt, would keep his manners intact even upon his deathbed. It was why his country did so well in the world, she reasoned, this conduct of decency and rectitude even in the face of extreme provocation.

'I had a visit from your friend Tomeu last night.'

Shocked, she could only stare at him.

'Well, that answers my first question,' he returned and sat down. 'I thought you might have known.'

'What did he say?' A thousand things ran around in her head, things that she sincerely hoped he had not told this Englishman.

'That you were married to his cousin. For a month.'

'A short relationship,' she gave back, hating the way her voice shook with the saying of it.

'Tomeu also confided that he himself had asked you to be his wife, but you had refused.'

All of the secrets that were better hidden. 'He was talkative, then.'

'Unlike you. He implied you were in danger here.'

At that she laughed. 'Implied? It surrounds us, Capitán. Three hundred thousand enemy troops with their bloodthirsty generals and an emperor who easily rules Europe.'

'I think he might have meant danger on a more personal level.'

'To me?'

When he nodded she knew exactly what Tomeu had said, for he had used the same arguments on her when she had broken his wrist.

'He talks too much and I did not ask for your help. It was you who needed mine.'

He ignored that sarcasm. 'He said the trip west might be difficult. The power your father holds has aggravated those who would take it from him, it seems. Including Tomeu.'

At that she smiled. 'When my father asks you again to aid the effort for Spanish independence, say yes, even if you have no intention of doing so.'

'Because he will kill me if I don't?'

'He is a man with little time to accomplish all he feels he must. To him you are either the means to an end or the end. Your life depends on how much honour you accord to your word, Capitán. My advice would be to allot it none.'

'A promise here means nothing?'

'Less than nothing. Integrity is one of the first casualties of war.' Alejandra held her mouth in the grim edge of a scowl she had become so good at affecting and did not waver. She was pleased when he nodded.

'When your mother was alive...'

She did not let him finish.

'We will leave here in a few days and head west.

There will be two others who travel with us and my father will provide you with a warm coat and sturdy boots.'

His own were cracking at the soles, she thought, the poorly made footwear of the English army was a disgrace. What manufacturer would cut corners for profit when the lives of its fighting men were at stake?

Honour. The word slid into the space between them like a serpent, pulled this way and then that, unravelled by pragmatism and greed.

'We will travel into the mountains first, so you will need to have the strength to climb.' Despite meaning not to, her eyes glanced around at the flat small space that lay between the olives. Hardly the foothills of the mountains. The questionable wisdom of her plan made her take in a breath.

She did not want Captain Lucien Howard to die in the wastes of the alpine scrub, made stiff by ice and cold by rain. She could help him a little, but with Adan and Manolo tagging along she understood they would not countenance anything that endangered safety.

He would have to manage or he would die.

She knew he saw that thought in her eyes because he suddenly smiled.

Beautiful. Like the picture in his English newspaper, the sides of his mouth and eyes creasing into humour. She wished he had been ugly or old or scarred. But he was not. He was all sapped strength, wasted brawn and outrageous beauty. And cleverness. That was the worst of it, she suddenly thought, a man who might work out the thoughts and motivations of others and set it to work for his advantage.

'I will be fit for the journey. Already I feel stronger.'

When he leant forward Alejandra saw the bandage at his neck had slipped and the red-raw skin was exposed. It would scar badly, a permanent reminder of this place and this time.

Lucien knew Alejandra worried about the wound on his neck, though she smoothed her face in that particular habit she had so that all thoughts were masked.

He imagined getting home to the safe and unscathed world of the *ton*, with war written on him beneath superfine wool. The hidden history on his back in skin and sinew would need to be concealed from all those about him, for who would be able to understand the cost of it and how many would pity him?

A further distance. Another layer. Sometimes he felt he was building them up like children's blocks, the balance of who he was left in danger of tipping completely.

Except here with Alejandra in the light of a Spanish winter morning, the grey-green of olive branches sending dappled shadows across them.

Here he did not have to pretend who he was or wasn't and he was glad.

Without her watching from a distance he might not have found the mental strength to try again and again and again to get up and move when everything ached and stung and hurt. She challenged him and egged him on. No sorrow in it or compassion. Both would have broken him.

Breathing out, he rose from the seat and stood. He was always surprised just how much taller he was than her.

'Tomorrow I will walk to the house.'

'It is more than two hundred yards away, *señor*,' she said back, the flat tone desultory.

'And back,' he continued and smiled.

Unexpectedly she did, too, green eyes dancing with humour and the dimples in both cheeks deep.

He imagined her in a ballroom in London, hair dressed and well-clothed. Red, he thought. The colour of her gown would need to be bold. She would be unmatched.

'If you walk that far, Ingles, I will bring you a bottle of the best *aguardiente de orujo*.'

'Firewater?' he returned. 'I have heard of this but have not tried it.'

'Drink too much and the next day you will be in bed till the sundown, especially if you are not used to the strength of it. But drink just enough and the power fills you.'

'Would you join me in the celebration?'

She tipped her head up and looked him straight in the eyes. 'Perhaps.'

Lucien spent the evening on the floor of his room exercising and trying to get some strength into his upper body. He could feel the muscles remembering what they had once been like, but he was a couple of stone lighter with his sickness and the shaking that overtook him after heavy exertion was more than frustrating.

So he lay there on the polished tiled floor and watched the ceiling whilst his heart rate slowed and the anger cooled. Just two months ago he could have so easily managed all that he now could not.

He cleared his mind and imagined the walk from the trees to the outhouse and back. He'd walk past the first olive tree and then on to the sheltered path with lavender on each edge. The hedges were clipped there and could not be used for balance and after that there were three steps that came up to the covered porch. Two hundred yards there and another two hundred back and flat save for the stairs.

Of course he could manage such a distance. He only had to believe it.

The marks drawn into the plaster beneath the windows caught his attention again. Closer up he could see they formed a pattern different from the one he had first thought.

There were many more indents than he had originally imagined, smaller scrawlings caught in between the larger strokes. Twenty-nine. Thirty-one. Fifteen. Days of the months, perhaps? His mind quickly ran across the year. February and March was a sequence that worked and 1808 had been a leap year. But why would anybody keep such a track of time?

A noise through the inside wall then also caught his attention, quiet and muffled. Plainly it was the sound of someone crying and he knew without a doubt that it was Alejandra. Her room was next to his, the thickness of a stone block away.

Rising, he stood and tipped his head to the stone. One moment turned into two and then there was silence. It was as if on the other side of the wall she knew he was there, too, listening and knowing. He barely allowed himself breath.

She could feel him there, a foot away through the plaster and stone, knew that he stood where she had stood for all of the months at the end of Juan's life; he a prisoner of her father's, a man who had betrayed the cause.

She could not save Captain Lucien Howard should Papa decide that he was expendable, so she needed to take him out of here to the west. The evening light drew in on itself, watchful, the last bird calls and then the quiet. Juan had lost his speech and his left arm, but he had lingered for two of the months of winter and into the first weeks of spring. She had prayed each day that it would be the end and marked the wall when it was not.

Her marks were still there, the indents of time drawn into the plaster, one next to the other near the base of the wall, and left there when he passed away as a message and a warning.

Betray El Vengador and no one is safe, not even the one married to his only daughter. Juan had died with a rosary in his hands. Her father had, at least, allowed him that.

A year ago now, before the worst of the war. She

wondered how many more men would be gone by the same time next year and, crossing her room, took out the maps of the northern mountains that Lucien Howard had upon him when he was captured. Precise and detailed. With such drawings the passage through the Cantabrians for a marauding army would be an easy thing to follow. She wondered why the French had not thought to search his saddlebags and take the treasure after leaving him for dead on the field.

Probably the rush of war had allowed the mistake. Not torture, but battle. Certainly the swords drawn against the Englishman had not been carefully administered, but made in the hurried flurry of panic.

She ought to deliver these maps into the hands of her father, but something stopped her. Papa did not need information to make his killings easier, no matter what she thought of the French. These were English maps, any military advantage gained belonged to them. On the road west she would give them back to the captain to take home and say nothing of them to her father. Perhaps they might be some recompense for Lucien Howard coming into Spain with an army that had been far too small and an apology, too, for his substantial injuries.

She felt tired out from her worrying, shattered by her father's reactions to the Englishman. She had hardly slept in weeks for the dread of finding him with his throat cut or simply not there when she hovered outside his chamber just to see that he still breathed.

She did not want to be this person, this worrier. But no matter how the day started and how many hours she could stretch it out between making sure he was neither dead nor gone, she also couldn't truly relax until the continued health and welfare of Captain Lucien Howard had been established.

A knock on the door had her standing very still and she glanced at herself in the mirror opposite. She looked as if she had been crying, her eyes red and swollen. The knock came again.

'Who is it?' Her tone was strong.

'Your father, Alejandra. Can I come in?'

Concealing the maps in a drawer, she wiped at her eyes with the sleeve of her jacket and rubbed her cheeks. If the skin there was a little redder, her eyes would not show up quite so much. Then she flicked the lock.

Enrique Fernandez y Castro strode in and shut the door behind him. Slowly. She knew the exact second he recognised she had been upset.

'If your mother were here…' he began, but she shook that train of thought away and he remained silent.

Rosalie Santo Domingo y Giminez stood between them in memory and sometimes this was the only thing they still had in common, their love for a woman who had been good and brave and was gone. Both of them had dealt with her death in different ways, her father with his anger and his wars and her with a sense of distance that sometimes threatened to overcome her completely. But they seldom spoke of Rosalie now. To lessen the anguish, she surmised, and to try to survive life with the centre of their world missing.

'The English earl is gaining his strength back.' This was not phrased as a question. 'I have heard he is a man of intellect and intuition. What do you make of him?'

'A good man, I think, Papa. A man who might do your bidding in London well if you let him.'

'He could be dangerous. To you on the way west. Others could take him.'

Alejandra knew enough of her father to feign indifference, for if she insisted on accompanying Lucien Howard she also knew that he would surely change his plans, so she stayed silent.

'Tomeu says he can read minds.'

At that she laughed. 'And you believe him?'

'I believe there might be more to him than we can imagine, Alejandra, and we need to take care that he knows only so much about us.'

'The house, you mean. The security of this place and the manpower?'

'Take him out blindfolded. I do not wish for him to see the gates or the bridges. Or the huts down by the river.'

'Very well.'

'And leave him in Corcubion, no further. You should be able to find him a boat to England from there and it is a lot closer.'

'Adan has family in Pontevedra.'

'Almost a week away by the mountain paths. I want you back sooner.'

'Very well.' Her mind reeled with the implications

of sending him from a town that did not have the protections of the others.

'Here is a purse.' The leather bag was tied with plaited rope and it was heavy. 'He costs me much, this British spy. If you feel at any time he is not worth the danger, then kill him. I have instructed Adan and Manolo to do the same. Anything at all that might bring trouble. You will leave here three days from now.'

'But he is not well enough, Papa.'

'If he can't walk out of here by then, he will never do anything else. Do you understand me, daughter? No more.'

'Indeed.' Her father wanted the English captive gone and if it could not be done with any sense of decorum, then he would simply get rid of the problem altogether. 'But we will leave when it is dark for it will be safer that way.' She needed to give Captain Howard time to acclimatise and the night-time would help. If they went late, it would mean only a few hours of walking.

'Good. I shall not see him before he goes for I am off to Betanzos before dawn on the morrow and will be there for a week. Give him my promise that someone will be contacting him. Soon.'

'I shall.'

He smiled at that, a quiet movement that made him look more like the handsome and kind father of old. It seemed so long since she had felt such kinship.

'Go with God, Alejandra.' He tipped his head and

left the room, the sound of his steps on the tiles outside fading.

She had three days to prepare the English captain for the gruelling walk, though now they would not go into the mountains, it seemed, but along the coast. That might be easier for him, but harder for them with the lack of cover. Juan's family, the Diego y Betancourts, inhabited this part of the land and they would need to take care to avoid notice.

Swearing softly, she thought of the difficult steps the captain had managed today. No more than a few hundred hard-fought yards till he needed to rest.

In three days he would not have that luxury. Extracting her rosary from her top pocket, she prayed to the Lord for strength, courage and perseverance. For both of them.

Lucien took in breath.

The new day was cloudless but cold and Alejandra stood beside him watching. Further afield he saw a group of others turn and stare.

'Don't come with me,' he instructed as she took the first step when he did. 'Wait here and I will be back.'

'The *orujo* will warm you, *señor*.' No 'good luck' or whispered encouragement. He was glad for it.

He was neither dizzy today nor light-headed and he had eaten a substantial breakfast for the first time in weeks. He was also aware of the heavy shadows beneath Alejandra's eyes.

Taking the first step, he kept on going. The hedges of lavender were at each side of him now, he could smell the scent of the leaves, heady and pungent. Then the small space of chipped stones and the three rising steps.

He stopped before them and redrew in breath. He was sweating and the bravado that he had started with had waned a little, the stairway requiring a lot more in effort than the flatness of the path.

There was no handrail, nothing to hold on to as he raised one foot and transferred his weight. One. Two. Three. The deck welcomed him and shaded him, another flower he had no notion of sending a pungent odour into the air all around.

When he turned he saw her, standing still against the olives in the distance, her hands knotted before her as if she had been certain he might fall.

He smiled and she smiled back, the journey now easier in its return.

He could do it, the steps, the pathway, the lavender hedges and then back to the trees where he had left her. He did not even need to sit down when he reached the olives, but stood there, snatching the hat from his head and taking the ornate glass cup that she had filled from her hand.

'Salud.'

'Good health,' Lucien gave back in English and their beakers touched, the cold of the tipple drawing trails across glass. He was elated with his progress and far less exhausted than he imagined he might have been. Tomorrow he would try for a longer distance and the next day more again.

'We leave in two nights for the west.'

That soon? The liquor burnt down his throat and touched the nausea that roiled in his stomach, but he would not let her see that as he took another sip.

Despite his success this morning he could not even imagine climbing into the foothills of the Cantabrians or the Galicians and pretending energy and health for hours and hours on end.

'If you lag behind, you will be shot. My father's orders.'

Finishing his drink, he held out his glass for more. 'Then I hope the firewater is all that you say it is.'

'Papa has enemies here and the French have not withdrawn. But we know this place like the back of our hands, the secret trails, the hidden paths, and we will be armed.'

'We?'

'Adan, Manolo and I.' She looked around as if to check no one else was close. 'You have your knife, Capitán. Make certain it is within easy reach and keep it hidden. If anyone threatens you, use it.'

'Anyone?' His eyes scanned her dark ones.

'Anyone at all,' she returned and finished the last of her *orujo*.

'Clothes will be brought to your room for the journey. And hair dye. The pale of your hair would give you away completely. Constanza will come and do it.'

'A disguise, then?'

He saw how she hesitated, the stories of men captured without their uniform and hanged perfunctorily so much a part of folklore. With a cloak over blue and white he might be safer, but those travelling with him would not.

'You speak Spanish like a native of this part. It will have to be enough.'

'Do you expect trouble?'

She only laughed.

The pleasure of completing the walk had receded a little, but Lucien did not want her to see it. Even the *orujo* was warring against his stomach, a strong dram that scoured his digestive system after six weeks of bland gruel.

'Can I ask you a question, Alejandra?' She nodded. 'What happened to your husband?'

The deep green of her eyes sharpened, bruising in memory. 'He betrayed us, so he died.'

The shock of her answer left him reeling. 'How?'

'The betrayal or the death?'

'Both.'

'It was almost a year ago now and it was winter and cold. There was a fight and my husband lost. He died slowly, though.'

'Three months' worth of slowly? It is his room I am in.'

'How could you possibly know that?' She had stepped back now and her voice shook.

'The marks on my wall. February had twenty-nine days in the last year only and March has thirty-one. I am presuming he died on April the fifteenth. I think you placed the marks there. To remember.'

'I did.' This time she held nothing back in the quiet fury. 'I drew them into the plaster every night I stood in his room and wished him dead. It was for money he betrayed us. Did you figure that out, too? For the princely sum of pesos and guns, enough to start his own army and replace my father. And me.'

'He confessed?'

'No. A shot through the head was not conducive to any sort of explanation. Papa only let him live so that he might understand his reasoning and to see who else was implicated in the plot.'

'Did El Vengador find others?'

'He died without speaking again.' Her answer came back with fierceness and Lucien could see in her eyes the truth of hurt. 'Though it seems he could still write. I had not known that.'

A minute later she was gone.

The words in the Bible had been her late husband's handiwork, then? Lucien wondered what he had done to Alejandra to make her hate him so very much.

Chapter Five

Sometimes the weather in Spain, even in winter, could be windless and dry.

But on this night, early in the first week of March, the gales howled from the north in a single blowing force, enough pressure in it to make Lucien lean forward to find balance. The rains came behind, drenching, icy and cold.

His clothes at least were keeping the wet out and the warmth in. He was surprised how comfortable his new boots were and pleased the hat he had been given had a wide and angled brim. He had long since lost the feeling in his bare fingers, though.

They had been walking for a good two hours and he'd managed to keep up. Just. Alejandra hovered behind him, Adan and the other man, Manolo, cutting through the bushes ahead.

'We will stop soon.' Her words were muffled by the rain.

'And make camp?'

'More like sleep,' she returned. 'It is too dangerous

to risk a fire, but the trees there will allow us at least shelter.'

He looked up. A moon was caught behind the heavy cloud, but he could see the dark shape of a line of pines about a quarter of a mile away.

He was glad for it, for although he carried very little in the bag on his back, his body ached with the prolonged exercise after such a sickness. He had not eaten much, either, his stomach still recovering from the effects of the *orujo*.

He knew Alejandra had slowed to match his pace and was thankful for it, the blunt warning she had given him still present.

Adan suddenly tipped his head. Alarmed, Lucien did the same and the sound of far-off voices came on the wind. A group of men, he determined, and ones who thought they were alone in these passes. A hand gesture had him dropping down and Alejandra crawled up beside him.

'They are about a quarter of a mile away, but heading north. Nine or ten of them, I think, with horses.'

She pulled the brown coat she wore across her head and dug into the cavity of dirt on the edge of their track.

Further ahead there was no sign at all of the others. He guessed they, too, had blended in with the undergrowth, staying put as the foreign party passed.

His eyes went to the leaves above them. Downwind. If there were dogs, they would stay safe.

Alejandra held her pistol out and her knife lay in her lap. He removed his own blade and fitted it into his fist, wishing he had been given a gun as well and rueing the loss of the fine weapons he had marched up to A Coruña with.

The rain had lightened now, beads of it across Alejandra's cheeks and in the long dark strands of hair that had escaped from the fastening beneath her hat.

He wondered if she had killed before. The faces of the many men he had consigned to the afterlife rose up in memory, numerous ghostly spectres wrapped about the heart of battle. He had long since ceased to mourn them.

The enforced rest had allowed his heartbeat to slow and the breath in him to return. Even the tiredness was held temporarily at bay by this new alertness. They were not French, he was sure of that; too few and too knowledgeable of the pathway through the foothills. A band of men of the same ilk as El Vengador, then? Guerrillas roaming the countryside. He could hear a few words of Spanish in the wind.

'It's the Belasio family,' Alejandra explained as he looked up. 'On their way back to their lands.'

'You saw them?'

She smiled and shook her head. 'I smelt them.' When her nose sniffed the air he smiled, for the rain and wind had left only wetness across the scent of winter and earth and she was teasing. Still, the small humour in the middle of danger was comforting.

'They are armed partisans, too?'

'Yes.'

'Then surely we would hardly be enemies?'

'There are no hard and fast rules to this kind of

warfare. We have guns they want and your presence here would have been noted.'

'Me?'

'There is money in the exchange of prisoners. Good money, too, and it is difficult to hide the blue of your eyes. You do not look Spanish even though you speak the language well.'

He swore. 'Where are we going?'

'Corcubion. It is a small harbour two days away.'

'I thought I had heard Muros?'

She shook her head and stood. 'My father and Adan are insistent on the closer port given your condition. Come, the Belasios are gone now and the trees are not far.'

Thirty minutes later they stopped beneath the pines. It was full dark and the rain had gone, though the intermittent drips from drenched boughs above were heavy.

'We will leave again at first light.' Adan, the older of the two men, stated this as he bedded down in the lee of a medium-sized bush and the other man joined him. A good twenty yards away Alejandra stayed at Lucien's side.

He knew there was bread in his bag and he pulled out the crust of it and began to eat. Any sustenance would see him through the next day and he needed all the energy he could muster. He wished he still had his silver flask filled with good English brandy, but it had gone with the rest of his things. The French, probably, when they had first caught him.

He did have a skin of Spanish red wine and he drank this thankfully. Alejandra simply sat there, neither eating nor drinking. She looked tired through the gloom and he handed her the skin.

Surprisingly she took it, wiping the mouth of the vessel with her sleeve when she had finished before giving it back.

'Do you want bread, too?'

She shook her head and arranged her bag as a pillow, fastening the cloak she wore about her and curling into sleep.

Overhead a bird called once. He had heard very few on the march up with the British in the lower valleys of the Cantabrians. But outside Lugo he had shot a substantial owl and sucked the warm blood from its body, because there was neither wood nor safety to cook it and he had not eaten for three days. Then he had plucked the breast and stuffed the feathers in his ruined boots to try to ward off frostbite.

He breathed out. Hard. It was relatively warm here under the trees and he had food, drink and a soft bed. The pine needles formed a sort of mattress as he lay down on his back and looked up. His knife he placed within easy reach, just outside the folds of his jacket.

'You are a careful man.' Alejandra's words were whispered.

'I have learnt that it pays to expect trouble.'

'It is my opinion that we will be safe tonight. The noise of the eagle owl, the birds you heard cry out before, is why we stop here. They roost in the trees above and are like sentries. If anything moves within a thousand yards of us, they will all be silent.'

'A comforting warning,' he returned softly, and her white teeth flashed in the darkness.

'Spain is like a lover, Señor Howard, known and giving to those who are born here. The bird sounds, the berries, the many streams and the pine needles beneath us. It is the strangers that come who change the balance of the place, the ones with greed in their eyes and the want of power.'

She saw the way he stretched out, his knife close and a sense of alertness that even sickness and a long walk had not dimmed.

She knew it had been hard for him, this climb. She had seen it in the gritted lines of his face and in the heavy beat of his pulse. His silence had told her of it, as well. It was as if every single bit of his will was used in putting one foot in front of the other and trudging on. The wine might dim the pain a little. She hoped it would.

He had removed his hat just before the light had fallen and the newly dyed darkness of his hair changed the colour of his eyes to a brighter blue. If anyone at all looked at him closely, they would know him as a stranger, a foreigner, a man to be watched.

'It is mostly downhill tomorrow.' The words came even as she meant not to say them, but there was some poignancy in one who had been so very sick and whose strength was held only by the threads of pure and utter will. He would not complain and she was thankful for it.

On her part all she wanted to do was sleep. His presence at the hacienda had left her fretting for his safety, mindful of her father's propensity to do away with problems and so for many nights she had barely slumbered.

Here at least Manolo and Adan were a good way off and Lucien Howard's knife was sharp. There was some ease in being next to him as well and she had made sure to place her blanket roll between the captain and the others. It was as much as she could do.

The birds above called and insects buzzed about them, zinging in the night. The music of a quiet forest unthreatened by advancing armies or groups of the enemy.

She felt the warmth of Lucien Howard's shoulder as she turned away and slept.

Lucien woke as the first chorus of general birdsong sounded. Alejandra was still asleep, her arm across his as if the warmth had brought it there in a mind all of its own. One finger was badly scarred and another had lost a nail altogether. The hand of a girl who had seen hardship and pain. The lines he had noticed before on her right wrist showed up as multiple white slashes in the dullness.

He remembered all the other hands of the women of the *ton* with their painted nails and smoothness and he wanted to reach out and take her fingers in his own with a desperateness that surprised him. In sleep she looked younger, the tip tilt of her nose strangely innocent and freckles on the velvet of her cheeks.

A wood nymph and a warrior. When a spider crawled up the run of her arm he carefully brushed it away. Still, she came awake on the tiniest of touches, from slumber to complete wakefulness in less than a blink.

'Good morning.'

She did not answer him as she sat, her hair falling in a long tousled curtain to her waist, the darkness in it threaded with deeper reds and black.

He saw her glance at the sky. Determining time, he supposed, and marking the hour of dawn. The steel in her knife's hilt had left deepened ridges on the skin of her forearm, so close had she held it as she slept. When her glance took in the empty clearing she looked around.

'Where are the others?'

'They went to the stream we can hear running, about ten minutes ago. I should imagine they will be back soon.'

Standing she packed her things away and kicked at the pine needles with her feet.

'It is better no one knows we were here. A good tracker could tell, of course, but someone merely passing by...' She left the rest unsaid, but the green in her eyes was wary as she turned to him. 'Spain is not a soft country, Capitán Howard. It is a land with its heart ripped out.'

'Yet you stay here. You do not leave.'

'It's home,' she said simply and handed him a hard

cooked biscuit, the top of which was brushed in a
sugar syrup. 'For walking,' she explained when he
looked at it without much appetite. 'If you do not eat,
you will be slower.'

He felt better now that it was morning, the old
sense of energy and purpose returning; perhaps it
was the change of scenery or the hope of getting back
to England soon that did it. His companion's smile
was also a part of the equation. Without the scowl
or the anger Alejandra Fernandez y Santo Domingo
was beautiful. Breathtakingly so, he supposed, if she
were to be seen in a gown that fitted and a face that
was not always filthy.

Where the hell was this train of thought going?
He pulled his mind back to their more immediate
problems.

'Do you have any idea on the movements of the
French?'

'Marshal Soult has taken Oporto and Marshal Vic-
tor and Joseph Bonaparte hold the centre and Madrid.
They seldom travel in small groups in this part of the
country anyway.'

'Because they are afraid of being picked off by
the guerrillas?'

'Would you not be, too, Capitán?'

Their travelling companions were back now and
Alejandra gestured to them to give her a moment as
she disappeared into the bushes in the direction of
the stream. Left alone with the two men, Lucien was
suddenly tense. Something was wrong; he felt it in
his bones and he was too much of a soldier not to take

notice. He had his knife out instantly as he turned to find the threat.

'Someone's close,' he said, 'to the east.' Manolo and Adan also drew their weapons and moved up beside him.

They came out of nowhere, a group of men dressed in a similar fashion as they were, the first discharging gun slamming straight into the gut of Adan. He fell like a stone, dead as he hit the ground, eyes wide to the heavens above in surprise. Lucien had his knife at the assailant's throat before the man could powder up again, slicing the artery in a quick and simple task of death. Then he did the same to the next one. Alejandra was in the clearing now, her knife out and her breathing loud. He stepped in front of her, keeping her out of the line of fire. Two more men, he counted. Manolo disposed of one and then fell against flashing steel. As Lucien advanced the last man simply turned tail and ran. Stooping to pick up a stone, he threw it as hard as he could and was pleased to hear a yelp further away. He'd have liked to have sent his blade, too, but he did not want to lose it.

The quiet returned as quickly as it had left, the shock in Alejandra's voice vibrating as she kneeled first beside Adan and then Manolo.

'Dios mio. Dios mio. Dios mio.'

Manolo clutched her hand and tried to say something, but the words were shallow and indistinct. In return she simply held his fingers stained in blood and dirt and waited until the final breath was wrenched from him. Folding his arms across his stomach and closing his eyes, she swore roundly and stood to see to Adan. With him she arranged the cloth of his jacket across the oozing wound at his stomach before covering his eyes with her handkerchief. The small piece of fabric was embroidered with purple and blue flowers, Lucien saw, a delicate example of fine stitchery from her past.

'It was the Betancourts. I recognised them from before, but we will revenge them. It is what my father is good at.'

With a deft movement she collected the discarded weapons and water bottles and covered the bodies of her fellow partisans with pine needles, reciting some sort of prayer over them with her rosary. Then she indicated a direction. He could see tears on her cheeks, though she brushed them away with the coarse fabric of her jacket as she noticed his observation.

'We have no time to bury them properly. Those who did this will be back as soon as the others are informed and they will be baying for revenge. Adan and Manolo would not wish to die for nothing, so now we will have to use the mountain tracks to go west and see you safe.'

She struck out inland, away from the sea, the breeze behind them. As they traversed along a river, making sure to place their feet only in the rocky centre of it for a good quarter of a mile, they saw the first scree slopes of the mountains.

She listened, too, every three or four minutes stopping and turning her head into the wind so that sounds might pass down to her, in warning.

Lucien knew inside that no one followed them. Always when he had tracked for Moore across the front of a moving army he had held the knowledge of others. Here, the desolate cold and open quiet contained only safety.

The Betancourts might try to follow them, but he and Alejandra had been careful to leave no trace of themselves as they had walked and the rains had begun again, the water washing away footfalls.

'You have done this before?' he finally asked when Alejandra indicated a stop.

'As many times as you have, Capitán. Who taught you to fight with a knife like that?'

'A rum maker in Kingston Town. I was a young green officer with all the arrogance associated with it. A man by the name of Sheldon Williams took the shine off such cockiness by challenging me to a fight.'

When he saw she was interested he continued.

'It was hot, too, mid-July and no breeze, the greasy smell of the sea in the air and a good number of ships in. He could have killed me twenty times or more, but he didn't. Instead he showed me how to live.'

'You fight like my father.'

'Is that a compliment?'

She shook away his question with a frown.

She couldn't take him home now, not with Manolo and Adan dead and a father who would place the blame on the Englishman's presence for it and kill him. The horror of their deaths hit her anew as a great wave of grief broke inside.

No. She would have to take him on over the Galician Mountains and down into Pontevedra in the hope that Adan's family might help them. A longer walk and one she had done only a few times before and always under guidance. Her whole body ached with the grief of more death, so senseless and quick.

She was on edge, too. The way Lucien Howard had slit the throats of those who had attacked them was so gracefully brutal and deceptively practised that she was wary. A man like this would make a dangerous enemy and alone with him she would need to be careful.

Still, she could not just leave him. Another thought occurred. He wore the sickness of exhaustion on his face and she noticed blood seeping again through the fabric of his jacket. From the wound on his neck, she supposed, the one that had not yet healed.

An Englishman alone in Spain would have no chance of escaping through any of the harbours on the east side of A Coruña. People here would be naturally suspicious, the scourge of the French having left a residual hatred for anyone new and different.

He spoke the language well, she would give him that, but his eyes were the light blue of a foreigner and the dye in his hair was already weakening. When she noticed the pale gold in the roots of his parting that small false truth of him firmed up resolve.

Rifling in her bag, she drew out the maps she had

found concealed under the last blanket of his dead horse.

'These are yours.'

He wiped his hands against his jacket before he reached out and took the offered documents, spreading the pages wide to ascertain they were all there.

'I thought them lost.' Puzzlement lay on his brow.

'They were trapped beneath your horse and I saw them as we lifted it off you. Did you draw them?'

'Partly. I had a group of guides and the information was collated over several months of travel. Maps like this have enormous value.'

'To those who would pillage Spain? The secrets of the mountains exposed to those who would want to rape it more quickly.'

'Or protect it.'

She laughed then because she could not help it. Once, she might have believed in the noble pursuits of soldiers. 'Good or bad? There is a fine line between each, Capitán. People die here because of armies. Innocent people, and a land in winter has a limit on the succour it can manage to harvest before starvation settles in. In the north we have reached that limit. Another season of battle and there will be nothing left in Galicia save for the freedom to starve.'

She had not meant to say as much, to give a man as clever as the one before her the true slant of her opinion. But she had ceased many months ago to believe in the easy spoils of war or the glory in it.

'Liberty and safety always come at a price, I'll give you that.' His eyes were threaded with weariness.

'And today Adan and Manolo paid for it dearly. The French will come and then they will go because there is no way they can stay here and live and people like the Betancourts will be swallowed up by bitterness and hate until there is nothing left of them, either. That, Capitán, is the true cost of valour. No one ever wins. Not for ever. Not even for a little while.'

'But is not simply accepting subjugation the true meaning of surrender?' The planes on his cheeks held the light and his eyelashes were the darkest of blacks against the pale of his skin.

Once, she had thought the same, Alejandra conceded. Once, before her mother and her husband and friends had all been consigned to the afterlife she might have imagined resistance to be worth it, to be honourable, even, and right. But no more. Her heart had been lost to the other side of caring months and months ago, before Juan even, before he had betrayed her and her father for the heady lure of gold and power.

A mishmash of promises had left her grappling for even one honest hope for Spain. All she wished for was peace and a rest from the war and blood that surrounded them. The face of Adan surprised by his death came to mind and she turned it away, unable to bear the image. It could have so easily been her. Or Lucien Howard. It could have been them tonight lying stiff on the cold earth with the pine needles across their faces.

'England is a soft country, Capitán, and far from

battle. If I were a woman of Britain, I should never leave it.'

'Come with me, then, when I go. You could be safe there.'

She was intrigued by his words. 'A large promise, *señor*. Too large to believe in, I am afraid, and if it is a choice between battle here or homesickness there, then I think I should always choose the former.'

Unexpectedly he reached out and took her hand and she wished that her nails had been cleaner or her skin softer. Stupid foolish wishes here out in the mountains with the scent of Adan's and Manolo's blood between them and a hundred hard miles to go.

'I appreciate that you are helping me to get home.' His words were quiet and for the first time she could hear a hint of foreignness within them.

It had been so long since someone had touched her with gratitude and kindness that she was overcome with a kind of dizzying unbalance. For a second she wanted to wind her fingers into his strength and follow him to England. The absurdity of that thought made her pull away and place a good distance between them.

'I would have done it for anyone.' But she knew it was not true, that small dishonesty. Right from the first second of seeing Lucien Howard on the battlefield above A Coruña, his long pale hair pinked in blood, she had felt a…sameness, a connection. Unexplainable. Unsettling.

The edges of his lips turned up into humour as he pushed a length of hair away from his eyes.

He held his maps in the other hand with a careful deliberateness and scanned the trees behind. A noise had caught his attention, perhaps, or a bird frightened from its perch. They were too high up for any true danger and the nights without cover were cold. Already the snowdrifts could be seen and if it rained again the ice would form. His breath clouded with the condensation and she felt a momentary panic about exposure. If it darkened and they could not find shelter...

'We have at least five hours before the night settles.' She wondered how he did that, reading her mind without warning and taking the words she was about to say.

A guide, he had said, for General Moore. Penning maps and alone before the main body of the English army as it ran before the worst storm in decades across the Cantabrian Mountains. Even looking at him she could see he fitted into this landscape with an astounding ease and mastery; a chameleon, hurt and exhausted, but as dangerous as they came.

He had bent to lift a dried acorn now, peeling off the husks to let them blow in the breeze. ''Tis nor-norwest. Another day and there will be heavier rain in it. Sleet, too, if the temperatures keep dropping. Do you know the way?'

Alejandra did not answer. If she got her bearings wrong, then they were both dead. There was very little civilisation between here and Pontevedra and already she was shaking.

Not all from cold, either, she thought to herself.

Anger was a part of it, too, that she should allow her worry for this man to override sense.

She could easily slip into the forest around them and disappear, leaving him with his wits to follow and the pine needles and oak leaves to bed down in. But she saw the fever in his eyes even as he held her glance, daring her not to comment, and turned to stride out before her. The bloodstain across his shoulders had widened and every so often a drip of crimson lay on the earth and bracken as he walked.

Chapter Six

An hour later Lucien knew he needed to stop, needed to lie down and reassemble his balance and his energy. His neck ached and the wound had re-opened; the warmth of blood had held the cold at bay for a time until it could do so for no longer. Now he felt the shivers even across the soles of his feet.

'We can camp here.' Alejandra's voice cut through his thoughts and he looked around. The clearing was undisturbed by civilisation, with a view wide down across the way they had just come. But most surprising of all was the tall tree tucked just before the overhang, the roots of it providing a shelter of sorts.

'Like a house—' she smiled '—with walls and a ceiling. I have used them before.'

'An oak?' The leaves and structure of the tree were not quite familiar.

She nodded. 'Spanish sessile oak. Different from English oak, I think.'

Lucien put down his rucksack and sat against it. If

he had been alone, he would have closed his eyes and tried to regroup, but he could see from the expression on her face that she was already worried by the tenuous nature of his health and he did not wish to add to her concerns. The hardness of the bark hurt and he leant forward a little. He needed to get his jacket off and some water on to the heat of the wound, but in the descending dusk and cold there would be little chance of such doctoring.

'You are shivering.'

He simply looked up at her, unable to hide the reaction of his body further. It was finished, this pretence. He couldn't have moved had his life depended on it, not even if a bunch of marauding partisans were to have charged at that moment through the trees.

'Leave me and go home. You'd have a better chance of surviving if—' She did not let him finish.

'I didn't take you for a quitter, Capitán.'

He smiled because that was what he might have said to her had the tables been turned.

'Besides, you have been hurt before just as badly. I saw the scars on your body when we brought you from the battlefields of A Coruña and if you can survive once, you can do so twice, or a thousand times.'

Her words rattled him. Had it been her who had stripped off his ruined uniform after the battle? He'd been nude beneath the covers when he had awoken in the quiet room that first time, a bandage the only thing covering him.

'Who undressed me?'

'Oh, I forget that you English have such a large

dollop of prudishness. War has changed things like that here.' She was rummaging through her bag, so Lucien was unable to determine her expression, though he could hear the humour in her voice. 'Take off both your shirt and jacket so I can see to you.'

He made no move whatsoever to do as she asked.

'Salve,' she explained as she found what she'd been searching for. 'Constanza gave this to me before we left. She said if the wound bled again and you had a fever, I was to make certain to use it.'

For just one moment Lucien thought to simply ignore her and lie down, but the throb in his neck was making his temples ache badly and he knew slumber would be hard to come by in such a state.

Hating the way his fingers fumbled, he unbuttoned the heavy jacket and then the shirt, the fabric of the latter sticking to his skin. When he tugged harder the coppery smell of fresh blood filled the air around them and he thought for an instant he might be sick.

The cold was helping, though, the breath of the mountains soothing and smooth. When Alejandra walked behind and laid her fingers against his shoulder to draw the last piece of fabric away, he started.

'It is off,' she said after a moment, 'and the bleeding has slowed.' Drawing a picture with her forefinger on his skin, she gave him words, as well. 'The cuts are deeper in the middle here than at each side and it is only those ones above your spine that have festered and still bleed.'

He'd been taken from the back. Lucien remembered the first pain as Guy had fallen.

Turning on his horse to fight, he'd drawn his sword quickly, but there had been too many and at too close a range. He had no true recollection of what had happened next save for a vague recall of place. The first true memory was on the field above A Coruña, waking to find Alejandra kneeling beside him and his steed's heavy head across his abdomen.

She washed the injury with cool water and blotted the blood with something soft. The salve held the smell of garlic, lavender and camphor and was cooling. Then she gave him a cup with herbs infused in water taken from a glass container within her rucksack. Its lid was of red wax.

'Stay still while I wrap your wound for protection.' Careful hands went beneath his armpits and then met at the middle. Her breath at his nape was warm and soft and he clung to the touch of it as she pulled the bandage tight.

'You are lucky this was not a few inches higher, Capitán. Nobody could survive a wound that severed the vein there and it was a near thing indeed.'

Close up the green in her eyes held other colours, brown, gold and yellow, and her lashes were long and dark. He had never had these sorts of conversations with a woman before, full of challenge and debate. He suddenly wished that they could sit here and simply talk for ever. The medicine, he supposed, the concoction of some drug that scattered his mind into foolishness and maudlin hope.

He stood unsteadily and put his clothes back on, watching as she arched up, her bag at her feet. A much more sizeable sack than the one he held, Lucien noted, angered by his weakness.

With her hat removed the long thick length of dark hair fell across one shoulder and down towards the curve of her waist. He glanced away. He would be gone in a matter of days and she would not be interested in his admiration. But the green eyes had held his with the sort of look that on any other woman might be deemed as flirtatious.

After a few moments she sat down opposite to him. When she gave him a strip of dried meat to chew he took it thankfully.

'The rain has stopped, at least, but even in good weather it will take us two more days to reach the port town of Pontevedra. More if you become sicker.' The impatience in her words told him she had little time for illness.

'Will your father not wonder where you are?'

'Papa has gone down to Betanzos for a week. I shall be home soon after, using the coastal route.'

'A quicker option when I am not with you, holding you back?'

Frowning, she observed him more closely. 'Are you very rich, Capitán Howard?'

Her question surprised him. Alejandra Fernandez y Santo Domingo did not strike him as a woman who would be so much enchanted with the size of one's purse.

'Your query reminds me of the debutantes in the court of London who weigh up the fortune of each suitor before they choose the most wealthy.'

At that she smiled. 'I was only wondering whether offering you up for a bounty would be more beneficial to our cause than the other option of sending you home. The rebel movement has a great deal of need for money.'

'I have an ancient pile in Kent and a town house in London. Expensive in their own right, I suppose, but not ready cash, you understand, and all entailed. Other than that...' He spread his hands out palm upwards.

'You are penniless?'

He did not mean to, but he laughed and the sound echoed around the clearing. 'Not quite, but certainly heading that way.'

'In truth, you are blessed by such a state, then. My fortune was what led me into marriage in the first place.' Her teeth pulled at the dry piece of meat. 'Papa chose Juan for me as a husband because he was older and a man of means and power.' Her words held a flat tone of indifference.

'And what happened?'

'I married him in the middle of winter and he was dead before the spring.'

'Because he betrayed your father?'

'And because he betrayed me.'

Her glance held his across the darkening space and Lucien saw all that was more usually hidden.

'So El Vengador dealt with him and you made the marks in the limewash to record his death?'

She nodded. 'I struck them off one by one by one. To remember what marriage was like.'

'And never do it again?'

Tipping her chin, she faced him directly. 'You may not believe this, but in my life men have liked me, Capitán. Many men. Even since Juan I have had offers of marriage and protection. And more.'

In the dusk he could so easily believe this, the deep dimples on her cheeks showing as shadow and her dark eyes flashing.

'But they also know I am my father's daughter and so they are wary.'

'A lonely place to be, that? Caught in the middle.'

'More so than you might imagine, Capitán.'

God. Such an admission would normally have sent his masculine urges into overdrive, but the sickness had weakened him and she knew it.

The moon had risen now, a quarter moon that held only a little light in the oncoming darkness. The noises of birdsong had dimmed, too, and it was as if they sat on top of a still and unmoving world, the tones of sepia and green and grey overwhelming. Far, far away north through the clouds and the mist would be the sea and England. Sitting here seemed like a very long way from home, though he felt better with the rest and the medicines, his strength returning in a surprising amount.

Lucien Howard was watching her closely and had been ever since leaving the hacienda, the roots of his hair in the rising night filled with the pale of moonlight.

If he had not been so sick, she might have simply moved forward and wrapped herself about him just to satisfy her curiosity about what he might truly feel like. Juan had been the sort of man who spoke first and thought about things later, but this army captain, this English earl, was different. Every single thing he said was measured by logic and observation and there was something in the careful cut-edged words he used that appealed.

'Are you married?' She had not meant to ask this so baldly and was glad when he smiled.

'No?' The small inflection he used lifted the word into question.

'Have you ever been?' She caught the quick shake of his head and breathed out.

'You are wise, then. Marriage takes large pieces of one away.' Alejandra was glad that he could not see her hands fisting at this confession. 'With the wrong person it is both a trap and a horror.'

She'd never told anyone this. She wondered why she was speaking of it now out here in the silence of night. She frowned, thinking that she did know, of course. It was the residue of shame and wrath that still sat in her throat as a constant reminder of humiliation. And it was also because of Lucien Howard's courage.

Her fingers found the cross she wore at her neck, the gold warming in her hands.

'A few people seem to manage the state of holy matrimony quite well.' He gave her this very quietly.

'A fortuitous happenstance that in my experience is not often repeated.'

The deep rumble of his laughter was comforting. She wished she could build a fire to see him better but did not dare to risk the flame. Her stomach rumbled after eating the dried meat and she longed for heartier fare, especially now they would be traversing the high passes instead of the faster and easier coastal roads.

She saw him abruptly turn his head, tipping it to one side and listening as he pushed himself up. Then his knife was thrown, a single flash in the almost dark, the metal catching moonlight as it rifled across the space in the clearing to fall in a heavy thump.

He was back in a moment with a large rabbit skewered by steel, his eyes going to the dark empty space before them. 'I will build a fire to cook it, but not here.'

Gathering dried sticks, he dug a hole in the ground a good ten yards away behind the trunk of the oak and bent to the task of finding flame.

Alejandra was astonished. She had never seen anyone kill prey with such ease. Even she, who was used to these woods and this clime, would not have aimed with such a precision through the dark. And now they would have a decent meal and warmth.

He was making her look like a woman without skill. Leaning forward, she took the rabbit and brought out her own blade, skinning it in a few deft swipes and laying it back down on a wide clean oak leaf that was browned but whole.

'Thank you.' His words as he threaded the carcass on a stick and balanced it across other branches he had fashioned into carriers. The flames danced around the fare, blackening the outer skin before dying down.

'Will you be pleased to return home, Capitán?'

She caught the quick nod as he rolled the meat above the embers. The smell of the cooking made her stomach rumble further and, hoping he would not hear it, she shifted in her hard seat of earth.

'Did your dead husband ever hurt you?'

The question came without any preamble and the shock of it held her numb.

'Physically, I mean,' he continued when she did not answer.

'No.' Her anger was so intense she could barely grind the lie out.

'Truly?'

He turned the rabbit again, fat making the fire flare and smoke rise.

'Truly what?'

'I am trained to know when people do not tell the truth and I don't think that you are.'

In the firelight his eyes were fathomless. She had never seen a man more beautiful than him or more menacing.

Just her luck to be marooned in the mountains with a dangerous and clever spy-soldier. She should tell him it all, spit it out and see the pity mark his face. Even her father had failed to hide his reaction when he had found her there, hurt and bound in the locked back bedroom at Juan's family house, a prisoner to his demands.

'I think you should mind your own business, Capitán.'

After this the silence between them was absolute and it magnified every other sound present in a busy forest at night.

Finally, after a good half hour's quiet, he spoke.

'Perhaps conversation will be easier again if you eat.'

Taking a small offering from the flame, he split it with his knife, laying it out on another leaf to protect it from the dirt.

Despite herself she smiled. Not a man to give up, she surmised, and not a man to be ignored, either. The rabbit was succulent and well-cooked, but his gaze was upon her, waiting.

'Do you ever think, Capitán, that if you had your life again you would do some things very differently?'

He took his time to answer, but she waited. Patience was a virtue she had long since perfected.

'My father and youngest brother drowned in an accident on our estate. It was late winter, almost spring, you understand, and it was cold and the river was running fast.' He looked at her over the flames and she could see anger etched upon his brow. 'I couldn't save them. I couldn't run fast enough to reach them at the bridge.'

'How old were you?'

'Fifteen, so old enough, but I made a mistake with the distance. There was a bend a little further upstream. I could have reached them there if I had thought of it sooner.'

Precision and logic. Everything he ever said or did was underpinned by his mastery of both. He had failed his family according to his own high standards, something that was the core of her shame, as well.

'If I could go back, I would have killed my husband the first time he ever hit me. I had my knife hidden in my boot.' She hated the way her voice shook as fury made speech difficult, but still she went on. '"Thou shalt not kill" is repeated in the Bible many times. In Matthew and Exodus. In Deuteronomy and Romans. I tried to take heed of the words, but then...' Her heart beat fierce with memory. 'The second death of hell is not the worst thing that can happen after all, Capitán. It's the day-to-day living that does it.'

He nodded and the empathy ingrained in the small gesture almost undid her. 'You are not the first to think it and you most certainly won't be the last. But you were made stronger? Afterwards?'

'Yes.' No need for thought or contemplation. She knew it to the very marrow of her bones.

'Then that itself is a gift.'

It was strange but his explanation suddenly eased her terror and the truth of the realisation almost made her cry. She had failed to be a dutiful wife. She had failed in her strict observance of the Bible. She had failed in bearing the heavy stick and fists of a man who was brutal in teaching marital obedience and subservience, but she had survived. And God had made her stronger.

For the first time in a long while she breathed easier. It was a gift.

'How long have you been here in Spain, Capitán?'

'Since August of 1808. After a few skirmishes on the way north we ran for the mountains, but the snow beat us.'

'It was thick this year in the Cordillera Cantabrica. It is a wonder anyone survived such a journey.'

'Many didn't. They lay there on the side of the steep passes and never moved again. Those behind stripped them of shoes and coats.'

She had heard the stories of the English dead. The tales of the march had long been fodder for conversations about the fires at the hacienda. 'Papa said a gypsy had told him once that the French will triumph three times before they are repelled. This is the first, perhaps?'

He only laughed.

'You do not believe in such prophesy, Capitán?'

'Generals decide the movements of armies, Alejandra, not sages or soothsayers.'

'Do you think they will return? The British, I mean. Will they come back to help again, in your opinion?'

'Yes.'

She smiled. 'You are always so very certain. It must be comforting that, to believe in yourself so forcibly, to trust in all you say.'

'You don't?'

She swallowed. Once she had, before all this had happened, before a war had cut down her family and left her in the heart of chaos.

Now she was not sure of exactly who or what she was. The fabric in her trousers was dirty and ripped and the jacket she wore had come off the dead body of a headless Hussar in the field above A Coruña. It still held the dark stains of blood within the hem-line for she had neither the time nor the inclination to wash it. A life lost, nameless and vanished. It was as if she functioned in a place without past or future.

Shimmying across to sit beside him, she took his hand, opening the palm so that she might see the lines in the flame. If he was wary, he did not show it, not in one singular tiny way.

'There are some here who might read your life by mapping out the junctures and the missing gaps. Juan, my husband, was told he would meet his Maker in remorse and before his time.' She smiled. 'At least that came true.

'Pepe, the gypsy, said that I would travel and be-come a hidden woman.' She frowned. 'He said that I should be the purveyor of all secrets and help those who were oppressed. Juan was not well pleased by this reading. His life ending and mine opening out into another form. I do remember how much I wanted it to be true, though. A separation, the hope of some-thing else, something better.'

His fingers were warm and hard calloused. She wished they might curl around her own and signal more, but they did not.

She couldn't ever remember talking to another as she had to him, the hours of evening passing in confidences long held close. But it was getting colder and they needed to sleep. It would be tough in the morning with the rain on the mountains and still a thousand feet to climb.

As if sensing her tiredness he let go of her hand and stood.

'The dugout might be the best place for slumber. At least it is out of the wind.'

But small, she thought, and cosy. There would be no room between them in the close confines of the tree roots. He had already taken his coat off and laid it down on the dirt after shifting clumps of pine needles in. His bag acted as a pillow and a length of wool she recognised from the hacienda completed the bed.

'I...am not...sure.'

'We can freeze alone tonight or survive together.' His breath clouded white in the last light of the burning embers. 'Tomorrow we will hew out a pathway to the west and take our chances in finding a direction to the coast. It is too dangerous to keep climbing.'

He was right. Already the chills of cold made her stiffen and if the earlier rain returned...

Finding her own blanket, she placed it on top of his. Then, removing her boots, she got in, bundling the other two pieces of clothing from her bag on top of the blankets.

Lucien Howard scooped up more oak leaves and these added another buffer to the layers already in place. Alejandra was surprised by how warm she felt when he burrowed in beside her and spooned around her back.

When she breathed in she could smell him, too, a masculine pungent scent interwoven with the herbs she had used on his back.

Juan had smelt of tobacco and bad wine, but she shook away that memory and concentrated on making this new one. He wasn't asleep, but he was very still. Listening probably to the far-off sounds and the nearer ones. Always careful. She chanced a question.

'Are you ever surprised by anyone or anything, Capitán?'

'I try not to be.' There was humour in his answer.

'You sleep lightly, then?'

'Very.'

Her own lips curled into a smile.

She finally slept. Lucien was tired of lying so still and even the cold did not dissuade him from rising from the warmth of this makeshift bed and stretching his body out in the darkness.

His neck hurt like hell and he crossed to her sack. The salve was in here somewhere, he knew it was. Perhaps if he slathered himself with the cooling camphor he might gain a little rest.

The rosary caught him by surprise as did the small stone statue of the resurrected Jesus. She carried these with her at all times? He'd often seen her fingering something in her pocket as they walked, her lips moving in a soundless entreaty.

A prayer or a confession. Her husband would be in there somewhere, he imagined, as would her father. Spain, too, would hold a place in her Hail Marys. He looked across at her lying in the bed of pine needles and old blankets. She slept curled around herself, her fist snuggled beneath her neck, smaller again in sleep and much less fierce.

Alejandra, daughter of El Vengador. Brave and different, damaged and surviving. One foot poked out from under the coverings, the darned stockings she had worn to bed sagging around a shapely ankle.

She was thin. Too thin. What would happen to her when he left? She'd have to make her own way home through the coastal route as she had said, but even that was dangerous alone. What was it she had said of the Betancourts? They hated her family more even than they hated the French. He should insist she go back from here and press on by himself, but he knew he would not ask it.

He liked her with him, her voice, her smell, her truths. He'd have been dead on the high hills above A Coruña if any one of the others had found him, an Englishman who was nothing but a nuisance given the departed British forces. But she'd bundled him up and brought him home, the same rosary in her bag cradled against his chest and her fingers warm within his own.

She'd stood as a sentry, too, at the hacienda when danger had threatened, his sickness relegating him to a world of weakness.

Jesus, help me, he prayed into the cold and dark

March night, *and help her, too*, he added as the moon came through the banks of clouds and landed upon them, ungainly moths breaking shadows through the light.

Chapter Seven

They saw no one all the next morning as they walked west.

Lucien would have taken her hand if he thought she'd have allowed it, but he did not make the suggestion and she did not ask for any help. Rather they picked their way down, a slow and tedious process, the rain around midday making it worse.

If he had been alone, he would have stopped, simply dug into the hillside and waited for better conditions.

But Alejandra kept on going, a gnarled stick in her hand to aid in balance and a grim look across her face. She stood still often now, to listen and watch, the frown between her eyes deep.

'Are you expecting someone?' He asked the question finally because it was so obvious that she was. Tipping his head out of the northerly wind, he tried to gain the full quotient of sound.

'I hope not. But we are close here to the lands of the Betancourts.'

'And the fracas yesterday will have set them after us yet again?'

'That, too.' This time she smiled and all Lucien could think of was how fragile she looked against the backdrop of craggy mountains and steep pathways. Gone was the girl from the hacienda who had dared and defied him, the gleam of challenge egging him on and dismissing any weaker misgivings he might have felt with his neck and back on fire and a fever raging. This woman could have held each and every dainty beauty in the English court to ransom, with her dimples and her high cheekbones and the velvet green of her eyes. Beautiful she might be, but there was so much more than just that.

Men have loved me, she had said. Many men, she had qualified, and he could well believe in such a truth. Angry at his ruminations, he spoke more harshly than he meant to.

'Surely they know it was your father who shot your husband?'

'Well, Capitán, it was not quite that simple,' she replied and turned away, the flush of skin at her nape telling.

'It was you?'

'Yes.' One word barked against silence, echoing back in a series of sounds. 'But when he came back from the brink of death it was Papa who made certain he should not survive it.'

'Repayment for his acts of brutality as a husband?'

'You understand too much, Capitán. No wonder Moore named you as his spy.'

He ignored that and delved into the other unsaid. 'But someone else knew that it was you who had fired the first shot?'

'In a land at war there are ears and eyes everywhere. On that day it was a cousin of Juan's, a priest, who gave word of my violence. No one was inclined to disbelieve a man of God, you understand, even if what he said was questionable. I was younger and small against the hulk of my husband and he was well lauded for his prowess with both gun and knife.'

'A lucky shot, then?'

She turned at that to look at him straight and her glance was not soft at all. 'He was practised, but I am better. The shot went exactly where I had intended it.'

'Good for you.'

A second's puzzlement was replaced by an emotion that he could only describe as relief. The rosary was out, too, he saw it in her hands, the beads slipping through her fingers in a counted liturgy.

'You have killed people before, too, Capitán?'

'Many times.'

'Did it ever become easier?'

'No.' Such a truth came with surprising honesty and one he had not thought of much before.

'"And he that killeth any man shall surely be put to death." Leviticus, Chapter Twenty-Four, Verse Seventeen.' Her voice shook.

'You know the Bible by heart?'

'Just the parts in it that pertain to me.'

'You truly think that God in his wisdom would punish you for fighting back?'

'He was my husband. We were married in the Lord's house.'

'He was a brute and any God worth his salt would not say otherwise.'

She crossed herself at the blasphemy as he went on.

'Looking too far back can be as dangerous as looking too far forward in life. In my experience it is best to understand this moment, this hour, this day and live it.'

'It's what got you through, then? Such a belief?'

'I'm a soldier. If I made it my mantra not to kill the enemy, I would have been dead long before we left the safety of Mondego Bay, near Lisboa. No, what gets me through is knowing who I am and what I stand for.'

'England?'

He laughed. 'Much more than that, I hope.'

He looked across at the land spread out before him, its valleys and its peaks, its beauty and its danger. 'Democracy and the chance of freedom might be a closer guess. Spain is in your blood as England is in mine, yet who can say what draws us to fight to the death for them? Is it the soil or the air or the colours of home?' Picking up a clump of leaves, he let them run through his fingers, where they caught the rising wind and spun unstopped across the edge of the pathway into nothingness.

'We are like these pine needles, small in the scheme

of things, but together...' His hand now lay against the trunk of the giant tree on the side of the track, its roots binding what little was left of the soil into a steady platform.

'Together there is strength?' Alejandra understood him exactly. This war was not about Juan or her father or her. It was about democracy and choice and other things worth the blood that spilled into death to defend such freedoms. And was not personal liberty the base stone of it all? Papa had never taken the time to understand this, the residual guilt of her mother's murder overriding everything and allowing only the bitterness to survive.

The waste of it made her stumble, but a strong hand reached out.

'Careful. We are high up and the edge is close.'

She wound her fingers through his and kept them there, wishing she might move every part of her body against his to feel the honour within him. Could life be like this, she thought, could one person be simply lost in the goodness of the other for ever, not knowing where one began and the other ended?

This was a kind of music and the sort that took your breath and held it there around your heart with an ache of heaviness and disbelief. Hope lay in the knowledge of a man who had not given up his integrity despite every hardship.

Such foolish longings made her frown. Her clothes were dirty and the knife that she carried in the sleeve of her jacket was sharp. This was who she was. A woman honed by war and loss and lessened by marriage and regret; a woman whose truths had long since been shaved away by the difficulty of living from one day to the next.

He could only be disappointed in her, should he understand the parts that made her whole. Carefully she pulled away.

'We should go on.' Her voice was rough and she did not wait for him as she followed the path down the steep incline above the mist of cloud.

She barely spoke to him as they laid out their blankets that night under the stars and the warmer winds of the lower country. She hadn't looked at him all afternoon, either, as the mountain pastures had turned to coastal fields and the narrow tracks had widened into proper pathways.

They had met with a sailor who was a cousin of Adan's and he had promised to take Lucien across to England on the morrow. He'd also offered them a room for the night, but Alejandra had refused it, leading them back into the hills behind the beach where the cover of vegetation was thicker.

'Is Luis Alvarez trustworthy?' Lucien had seen the gold she had pulled from her pocket for the payment and it was substantial, but he had also seen the pain on the old man's face when Alejandra had told him of Adan's death.

'Papa says that those who make money from a war hold no scruples, but I doubt he will push you overboard in the middle of the Channel. You are too big, for one, but as Adan's kin he also owes the dead some sort of retribution.'

'That is comforting.'

She laughed and he thought he should like to hear her do it more, her throaty humour catching. Tomorrow he would be gone, away from Spain, away from these nights of talk and quiet closeness.

'Being happy suits you, Alejandra Fernandez y Santo Domingo.' Lucien would have liked to add that her name suited her, too, with its soft syllables and music. Her left wrist with the sleeve of the jacket pulled back was dainty, a silver band he had not noticed before encircling the thinness.

'There has been little cause for joy here, Capitán. You said you survived as a soldier by living in the moment and not thinking about tomorrow or yesterday?' She waited as he nodded, the question hanging there.

'There is a certain lure to that. For a woman, you understand.'

'Lure?' Were the connotations of the word in Spanish different from what they were in English?

'Addiction. Compulsion even. The art of throwing caution to the wind and taking what you desire because the consequences are distant.'

Her dark eyes held his without any sense of embarrassment; a woman who was well aware of her worth and her attraction to the opposite sex.

Lucien felt the stirring in his groin, rushing past the sickness and the lethargy into a fully formed hard ache of want.

Was she saying what he thought she was, here

on their last night together? Was she asking him to bed her?

'I will be gone in the morning.' He tried for logic.

'Which is a great part of your attraction. I am practical, Capitán, and a realist. We only know each other in small ways, but...it would be enough for me. It isn't commitment I am after and I certainly do not expect promises.'

'What is it you do want, then?'

She breathed out and her eyes in the moonlight were sultry.

'I want to survive, Capitán. You said you did this best by not thinking about the past or the future. I want the same. Just this moment. Only now.'

His words, his way of getting through, but she had turned the message in on itself and this was the result.

He should have stood and shaken his head, should have told her that the decisions made in the present did affect the future and in a way that was sometimes impossibly difficult. If he had been a better man, he might have turned and walked into the undergrowth, away from temptation. But it had been almost a year since he had slept with a woman and the need in him was great.

'You are not promised to another in England? I should not wish to harm that.' Her question came quietly and he shook his head. 'Then let me give you this gift of a memory, for my sake as well as your own.'

Her fingers went to the buttons on her shirt and she simply undid them, one by one, parting the cloth. Then she leant forward and took his hand, placing his

palm across the generous swell of her breast beneath
the chemise. The heat there simply claimed him.

She smelt of flowers and sweetness, and the silk
of her undergarment against his hand was soft. Her
hair had fallen, too, over her shoulder, unlinked pur-
posefully from the leather tie she more normally fastened it with, the dark of it binding them into the
shadows of night.

Her nipple was hard peaked, risen into feeling,
and the white column of her throat was limber and
exposed, a holy cross in gold hanging on the thin
chain. He could just take her, like this, Alejandra
Fernandez y Santo Domingo with all her beauty and
her demons, offering herself to him without demand
of more.

'Hell.' His curse had her smiling as she brought
the blanket around them, a cocoon against the winter cold.

Her hands were on his neck and his chest, feeling
her way. He hated how his breath shook and how the
certainty that was always with him was breached with
the feel of closeness.

She filled him up with hope and heat, and even
the ache of his wounds were lessened by her touch.
For so very long he had been sore and sick and lonely
and yet here, for this moment above the sea and in
the company of a woman he liked, he felt...complete.

Such recognition astonished him as his thumb
nudged across her nipple on its own accord in a
rhythm that was ancient. He felt her stiffen, felt her

fingers tighten on his arms, the nails sharp points to his skin.

'You are beautiful, Alejandra.' His member pushed against the thick fabric of his trousers.

Lifting up, he steadied her against the trunk of a pine, the blanket behind them a shield against the roughness of bark and a buffer of warmth. There was no time now, no dragging moments, no hesitation or waiting. Undoing the fastening of her trousers, he had them down around her knees before she could take a further breath and then his fingers were inside her, sheathed in warmth and wetness, the muscles there holding him in, asking for more.

'Lucien?' Her voice. Whispered. 'What is happening? What is this that you are doing to me?'

'Love as we make it, sweetheart. Open wider.' When she did as he asked he found the hard bud of her centre and pressed in close.

Her shaking was quiet at first, a small rumble and tightening, and then growing. He held her there in the night air and the moonlight and brought her to the place where the music played, languid and true, a rolling sensation of both muscle and flesh.

She was not quiet as she called his name, or gentle as she held his hand there hard inside, wanting all that he would give her, the last edge of reason gone in the final flush of orgasm.

He smiled, his gift to her new philosophy of living for the now and one that would make it easier come the morning. He wished it could have been different. He wished he could simply follow where his hand had been. But there was danger in such abandonment, the least of which was an unwanted pregnancy.

As she slid down the trunk of the tree to sit at the base of it, her knees wide open, he thought she had never looked more beautiful or more content. The smell of her sex was there, too, and he breathed in and savoured it.

'That has never happened before. To me.' Her words, quiet and tearful. Her eyes were full of unshed moisture as he moved his forefinger and the clench of her muscles echoed in answer.

'This?'

'Yes. It was exactly right.'

She was asleep before he had the blanket about them, her head cushioned against his chest. Uncoupling his hand, he sat there and tried to work out what the hell had just changed inside.

Usually sex to him was a quick thing associated with relief and little else and he left afterwards with a small but definite guilt.

But here tonight, when he had not even found his own completion, the tight want in his being was unquenched.

He prayed that this might never stop, this now, here in Spain with Alejandra in his arms. Above them in the gap of cloud a shooting star spun across the sky and he wished upon it with a fervour that shook him.

'Lord, help us.'

It was as much as he could do in this arena of war with a boat waiting to take him home on the morrow and a back full of wounds that were worsening.

Left in his company, she would be compromised and tomorrow when she woke he knew there would be difficulties. In the harsh light of dawn reality would send each of them their different ways and back into lives promised elsewhere. It was how life worked.

Lucien thought of his friends at home and his family and the ancient crumbling estate of Ross that would need a careful guidance if it were not to fail completely.

He could not stay in Spain. He could not live here. But his arms tightened about Alejandra and he breathed her in.

She came awake so abruptly she jolted and felt him there beside her, lying in the warmth of their blanket fast asleep.

In the early spread of dawn his hair looked lighter again. It was as if more of the darkness had been rubbed away, leaving large swathes of the pale that were caught now in the new morning.

She swallowed back the heaviness in her throat and stayed perfectly still. In sleep Lucien Howard looked vulnerable, younger, the lines of his face relaxed into smoothness. The heavier shadow of a day-old beard sat around his jaw, a play of red upon fair bristles.

She had never lain with a man like him. Juan had been dark and hairy and thick. This English captain was all honed muscle and lithe beauty, reminding her of the statues she had seen once years ago when her mother and father had taken her to Madrid, the marble burnished smooth by time and touch.

She had been astonished at the way he had made her feel last night—still felt, she amended, as the memory lifted her stomach to a tight ache and she moved against him. She wanted again to feel like that, tossed into passion and ecstasy and living in the blinding moment of joy.

He stirred and turned towards her, his hands coming around her in protection, and her fingers found the buttons of his trousers and slipped inside. His flesh was warm and smooth and for a moment she wondered if what she did was right, this plundering, without his consent. Still, as her hands fastened about him the flesh grew, filling the space with promise.

No small measly man, either. No quiet polite erection. Already her hips were moving and her legs opened at the same time as his eyes.

Pale and watchful, the very opposite of his vibrant quickened appendage. The surprise came next, creeping in with a heavy frown.

'You are sure?'

In answer she simply drew him over her and tilted her hips and the largeness of Lucien filled her completely, stretched to the edge of flesh, pinning her there as he waited.

'Love me, Alejandra,' he said and drove in further.

'I do,' she replied, and it was only much later when he was gone from her that she understood exactly what such a truth meant.

He was not gentle or tentative or hesitant. He was pure raw man with the red roar of sex in his blood and a given compliance to take her. She had never felt more of a woman, more beautiful, more cherished, more connected, more completely full.

The way he made love was unlike anything. He used his hands and his mouth and his body wholeheartedly and joyously, as if in the very act he sacrificed his reserve in real life, nothing held back, nothing hidden.

And this time he came with her to the golden place far above, the place where their hearts were melded into one, cleaved by breath and flesh, joined in the sole pursuit of rapture and escape and fantasy. Delivered into euphoria. Like a dream.

The shaking started as quietly as it had done before, at first in the very pit of her stomach and then radiating out, clenching and tight, her breath simply stopping as it spread so that her back arched and she took what he offered with the spirit that it was given, with honesty and pleasure and something else that was more unnameable.

And then the tautness dissolved into lethargy and the tears came running down her cheeks in the comprehension of all that had just occurred and never might again.

She could not ask him to stay, there was no place safe here for him, and she knew she would not fit into the polite and structured world of an English earl.

This small now was all the time they would have together, close and real, yet transitory. She found his hand. She liked the way he linked their fingers.

'I will come back for you. Wait for me.' His words

whispered into the light, the promise within both gratifying and impossible.

'I will.'

She did not think that either of them truly believed it.

Chapter Eight

She was there and not there in the ether of pain and sickness, close beside him in memory and in loss.

'Alejandra?' Her name. Strangely sounded. There was something wrong with his voice and he was burning up.

'It is me, Luce. It's Daniel.' The feel of a cloth pressed so cold it made him shake, first across his brow and then under his arms when they were lifted. Gentle. Patient. Kind. 'You are back in England now. You are safe. The doctor says that if you rest...' The words stopped and Lucien opened his eyes to see the familiar pale green orbs of his oldest friend, Daniel Wylde, slashed in worry.

'I...am...dying?' His question held no emotion within it. He did not care any more. It was too painful and he was too weak, the wounds on his neck making breath come shallow.

'No. Have some of this. It will help.'

A bitter drink was placed between his lips and his head raised. One sip and then two. Lucien could not remember how he knew this taste, but he did, from somewhere else, some dangerous place, some other time.

'You need to fight, Lucien. If you give up...' The rest was left unsaid but already the dark was coming, threading inside the day, like crows in a swarm before the sun. Wretched and unexpected.

'You have been in England for six weeks. I brought you up to Montcliffe three days ago. For the air and the springtime. The doctor said that it might help. He stopped the laudanum five days ago.'

'My mother...?'

'Is in Bath visiting her sister. Christine made her take a break from nursing you.'

Lucien began to remember bits and pieces of things now, his family gathered around and looking down on him as though the next breath he took would be his last one. He remembered a doctor, too, the Howard family physician, a good man and well regarded. He'd been bled more than once. A bandage still lay on his left wrist. He wished he might remove it because it was tight and sore and because for a moment he would like to look at himself as he had been, unbound and well.

Alejandra.

The name came through the fog with a stinging dreadful clarity.

The hacienda and the Spanish countryside tumbled back as did the journey across the Galician Mountains. He shut his eyes against more because he did not wish to relive all that came next.

'I thought you'd been killed, Luce, when you did not arrive on the battlements by the sea to get on to the transports home. Someone said they had seen you fall on the high fields, before Hope's regiment. I could not get back to look for you because of my leg—'

Daniel broke off and swallowed before continuing.

'We'd always sworn we'd die together. When you didn't come I thought...'

Lucien could only nod because it was too hard to lift his arm and take Daniel's hand to reassure him and because the truth of battle was nothing as they had expected it to be. So very quick the final end, so brutal and incapacitating. No room in it for premade plans and strategy.

He came awake again later, three candles on the bedside table and a myriad of other bottles beside them.

Daniel was still there, his collar loosened and eyes tired.

'The doctor has been by again. He will come back in the morning to change your bandages as he has taken a room in the village with his brother. He said that I was to keep you awake and talking for as long as I could tonight and he wants you up more. Better for the drainage, he said. I have the same instructions.'

'You do?'

'I took a bullet through the thigh as we left A Coruña. It seems it is too close to the artery to be safely excised, so I have to strengthen the muscle there instead if I am to have any chance of ever walking again without a limp.'

'Hell.'

'My thoughts exactly. But we are both at least half alive and that is better than many of the others left in the frozen wastes of the Cantabrians.'

'Moore is there, too. A cannonball in Penasqueda. He died well.'

'You heard of that. I wondered. Who saved you, Luce? Who dressed your wounds?'

'The partisans under El Vengador.' His resolve slipped on the words.

'Then who is Alejandra? You have called for her many times.'

The slice of pain hit him full on, her name said aloud here in the English night, unexpected.

'She is mine.'

They had come down in the morning across the white swathe of a winter sun, warmer than it had been and clearer. Alejandra walked in front, a lilt in her step.

'You thought what…?' she said, turning to him, the smile in her eyes lightened by humour. Girlish. Coquettish even.

'I thought you would be regretful in the morning.'

'Of making love?'

'With a stranger. With me. So soon…'

The more he said the worse it sounded. He was a man who had always been careful with his words and yet here they fell from his mouth unpractised and gauche. Alejandra made him incautious. It was a great surprise that.

She waited until he had reached her and simply placed her arms about his neck.

'Kiss me again and tell me we are strangers, Capitán.'

And he did, his lips on hers even before he had time to question the wisdom of such a capitulation here in the middle of the morning. She tasted like hope and home. And of something else entirely.

Tristesse.

The French word for sadness came from nowhere, bathed in its own truth, but it was too soon to pay good mind to it and too late to want it different.

'Only now, Lucien,' she whispered. 'I know it is all that each of us can promise, but it is enough.'

He looked around, his meaning plain, and she took his hand and led him off the track and into a dense planting of aloes.

'It will have to be quick. I am not sure how safe...'

He didn't let her finish, his fingers at her belt and the trousers down. His own fall was loosened in the next seconds and he lifted her on to his erection, easily, filling her warmth and plunging deeper into the living soul of delight.

Nothing compared to this. Nothing had prepared him for it, either, the response of her flesh around him, keeping him within her, quivering and clenching.

He had always held a healthy appetite for the women he had coupled with, not too numerous, but not a puny number, either. Always before he stayed in charge and detached, as though at any moment he had the capacity to pull away and leave. Only momentary. Only casual. He never lingered to hear the inevitable tears or pleadings, preferring instead to depart on his terms, before closeness settled.

Until here and now in the shifting allegiances of war when it was both impossible to stay and dangerous to leave.

His hand cupped Alejandra's chin and he slanted his mouth across the fine lines of her. He wanted to mark her as his, in a primal demarcation of possession. Just as he wished to plant his seed in a place where the quickness might take and grow and be.

The very thought made him come, hot into her, the pulse of desire, the sating of want. He pumped the heart of himself into her womb and held her still so that there might be a chance that part of him would live in her and she might remember. Him.

Dangerous. Stupid. Impossible.

But the rational side of him was gone and in its place stood such a shaking want he could follow no other master.

She had closed her eyes now, as her own orgasm strengthened, panting and tensing as it took her, the flat planes of her stomach as jerky as her breath. He liked listening to her edge of surprise, the red whorls on her throat only emphasising all she had allowed him as the waves of release billowed.

She tried to say something afterwards, but he stopped her because he knew what the words might be and he was not ready to hear them, feel them, know them. Not here in the centre of chaos and pain and delight.

She needed to be away safe and his presence could only harm her if they were found together. Already those on the waterfront might have talked; a stranger with the daughter of El Vengador coming down from the high hills and unaccompanied. Small ports like this did not allow the shelter of anonymity or the chance to disappear unnoticed into a crowd and stay hidden.

As though she could sense him thinking she pulled away, quick fingers retying her buttoned fall. She did not look at him, either, a faint redness tingeing both her cheeks. He could smell the scent of loving between them, pungent and raw.

'We should go, Capitán. The tide will not wait…'

'And you? How will you get home from here?' He could not help but ask, though he held no mandate to shape her future.

'The way I always do. Easily.'

He wanted to believe that. He did. He wanted to think that after he had boarded the boat to England she would simply walk down the path towards home, unmolested, unchallenged.

And if not…

He shook that thought away and took her arm. 'If you are ever in trouble, send a letter and this to the Howard town house in Grosvenor Square. Do you understand? Address it to the Earl of Ross and mark it as important.' His warm signet ring sat in the centre of her hand, pulled from his finger as the only possession he could bestow on her that was truly recognisable.

She nodded, her eyes had faded into a flat dull green, though her fist curled around the crest engraved in gold.

Alejandra knew as a certainty that an important English earl would have no place beside the daughter of one of the most infamous guerrilla leaders in the northern parts of Spain. A woman who had been married once badly and who had killed and fought and maimed. For freedom, she told herself, but each time took more of her soul and now there was so little left of it Alejandra was afraid. He had not asked about the marks on her wrist, either, the scars of hopelessness and betrayal. The way out.

She would not contact him, she knew that as certainly as she did her own name, but she would keep the ring. These were the last moments that they would be together and she was glad for the wet of him there inside her body, to hold on to and to remember.

The blood was seeping through his clothes again, a dark stain against the navy of his borrowed jacket. She knew how much it would be hurting him.

'Only now,' she whispered at his back. Only this time, she chanted inside herself as the path wound its way down towards the port and to the bright emerald of the sea. He needed medical help and he needed it fast for the heat in him last night had not been all from ardour. A few days to the coast of England in fair weather. 'God, please let it be enough. Please deliver him from his troubles.'

Luis Alvarez was ready to leave, his cargo secured and his sails unfurled. Another man she had not met reefed the ropes at the back of the boat and moved a pile of canvas.

'Is there luggage?'

'No.' Lucien Howard had finally found his voice again. 'My sister married an Englishman and is sick. I need to be there quickly.' She was glad he spoke the Spanish with such precision, for Alvarez seemed to accept his story without pause.

'Come aboard, then.'

She turned towards him and folded her hands across her chest. She was glad this was such a public space, glad that he would not touch her, glad that it was only a matter of minutes before he was gone. Because she could not have borne a dragged-out good-bye. Not after the night and morning that had just been.

'Safe journey, then, Lucien.'

'And to you, too, Alejandra.'

She stepped back and so did he, one foot and then another until the gap between them was such that even had she wanted to she could not reach out and touch him.

Then he was on the boat, gold and black hair blowing in the breeze as he removed his hat.

The noise of ropes stretching and shouts, the slap

of water when the vessel turned into the current, shadows and light as the sails slid into shape, filling with wind and then movement.

One yard and then ten.

She did not raise her arms or shout goodbye, but stood there, silent, caught between hope and despair.

'Only now,' she whispered to herself as the shape of him grew blurred by distance and was gone.

His sister, Christine, was there the next time he awoke, her hand across his on the spotless counterpane of his sickbed. She had been crying, he could see it in the swollen redness around her eyes.

'I might live, yet.' It was all he could think of to reassure her and she looked up, a frown across her brow.

'You think that is why I sit here and weep, because you are bound for heaven any moment?' There was sadness in her voice. 'You will recover, Lucien, though the doctor said it might take a while.'

'Then why are you crying?'

'Joseph died before his regiment reached Betanzos. The cold, I think, and a lack of clothing. I got the letter the day after you arrived home and I have heard the stories.' She lifted her hand and showed him a heavy diamond in white gold. 'He had asked me to marry him when he returned and I was waiting...'

'God, Joe Burnley is dead? I am sorry for it.'

His sister detested profanities and she pursed her lips in that particular way she had done so all of her life when one of her brothers annoyed her.

'What? You never swear in your bed at night when no one is listening, Christine? Never rant against the unfairness of it all?'

As she shook her head he laughed and was surprised at how hoarse such humour sounded. 'Then I think you should start. That truth at least is universal.'

'You are so much more cynical than you were, Luce.'

'A failed military campaign does that to one, I should imagine. All the mistakes and the damned waste of it...' He drew in breath. Once he started on the debris of war he might never stop and his sister should not need to learn that her betrothed had died because of an error. Let her imagine bravery and courage and valour instead. Let her think the British expeditionary force under Moore had had a firm plan and a fine higher purpose.

Closing his eyes, he was glad when he heard her stand and leave the room. Grief was a lonely companion after all, hers and his, unexplainable and constant. He imagined Alejandra here looking down upon him, willing him better, challenging him to fight. But his strength had left him ever since he had stepped on to that boat in the harbour of Pontevedra and all he could feel now was an ache of aloneness.

Dislocated and adrift.

The skin on his wrist where the doctor had bled him pulled against the stitching of a blanket and began to bleed again through the bandage as he raised it. One drip and then two against the snowy white of the sheets. He was suddenly reminded of the scars on Alejandra's right wrist, precise white lines that looked deliberate and lethal.

Where was she now? Was she safe? Was she home with her father or out on the hills above A Coruña again scouting? He'd get someone from the intelligence sector to find out the situation there. He'd ask Daniel to organise it come the morning. Then he would return and look for her. That thought allowed him to close his eyes and sleep.

Four weeks later Lucien was back in London and up walking short distances. Oh, granted, he did not have his full energy back or the same sense of well-being he was more used to but he was out of bed and dressed and for that he was grateful.

When Daniel turned up at the Howard town house early after breakfast, though, Lucien knew something was not right. Excusing himself from the table, he bade his friend follow him to the library, away from the ears of others in his family because already he had a fair knowledge of what this visit might be about. 'You have had word from Spain?'

Daniel handed him a sealed missive, but his face looked drawn.

'Is it bad news?' The flat question was asked in the face of disbelief.

As his friend failed to answer Lucien ripped apart the missive, unfurling the page so that the tall spidery writing could be better viewed.

*I am sorry to inform you that the Hacienda of
Señor Enrique Fernandez y Castro was razed
to the ground on the second week of March
1809 and all the occupants within it appear to
have died.*

    These occupants are listed as:...

Both the names of Alejandra and her father were
amongst those missing.

Lucien looked up. 'You knew?'

'They told me to make sure you were sitting when
I gave you this.'

'Gone.' He read the names again and then again,
as if on another try the words might have changed,
releasing Alejandra from the spectre of fire.

Crossing the room, Daniel extracted two glasses
from the mahogany cabinet, pouring a generous
brandy in each. Handing one over, he sat on the
leather chair opposite.

'Tell me about her, Luce. Sometimes talking helps.'

Could anything truly help? Lucien wondered as
the grief of his loss broke through. 'She was brave
and beautiful and fought for my health harder than
even I did at the time. She found me the morning after
the retreat, under the dead carcass of my horse, and
brought me home.'

'Courageous indeed, then.' Lucien liked the way
Daniel said that, his tone full of thought and truth.

'She brought me down to the port of Pontevedra
and got me on a boat. Then she returned to the hacienda.' He took a long sip of the brandy. 'To die in

a fire. I should have insisted that she came with me, to England, where she might have been safe, but she had made it clear Spain was her home and I was...' He stopped.

What? he wondered. What exactly had he been to Alejandra?

'Did you love her?' Brandy words. Careless and exposed and demanding answer.

'No.' Lucien felt his insides curl into grief because he could not say it, could not let the truth become his reality. His fist brought the paper into a tight ball and he was shaking. Fiercely. He wondered for a moment whether this was what it felt like to die of shock. He'd seen others take the same path and it had always been quick.

But then Daniel was there, taking the glass from his hand and lifting him in arms warm and solid on to the sofa to one end of the library, a blanket shoved across the cold.

'Should I get a doctor, Luce?'

'Don't.' He had found his voice again and his wits. Uncurling his fist, he let the paper drop on to the floor, where it sat quiet and tiny, the penmanship unseen. 'Can you burn it?' He didn't want to read it again and find her name there on the third row down.

Her middle name had been Florencia. He had not known that. There were a thousand things he had not known of her and now never would.

When Daniel did as he asked Lucien watched as the paper caught alight in the grate, a small flare of yellow and orange and then gone.

'Was it Alejandra who had your hair dyed black?'

'Yes. She thought it was safer that way. Less obvious. Another protection.'

'I should have liked to have met her. Your woman.'

'Mine.' Now he could not stop the tears that fell unheeded down his cheeks and into loneliness so deep and painful he thought he might never survive it.

Chapter Nine

London—1813

The widow Margarita van Hessenberg was beautiful, clever and wealthy and she was a good friend of Daniel's wife, Amethyst, a woman Lucien both liked and admired.

Lucien had seen her from a distance many times, but of late she had sought him out, to ask an opinion of a book or a play or a painting. A cultured woman with an enquiring mind and a curious nature.

Today in his arms in the Harveys' ballroom Margarita was speaking of the Turner painting that had surfaced at the Royal Academy's summer exhibition at Somerset House last year.

'It was widely praised as magnificent and sublime by any critics who mattered. But for myself the axis of perspective seemed to break with the traditional rules of composition and I could not quite enjoy it.'

Lucien knew that Margarita was an artist and was

said to be most practised, but still the painting of the ancient Punic Wars had released something unexpected in him when he had gone to see it.

The image of Hannibal and his army crossing the Maritime Alps with the Salassian tribesmen thwarting them had had a familiar sense to it. The forces of nature he determined, and the smallness of man, caught in war and snowstorms. For a moment he had been transported to his own hell, marching the icy passes between Villafranca and Lugo, the road one long line of bloody footmarks and corpses.

Turner had rendered exactly the despair of soldiers and the loss of compassion. He had placed in the strokes of a brush the exhaustion there, too, and the pain of struggle.

'You are most quiet, Lucien. Do you hold a differing opinion?'

'I liked its power. I liked its terrible truth.'

Her hands tightened across his back as she moved closer. 'Will you come home with me tonight and stay?'

This was whispered in his ear in a sultry tone and the hairs on his arms stood up at the invitation. It had been so long since he had last bedded a woman.

He should say yes; already he could see Daniel and Amethyst beside him, the hope in their eyes shining like beacons. Gabriel Hughes was there, too, to one side of the room with Adelaide, his new and most interesting wife, and they, too, looked pleased for him.

They all wanted him to be as happy as they were and as content with life and love and hearth. For a good two years now, after the Higham-Browne fiasco, they had paraded one sterling woman after another in front of him, at dinner parties and balls and also at more private soirées especially manoeuvred to make everything conducive to a successful affair of the heart.

And for all that time he had pleaded excuses and found escapes, unwilling to remember all that he only wanted to forget.

Alejandra Fernandez y Santo Domingo.

Even here she haunted him, amongst the laughter and the dancing, sadness the only honest emotion in his breast. Four years of loneliness. Four years of self-inflicted isolation. Four years of a grief that he could not shake.

And suddenly it was enough.

'Yes, I would like that.' He swallowed and felt the dry fear of the answer in his mouth curling into panic.

'Thank you.' Margarita was clever in her reply. If she had said anything else, he might have bolted, but the sweet gratitude in her words touched him.

'I am not a woman prone to asking men to my bed, you understand.' He smiled as her breath warmed the skin on his neck. 'Once, I was married to a man I loved with all my heart and when he died I could not understand who I was any more. But with you...' The words slid into a silence as he nodded and the music soared in the air above them, promise and hope within its melody.

* * *

The substantial van Hessenberg town house was darkened with only a few candles still alight as she led him through the reception area and up the stairs to a room that was painted as a garden, murals on each wall by the windows.

'This is my folly, Lucien,' she said softly. 'I missed my flower beds in Essex and sought to bring them here.'

'Inanimate and permanent? No watering needed.'

She laughed at that and moved closer. 'That is what I love most about you, Lucien. You are a man of few words, but all are well chosen.'

Her fingers went to the tie of his cravat, unwinding it slowly and discarding the length of it on the floor. He watched the white cloth fall and thought of the scars she would soon see, across his neck and back, thick and ugly and red.

'Perhaps we could have a drink first?' The quiver in his voice worried him.

'Of course.' She had heard it, too, he thought as she broke away to find glasses and a bottle of champagne.

An 1811 Veuve Clicquot and the very best of that vintage. He finished almost half the glass before he took a breath and Margarita filled it again.

'I went there once, you know, to France, to sample the wine in the cave itself. It was magnificent.'

Only the best, he thought. Gowns. Rooms. Wine. Travel. His mind wandered to the dishevelled clothes of Alejandra, torn and dirty as they had marched through the mountains. He remembered the home-brewed *orujo*, too, and small dugout spaces between tree roots, where they had fashioned beds in pine needles under the endless Spanish sky.

He felt less here in a room of so much more. He felt less certain and less strong and less sure. He took in breath and turned to the window, watching the lights of London town and Margarita's reflection in the glass as she walked up behind him.

And he knew without doubt that this was wrong, that he was wrong, that the closeness he had known with Alejandra would not be repeated here.

'I need to go. I am sorry.'

She took his words with calmness and dignity. 'Then I hope you will be back...some other time. You would always be welcome.'

He nodded because the pretence of it was expected and because anything to allow him the chance to depart with some dignity was to be snatched at. He picked his neckcloth up from the thick burgundy rug as he strode to the door.

Once outside the house his desperate haste seemed to slow. He was free. Of the cloying room. Of sex. Of expectation. The night air calmed him, the first hint of winter on the breath of breeze. He should have stayed in Pontevedra or he should have insisted Alejandra go with him to England. He should have done anything other than what he had done, simply getting on that boat home and leaving her to die less than a few days later in the fiery inferno of her home. He missed her. He missed everything about Alejandra Florencia Fernandez y Santo Domingo.

'Jesus, help me,' he whispered as he walked. 'Please, please help me.'

White's was still open. He thankfully found a seat in a secluded alcove and, ordering a drink, leant back against the soft leather.

'Lord Ross?'

A man Lucien did not recognise stood there.

'I am Captain Trevellyan Harcourt, the son of Major Richard Harcourt. I think you might know him?'

'Indeed.' Lucien clipped the word, hoping the young fellow might simply leave it at that. He did not feel like chatting after such a personal and intimate failure.

'The thing is, sir, I have only just recently returned from the Iberian Peninsula. I have a commission in the Seventh Light Division under Wellington, you see, and was sent home because I was injured. Not badly, but enough,' he carried on and smiled.

Lucien could not see where any of this was leading, but he listened because there was something in the young man that others might have seen in him. Dislocation, he supposed, and struggle. Gesturing for Harcourt to sit in the chair opposite, he ordered another brandy.

'I was there myself under Moore, five years ago, in the first campaign.'

'A difficult time, sir, and although the push into Spain was ultimately a retreat it was also important. General Moore paved the way for us.'

'A forward-thinking opinion, Captain Harcourt. There were many who would not be so generous.'

'I take it you made the long march north, then, up to the coast, my lord, and the Bay of Biscay.'

There was a tone in Harcourt's voice that had Lucien sitting up straighter. He knew the sound of a man fishing for information, sifting for details. My God, it had been his job for all the years of his commission with the British army and a prickling awareness of something being important began to rise.

'Why do you ask?'

Harcourt sat forward, one hand delving into his jacket. 'I found this on a finger of a homeless drunk I had a contretemps with and I recognised the insignia. The Ross crest. Your coat of arms, sir?'

Time simply stopped for Lucien. Dead still. Like a crack in the fabric of his world, one moment this and the next one that.

It was his ring, the one he had given Alejandra all those years ago with the strict instructions to contact him if she ever needed help.

She hadn't done that.

Yet here it was again, a little less shiny and a deep scratch across the bottom of the crest. To determine whether it was gold or not, he presumed, to see if the worth of it held value. How the hell had it escaped the fire?

'It is mine.' Lucien felt his heart race. 'You found it on a drunk, you say?'

'I did. He was a man of dubious means and had a propensity for thievery. I am guessing that the ring was stolen, too, by the looks of him. From you?'

'Where exactly did you come across it?'

'In Madrid, sir, in one of the older barrios there. I cannot remember which. I would not have thought you to come through the city under General Moore.'

'I didn't.' He did not want to say more. 'I will pay you for the return of the ring, of course...'

'I am a commissioned officer, sir, and you were one before me. I should not accept any recompense for returning property that was so patently yours in the first place and one that cost me nothing more than a slight shove to acquire.'

'Then I thank you.' Already Harcourt was rising as his name was called from further down the room; friends, Lucien supposed, waiting for him and wondering why he tarried. Lucien stood as well and shook his hand.

'I am indebted to you. If you ever have the need of a favour...' The other man bowed slightly and moved off.

Left alone, he reached down and took the ring in his fingers, clasping it gently and well. How had such a valuable piece been lost from Alejandra's possession before ending up in the biggest city of Spain? Turning the gold into the light above, he saw a mark on the inside band, an inscription that had not been there when he had given it to her.

Only now.

'God.' A wave of heat washed across him and he sat down.

Had Alejandra survived the fire? She would have had neither the time nor the place to have an inscription engraved on the road back from Pontevedra. Had she somehow turned in another direction and gone south?

His fingers closed down over the ring and he hated the way they shook.

'Please, please let her be alive.'

Luis Alvarez looked more than a decade older when Lucien finally found him, outside a tavern on the very edge of the port road of Pontevedra.

He'd come by boat from Portsmouth the day before into Vigo and taken a horse on the paths north, careful of strangers and mindful of jeopardy. The war between France and Spain still raged in the north, but the direction of the battles has been pulled east towards the Pyrenees.

The old man's face crinkled further as he recognised him. 'I took you over to England once,' he said. 'The friend of El Vengador's daughter?'

Lucien nodded, ordering a round of drinks and paying.

'I heard that Alejandra Fernandez y Santo Domingo had died in a fire at the hacienda.' He tempered the question in his voice and watched the man directly.

'Aye, a tragedy that. Enrique Fernandez y Castro

for all his violence was a good man once. Rumour says it was an act of revenge by his daughter's dead husband's family. An eye for an eye...' His voice fell as he looked around. 'But she was not long gone from here when the atrocity happened and I wondered...' He stopped.

'You wondered what?'

'I wondered if she had escaped it and disappeared altogether for the charred bodies of those left were burnt beyond all recognition and form. It was said someone saw El Vengador's daughter in Madrid a good six months after the fire and another swore she resided in Almeida, but by that time the heart had gone from the hatred of the Betancourts and they just let it go.'

Lucien turned the ring on his finger as the man carried on.

'People say things and see things that are not real. Like the dye in your hair. It was black once, if I recall. Now it is the colour of the sun.'

Placing his glass down, Lucien spoke slowly, feeling his old self coming back, the man that he had been here once. The soldier. The spy. The careful gatherer of information, no scrap of it too small or unimportant.

'Do you remember the exact date of the fire, *señor*?' It had never been noted on any of the reports.

'The tenth of March,' the older man replied. 'My birthday. We were out celebrating when we got the news.'

Lucien quickly calculated time and distance. He

had left Spain on the fifth of March. That left five days from Pontevedra to A Coruña. It could be done if she had used the coastal road, but it had rained hard that night out in the Bay of Biscay. Had it done the same here, slowing everything?

'Do you remember what the weather was like that evening?' He held his breath as the old man thought.

'It was pouring earlier on, but it had cleared by midnight. We walked home from the tavern without getting wet, but the mud underfoot was deep.'

The rain meant Alejandra would have had to be more careful. It meant that she might have sheltered, too, in one of the overhangs of a cliff or beneath the gnarled roots of trees until it passed. Unless she had simply pushed on undeterred and met her maker in the hot flush of flame.

He wondered how long she had stood on the wharf watching him go. Others might have seen her there and could remember. He phrased his next query carefully.

'Your son helped you on the docks, didn't he? He was there the day we left, tidying the last of the cargo that you had delivered. A large youth with a beard?'

'Indeed. He is there.' He pointed towards the bar and the same barrel-chested young man materialised from within the forms of others.

'Might I talk with him for just a moment?'

'Keep your voice down, then, if it's questions you are asking. Bringing up the past can sometimes cause problems around here. Xavier. A word, if you please.'

The lad came quickly, a full tankard in hand, and

sat by his father. Side by side there was more of a resemblance than Lucien had previously thought.

'Do you remember the daughter of El Vengador, the beautiful young woman who came to the wharf that day with this man?'

Dark eyes flicked across him. 'Yes.'

Lucien took over.

'Did she stay here long in the village after I left with your father?'

'*Si*. She sat against the mooring post and watched the ocean for all of the next few hours, and she was sad. Not crying, but I could tell she was near to it.'

Lucien's heart lurched and fell to the very pit of his stomach. 'And then?'

'She left just after dusk. She went up the high path and into the hills. I thought she would take the low road, but she didn't. It was raining and there was the promise of more.'

And suddenly Lucien knew. Right there and then with the sound of drunken voices in his ears and the smell of cheap red wine all around. Alejandra was alive. Breathing. Somewhere. The inscription inside the ring was confirmed by the words of these men here.

He put down his glass and stood, leaving two gold coins for father and son as he departed. Then he went up into the high road past the last cottage and into the hills.

He felt Alejandra with him, in the stillness and the smell of earth. He touched the rough bark of an oak and then sat beneath it, the news of her safety so very new he felt dislocated. The dark enveloped him like a blanket as he thought of her smile and her softness and her honesty.

He would find her if it took the rest of his life to do so, but first he needed to return to England for he had good contacts in military intelligence and with the British Service. Aye, he would need all the help he could get to find a woman who had never once written to him and yet who had inscribed the words *only now* into gold.

'Word has it you are going to Spain again to look for your Spanish rescuer?' Daniel asked the question as they walked along Regent Street after seeing a wine merchant who traded just off it.

'Who told you this?'

'Gabriel. He still holds contacts in places one would not think him to have. He said you had already been in at the British Service and that you were certain she was still alive.'

'I am.'

'I hope you will not be disappointed in what you find out, Luce. If she had wanted to see you again...' He stopped.

'I am relatively easy to contact,' Lucien finished off the thought for Daniel. 'I know this, but there is something that is wrong...'

'Clara Higham-Browne's sister was asking of you, too, the other day. I saw her in the park riding and she stopped me. I do not think that family will ever forgive you calling off your betrothal at such a late notice.'

'Clara wanted things I could never have given her. One day she will probably thank me for it.'

'I warned you off her right from the start, if you remember. She would have tied you in knots and fastened on to the side of you for ever without conversation or cleverness. Boredom would have killed you when her beauty wore off.'

'Perhaps.'

Lucien had asked Clara Higham-Browne to be his wife for all the wrong reasons. For loneliness and for a place in the world. Even to please his mother, he thought, if he were honest. Nothing of lust or love or plain damn want. The hitch in his heart made him swallow.

Alejandra.

Her hair down and her shirt open and her hands finding the places in him that melted at her touch.

'How long will you be gone? When do I need to start worrying that you might not be back?'

Daniel's query brought a smile to Lucien's face. 'A month at the least and two at the most. I will be in Madrid.'

'Does your mother know why you are going?'

'No. She was the one who was most taken with Clara Higham-Browne and her family. Mama thought the viscount's daughter would settle me down, make me stay here in England, keep me taking part in the politics of London and the affairs of society. She does not want me back in Spain at least, for a fortune teller once told her I would die there and she is convinced it will come true seeing as I very nearly did. I never gave her the story of Alejandra or the aftermath of A Coruña for she is a woman who likes her children to be near and has a need for the order of her world to be in place. Anyone who challenges that is a threat she wants no part of and she worries until she is sick with it.'

'You truly think you can locate this woman after so many years? In all of Spain?'

'In Madrid. Someone might know something and all it takes is one piece of luck.'

'Good or bad, Luce. Margarita van Hessenberg asked if I had spoken with you. She seemed to think you would visit her again soon. Unfinished business, she said, and I gained the distinct impression she was speaking in the currency of lust as well as the gentler one of hope.'

Lucien turned his head to the sky and felt the sun on his face. 'It is entirely my fault that I let her down. I thought we could be more than friends, but...' He stopped and lowered his voice. 'I need to find Alejandra, Daniel, even if it is just to understand what was between us in order to move on.'

'What of the manufacturing businesses you are so heavily involved in now? Who will look after those while you are away?'

'They will run themselves, Daniel, for I pay the managers I employ well.'

'They seem damned lucrative.'

'They are, though my mother still has her doubts about dealing in trade despite the accrued wealth.'

'Beggars cannot be choosers, Luce.'

At that they both laughed.

Lucien leant back on the balcony of the generous room he had been allotted by the Duke of Palma at his country seat on the outskirts of Madrid.

He had arrived four days ago and walked about the town, feeling the warmth, exploring the central barrios and the palace and the marketplaces in the Plaza la Cebada and San Andres Square, and all the time asking questions that might lead him to Alejandra.

An acquired military intelligence had led him to a man in the district of Puerta Bonita in Carabanchel and this meeting had resulted in the name of a woman who was helping the British cause by sending sensitive information through the closed channels of intelligence.

Señora Antonia Herrera y Salazar was a prostitute in a brothel on Segovia Street in the barrio of La Latina. He had had a discreet servant of the Duke make an appointment with her in two days' time under the false name of Señor Mateo, hoping to procure enough privacy to further his questioning.

If Alejandra was here, she would be helping Spain and its cause of independence, he knew she would be. She would be in hiding, too, for those who had killed her father were dangerous and she would not wish for them to find her here.

Perhaps this woman might have seen her or knew

of her. He had to be careful with any physical descriptions because the work was sensitive and dangerous and he did not wish for her to be hurt because of such questioning.

He would tread lightly and hope for some further clue to follow. He glanced down at his newly returned signet ring and felt the hollow ache of loss.

Chapter Ten

Señora Antonia Herrera y Salazar briskly tied the ribbons of her new bonnet beneath her chin and bent to reassure the old woman before her, tucked warmly into a large bed.

'I will only be gone for an hour, Maria. My appointment is at two.'

The lined face lightened. 'You have the papers regarding the loans?'

'I do.' Her fingers touched the soft leather of her bag. 'The numbers in the ledgers are heartening, as well. I looked at them all last night and compared them to our takings at this time four years ago.'

'We have come a long way, then. You and I.'

Kissing the offered cheek, Antonia stood. She could hear the carriage slow at their doorstep and did not wish for any tardiness.

'How do I look?'

'Beautiful. But then you always did, my dear. A companion fit for a king. The younger Señor Morales shall agree to all our requests, I am certain of it. He shall be smitten by you.'

Outside, the driver's eyes widened as she let herself into the hired hack. She had dressed today in the most sombre of all her clothes and yet still she felt exposed somehow, back in the ordinary world of the lives of others.

'I wish to go to the Calle de Alcala.'

They needed a loan because there was no way of expanding their premises without more money and without some form of enlargement and modernisation the Santa Maria *burdel* was doomed to failure.

Other establishments had come to the streets around the port in the past few years and they had not all been fair, the quest for riches in the trade of flesh speaking a language that held no moral scruples. Competitors had tried to poach the women who worked for her and frighten her customers. They had spread rumours and threatened her with retribution.

But Antonia had not buckled and she had never let anyone in close.

Not one. Not even Maria.

She had been good at the details and possibilities that came with running a business. Already she had paid back her first loans and saved a good bit besides. Alberto Morales, the manager of the loan company, had been a helpful and valued friend, but the old man had died suddenly a month ago and she had heard it said his only son was nowhere near as generous with his lending. Smoothing down the heavy fabric of her skirt, she swore beneath her breath. 'Only now,' she whispered to herself and liked the calm that seemed to emanate from the two simple words.

Her mantra. The way she lived. Her pathway through difficulty and disappointment. No future and no past. This moment. This second. This heart-beat of hope and ambition.

Pushing away anything else, she paid the driver and alighted, the stairs leading to the front entrance of the stone building steep and solid.

After introducing himself to her, Señor Mateo Morales got straight down to business.

'Your way of life is rather a chancy one, Señora Herrera y Salazar. I should have imagined my father must have told you that many times.'

'He did not, *señor*. He looked most favourably at my substantial line of credit and often said that if all his customers were as honest as I—'

A well-manicured hand waved in the air and cut her off. 'You are a woman without a husband and one of dubious reputation and residency.' He flipped open the pages of a thin book before him. 'Twice you have not paid on time, and once it was a good month until we received any redress. I am not certain whether I wish to continue my father's arrangements at all.'

Antonia felt as if she had been kicked in the stom-ach, hard and unexpected. Right from the first day of coming to Madrid, from the first hours of uncer-tainty and dread, she had known she would survive. But this…?

'Our credit is good, sir. More than good.'

'Our?' He leant forward to read through a page, thin glasses balanced on his nose. 'Oh, yes. I see Señora Maria Aguila is one of those who sing your praises. She, of course, has her own detractors.'

Antonia remained silent, wishing now that the younger Morales might simply say yes and then she could leave, but the atmosphere in the room had changed somewhat and it changed again as he came to stand beside her. Too close. She could smell the brandy on his breath and the lavender imbued in the fabric of his clothes.

'There is a way in which you might make me consider your application a little more favourably if you will, madam.'

She knew what he might say before he said it, the thin grey voice expressing his idea of a good deal without waver.

'If I could visit you, say, once a week for…services, I might be persuaded to look at your request differently.'

'Visit?' She needed to make sure she knew exactly what it was he meant.

'Become a patron of your brothel, madam, and a good paying one, too. I shall be discreet and polite. I am unmarried, you see, and most upstanding, but sometimes…well, sometimes I have the need of relief. I would require all this to be most confidential.'

'And we could well accommodate those desires, Señor Morales. I have a number of girls and women who…'

'No. It is you I want.'

Antonia swallowed. 'You do not know me, sir. At all.'

'But I have seen you for years coming here in the company of my father and I have admired you.'

'I do not think…' She stopped as he leant back to shut the book on his desk with a bang, a frown covering his brow.

'Send me a message when you have considered my request, *señora*. Perhaps when you have had longer to think about it you would be more willing.'

Antonia nodded in order to buy herself some time. Maria was old and sick and the twenty or so girls she employed depended on her for their livelihoods.

'There are other places I could go for a loan, *señor*.'

'Other places that will not touch your business proposition without word from me, *señora*.'

Blackmail. That was how the world ran. I give you this and you give me that. Moneylenders by nature were narcissistic and vain.

Only now.

'Good day to you, sir.'

Without a promise she turned for the door and walked through it, making certain it slammed hard as she left. The man outside sitting at a desk looked up in surprise at her, but she made herself smile. She had learnt the important lesson of putting a bright face over adversity a long time ago.

'How did it go, my dear? Did we get the loan?'

'The son of Alberto Morales is a charlatan and a cheat and he had the temerity to say that he would only lend me the money if I…' Antonia stopped and brought out the carafe of red wine from the cabinet to one side of the room, pouring herself a generous libation.

Maria's laughter was as honest as it was surprising. 'You are a brothel owner, my dear, not a high-born lady. What did you expect?'

'A business meeting,' she returned with feeling. 'A man who may have acted with more professionalism.'

'I built this place up on consensual favours, Antonia. When I started my body was all I had in the world to barter with and it was a good commodity. Do not be too prideful.'

'I am not for sale, Maria.'

'Not yet, perhaps. But the world in which we live is changing and if you want to continue on here in the capacity that you have been, then a sacrifice is often worth the payment. It is work we have all done, after all, and in the safety of this place it need not be as bad as you think it. A quick tumble with a man who is wealthy, harmless and clean. I can think of worse ways to spend an evening.'

Turning to the window, Antonia looked out. There were beggars across the street, a woman and two children who looked as though they had not eaten in a week. Madrid took in such fallen souls on a regular basis, from the poorer urban outskirts and from other towns on the rural plains and hills when the rains failed and the crops did not come in.

This was the truth of poverty, the line between life and death blurred and thin. Once under another name she might have had choices and options, but here in the old city of Madrid they had narrowed. Oh, granted, she could sell off some furniture and other personal belongings, but the rental on the building was high and nothing would cover the refurbishment costs other than a loan.

She was a brothel owner and soon, very soon, she would be a whore, as well. She knew it would have to come to this eventually, knew that the old ways and beliefs would one day become impossible.

'Very well.' Antonia heard the words come from her mouth as if at a distance. 'Arrange the meeting for the day after tomorrow with Señor Mateo Morales and I will make certain we get a renewal of the contract.'

As she turned, her eyes caught her reflection in the mirror above the mantel, a woman who looked stern and cold, the dyed red of her hair harsh against her face. She could not see what would possibly attract any man to her.

'I want for you to be happy, Antonia, but that cannot happen if we are forced on to the streets.'

'There are more important things in life than being happy, Maria.'

'Important things like the secrets you take from the French, you mean.'

'You know of this?'

'I know of the way you go through the bags and jackets of the French soldiers who come here. I see you watching them, too, and there are rumours...'

'Rumours?'

'It is being said that a beautiful aristocrat is aiding the cause of Spanish freedom on the city streets of Madrid. With Joseph Bonaparte installed in place of the Bourbons and the large portion of Spanish lands under the jurisdiction of the French there is great danger, Antonia. And well you know of it.'

Antonia was struck dumb. She had always been so careful in her clandestine activities. She had worn a blonde wig and talked in the old High Castilian, her face hidden beneath a large hat and dressed in the clothes she had left the north of Spain wearing all those years before.

Capitán Lucien Howard.

He came to her more often now in dreams, which was an odd thing given she had cried for him for at least eighteen months after the fire. It was the days then that were hardest to get through. Now it was the nights.

'Who else knows…here?' The admission was whispered and she was pleased to see Maria shake her head.

'No one. I am old and I sleep badly. I see things that others would not and I worry for you. So alone. So bitter. Is there anyone at all whom you might turn to for help?'

Once, there had been. In the first months of losing her father, her lands and her heritage she had sent three letters to the Earl of Ross. She had kept the ring, though, safe and sound in the pocket of her only jacket, because she could not truly trust another with it.

And she had waited in the hills above the small port of Pontevedra for him to arrive. Month after month until it was too dangerous to tarry further and she had sickened from living in the damp.

He had not come then and he had not come later in Madrid when the fourth letter had gone, paid for in the pawning of her favoured knife so that the postage was secure and the missive had the best of all chances of being delivered.

She had written of her pregnancy and of her need for help. She had put her heart into the words of entreaty even though she knew her English was poor.

The returned mail had been short and to the point, the crest of the Ross title embossed on to the thick paper.

Do not write again. I shall receive no further mail from you. If you persist in these false claims, I will have my legal team draw up a case against you.

The signature had been Lucien Howard's and the wax seal had been exactly the same as that in the gold of his signet ring.

Then a few months later in the reading room of the library in Madrid she had seen a story of him in an English newspaper. The Earl of Ross was to be married to a woman called Lady Clara Higham-Browne, the daughter of a viscount and reputedly very beautiful. The article had made much of stating that both sets of parents were old family friends and that everyone concerned was most pleased. Alejandra had read it through a number of times, memorising each and every word and understanding that the union would protect the old solid lines of aristocrats who had marched, heedless of any lesser beings, through the centuries.

Her birthing pains had come late in a night in the autumn, a welcomed child, a reminder of all that had been good. But the baby had breathed and then stopped. A boy child and perfect in every way save for size.

After that she had forgotten the promise of the English captain, his troths lost into deceit and distance, and she had thrown her hand in with Maria. A year later the signet ring had been stolen from her chamber at the brothel and she had tossed her rosary into the murky depths of the Manzanares River because she had lost her faith in God and Jesus and hope.

'It could be worse, Antonia.' Maria's voice broke into her thoughts. 'We could be out on the street and homeless. As it is we have fresh beef for dinner and beans from the garden. Life is best lived in the moment, my mother used to say, and I think she was right. Besides, if worst comes to the worst, I can always pawn my pearls and they are worth at least a few months' grace from rent.'

Time was bought in tiny allotments now, here in Madrid on Segovia Street, in La Latina on the land where an Islamic citadel had once stood. The narrow busy streets opened out on to large tree-lined plazas full of tall colourful houses with Arabic-tiled roofs and elegant iron-fretwork balconies.

Home. Safe. Surviving.

Maria was right. There came a time when the line you had once drawn in the sand was shifted and changed.

Señor Mateo Morales, the son of Alberto Morales, was not a bad man or a violent one. He was unmarried and he had needs. If she wanted to keep the brothel, she would have to meet those needs and it had been a long while since she had had enough money to do exactly as she willed.

Morality and integrity were the luxuries of the rich and they were indulgences she could no longer afford to rely upon. Breathing out, she felt her heart break quietly, just a soft slice of pain and then nothing.

Antonia thought she might be sick as she dressed in the light gossamer nightdress that was barely there. Eloisa had fashioned her hair in a series of curls and put on the make-up, thick and garish.

Like a disguise, she mused, like an actress on the stage playing a part. She had so many bracelets around her right wrist and left ankle that whenever she moved she made a sort of music. A harlot's tune. Maria had oiled her skin so that it glowed.

Señor Mateo Morales had asked for an hour. To talk, Eloisa had said, and as the servant dispatched to arrange the appointment he had been grand and stand-offish she had not wished to question him further.

The master did not wish to be kept waiting and he

did not wish to be interrupted. The manservant had been most particular about all he did not wish. Privately Antonia thought the younger Morales sounded rather commanding in his stated wants, the thin unpleasant man she had met a week before not quite adding up to one with so many distinct needs.

She looked at the clock in the corner, a few minutes before ten, and swallowed. She was not a young girl and she was not a virgin. She was a twenty-six-year-old widow with scars on her right wrist and a larger one on the top of her left thigh. Imperfect. Jaded. Damaged.

Such thoughts settled her. She could do this. She could. One night a week with a man who was not an ogre or a pervert. One night a week to save all of those who lived in the *burdel* high on the ravine of the San Pedro River before it flowed into the Manzanares.

Footsteps and a knock on the door. A warning. She had insisted on the courtesy because she did not wish to be surprised.

Making her way over to the window, she looked out over the streets and plazas and the outline of the old La Latina hospital a good mile away.

'For all have sinned and fall short of the glory of God…' She had not recited the verses of the Bible in years and she wondered why she did so now. There was no salvation to be had in any of it.

The room was darker than he expected, a single candle burning on the mantel and the rest of the chamber dim. Lucien waited until the servant departed before shutting the door and hesitated again as his eyes grew accustomed to the light.

It was a large and well-appointed room, a place of a well-to-do courtesan, he supposed, the smell of floral oil in the air and some other perfume he did not recognise. Musk, perhaps, or the heavy sweetness of jasmine?

The whore he presumed to be Antonia Herrera y Salazar was standing against the window with her back to him, the gauzy wisp of a petticoat covering little and myriad silver bangles on her right arm. Her hair was bright blood red and fell to her shoulders, the curl of it formal and lacquered. Pearls hung around her neck in one long and drunken strand, the clasp of them hooked into the strap of her chemise to make them skewed.

Rather than speaking he simply stood there waiting for her to turn. Ten seconds and then twenty. She was small, he saw, and thin. All the skin on her arms had prickled into fear.

'I should tell you before we go to bed that I expect you to honour your promises, Señor Morales.' Her voice was high, stretched out into some tone that was forced. The accent was that of León and the north, but edged in the theatrical. 'And I do not allow kissing.'

'Morales?' He could not understand just who it was she alluded to. 'Perhaps there has been a mistake, *señora*. I am here just to talk.'

At the sound of his voice she whipped about, the look of surprise turning to horror before she had gone halfway and then changing again into unbounded anger fired in fear.

'You.' Her mouth was open and her green eyes were wide with shock.

'Alejandra? My God.' He was across the room and taking her arm before he knew it, the velvet of her skin, the grace of bone and flesh. She shook away his touch as if it burnt. 'You are a...a...?'

He could not quite say it.

'Whore.' She supplied the word without compunction, the outline of her breasts so very easily seen against the candlelight. Fuller. More womanly. For a moment through the make-up and the hair dye, through the bangles and the wisp-of-nothing cloth, he completely lost the woman he had once known. 'There are worse ways to survive, Capitán, much worse ways than you could ever know and this is my home now.'

God. He thought he might be sick right there on the bed draped in velvet and covered in pelts of fur. The small cloth on the sideboard told of some cleansing ritual and the oil she wore was so strong it felt as if it clung to him, as well; an essence of ruin.

'Why? You could have been anything or anyone and instead...'

His hands spread across the air in front of her, expressing all that words could not.

'Instead I am this.' Narrowed eyes flickered and flattened, a rise of blood on her cheeks. 'I have survived, Capitán. I have been made stronger by adversity. I am Madam Antonia Herrera y Salazar now, a courtesan and a different woman from the one you knew.'

She lifted a glass to her lips, brandy by the colour, and drank all that was left, trying to dismiss him. But he could not let it go at that. He needed to know what path had brought her here to this choice of a brothel in the backstreets of one of the poorer barrios.

'You had an uncle—'

'Who is dead.' She did not let him finish.

'Then the ring I gave you?'

'Was stolen.' She laughed then, a deep and throaty sound. 'I do not want you here, my lord, paying for a service I once gave you for free whilst preaching on the ways I could have saved myself. I have many customers who like the person I have become, so perhaps it is wiser that you depart. There are others here who could see to your needs and a line of waiting patrons who can most certainly attend to mine.'

Her glance fell to the crotch of his pants and he knew that the erection there was obvious.

'Girls or boys, Capitán? The Santa Maria *burdel* has a large and varied choice. As young as you want them, or as old.' Her voice was hard and brittle and foreign.

Horrified, he could only look at her. The earrings she wore were ludicrously large and made of cheap-cut glass and her breasts spilled over the edge of the thin lace, the nipples darker than he remembered; in mockery and in parody. She was like some tarnished version of what she had been and he could hardly see the girl he had known in the swollen pout of her lips and the unfocused bitterness in her eyes.

He could smell a herb in the air that he recognised and was appalled. 'Drugs? Do you use these now, too?'

'Laudanum. It relaxes the body and fortifies the soul. A useful elixir in my kind of work and I swear there are times when I simply cannot get enough of it.'

Lewdly she spread the silk in her nightdress so that he saw the bare skin of her sex and hope drained from his face when she smiled, the red from the thickened wax she wore on her lips staining her teeth.

He turned for the door and kept on walking.

Chapter Eleven

Alejandra came to in her bed, a wet cloth across her forehead and Lucien Howard gone.

Maria was sitting there, the full light of the midday upon her. 'You took too much of the laudanum last night, Antonia. It has that effect on one who has not tried it before. I warned you one twist of it was ample, but you took three.'

A headache split the day into jagged pieces and she shielded her eyes from the light whilst directing Maria to pull the curtains closed.

'I only took one before my…customer got here and then two more after he had left.'

'Señor Morales does not look like any moneylender I have ever had dealings with. He also does not look like a man who would have the need to pay good money for a woman's company.'

'He isn't Mateo Morales, Maria. Eloisa placed him down as such in the book of appointments and the error was not corrected.'

'Who is he, then?'

'A soldier. An Englishman. My lover. Once.'

'And now…?'

She turned away and let the pillows envelop her. Now she had no idea what he was to her or she to him.

Instead you are this.

His words. The ones that had ripped the heart out of any forgiveness or hope and she had played to his disappointment like a master, pushing him back and keeping him there.

A thousand days of distance had shaped each of them differently and whereas once those differences had fitted them together, now they only tore them apart. In damage and in pain.

One could only be the sum of one's regrets and hers were many.

Clasping at her stomach she breathed in. Their child. She had called him Ross for his father. He had been two minutes old when he took his final breath and the little grace that had still been in her had been extinguished completely. Every day since she had visited the cemetery.

'I will not see Lucien Howard again.' The anger in her tone was threaded in sorrow.

'Then if he comes back, I shall say you have left the house, Antonia. An uncle in Almeida perhaps might be advisable, or a cousin in Cadiz. I have family in both places. I can give him those directions.'

'Thank you.'

Alejandra was gone when Lucien arrived the next evening at the *burdel* on Segovia Street. 'She has gone to Cadiz,' the old lady said, and he had no reason to disbelieve her story. 'She said to say she thought it was for the best, for both of you.'

'I see. She has a place there?'

'Of course. A beautiful woman is always welcome wherever she goes. It is in the nature of men to want to protect such loveliness.'

'Another brothel, then? Like this one? Interchangeable?'

'Antonia was not born with a silver spoon in her mouth, *señor*. Perhaps she enjoys the work. Or perhaps she just needs it.'

'Tell her I will wait in the reading room of the library on the Paseo de Recoletos. I will be there every morning for the next month and if she would like to talk I would like to listen. Give her this. It was hers anyway.' Taking the signet ring from his pocket, Lucien laid it on the small table to one side of the foyer.

The old woman looked shocked as she reached for the gold ring. 'This is yours?'

'It is. I am Major Lucien Howard, the sixth Earl of Ross.'

'Ross?' His title was repeated in a strange manner, almost breathless. 'I will make sure she receives this message, my lord. I promise it on the name of Our Lord and for her sake I hope she will come to you at the library on Recoletos.'

'Can I ask you something, *señora*?'

He waited until she nodded before going on.

'Do the French soldiers come here, to this place?'

'They do, sir. Often.'

'And are you a supporter of Napoleon and his brother Joseph's hopes for the Spanish throne?'

The silence was telling. Spain was a dangerous place these days to confess otherwise to a stranger.

'Thank you.'

He turned towards the door and let himself out, through the garish velvet hangings and a row of poorly painted golden statues. Valour came in different ways, he suddenly thought, and he was sure Alejandra was still here in Madrid for he could feel her close. Looking back at the facade of the house, he hoped he might see movement at the windows, but there was nothing, no telling shadow or twitching curtains.

Was El Vengador's daughter sleeping with the enemy in order to help Spain? He imagined it highly likely as he hailed his carriage. She had been expecting another in his place, that much was sure. Señor Morales was the name she had uttered and he resolved to find out more about the man. Señor Mateo Morales perhaps, for that was the Christian name he had given for the rendezvous. For this moment she might be lost to him, but there had been something in her actions that had spoken of desperation. And sadness.

Tristesse.

As the horses pulled on through the busy streets of La Latina Lucien swore that he was damn well going to find out what had happened to bring her to this brothel and in a disguise that spoke of hidden danger and hardships.

* * *

On the fourth day after the meeting with Lucien Howard, Alejandra went to the pawnshop on Calle Preciados and got the next three months' rent for the sale of the ring.

It bought her another ninety days and she was not sorry to sell it for it meant nothing any more and she could no longer bear to look at such a false circle of promise.

Lucien Howard had given the ring to Maria as a means of apology, she thought, as an ending and a way out. Guilt was there, too, probably, given all that had happened between them. Well, she would take it in the spirit it was given and the pesos realised by the gold would allow her the time to think and plan and be.

Maria herself had been uncertain about such an action because she had fallen heavily under the spell of the English captain.

'You are too stubborn, Antonia. So stubborn you no longer know what might be good for you any more. I do not understand why you will not go to the Paseo de Recoletos and at least speak with him, for he seemed a most reasonable man. I am guessing that he was the father of your child. The sixth Earl of Ross? He gave me his title.'

'My child is gone. Dead and buried. If Lucien Howard had wanted to find me, he could easily have done so. I sent my address and a letter to his home in England, but he did not want contact and he wrote back to say so. It is too late now. For both of us.'

'Because he thinks you a whore?'

'No,' she bit back quickly. 'Because I am one.'

'But you have never...'

'I have drugged French soldiers for my own purposes. I have stolen documents and personal letters and have had no compunction at all in sending these on to those who might pay me well for them. I have taken girls into this house and set them to work in a way that I knew in my heart was wrong.'

'You have always been too hard on yourself, Antonia, since you first came here four years ago.'

'Because once I was not this person. Once I was better and Capitán Howard only remembers that woman.'

'Does he know you have sent useful intelligence to the British army here? Does he know the girls you employ are well cared for? Does he know the streets in Madrid are a dangerous place for the homeless and the vulnerable and the aged? So dangerous you decided to help by taking them in?'

'He is an earl, Maria, an earl who has a high place in English society. I would only be a hindrance to him, a liability because I am no longer a person he could even like.'

She did not say that her body was different, too, with the birth of Ross. A vain and vapid thing, but still it was there, lurking in the background. No longer young or beautiful. The past four years had seen to that.

'Ross.' Her child. The pain of his name spoken loud had her bending over and sitting. She would not cry. She had run out of tears years ago and Lucien Howard was as good as dead to her.

The vanity of imagining he was here to rescue her, to love her, to take her in his arms and hold her safe was a stupid one. He had been in her room to buy the services of a whore for an hour and no amount of argument could make that different. He was married, too, though she had seen no rings upon his hands when he had visited her.

No. She could not weather another betrayal from a man she had always thought of as honourable and her past would crucify them if she allowed a new closeness.

It was the right thing to do this, for him and for her. She just prayed he would leave the city soon.

The French soldier was fast asleep and would be for some time with the help of the laudanum she had administered. Eloise, one of the younger girls, was in his bed curled around him to keep him quiet whilst she rifled through his clothes behind a curtain hung specially to one side of the room for just this purpose.

It was so easy to catch them off guard, these boys, Alejandra thought, so simple to allow them a few indiscretions whilst toasting king and country and their hopes for an empire that would rule the civilised world.

There was only a small paper in his pocket as she went through the jacket and it was in code. She had seen these before, the jumbled nonsense of war secrets written so that no one else, save the proper receiver, could understand them.

Sitting at her armoire, she meticulously copied the scrawl, making certain that every letter was exactly the same and that each line reflected precisely what was written there. The English would pay well for this and the soldier for all his youth had a jacket with many decorations upon it.

Tucking the letter in her diary and placing it in the secret drawer at the back of her desk, she returned the original document to the particular pocket it had come from and signalled to Eloise that her search was finished. He would wake soon and then…

The door was torn open and it hung drunkenly on its hinges. There was the sound of crying and screaming from further within the house and a group of French soldiers here in her room.

'Come here.' The first man gave the order and Eloise scrambled to her feet to hide behind Alejandra as two others came forward. In her nightgown the young girl was at a distinct disadvantage, the thin lacy fabric of the thing stretched across her breasts so that everything was exposed.

'It is me you need to speak with, *monsieur*. The girl here is young and an innocent—'

The older officer slapped her across the face, hard, and Alejandra tasted blood and fear at the very same time, though she was pleased when Eloise was allowed to run from the room.

'It is you I particularly wish to speak with, Señora Antonia Herrera y Salazar.'

His glance took in the young soldier naked upon the bed and the clothes he had been in folded neatly across a nearby chair. He found the document within a moment and held it up to her.

'We have word that you are a spy for the English and that you are using this place as a means to steal intelligence from any military man who has the misfortune to use your establishment. You drug them? Is that how it is done?'

'No.' She sought for feminine wiles and abject terror. 'I am only a working woman and he is asleep.'

'Wake him up.' A barked order to a fourth man, who promptly shook the boy on the bed violently. He remained in slumber.

The first man hit her again. She felt the smack of his hand across the bridge of her nose and wondered if perhaps it was broken. At least he had not smashed in her teeth.

Maria was suddenly there, the old woman fighting her way through the crowd with her stick raised.

'Leave her alone. She has done none of the things you say she has. She is a good girl and—' Someone pushed her away and she fell, slowly, one moment there with her anger and her concern and the next falling, her head striking against the sharp brick corner of the fireplace as she went down and then silence.

It was as if Alejandra was in a play, not quite real, the fantasy of horror and blood and glassy eyes. Death held a look that she had seen many times over and here it was again in her room, beside the thick burgundy velvet of the curtains and on the waxed boards of the floor, the polished stick turning in its own macabre circle before it slowed and stopped.

She tried to get to her, to pull away and cradle the woman who had taken her in, pregnant and terrified all those years before, to give her a home and a place of safety. But the older man simply walked forward and without saying a word removed his pistol from his pocket and slammed it down across the back of her head.

She woke in a cell and she was naked. It was dark and she was shivering violently, from fright rather than cold, she thought, though small tufts of straw were the only barrier between her and a rough dirt floor.

Maria was dead. It was finished, this part of her life, and she had heard what happened to women prisoners taken by the French. Many did not return and if they did they were seldom the same. War held a violence that would never have been acceptable in peacetime and a spy couldn't expect a pleasant time of it. They would have found the copied note by now and the laudanum held enough evidence for them to be certain of her guilt.

She had not been raped yet. Her head was sore and there were scratches on her breasts. Her nose ached and her cheek stung, but apart from that... She ran her fingers across herself just to check and found nothing more than a badly split bottom lip.

It was either very late or very early, the darkness complete and thick. The cell held no window and the walls were all of stone. She wondered if she could start digging, but the ground was as hard as any rock and she knew that she would need to conserve her energy for what would come next.

She was not afraid of dying.

That thought came with a surprising certainty. There was nothing left here for her now that Maria was gone and Ross was there on the other side waiting.

She wished she might pray, might find the words that used to mean so much to her, the guidance and the truth, but even as she started to recite the Apostles' Creed she stopped. God would know she did not mean them, could not mean them, because her heart had been shut off to that succour for years, the falsity of it so very obvious.

A noise held her still, a small quiet sound that came from the left down a dark corridor. And then Lucien Howard was there on the other side of the heavy iron gate, dressed in black like a shadow, a slouchy hat pulled down low across his hair.

'Shh.' He did not say a word as he lifted the lock and fitted it to a thick wire he held in his hands. Two seconds and the catch released. Opening the door, he drew her out, whipping a blanket around her shoulders and head so that she was like a wraith in the night. He wore gloves, thin leather ones that felt warm against the skin of her arms where he held her.

She could barely see where they were going it was so black, but he moved like one who could find the way and soon a new corridor appeared.

'This way.' His first real words. She stood on

something and it cut her foot. She felt the slice of it and the pain, but did not say a thing.

Then he was lifting her through a window and out into the cool of night, where she fell a good few feet on to the softness of long grass and earth and rolled to the bottom of an incline.

They ran as fast as they could go across the wide openness of the ground around the building, away from the high stone walls and silence, up into the hills and early-morning light, stopping only as the cover of the bushes became thicker.

'Hell.' He was looking at her foot and the trail of blood she had left behind her. 'When did this happen?'

'In one...of the...corridors.' She was so breathless she could hardly give him answer. He simply pulled her up then and wrapped his cloak about her foot and carried her on into the morning until they reached a stream.

'Stay in the middle of the water and don't touch any of the branches.' He did not wish for broken twigs or torn leaves, but she understood that well and was careful in her progress.

One hour and then two and then two more, the sun full up into the sky now and her throat burning with thirst. They had left the river a few hours ago and were now well out into the countryside. The water had stopped the bleeding and all that was there now was a dimpled white jagged line of skin, sealed off by the cold.

He handed her a flask he'd filled from the stream

and she drank until he took it off her and drank himself. Then he turned to her, the look in his eyes angry and distant. She tucked the blanket over her shins to cover any piece of skin that was showing.

'Right. Now, Señorita Alejandra Fernandez y Santo Domingo, you are going to tell me exactly what the hell just happened and why you were in a Spanish brothel pretending to be a whore.'

'Pretending?'

'Enough.' This time she heard more than only indifference. This time the man she had known in the north of Spain was back, too, careful, still and clever. 'I came to save you from the French because you did the same for me, once, but it seems you have been selling secrets to the British army for the past three years.'

He brought a paper from his pocket and she saw it was the same coded document she had copied out... yesterday? Or was it the day before?

'It is a wonder the French didn't find this. A secret drawer in a desk is hardly difficult to locate. A woman at the brothel told me you were the owner and that you did not service patrons.'

'Did she also tell you Maria is dead, the old woman who I work with? The French soldier killed her so easily when...' She stopped because she could not go on. 'What now? What happens to me now?'

'I am no longer with the military for I resigned my commission after A Coruña, but I will take you to the British in the north. You will be safe there.'

He promised her nothing more. He had saved her

because she had done the same for him and now...
now they were people travelling in directions that
the other could not follow. Still, she could not quite
give up.

'I wrote to you. In England. But you know that.'

His head tipped and he stilled. 'No letter ever
found me. When was this?'

'After you left Pontevedra. And then again when I
first arrived in Madrid. I wrote to tell you...' She just
could not go on. Not like this, not in fright on the run
and a scowl on his face. Not when he was looking at
her as if she were a stranger, a foreigner, a woman
whom he no longer recognised.

Ross deserved more than that, more than a quick
mention and an instant dismissal. Someone had written back to her, though, and if it was not him...? His
family, perhaps, horrified that a girl of no title who
wrote in broken English might claim the Earl of Ross
as the father of her illegitimate child.

'I was sick for a long time when I arrived back in
England. Perhaps the missive was lost.'

'Perhaps,' she murmured back and took in breath.
She'd burnt the letter she had received from London
with the seal of an important earldom upon it and the
words that had broken her heart.

Suddenly it all seemed like a long time ago and she
was so tired she felt as if she would just fall down to
sleep for a hundred years, like that princess in a folk
tale her mother had told her once.

But she was not a princess. She was a runaway and
a traitor. She was also broke, naked and hurt.

'You need to sleep.' He had been able to do this before, to read her mind and find the solution to the problems of it. 'I will find you some clothes at the next town we come to.'

'Thank you, Lucien. For everything.'

Even if it was not love that had brought him to the French prison she could not imagine what might have happened in the morning if he had not come. The hugeness of such a risk made her stomach feel sick. If they had captured him, too...

She wished he might touch her as he used to, just once, but he did not. The scowl on his face was distinct.

They had moved nor-nor-west at night when dusk fell and the moon rose. He had found her clothes and boots in a small village in the afternoon of the first day and she was dressed as a lad because it was less conspicuous and much safer. The next morning they boarded a public coach going north on the Burgos Road.

He seldom really looked at her, his whole being focused on the journey and their safety. The intimacy that they'd had was gone and in its place sat a shared wariness.

She did not mention the letter and the reply and he did not ask her anything of her time in Madrid. A strained truce of acceptance ensued, the fragile new shoots of trust too young and small to be battered again by revelation and survive.

They skirted around other more impersonal issues, though mostly there was silence.

The fire at the hacienda came up on the fourth day of travelling as they moved north from Burgos and towards the coast.

'I thought you were dead. The documents of the fire I saw in London mentioned your name beneath your father's. There were no survivors. No one was left.'

'It was the Betancourts,' she said, lifting her glance to his. They were sitting beneath the overhanging boughs of a large oak just outside San Sebastian and it was almost dusk. 'The family hated us after Juan's death and I think they saw their chance and took it. The fight that killed Manolo and Adan was a part of their revenge, I suppose, as well. Did your report mention what happened after the fire?'

'No.'

'Not everyone perished in the house. When they came out from the hacienda they were shot and their bodies tossed back into the flames.'

'Where were you when this was happening?'

'Returning on the high pass from Pontevedra. It had been raining heavily and I had to wait until the weather cleared to get through.'

'Then who told you of it? Of the aftermath, I mean. Of the fighting?'

'Tomeu escaped and he came to find me. He was burnt badly, trying to save my father, and died four days later for I had very little to tend him with and dared not risk going down into the village again. I spent a night watching the house from the hill behind after he had passed and saw that the land was empty, of men and livestock. Then I left.'

'You went alone?'

'I did. I travelled south to Madrid and cut my hair and bleached it. I found new clothes, a new voice and a new name.'

She did not mention the fact that she had returned to Pontevedra and waited many more weeks for him in the hills above, praying to God all the while that he might come back and save her.

In the last light of the day Lucien saw other truths that she was not saying, darker honesties that left the green of her eyes locked in hurt.

The colour of her hair was a bright and artificial red. He wished she had left it just as it was, long and dark and shining. He wished, too, that she might look at him properly, the furtive short glances beginning to annoy him. Only a few times had she lifted her chin and met his eyes directly, but the challenge and the strength he had always associated with Alejandra Fernandez y Santo Domingo was gone, an indifferent resignation at her lot in its place. A watered-down version of the girl he had once known, wary, plaintive and sad.

Her hands, too, were so much more still. Her rosary was missing and when she spoke her fingers hung now by her side, lifeless and quiet. Each nail was coloured in a redness to match her hair, though the paint was chipped badly with the exertion and hardships of the past days. He wondered how one removed such lacquer so that the vestige of anything left was gone. She had worn gloves in the carriage up to Burgos and a large cloth hat that had hidden most of her face and hair. She walked like a lad and acted as one, too. A chameleon, changed beyond belief.

Her right wrist was still crossed with the scars he had seen there before and although she saw him looking she did not try to hide them as she had always done in the hacienda above A Coruña or in the mountains of Galicia.

This is me, she seemed to wordlessly say. *Battered and ruined. Take it or leave it. I do not care.* The buttons on her shirt were done up to her throat in a tight marching line despite the heat and the collar of the jacket she wore at night was raised around her neck. Concealment. She wore it like another set of clothes.

'Did you bury your father?'

'No. I left him where he was, for all the bodies were charred beyond recognition and I could not risk being seen there. When I travelled the acrid smell of burning followed me for miles.'

He thought she might cross herself or recite some appropriate and known verse of the Bible, but that was another difference. In the five days of her company he had not seen her once murmur a Hail Mary or hold her hands up in silent prayer.

It was as if the changes in her appearance outside were mirrored in the inside traits. She had never asked him even one personal question about his own recent past.

'Do you still carry a knife?' His own query was out before he could stop it.

'No.'

'Never?'

For the first time in his company since leaving Madrid she smiled, a nervous and measured humour, but undeniably there. He was heartened by it and pressed on.

'You have lost the skill of wielding a blade?'

'More the inclination, I think, Capitán.' A quick surge of anger accompanied her reply. He covered the silence quickly.

'I do not know whether to be relieved or concerned by that.'

'At least you have no worry of a dagger through your ribs in the dead of night.'

Only in my dreams, he thought and stood, the conversation getting too close to the bone.

He had wanted her before and he still wanted her in the way a man needs a woman. He shouldn't and he hated that he did, but there was no help for it.

'It is time to go.'

Scuffing at the ground in which they had lain, he picked up his bag. The bruises on her face were fading and the black beneath her left eye was changed to a lighter tone. Her bottom lip still looked puffed and split, but he'd had the same at A Coruña after the battle and he remembered that had taken a long while to heal.

All in all she had been lucky. At least they had not used their knives on her and everything would mend. The sunset tonight was a vibrant yellow, the branches of the trees outlined in the stillness so that every leaf could be seen against the glow. A moment in time and yet out of it, he thought, a moment remembered for its quiet peace and beauty amongst all the danger, chaos and change.

Chapter Twelve

Lucien Howard had always had that knack of full certainty, she thought as she watched him check his compass and look up at the sky. He had been the same in A Coruña, and on the road across the Galician Mountains, and here he did not falter or hesitate as he pushed forward through the scrub-filled hills in the moonlight.

She had no idea as to where they were headed, but he had said he would take her to the British camp and she knew the army under Wellington to be somewhere in the vicinity of the northern coast towards the east.

The smell of smoke was barely noticeable at first, a slight wisp of burning on the air. She knew he had smelt it, too, for he stopped, his face lifting into the wind.

'San Sebastian is on fire.'

Shocked, Alejandra could only nod, for tall billows of smoke crested a hill, the black height of it denoting great damage. They could hear no gunshots or sounds of fighting, though, as they crouched down on the top of the hillock and waited, the early-morning sun on their backs and a thousand questions unanswered. Below there was the movement of people along the streets and the carts of an uninterrupted trade.

'It is over, the battle. I think it's the vanquishers who have started the fire.'

'The English, then? They have won it?'

'If they had not, we would see them still outside the fortified southern walls or across the estuary of the river. It is Rey who is the general in charge of the French here and they have used the ancient fortifications well for defence by all accounts. But Wellington has over nine thousand men from Oswald's Fifth Division and a good number of Portuguese troops to boot and Rey has only just on three thousand. So San Sebastian was always going to fall if Soult didn't have the means to defend it, which he hasn't for word has it they are a lot further east in the foothills of the Pyrenees.'

Such words told Alejandra that Lucien Howard was still involved in the military somehow. She stayed silent whilst he removed a small looking glass from his bag and pieced it together before aiming it towards the city walls.

Finally he stood. 'Come. We will go down and make ourselves known for I am fairly sure it is the English who are in charge.'

The town was reeling with drunken riotous mobs of British soldiers, the brandy and wine flowing freely in the streets.

Lucien made certain that Alejandra stayed close behind him, glad she was dressed in her lad's clothes. Down nearly every alleyway and small lane there was evidence of violence, men with their throats cut and the screams of young women heard. Rape had a certain sound to it unlike the silence of murder.

When a half-clothed girl ran into him as she tried to escape a trio of drunken English louts, Lucien held her arm so that she did not fall.

'Help me.' The words were only mouthed as though sound had been taken from her in shock. Pushing her behind him, he confronted those who stood now watching.

'She's our Spanish whore. Give 'er back and get yer own, guv. There's plenty of 'em here.'

Drawing his pistol, Lucien pointed it straight at the heart of the biggest man.

'You'll have to take her from me first.' All these soldiers understood was aggression and his anger had surfaced in a red-raw fury.

When the same man came forward with a knife, Lucien simply shot him above the knee, in a fleshy part of the leg, a small injury that would not permanently disable him, but would certainly hurt. Then he lifted his gun to another behind, threatening to do the same again.

'Good shooting.' Alejandra's voice was close.

The piercing screams of the girl between them almost drowned out the barrage of swear words directed at him by the departing English soldiers, yet as chaos consumed them Lucien was more and more aware of the calm surrounding Alejandra. She did not flinch or pull back. No, she stayed right behind him, resolution to aid him well on show, even weaponless.

No doubts. No misgivings. She had taken the Spanish girl by the hand and was trying to give her comfort, settling her with quiet words of strength.

'They are gone now and they won't be back.'

She could not say more for at that moment an older man came from a house a few yards away, tears streaming from his eyes.

'I thought you were dead. I thought that you had been taken away.'

'Papa.' The girl rushed into his arms. 'This man saved me. He shot the drunken soldier and frightened the rest.'

'Then I thank you, sir. My daughter is all I have left and without her...'

More shouting further away had them turning and the pair disappeared into their house, the heavy door closing behind them. Lucien hoped such a protection would be enough, but he doubted it. He had never seen such lawlessness and lack of organised control in all his years in the army. He turned to Alejandra, her green eyes watchful and the fury all about them still.

'We'll need to find Wellington and his aides, for he will know me, but this is a dangerous place, Alejandra, so stay close.' Reaching into his bag, he brought out a knife he knew she would recognise, wicked sharp, the heft smoothed from years of use.

'Take it and don't hold back if you need to use it.'

* * *

The look and the feel of the weapon in her fingers was familiar. For so long she had carried a knife. Until Madrid when death had reduced her to not caring whether she lived or died and so such protection was immaterial.

For a moment, though, some small thing came back, some stronger sense of herself, a knowledge of who she had been once. Before. It was the knife she had given him at the hacienda in the very first days of his arrival there.

'If anyone attacks you, kill them. There are no rules here save anarchy and it is a choice between your life or theirs. An eye for an eye and a tooth…'

'I no longer believe in any of that.'

'God. Jesus. Heaven. Hell?'

'Hell, perhaps, but none of the other.' The feeling in her throat thickened as she said it. Once, religion had been her backbone and her strength. Now it was lost to her, through both choice and circumstance. 'Look about you, Capitán, and tell me, is there a God here, in this?'

'Maybe,' he replied. 'Maybe in the lesson of it for next time, I think.'

She glanced away because in his simple philosophy she saw the truth of who she had become and also of who he was.

She wanted to ask him then what his life had been like across the past four years, but she did not. Safer that way, she thought, holding on to her distance like a shield as she positioned the knife in her fist.

The wholeness she had felt with him all those years ago was creeping in again. Unexpected and wonderful. The fears and struggle of life seemed to melt away in his company and all she felt were the possibilities. Swallowing down the hope of it, she followed him into the town proper.

'It's a damned mess, is what it is.' Ian MacMillan, an aide of Wellington's, had taken them into the house used by the officers on the far side of San Sebastian. 'Our casualties were high in the first onslaught from the beach because although the town wall was breached there was a second inner *coupure* that meant those sent in were trapped in a no man's land. Many died there and the anger has lingered. This is the result.'

'The wine and brandy has something to do with it, too, I am guessing.' They'd seen casks on the street upturned and abandoned so that the liquid was running in the gutters, the colour of blood.

The other man nodded. 'Indeed, the place was full of booze and the men have run amok, pillaging, burning and killing. Some of the officers tried to stop them, but they were either ignored or threatened. Sanity is long gone.'

'And it will be this way until the alcohol runs out.' Lucien stated this quietly as he looked out the window across a plaza filled with violence. 'Where are the French now?'

'General Rey and his men have retreated to the hill of Urgull, a small garrison on the mound above the beach. The Marquess of Wellington is expecting them to ask for terms as they are surrounded, and as I think he has not the heart, after this, to beat them down further, he will agree.'

'It's been a long campaign, then?'

'As long as yours was, sir, under Moore. We heard about the difficulties in that one.'

'At least you have had your victories.' His humour was measured as the sounds of those outside filtered into the room.

Captain Howard was not dressed as a soldier, but anyone looking at him could tell he had been one. It was inherent in the way he stood and spoke and in the questions he asked. He was not bent down by life or death or even by what had happened here. He had saved a young girl today from being raped and shot a soldier in the knee and yet he had made no mention of this to anyone.

Honourable and good. That was who he was and the anger that had built a tight knot about Alejandra's heart began to loosen.

'Would you and your lad like a bed here tonight? It might be safer than taking your chances out there at least.'

It was getting late and a storm looked to be brewing to the north. Lucien caught her eye in question and she nodded.

Four hours later they were finally alone, the dinner an early one and quickly taken.

Two beds stood against each wall and although

the room was small it was cool, a band of windows along one side open to the night and two storeys up.

With the candles burning and a bottle of wine on the table between them this place was the most luxurious and private accommodation they had had since leaving Madrid, but it made Alejandra feel nervous. With her anger slipped a notch she could no longer latch on to fury as a way to keep Lucien Howard at a distance. Yet he had not in one word or touch signalled he wanted more than the relationship that prevailed.

Cordial. Wary. Polite.

Taking off her hat, she fanned her fingers through her hair and spread the heavy heat of it out before tying it up with leather.

'Will you dye it again?'

This was the first truly personal question he had asked her.

'My hair?'

He nodded and sat down on the opposite bed watching her. 'Do you prefer it that way?'

'The blonde I used to have was worse.'

At that he laughed.

'Maria insisted on the red because her daughter had been one. She had bottles of the stuff left after Anna passed and I suppose I was her substitute.'

'How did she die?'

'Giving birth. It is a dangerous thing to do and sometimes a mother can perish, or a...'

Stopping herself by sheer dint of will, she felt the tremble of loss run over her heart. A child could die, too. So very easily. Her child. Their child. Left in a nameless grave in a cemetery she might never be back to visit.

And yet here…here the disasters of life were unfolding about her, too, and Lucien had kept her safe, untouched, whole. The fright of the young girl had shocked her, the relief of her father amidst screams and shouts of other victims in all the corners of the town underlying the terror.

Death visited unannounced and with little warning. One moment here and the next one gone. Like Ross. Like her father. Like Maria and Tomeu and Adan and Manolo and her mother. It took no account of honour or fairness. It just was.

Five days ago she had cheated it in the dank and cold prison cell on the outskirts of Madrid and tonight she lay above the chaos and looting in San Sebastian, yet cocooned in safety.

Lucien Howard was sitting with his back against the wall, having removed his boots and jacket. His knife was laid down next to him, in the soft leather in which he sheathed it. 'The battle for the freedom of Spain is nearly won.'

'At a great cost to the town of San Sebastian,' she replied, watching him frown.

'"Only the dead have seen the end of war",' he quoted. 'Plato said that more than two thousand years ago and it still holds true today.'

'The philosopher?' She had heard of him but had read none of his treatises. 'You are a learned man,

Capitán, yet you are not a soldier any more? You no longer march with your army?'

'No. One needs heart to fight well.'

'And yours is lost? Your heart?'

He met her gaze at that and for a moment through the final slash of light before the darkness fell she saw what war had cost him. It was written on his face in sadness and loss. As it probably was, just as distinctly, on hers.

Turning away, she pulled back the sheet and kicked off her own boots even as she fashioned a pillow from her jacket. She was glad for the night-time and the privacy it afforded as she lay down.

'What will happen next, do you think? With the English forces?'

'It is most likely that Wellesley will chase General Soult across the Pyrenees and back into France and Joseph Bonaparte will be sent home from Madrid as the support for Napoleon crumbles. Another year should do it and then there will be nothing left of the little Emperor's pretensions.'

'Just dead people,' she said quietly, 'and sadness.'

He wished he could have gone outside and walked, but he did not want to leave Alejandra here alone and so he lay back in his bed by the window and watched the clouds instead, scooting across the moon and running just ahead of a storm.

What the hell was he to do with her now? He could not simply hand her over to the British army's safe-keeping with the confusion here and the French less than a mile from where they lay. Her disguise was at best tenuous and he had the suspicion the aide to Wellington who had shown them to their room had already understood the lad who accompanied him was indeed a lassie.

Lifting a glass from the table, he drank some of the wine, a fine and full-bodied red with a strong hint of something he could not quite define.

Like Alejandra, he smiled and looked over to where she lay.

He had watched her sleep in the hills after A Coruña and she still slumbered in the same way, curled up on her side with one hand under her head. The bandage on her foot was dirty where she had kicked off the sheets to allow a freedom and he vowed to find a medic on the morrow to get it checked.

She had not complained. Not once. She had hobbled on the foot for miles and shaken her head when he had asked her if it was painful. Her lip looked better today, too, and the bruises on her face were harder to see.

He could not imagine one other woman of his acquaintance making so little fuss about injuries and wounds. There was an old square of mirror in the room they were in propped up against a shelf by the door. He had not seen her glance in it even once.

Outside the sounds of the night were receding into silence. He wondered what Wellington must think of such pointless aggression, how he squared off his triumphs with such defeats. He was glad he was out of it now. Once, he had not been.

Once, after A Coruña and Alejandra, all he could think of was going back into battle and losing his life for a cause that was worth it.

He closed his eyes and rested his head against the rough boards that lined the room, her soft sleeping breath coming to him across the space between them.

He couldn't leave her here. At least of that he was sure. If Wellington could not offer her a safe haven, he would take her to England with him. He smiled at the thought, imagining what the tight-laced English society doyens might make of Alejandra Fernandez y Santo Domingo and she of them.

He was certain Amethyst Wylde would like her and Adelaide Hughes. His sister, Christine, would also enjoy the company of a woman who did not simper or flirt or pretend.

His mother, of course, would take some convincing given her loathing of anyone Spanish, but that was a worry for another day.

He laughed to himself, thinking that he had planned out a future for her that she herself had taken no part in. Indeed, she looked as if she would be off in a flash if he did not watch her, gone into the ether and another life that he would have no notion of. Yet with her time in Madrid finished and her safety in A Coruña and the northern coast uncertain she was running out of locations to make a home from.

'You are still awake?' She had stretched out and, in the dark, her lurid hair looked less red. 'It's very late, I think.'

'I like the night. It's the quietest time of the day.'

Without the need to directly look at each other talking was easier.

'I saw a story of you once in an English paper about a girl you were to marry.'

'I didn't.'

'Pardon?'

'I didn't marry her.'

'Why not?'

'I could not give her what she needed.'

Now she sat herself up, her rolled jacket tucked in behind her, and was trying to peer at him through the gloom. 'And what was that?'

'Love. Honesty. Even the truth was beyond my capability. I took the blame of it all, of course, and I think in the end she did not suffer overmuch. Her parents took her off on an extended tour of the Continent virtually straight away and when she returned a good year later it was on the arm of an Italian count who had much in the way of wealth and devotion.'

Alejandra was amazed that he might have told her such a personal thing. She was also unreasonably angry. For him. 'Was your heart broken even a little?'

He laughed at that and shook his head. 'I was relieved. A lifetime is a long while to spend with someone…'

'Who could not love you in the same way you loved them back?' She finished the thought for him.

'Yes,' he said. 'Just that.'

The moments of quiet stretched out, but now it held

a lot less restraint and much more warmth, their lines of communication more fluid and real.

'What happened to my signet ring? I left it with the old lady at the brothel and asked her to give it to you.'

This question was unexpected. 'I sold it. Señor Morales was pressing me for the loan repayments and it was valuable.'

'Mateo Morales? The man you thought was me that night in Segovia Street?'

'He is a moneylender and he was going to call in the loans unless I…' She stopped and wished she had not said anything, but he carried on anyway.

'Unless you slept with him?'

'I would have, if you had not come. Do not think that I wouldn't have. I am not the innocent I was before, Capitán.'

His smile surprised her. 'You shot your husband, Alejandra. You knew how to use a knife as you traipsed across the killing fields of war as the daughter of the guerrilla leader El Vengador. What part of that implies innocence?'

'I was not a prostitute then.' Her voice was low.

'And you are not one now.'

'I loved God and Jesus. I believed. I had faith and now I don't. I threw my rosary into the river.' This she said in the hushed tone of the truly dreadful, the worst possible confession she might make.

'Buy another one, then. Begin again.'

She swore. 'The people here, Capitán, those who have been maimed or raped by a force that was supposed to free them, know how impossible it ever is to go back, to be who you were before. The cost of life is sometimes just too much to pay, don't you see? Some things that are broken just cannot be fixed.'

She thought of Ross and the hospital of La Latina, cold and quiet and bare. She remembered walking home without him, the rain in her boots and the tears on her cheeks. Maria had been there when she got back to Segovia Street and she had set a fire and rubbed her feet and put her to bed beneath the warmth of a duck-feather eiderdown, tucked around both slumber and pain.

But she had woken up a different person: harder, angrier, less able to believe in the goodness of anything or anyone.

'How old are you now?'

'Twenty-six.'

'So you are saying that you will be this broken for all of your life. Fifty or so more years of anger and guilt?'

Now, this was new. He was not telling her that what had happened to her was not her fault. No. He was telling her to sit up and take responsibility. And live. Perhaps he was right. Perhaps it was the secrets she carried that kept her from life, the dreadful creeping sadness that had emptied any joy. What was that saying Maria had recited to her on numerous occasions? Shared sorrow is half a sorrow. Perhaps it was the case with the right person?

She took a shaky breath and made herself speak.

'We had a son, you and I, a little boy and I named him Ross. After you. He lived for two minutes and then he simply stopped breathing. The nurse said that happens sometimes when babies are very little because their lungs are not formed or just perhaps because God wanted them back again.'

'God.' His expletive was shocked.

'He had dark hair and he was tiny. Too tiny. He had a purple birthmark on the very top of his left arm, just here, and he was warm when I held him until he wasn't.'

'God,' he repeated, the stillness in him magnified by the night.

'I sent you a letter, with the postage paid through the correct channels of communication. A month later I had a reply back. It said do not write again and that if I did you would set the law upon me for making false claims. It held your seal in wax and your signature.'

He stood and walked to stand by her bed. 'I did not send the letter, Alejandra. I swear it by all that is holy. If you believe nothing else of me, at least believe that.'

'I do.'

The anger in him vibrated, coldly held under control by sheer and utter force. She could see the way the knuckles of both fists were pressed white. 'Ross, you say?'

'Yes.'

'A strong name that claimed his birthright.' There was a catch in his voice, a tremor, each word enunciated with tremendous care.

'He did not suffer at all, at least there was that. He looked just like he was sleeping.' She suddenly wanted to comfort him, this soldier who had fought his way all across Europe and was still fighting, injustice, wrongness, terror. 'He died peacefully in my arms on October the second. At six minutes past eleven at night. It was raining.' Specifics. Details. She remembered each and every one of them as if they had been engraved in blood upon her skin.

'We will bring him home.'

'Pardon?'

'We will bring him home to England and bury him at Linden Park, my family seat at Tunbridge Wells. At least he won't be alone then.'

'You would do that?'

'He is ours, Alejandra. He needs to be with his family.'

Ours. No longer just hers. A shared sadness.

And just like that a dam long held back by hardship and circumstance began to crack; the water at first a tiny drip and then a stream and after a river in full flood and rushing across the bleak landscape of her emotions. She stood, only thinking to escape, but he was by her in a second, letting her cry against his warmth and strength. And she did cry for herself and for Ross, for Lucien and her father and mother and for Spain. For San Sebastian, too, with its deaths and its violence, and for Maria, who had only ever tried to help her.

She could not remember a time when she had done

this before, to just let go, no longer trying to control things.

He mopped her eyes finally with the edge of his sleeve, her hair wet, too, from the exertion and her heart sore.

'Who was there to help you, Alejandra?'

'Maria was there after he died and she said that I had only two choices, to go on or not to go on. The brothel needed a younger hand, a steadier one, and I found I was good at the business side of things, tallying the finances and seeing that the house was... in order. Even in a brothel there is some sense of arrangement and structure, you see, Capitán, and it had long been left to run down.'

'You became Maria's right-hand woman?'

'I did and it was an honour. She had no one left and neither did I.'

'And so you wrote the letter for help?'

'No, it was for the truth I wrote. For Ross. Not for me. I wanted you to know that he would be...that he would have a life and a name and a time.'

His ripe curse had her hands rising up to her chest, about to make the sign of the cross, but she stilled them. To ask the Lord for help now was hypocritical and disingenuous. She could not expect it, not after so long of turning away from his ministry.

'Did you keep the letter?'

She shook her head. 'Everything that I had left of you is gone.' With that she moved away and lay down on her bed, turned towards the wall. She did not want false promises. She did not want him to capitulate only in pity. She was glad when he did not speak again.

When she woke he was missing from the bed by the window, his bag neatly packed and the blanket pulled up. Outside it was blue, the rain and storms across the past few days disappeared and the temperatures warmer again. Hot, in fact, she thought as she loosened the few top buttons on the man's shirt Lucien had given her.

For the first time in a long while she felt hungry, as if she should eat well before greeting the day. Another difference. She folded her jacket into the small sack she carried and put on her boots before washing her face in the cold water someone had left in a china bowl on the table between the beds. Her heel ached and although she had tried to wash it when she could, in both rivers and smaller streams, an inflammation had set in.

Then Lucien was there, offering bread and cheese.

'We can't stay here in San Sebastian. Wellington has his own worries and there are no boats in the harbour to take us north.'

'North?' She could not quite understand what he meant.

'England. You can't go west because of the Betancourts and the south and east are still controlled by the French. We should have safe passage towards Bilbao, though, in the smaller ports on the Costa Vasca.'

'I cannot come with you to England. How would you explain me to your family?'

'We will think on that on the road,' he returned and lifted up his bag. 'When you have finished breakfast we will go.'

An hour later they were riding through the countryside on two steeds Lucien had managed to procure.

The closeness of last night had not been lost altogether and the tight dread of her life seemed to have been unwound a little. Lucien had not left her in San Sebastian and he had promised to bring Ross home. For that alone she was grateful, but there were other things that ran around her body and in her mind that owed no tether to simple gratitude.

When he had held her last night against him in comfort she had wanted what they had enjoyed on the high passes of the Galician Mountains, to feel him inside her once again, to know the passion and the glory of a connection that she had never forgotten.

She looked away from him so that he would not see that which burnt in her eyes. But when she glanced up at the sun streaming through the trees and leaving beams of light on the air she felt hopeful.

The word surprised her. It had after all been so long since she had once felt that.

Lucien watched the landscape about him. It was still dangerous to ride through these passes without an escort from the military, but Wellington could not spare any men and Lucien did not wish to wait for a week or two until he could.

So he was cautious and wary as the miles passed, checking distance, listening for sounds and watching the horizon for any sign of movement that could be risky.

He felt flattened from her news of their baby son, all his defences down and the loss of what could have been. He was also furious that she had written to him when she was pregnant asking for help and that somebody had sent an answer back refusing it.

His mother, probably. The wrath inside made him shake.

'Where do you live when you are not in London?' They'd slowed the horses to give them a break and so were able to talk.

'At Linden Park, in Kent, to the south of the city,' he qualified as she frowned.

'And your family is there? You said once that there were lots of them.'

'Two brothers and my sister, Christine. And my mother. The estate had been left to run down, so that is why I left the army, to try to build it up again and make it prosperous. I am having some success with manufacturing.'

And he was. The textile business had become most lucrative and the power mills and new technology meant everything could be done faster and better. He had poured what was left of the family fortune into the sector, and so far the odds looked to be paying off.

Business. Profits. Manufacturing. Why was he

not asking more personal questions of Alejandra or simply getting off his horse and dragging her into the substantial undergrowth around them to see if they could rediscover all they had felt before? He wanted her with such a violence he could barely breathe and it worried him.

Last night had been a revelation, but he was wary, too. He needed to get Alejandra to England first and home to a place where she would not be able to simply disappear. He no longer trusted that she would not flee in the environs of her own land given that the freedom from Spain's independence was creeping back in.

She had always said she would never leave Spain, but if he brought Ross to England, would that not engender a different loyalty? A base. A place to put down roots and grow from?

He could not afford to harm the small trust that was developing between them by going too fast, by expecting too much closeness.

Hence he turned the subject to other things.

'When I left Spain after Pontevedra the boat hit a storm in the Bay of Biscay and it took us a lot longer to reach England than Alvarez had imagined. At times I wondered if the ship would not just sink into oblivion.'

'And your wounds? How did you fare by the time you did reach it?'

'Badly. I was ill for a long time and then convalesced at Montcliffe, a friend's family seat in Essex. Daniel Wylde. He was in Spain with me.'

She nodded. 'You spoke of him in your fever dreams at the hacienda, calling him to help you. And of some others. Francis and Gabriel. Like the angels in the Bible,' she qualified and reddened. It was the first religious reference he had heard her make since he'd met up with her again.

'I grew up with them all. Daniel has a wife now called Amethyst and children and Gabriel is married to Adelaide. They are not women who covet society and its frippery.'

The fright and distance in her eyes was evident. Once, he had imagined Alejandra in the city with her bravery and confidence dressed in a fine gown, but now…all he saw was fear and uncertainty, the red in her hair strangely contrasted against the sheen of her skin.

But she had smiled four times today, which was twice more than she had yesterday and four times more than the day before that.

He did not want her to meet his family looking beaten. He wanted her to lift her eyes and become the woman she once had been.

The small port town of Bermeo came into view towards the late afternoon and as luck would have it the tide was in and they managed to find passage to England on a fishing boat that would leave in an hour.

Lucien was pleased to pay the fare and pleased, too, for the hammocks slung on the deck that were to be theirs for the two-day journey. Alejandra had barely spoken to him and he knew without being told that she was more than wary of finding herself in England.

Chapter Thirteen

London

'I did not realise that she was a woman you had strong feelings for, Lucien. I thought she was a charlatan cashing in on a quick way to an easy life, a woman who would hoodwink and dupe you with the threat of a pregnancy. That was what I thought.'

His mother was crying, large tears falling down both cheeks.

'But to never consult me on it. To simply burn the letter and never tell me anything at all? It is that I cannot forgive you for.'

He had confronted his mother about the letter after introducing her to Alejandra. The meeting had been tense and he could see on her face that she had recognised the name. After taking Alejandra to the library and asking the maid to bring her refreshments Lucien had gone back in order to find out the exact story.

'I know it was wrong, Lucien, but you were so sick

I thought another problem might simply finish you off. I was going to talk to Daniel Wylde of it, but he was never here in London, what with his leg and the problems he was facing at Ravenshill Manor, and after a time…I felt ashamed. Too ashamed to ever bring it up again even when you were better.'

'She lost the child. Our child. Your grandson. Alejandra named him Ross. He was too little to live.'

A fresh wave of tears had him almost feeling sorry for his mother, but he refrained from moving towards her because the anger that had stifled him all of the journey home was still too raw and fresh to dismiss. He wanted her to be as hurt as they had been.

'Do you think that my reply might have caused…?' She did not finish, her face an ashen white.

Of a sudden Lucien's anger changed to grief and he could no longer say what he thought he might have.

Turning, he simply walked out the door and back to the library. Alejandra was there, sitting on a chair by the fire, and he thought that although it was not very cold, to her it must seem so.

The gown he had found in a shop in Bournemouth which had been serviceable and appropriate there was old and tatty in London. The colour did not suit her, either, the orange against red only bringing out the garishness of both clashing shades.

'She does not like me? Your mother. She did not look happy at all when we arrived. I am sorry for it.'

'Don't be. She is a woman who takes a while to warm to those she does not know. We will leave for Linden Park on the morrow, but you will need a chaperon.'

'A chaperon?'

'In England it is not done for a young unmarried lady to spend time alone with a man.'

'But we have been alone for nearly two weeks now.'

'The very height of scandal,' he returned, 'and better not to mention that to anyone at all.' She smiled. 'My sister, Christine, will come with us to Kent and also my aunt. Mama will no doubt venture down at some time, too, but for now...'

'She was the one who sent the letter, wasn't she?'

He nodded. 'She had a dream I would die in Spain and she thought...'

'To save you from harm. A mother's prerogative, I should suppose, to try to protect her son.'

He shook his head. 'No, it was unforgivable. If she had been honest, I could have been there to help you when Ross was born.'

For the first time since he had found her in Madrid she stepped forward and touched him willingly. One finger placed gently against his lips.

'You are here now. It is enough.'

'Enough for what?'

'For me. This now. For being here with you and safe in England.'

He took her hand and held it to his heart, liking the warmth of it and the littleness. The pulse in her wrist beat fast.

'I am not sure of anything any more, Lucien,' she

whispered, but she did not pull away. 'I am not sure of who I am or of what I might become. I used to be more sure, but now…it is cold in this land and grey and all I can be to you is a…nuisance…'

The last word was whispered as if it were too terrible to say louder.

'I bled a lot when Ross was born and the doctor who attended me at the hospital said…' She took in a breath and kept going. 'He said I would probably never have another child. It could be true.'

The green in her eyes burnt with shame and sorrow.

'So you see your mother is right. I should not be here with you like this…' Her hands ran across the shabby fabric of the dress before rising to her hair, pulled from its fastening after a day's hard ride from the coast. 'I cannot fit in here even if I wanted to.'

As he was about to answer the doorbell rang and voices were heard booming over the silence.

'Where is he?'

'Where's Luce?'

When the door opened, a man and two women spilled into the room.

They were all beautiful. That was Alejandra's first thought. Beautifully dressed, beautifully presented, beautifully English, their manners instantly harnessed into politeness as they caught sight of her standing by the fire.

'You are Alejandra?'

The tall man with pale green eyes came forward first. He limped slightly and had the air of a soldier.

'My God, Luce actually found you? I never thought he would.'

Lucien had now moved over to her side. She felt his presence there and was pleased for it.

'Alejandra Fernandez y Santo Domingo, this is Daniel Wylde, the Earl of Montcliffe, his wife, Amethyst, and my sister, Christine Howard.'

The two women smiled, but there was puzzlement on their faces.

'Is most nice to meet with you.' Alejandra hoped her grasp of English was correct. It had been so long since she had spoken the language aloud with her mother and Rosalie herself had not been in any way fluent.

Both women acknowledged her and then Christine spoke again. 'You are the one who dyed my brother's hair? In Galicia? He cut it off short when he returned to England to get rid of the black and he looked like a scarecrow for weeks and weeks after.'

'Scarecrow?' Was that a good thing or a bad one?

'Espantapájaros.' Lucien supplied the word in Spanish and it fell into the library like an interloper. Every tome here was in English, she'd looked at the shelves when he was in with his mother, and there had not been a single title in Spanish.

'It was a protect,' she qualified, tripping on the last word as Daniel Wylde moved forward and spoke.

'Well, we thank you for it, Alejandra, for rescuing Lucien in Spain and saving his life. He is dear to us, you see, and without him...'

'Is my favour to do. He helps me also from the French. I am agree he is good man.'

Por favor, que me entiendan.

Please, let them understand me.

The words ran under everything she said even as Christine Howard reached out her hand and laid it on Alejandra's arm, her smile warm.

'Do you have other clothes with you? Other things to wear? My brother is obviously lacking in his duties in finding you such a gown.'

'Lacking?' She did not know this word at all and looked to Lucien.

'Le falta.' A further Spanish translation. 'Don't tell her of the breeches in your bag or the man's shirt.' This was also said in Spanish and very quickly. 'Christine will never let me hear the end of it if you do.'

Watching Lucien Howard at a disadvantage in the presence of his sister made her smile. 'I leave all my clothes in Madrid,' she said slowly and saw the relief on his face.

'Like a red rag to a bull,' Amethyst drawled and everyone laughed.

Why should they speak of bullfighting? Alejandra thought, trying to understand the humour. They were brutal and bloody and she had never enjoyed the spectacle. Surely here in the mannered salons of England such a thing would be abhorrent. She turned again to Lucien for explanation and he gave it slowly in English.

'My sister is a woman with a love of fashion and it

would give her great pleasure to help you choose other clothes. It is both her calling and her downfall,' he added and laughed. 'No one ever quite measures up.'

'Ignore Lucien. She has a gift for it, I promise.' Amethyst said this. 'Though I think you will not need much help at all.'

'Except with your hair.' Christine reached out a finger to touch her head. 'May I?'

Bemused Alejandra nodded.

'This is not your natural colour, surely?'

'No. Is dark, not red.'

'Much better then for such a shade would suit your eyes and skin. Did you cut it yourself?'

'Yes. Many times.' She wondered if she should have said that or not, but Lucien's sister seemed most adept at identifying faults. She frowned, too, at the scars on her right wrist as the sleeve of her jacket fell back and even the last remnants of the red paint on her nails was noted.

A poor specimen, she probably thought. Lifting her chin, though, she met Christine's eyes directly and this time real humour marked the light blue. Like Lucien's eyes, only darker, and threaded at the edges in gold. Were the Howard siblings all as beautiful as these two, she wondered, or as forthright?

'Perhaps we could start now, Alejandra.'

'Start?'

'My room is close and I am certain we could find something more suitable to dress you in. Amethyst will help us, too, and my maid is very useful with a needle.'

Lucien would not come with her, she was sure of it, and the thought made her hesitate. But still this dress was an ugly colour and the shoes were most uncomfortable. If they talked slowly, she would manage.

A moment later she found herself bundled away from the sanctuary of Lucien and his library.

'So the fire was mistaken intelligence, then?' Daniel sat on the chair before the desk and made himself comfortable.

'No. There was a blaze, only Alejandra had not returned from Pontevedra, the port she had taken me to, and so she escaped it. Her father died, though, and the house was razed along with many of the men living there.'

'Was it the French?'

Lucien shook his head. 'It was another guerrilla family who lived close by. Old rivalries,' he explained and poured them both a drink. He would not say anything of Alejandra's first husband or the revenge his death had incited.

'She is very beautiful, your Spanish lady.'

'Yes.'

'And very unprotected. The scandal would be huge if anyone were to find out how long you have been in each other's company. Unchaperoned, I am presuming.'

'It's why I didn't just head to Linden Park from Bournemouth, but came straight to London. With luck no one need know of her past.'

'Where has she been living since you returned if

her home was gone? The perpetrators were undoubtedly still on the lookout for her, so I am presuming she had to hide somewhere.'

'In Madrid.' Lucien smiled at Daniel's deductions.

'But she never thought to contact you?'

'No.' He took a decent sip of brandy and swallowed it.

'Because she found another protector?'

Lucien shook his head.

'I am certain she would have had no lack of men interested in helping her. What did she do for money, then, after her home was gone?'

'She ran a business in La Latina, one of the central barrios in Madrid.'

This time it was Daniel's turn to laugh. 'No wonder Amethyst liked her so much. What sort of business?'

'A brothel.'

'Hell.' He repeated the word again and stood. 'Under her own name? That could be difficult.'

'No, under a different one.'

'Another identity, you mean? A dangerous occupation, I imagine, for a small and beautiful woman.'

'She used the place as a way to extract information from the French customers and move the intelligence on to the British. It was a cover.'

'Even more dangerous, then. Lord above, Luce, she sounds like the perfect match for you. Don't you dare let her get away.'

In answer Lucien simply poured another drink and hoped Alejandra was not going to be too overcome by the ministrations of Christine and Amethyst.

* * *

She had never been particularly worried about her body in front of others and when the maid peeled off her gown to discover nothing at all beneath it, she simply stood in the centre of the room naked.

Christine and Amethyst on the other hand both blushed.

'Oh.' Christine reached for a blanket on the bed and wrapped it around her bare shoulders. 'Well, I think we shall have to remedy your lack of under-clothing immediately.'

Lack. *Falta*. Alejandra struggled to remember Lucien's translation.

'Though I must say with a figure like yours you will be a pleasure to dress.'

Amethyst Wylde began to giggle. 'It looks like you go in the sun without clothes, Alejandra?'

She nodded. 'A long time before when I am a girl. Is hot in Spain.'

'How wonderful,' Christine suddenly said. 'I have become so very sick of all the rules in England. Your Spain sounds like just the place to live.'

And then it was easy. Feeling less different and tense, Alejandra began to remember more of her English and reply without so much trouble.

They were kind women, good women, and the clothes Christine took from a wardrobe, which stretched the whole side of one wall, many and of fine quality.

Christine ordered a maid to bring hot water, to which an infusion of lavender was then added. It made

Alejandra feel as if she was home again amongst the aloes and olives and lavenders, such water, the feeling growing as a cloth was brought across her body and the grime and sweat from days and days of travel was washed away.

Then there was a linen chemise brought out from a box and wrapped in tissue and a cotton stay was fastened above, her breasts folded into the fabric. A petticoat came next, draped across her bareness, the bodice tight and the skirt generous. The soft feel of silk was wonderful as white stockings with garters of ribbon were pulled to her knees.

'This is just the beginning, Alejandra. Now we must decide on a dress and I am certain that you would suit bold colours in a gown. Like this.' Reaching over for a vivid red dress from her cupboard, Christine peeled away the calico. 'Or this.' Another gown joined the first, royal blue and frothed with lace, and then a third in green and gold.

'They are all beautiful.' Alejandra could not believe the softness of the fabric or the fineness of the stitchery.

'I make them,' Lucien's sister said quietly. 'The Ross estate is trying to gain back what it has lost financially and though Lucien is doing a grand job the money does not yet run to a large budget for gowns and the suchlike. So this is my effort to appear more than we are.'

'You make the dress of yourself?'

'With the help of my maid, Jean, and her mother mostly. But I love the feel of fabric and the possibility. It would be better if you kept that bit of knowledge private, though.'

'To tell no people of your cleverness?'

'The *ton* is a group who believe any labouring should be done by the lower classes. They do not believe a woman should earn money or work a day in her life at any interesting job.'

'Oh.' Alejandra was taken aback by the notion.

'I ran a timber company for years and now we have a most successful horse-breeding business.' Amethyst's words were soft. 'Outside of London one can be just who one wants to. People find their places and no one complains as long as you are careful.'

'And you are?'

'Decidedly.'

It was almost like at the hacienda. There were rules to break and others not to and if one kept inside the forbidden boundaries one could be...free.

Christine went even further. 'My brother is not a man to restrict others in doing what they want to for he himself has lived outside the narrow confines of propriety for years. So talk to him and find your own pathway here, Alejandra, and you might be surprised and delighted with what you are offered.'

Turning, she brought the green-and-gold gown away from its hanger. 'But for now we need to make you look unmatched. Firstly, though, we must do something about your hair.'

Lucien could not believe that Alejandra was the same woman Christine and Amethyst had whisked away two and a half hours earlier.

Gone was the shabby orange gown that had drooped across the neckline and sagged at the back and in its place was a stunning green-and-gold creation that held a froth of lace on its bodice, highlighting the rounded swell of bosom and velvet skin.

Her hair was different, too, the strands wrapped across each other and secured in curls and waves around her face, giving the impression of its previous length and shine. It was no longer the gaudy red, either, but more like the hue he remembered.

However, it was the look in her green eyes that had changed the most, for the ragged urchin of wariness and carefulness was replaced by a woman who was beautiful. And she knew it.

The words she had given him years ago on the high hills of the Galician Mountains came to mind. Many men have liked me, she had said, and even then he could well believe it true.

But now? Like this? God, she would stand out in society like a rare and exceptional jewel. The very thought was enough to bring him to his feet.

'We will leave for Linden Park in the morning.'

Lucien Howard did not like her transformation for some reason. The frown on his face was deep and he looked anywhere but at her as he spoke of his plans for moving south to his family seat in Kent.

Perhaps he thought her murky past might catch up if they stayed in London or maybe he was ashamed of her lack of English. Whatever it was he did not say a word about the things his sister had done to make her look…better. His friend Daniel Wylde, however, was more than effusive.

'You are a magician, Christine. My wife is always saying you are such and today proves it. The men of the *ton* will be champing at the bit when they see you.'

'Champing…?'

Lucien leant forward to explain. 'They will lay their hearts at your feet. Beauty holds a great deal of sway in London society and a woman here barely needs anything else to flourish.' His words were laced with irritation and also tiredness.

They had hardly slept since they had left Spain and he'd had a lot less sleep than she. Every night on the boat in her hammock when she had awoken in the dark he had been there, sitting and observing the horizon to keep watch.

She had napped, too, for a good many miles as they came north from Bournemouth in a hired coach, where a doctor had been summoned to see to her foot in a private room at a tavern on the way. The medic had not been gentle. The pain of his ministrations and the effect of the brandy Lucien had offered to dampen the agony had left her exhausted and she'd slumbered in his arms as they had wended their way up to the city of London.

But now here with her foot feeling so much less painful, and her hair and clothes so very fine, she wanted Lucien Howard to recognise the difference, to see her as she once had been many years before, the only daughter of a wealthy and noble Spanish family with a generous dowry and all the chances in the world to marry well.

Half a lifetime ago. The elation dimmed somewhat as she counted back the years. Perhaps this new persona was as false as the last one with the lacy gloves covering the scars on her right wrist and a dozen silver bracelets. She knew Christine and Amethyst had seen the old wound on her left thigh, too. They had looked shocked at the sight before hiding it, but this damaged woman was her as well, marked in danger, formed by war and honed in shame.

'We will come down next week, Lucien, to see you. There is a man in Orpington who has a fine roan mare for sale that I wish to take a look at.'

Daniel Wylde's voice cut into her thoughts.

'We will bring Adelaide, too.'

'Is she still running her clinic in Sherborne?' Lucien asked this, interest in his eyes.

'Yes. Gabe is having a lot of success in new practices of farming and they are halfway through rebuilding Ravenshill Manor. If he can get away we could bring him down. Francis may be able to come, as well.'

Friends, thought Alejandra. Daniel. Amethyst. Christine. Gabriel and Adelaide. Francis. She could not remember a time when she had even had one true confidante her age. A fault that, probably. Another lack her life was full of. England seemed to underline all that she was not.

When she saw Lucien observe her with concern in his face she smiled, a brittle pretend grin that felt wrong in its falseness, but it was suddenly all that she had left. She was adrift here as surely as she had been in Madrid, the future uncertain and the past defining her.

She was glad when the others gave their goodbyes and left, the concentration needed for speaking a language she was not fluent in exhausting.

'They are good people, Alejandra. Real people.' He looked at her with question in his eyes as she raised her left arm, the silk tight against her skin.

'But where does a knife fit in a sleeve such as this?' Her leg bent next. 'And what manner of woman could ever escape quickly in these shoes?'

'It is seldom one has the need to whip out a knife in London, but be warned. Words are the choice of weapon ladies and gentlemen of the court use and they can be as cutting.'

'And therein lies the problem. I can barely understand a simple sentence, let alone one that might slay me.'

He began to laugh. 'Beauty is enough here, believe me. Just let that do the talking.'

'You think that I am? Beautiful, I mean?'

He stepped back and nodded, though the same wariness she had seen before was more than apparent.

Hope rose inside her breast and into her throat, making her swallow away tears, the pale blue of his eyes touching her in all the places she wanted his hands to be. Strangers and lovers. And friends, too, once. The sun slanting in the window frosted his hair with gold and silver.

'If people here were to ever know who I had been...' She left the rest unsaid.

'Scandal has its own deficiencies. If you don't care enough about the gossip, it is fairly self-limiting.'

'Like you don't...care, I mean, about what others say?'

He smiled.

'I doubt whether the girl who watched me walking along the paths of lavender at the hacienda of her father would have given it a second thought, either.'

'I am not certain if that girl was ever real, Capitán.'

'No?'

'Once, I was braver, but loss has the tendency to take that away.'

'To live is dangerous, Alejandra. And to love.'

She was silent. *It was. It once had been.* Here in London he was far more the earl than just a plain soldier and anything between them before was now caught in such a difference.

The perfume Christine had applied most liberally was strong and she had the beginnings of a headache that made her feel slightly nauseous. The love of a man. The love of a child. The love of a country. Each one of these was fraught with the possibility of loss and each one of them had been snatched away from her so very easily.

There was still the problem of his mother, too. She did not wish to be the reason for some difficult family rift. Her own had been the masters of that particular downfall.

But Lucien was looking at her as if she were

beautiful and unflawed and honourable and when he stepped forward to take her hand she felt the same shock of awareness she always felt when he touched her.

'Take a risk,' he said quietly. 'Take a risk, Alejandra, and live.'

And so she did, moving forward, feeling his warmth and then his hand lifting her chin, the pale eyes close and questioning. Only now in a world of books and silence, the sound of breath, louder, raw, desperate, and his mouth then against her own, slanting, wet and hard.

Her neck arched and she opened to him, his tongue and teeth upon her, no small query now, but only taking. She could barely breathe or think, the weightless truth of wonder and rightness.

Home. With Lucien.

Her own hands came up to his hair, threading through the gold, entwined and pressing close, and the old magic that had got her through four years of hell returned, roaring against weakness and replacing doubt.

She loved him. She did. She had loved him from the very first second of finding him unconscious on the high fields of battle. A connection, a communion, a man who was her other half of living.

Take a risk and live, he had said.

She pulled back a little and looked him straight in the eyes.

'I will love you for always and I will never stop.'

'Marry me, then, Alejandra. Be my wife.'

She was speechless, shock tightening her throat as tears welled. She allowed them to fall down her cheeks and on to the green-and-gold silk of her beautiful gown.

'Yes.' No thought in it save delight and hope.

And then it was easy kissing, soft and honest, quiet in the way of disbelief and wonder. He would be hers for ever as everything and everyone else had not been, her husband, her lover, her friend.

'You are certain?'

'More certain than I have been in my entire life. Right from the beginning it was only ever us.'

'Us,' she whispered back and, standing on tiptoes, she found again the warmth and sweetness of his mouth.

Lucien wanted her. It was all he could think of. He wanted to be inside her. He wanted to know the pounding fury that had haunted his every moment since their trysts on the road down into Pontevedra from the high hills of the Galicians. Every other woman ever since had been irrelevant and shadowy and he had struggled for four years with intimacy and honesty and desire.

His member was rock hard against her, the physical embodiment of his desperation, and he did not try to hide it. He could not. He pressed against her and let her feel the extent of his need even as his hand slid beneath the green-and-gold silk of her bodice, undoing the buttons and cupping one round and full breast.

'You are mine, Alejandra, and I will be yours, too, for ever.'

In answer she simply pulled the gown from her shoulder and allowed him everything.

He suckled hard and felt her gasp, but he could no longer be careful. His teeth closed over the nipple and her nails scraped down the back of his neck, drawing blood, he thought and smiled.

They would mark each other again as they had done before, in ownership and in power. Already the red whorls of where his mouth had been were drawn into her skin.

He wanted to lift her up and take her to his bed, through the corridors of the town house, past his mother and his family, ignoring all of them to assuage the pounding beat of his heart that drummed in his ears.

But he could not because by doing so he would ruin his one chance of getting it right this time, of doing it properly, of cherishing her and protecting her in all the ways that he had failed to do so before in Spain.

He did not want another child out of wedlock, either. He wanted his friends there to witness his wedding and his mother watching to understand the love he brought to his wife. He wanted it beautiful and honest. He wanted to say their vows in the Linden Park chapel in front of God because he knew right there and then that Alejandra needed that. She needed to be back in the fold of religion in order to be whole. And so did he. With family and friends. Together.

Repositioning her bodice, he brought her in against him and took a breath.

'When we are married we will finish what we have started here. I promise. I want to be married at the chapel in Linden Park and the ceremony shall take place as soon as the banns are read and a dress is made.'

'A dress?'

'I hope the Church of England is suitable for you, my love, for this time we will be wed by the grace of God. This time it will be perfect.'

Dinner that evening was a strange mix of elation, tension and shame. Lucien's two younger brothers were at the table as were Christine and his mother.

The Countess of Ross had been crying, Alejandra could tell, and she held herself stiff and silent as news of the forthcoming wedding was given by Lucien.

Christine was the most excited, all her chatter about the gown she would design and of how she had seen a picture of a beautiful woman in Boston with exactly the dress she could imagine Alejandra in. The boys watched her covertly, blushing when she glanced at them and hardly talking.

Young men were always simple, she thought to herself and smiled as Lucien took her hand there at the table and held it firmly.

'We will be married at Linden Park in the chapel. We do not wish for a big wedding, but the Wyldes will come as well as the Hughes and Francis St Cartmail. And all the aunts, of course.'

'What of the Bigley cousins and the Halbergs? You will have to ask the Kingstons, too, for they would be most upset if they were not invited.' Christine chattered away and the list of potential guests became larger and larger until Lucien drew her ponderings to a close.

'We will have who we want, Christine, and that is the end of it.'

'And the banns will need to be posted?' This was the first thing the Countess had offered all night.

'I will make certain they are when we go down to Linden Park tomorrow.'

The older lady nodded and twisted the kerchief that she held in her hands this way and that.

'Are you of the Anglican faith?' This question was directed at Alejandra.

'No. I was Catholic, Lady Ross.'

Christine frowned. 'Was?'

'I have not much being in church for few years.'

'Because your faith was tested and found wanting?' These words came from Lucien's mother and they were barely audible.

'Tested?'

Lucien translated and the silence about the table was heavy.

'I did believe. Once. I hope this will come again.' It was all she could say with any sense of truth.

'I hope so, too.' The Countess gave these words with a great sincerity and Alejandra smiled at her. Perhaps things would be all right one day between them. She could only hope.

When the meal was complete Lucien excused them both and took her out into the small garden behind the house. It was a warm evening, the promise of a late summer in the air, and bells rang from some-where close.

They came together easily, his arms wrapped about her.

'I want you so much that it hurts.' No pretext. No hidden meaning. She felt that want, too, and bit down on it.

'How long?'

'Three weeks.' He knew exactly what she meant. 'I have to go north for a few days this week for there is business that needs my attention after being away for so long.'

'Of course.'

'It might be better, too.'

'The distance?'

'The temptation,' he returned and kissed her hard and quick before moving back. As he turned she saw the marks of her nails across the skin at his nape.

'It will be a church wedding?' She had been sur-prised when he had said that at the table given what he knew of her faith. 'I am not entirely sure I should even be in a house of God, making promises.'

He began to laugh. 'Mama betrayed me in the worst way possible and she is at the chapel most days. Christine shared a bed with the man who was sup-posed to be marrying her, but he died instead, and I have killed more people than I can even remem-ber and yet I am not rebuffed. What exactly is your crime, Alejandra? What is so terrible about what you have done?'

'I have given up on God,' she returned without a second's thought.

'Yet he brought you to me, to love again. Perhaps after all he did not give up on you.'

'Lucien?'

'Yes.'

'Never leave me. Not ever.'

'I won't, my love.'

Chapter Fourteen

There were white roses on the end of every pew and
more in large vases by the pulpit with blue and yellow ribbons tied in generous bows. Christine's work,
Alejandra supposed, nothing left to chance.

Her dress floated about her legs, the soft blue silk
embellished with flowers, and in her hair was a gar-
land of fresh white rosebuds.

But it was Lucien she looked at, standing tall and
still at the top of the aisle, Daniel Wylde beside him.
He was dressed today in unbroken black and it made
the pale of his hair lighter and even more beautiful.
His eyes were full of promise as he watched her walk
towards him and when she reached him he held out
his hand.

And at that moment with the sun coming through
the stained-glass windows in slivers of colours and
an organ playing a hymn she knew and loved; with
the scent of rose petals and the warmth of family and
friends all around her, Alejandra felt a shifting, an
easing, the warmth of belief coming back into her

heart like magic. Celestial magic. Unexplained and beautiful. She could even feel Rosalie there beside her and her father and Maria and Tomeu and Adan. And Ross in the strength of Lucien's grasp and in the love on his face.

Perfect. This was a perfect moment that she would never forget and God had given it to her. After all the sorrow and hurt there was wonder again and grace.

Lucien had known it with his insistence on such a wedding, celebrated with all that was good in the religious form and in the Church of England.

She was home. Here. Understood and known. When the music ceased she looked up into his eyes and smiled.

'Thank you,' she whispered.

'You are welcome, my love.'

Only now. Glancing at the minister, she gave him greeting and waited for the service to begin.

She was suddenly nervous, more nervous than she had ever been. He had not seen the scar on her thigh, not properly before, and it had been a very long time since they had last come together. Her wrist, too, was something he might ask about and there were marks across her stomach that had not been there last time.

Ross.

This was another fear. A baby or the lack of one. She could not quite come to terms with whether she would want to be pregnant again or would dread it.

It was late now and she had left Lucien downstairs in the large drawing room at Linden Park. Everything about this place was huge. The house. The gardens, the staircases, the ponds. Even the bed behind her. Their bed now, a large four-poster with a draping of gauze around every side of it.

The only small thing was the wisp of lace nightgown Christine had given her for her wedding night. She wondered if she should be wearing it at all as it reminded her a bit of the clothing in the brothel on Segovia Street.

Another worry loomed. What if that was all he could remember? The drugged and angry Antonia with her lewd actions, cut-glass earrings and blood-red hair.

She glanced in the mirror and was momentarily heartened.

Her locks now were so much darker and shinier, a result of a shampoo Adelaide Hughes had concocted for her in her house in Sherborne and a good-quality hair dye. She had been eating better, too, and the thin angular bones of Spain had been softened somewhat here into more feminine curves.

Lifting one finger, she carefully touched the diamond ring Lucien had pledged his troth to her with. Substantial and permanent.

It was all enough. She was enough. Footfalls on the boards outside had her glancing worriedly away from the mirror.

And then he was there, completely dressed, the dark of his clothes a contrast against the pale of her lacy white nothingness. He held a small box in his hands and he gave this to her without touching.

'For you, Alejandra.'

She had not thought to buy him a gift. Was this an English custom that was expected?

But when she opened it she forgot about all her fears and gasped in delight.

'A rosary?'

'Of jets. I found it in a shop on Regent Street and thought of you. Like your old one, if I remember correctly, the one you used constantly in Spain.'

'The one I draped across your chest as we took you from the battlefield.'

'The one you brought with you on the march west to take me to the boat. It was always so much a part of you I thought you ought to have a replacement.'

'It is beautiful.' The beads slid through her fingers in the same old familiar way, the words in her head as they always had been and joy in her heart.

'I will treasure it.'

'Oh. I nearly forgot,' he suddenly said. 'My mother also sends you this.' Digging into his pocket, he brought out a small fat statue of polished jade.

'What is it?'

'A fertility god from the ancient Chinese, but she swears it will work. She had six children and her mother had seven and they all attribute such abundance to this.'

'It is an old heirloom, then.'

'Indeed.'

'She wants us to have another child?'

'She most certainly does. She believes she had some hand in Ross's death and blames herself for it.'

'She shouldn't. He came too early. I do not think anyone could have stopped that from happening.'

'Would you tell her that, perhaps, when you feel ready to?'

'Yes.'

'Would you tell me it, too, over and over, so that I might know...?' He stopped and she heard the tremble of self-blame in his voice, the first time ever she had heard him anything but certain.

'Make another child with me, Lucien. Tonight. So we all can live.'

God, she was brave, Alejandra, his wife. He noticed the pulse in her throat was fast and shallow and yet still she would offer him absolution and forgiveness.

The lace nightdress she wore was very little. He could see the scars on her wrist and the larger one on her left thigh. He had touched the raised skin before once when he had taken her on the coastal path less than an hour before they had been parted in Pontevedra. He wondered who had hurt her so badly. Her first husband, probably, but the hacienda had been a dangerous place, too, as had the brothel in La Latina.

He needed to be gentle with her, but already a desperate need was rising.

He hoped they might have a child and that there would be something left of them when they had gone, but if they could not, then that was fine, too. He had Alejandra, finally, bound by law and church to him. For ever. It was enough.

Reaching out, he ran a finger across her cheek and then down her neck and on to her shoulder. The same awareness he always felt when he touched her made him smile. She had filled out, her curves more noticeable in the month since they had left Spain. Her hair had grown a little, too, reaching past her collarbones now, a curtain of shiny dark silk.

'You are so very beautiful,' he whispered, and she leant in to kiss him, on his cheek, on his chin and then on his lips, her mouth finding him with her tongue. No quiet kiss this, but a full and sensual onslaught. He was completely dressed and she was in less than nothing when one of his hands threaded between her thighs and came into her secret place with a hard intent.

She groaned and arched her head so that her eyes fell into his own, sparked with desire. He could see his movements in the verdant green, flickering as he pushed deep and her swollen flesh opened further.

'Love me, Lucien,' she murmured, her hands now at the buttons of his jacket and then his shirt. The neckcloth was unwound and his trousers fell.

He stepped out of them and lifted her, legs wound about his hips keeping him close, and then the softness of the mattress was beneath them, the thread work of the quilt under his knees. Pulling the gauzy hangings around the bed, they were caught in their own private space, the candle blurred and the fire a soft glow across the room.

He could no longer hold back, he needed her with the sort of desperation that held no stopping. Opening her thighs, he simply plunged in, the wet warmth welcoming and tight.

Their breathing was louder now, hoarse in the quiet and building upwards to the place where release came quick, beaching waves of pleasure cleaving them to the other and claiming what each craved, made one by the ecstasy. Alejandra shook afterwards when the tightness had waned, shook in his arms and tipped her head to his.

And this time when he kissed her it was quiet and gentle, languid and heavy, open-mouthed and closed. They were still connected, still joined, the seed he had spilled thick inside her and the last shuddering spasms of muscle not quite yet gone.

Taken. His. Even the thought kept him hard and he pushed in with purpose.

'Again?'

He nodded, his hand wrapped around her buttock as he lifted her against him, changing the angle, and when she finally cried out with the relief of orgasm he simply covered her mouth and took the breath of her to mingle with his own.

She felt heavy, swollen and full, the small wisps of lace torn from her body with the movements of their lovemaking so that what was left of the nightgown lay limp on the counterpane of bobbled silk.

And she still wanted him. Inside her. Pleasuring her in that particular way he had that defied all she had ever known of sex. She was a wanton. The thought pulled her lips upwards and one hand fell across her breast, a budded nipple hard between her fingers.

Then his mouth was there, suckling, using her breast as a babe might as she held him tight against her, fingers threaded through the hair at his nape. She wanted to nurture him and feed him. She wanted to bring him into herself where no one else might touch them and where they would never again be apart.

There was pain there, too, and she relished it when his teeth grated across the softness because it told her she was alive and here and protected. She leant across him and bit him on the shoulder, not quite drawing blood.

Then he was above and turning her, drawing up both hands and tethering her small fingers with his own.

Helpless surrender. He took her exactly as he wanted and she loved every moment of it.

Roughness had a different appeal to the soft and in it she felt the loosening of her past, the brothel, the deaths, the danger. She was small and he was large. He was pale and she was dark. He was hard and she was soft. She relished the differences as he showed her the mastery of his sex.

And afterwards he knelt between her legs and used his mouth to soothe her, to cool her, to sup at the well of womanhood as only a husband could do, healing the anger, accepting the past.

A lesson in loving that wrapped about her heart. Pain had many names, she thought, and one of them was Lucien. If she ever lost him again, she would die.

* * *

She woke in the night late and disorientated. Lucien stood against the windows, looking out, though he turned as soon as he perceived her watching him. His body looked like a statue of burnished marble, an erection stiff against the moonlight.

When she joined him he came into her from behind, their reflection surreal. It was cold against the glass, her breasts against the shiny hardness making each nipple bud. He did not hurry, either, but changed the rhythm of his penetration just as she was getting used to the last one. To lengthen the timings. To heighten the need.

'Please?' she whispered.

'Wait,' he said.

'Now?'

'Soon.'

And then it was there, intense and fragile, the wrenching truth of the together plucked from apartness as she felt his seed within and his teeth at her neck.

'I love you, Alejandra.' The words shivered across her nakedness and fell into the dark.

'How did you ever find me in that prison in Madrid, Lucien?'

It was almost dawn and the few hours of sleep they had managed was enough to allow them comfort.

'I knew the French used the place for interrogations and I'd found an old copy of the plans in the reading room on the Paseo de Recoletos. I was there every day waiting for you to come, so I had a good many hours to look.'

'You thought I would be caught?'

'Well, if I had heard the rumours of a woman who stole the French secrets, then I was certain the French would soon be likely to, as well. Nothing is sacred in the cut-throat world of espionage and so I felt it would pay to be prepared.'

'It was still a risk. Even with all that preparedness.'

'A risk I am glad I took.'

'I thought I would die. I thought they would rape me, too. I was not at all certain that when they did I could keep quiet, either.'

'You might be surprised at that. After a certain amount of pain it all begins to feel the same.'

'It was like that with your back? The scars are fierce still.'

He laughed. 'I do not even have the inclination to remember them, Alejandra. It is finished with, that time, and I am thankful.'

'Only now?'

'England is a quiet place and many here don't like to be reminded of the chaos in other lands. I have not shown anyone save the doctor my scars.'

At that she laughed. 'Your sister and Amethyst were not particularly worried to see the remnants of the wound on my thigh.'

'They each have their own skeletons, though. It is those who have never been touched by strife or war who make the most fuss.'

'Juan tied me to a horse and dragged me around a field. The root of a tree gouged my leg.'

The shockingness of it fell into the room like a stone, but she wanted to tell him of it all. He deserved to know.

'I was too independent, he said. Too inclined to do what I wanted. He needed me submissive and docile. My father found me in the back room of Juan's house. The wound had festered badly, you see, and I suppose Juan was ashamed of being such a bully. He did not allow anyone near me and I got sicker and sicker.'

'Then I am glad you are a good shot. The bastard deserved what was coming to him.'

'Tomeu gave me the gun. It was my job to see him punished, not my father's.'

'I knew I liked him.'

Alejandra snuggled into the warmth of her husband. 'You see, that is why I love you. You allow me to be me.'

Reaching over, she picked up the rosary from the bedside table and cradled it in her hands. 'I shall say a Hail Mary for Juan Betancourt and forgive him because otherwise...'

'You never forget.'

'Will they accept me, do you think, as your wife? Those in society, I mean. I should not wish to make it difficult for you to go to London.'

He shrugged his shoulders and laughed. 'After last night, Alejandra, nothing you could ever do would make it difficult for me.'

* * *

He couldn't get enough of her—that was the trouble. He could barely breathe properly when he was away from her and the duties of his earldom and manufacturing business had called him to London three days this week alone.

Their nights were what he lived for, losing himself inside of her, two becoming one as the long summer nights shortened and the first coolness of autumn appeared.

Tonight they had walked to the lake that stood in front of Linden Park and made love in the boathouse at the end of the pier. With the water lapping around them and the moonlight on Alejandra's naked body, Lucien brought her on to his lap and wrapped the blanket around them both, her legs to each side of him.

A quiet coupling, watching each other as the rhythm quickened, seeing the love in her eyes and the smile on her lips.

She was so very beautiful, her breasts moving with his pushes as nipples tightened by want. Soon he would suck them and she would whisper into his hair with soft words of Spanish. Protecting him. Wanting him.

He wondered what it would be like when her breasts were filled with milk and her belly lay swollen with babe. He wanted lots of babies, lots of family, the final expression of their love made physical. But even if they could not conceive he would be happy. With her.

When he smiled she saw it.

'You are happy?'

'I am,' he returned.

'With this?' she questioned, tipping her hips.

'Are you?'

'In the brothel I felt sick every time I would have to go into the room of a French soldier, to search his clothing, just in case something went wrong.'

'Did that ever happen?'

She shook her head.

'But with you…with you I don't think.'

'You just feel. This and this.'

'And this,' she added, her tongue winding around the lobe of his ear and down to the nape.

Chapter Fifteen

'There is a problem, Luce.' Daniel leant forward in the leather wing chair where they were tucked into an alcove in one corner of White's on St James's Street a month or so after the wedding.

Lucien frowned and finished his drink. 'What is it?'

'The brother of Sir Mark Walters has been telling all who will listen that you cohabited together outside of wedlock as you travelled from Bournemouth to London.'

'And how does he know this?'

'He was there as you landed from Spain, Luce, and he recognised you. It seems he is an artist of sorts and fashioned a drawing. A picture has just been published in a tatty broadsheet and it has had numerous reprints.'

'Do you have it?' Suddenly Lucien knew exactly what the problem would be. Alejandra had been dressed in her lad's clothes as he had carried her to the conveyance at the dockside because her foot was too sore to walk.

'I do.' Daniel brought forth a sheet of paper and unfolded it, the faded lines taking nothing away from the rendering.

'Hell.'

The drawing was every bit as damning as Lucien thought it might be and it was verified as the truth by Viscount Radford, a man who held no love for the Howard family.

'Damned if I admit this and damned if I don't? Can it blow over?'

Daniel laughed. 'Everything can eventually blow over, I suppose, but the fact that you might spend the next years as outcasts is one you might consider. Especially if you have children.'

'Has Amethyst seen this?'

'She has. She said when she was vilified by the *ton* over the furore of her first husband she was glad we all stood together. You are surrounded by friends with lofty titles, Lucien. Perhaps you should use us.'

'Beard the lion in his lair, you mean?'

'Your sister can have us all looking most presentable and Gabriel has already sent out the invites to his ball. A venue, so to speak, that is neutral and sympathetic. He could make certain the doubters are there.'

Leaning back, Lucien pulled his hands through his hair. 'I don't know if Alejandra is ready for this. If she is vilified anyway...'

'Then you are in exactly the same position as you

are now and at least you will know what you are up against.'

'I'd like to hit Walters and Radford right now. Hard.'

'Which would be playing right into their hands and everyone will think it true.'

Daniel was right. He had to be cleverer than that. He had to laugh at the accusation in such a way that people would begin to question its validity. Alejandra looked less and less like the girl he had found again in a Madrid brothel and more and more like the well-born lady that she was.

If they all stood together, it might work.

He just had to convince his wife that the charade was actually worth it.

Alejandra was sick when he arrived home from the city and lying on the bed in their room, a cold flannel across her brow and the curtains drawn.

He had never seen her look so lifeless before and pulled up a chair in front of her. Had she heard the rumours already? He was pleased when she smiled and sat up, her arms wrapping about his neck.

'I missed you, but I think I must have eaten something last night that did not agree with me for I have not been feeling well. How was your day?'

'I saw Daniel at my club.'

She frowned and pulled back. 'Is there something wrong, Lucien?'

'This.' Leaning back, he took the broadsheet with

their likenesses from his bag and laid it out on her knees.

'He is an accomplished artist, unfortunately, Mr Frank Walters, the man who drew this. If he'd been less talented, it may not have mattered. His friend Viscount Radford is verifying his story and he is the son of a man who felt my father duped him in a business venture.'

'And it does? Matter, I mean?'

'I'm not sure. If we do nothing, it might just go away.'

'Or it might not?' She took his hand in hers and he liked the warmth. 'So you think attack is the better option? It's fight or flee?'

Lucien laughed. 'Nothing that dramatic, thank goodness. He can't touch us here in Kent, but...the *ton* has strict punishments for those who might flout their rules, Alejandra, and premarital sex is one of the big ones.'

'But we didn't... Not that time...' She blushed and stopped.

'You were unchaperoned. That is enough. If we do go to Gabriel's ball, though, as we had planned to, Daniel and the others will stand with us.'

'In support, you mean?'

'With my family title and with the Hughes' and the Wyldes' and St Cartmails' support, too, it might well be enough to put this to bed so to speak. Besides, we are married now and so as a scandal it is not as juicy as the one that would have ensued if we were not.'

'How many people will be there?'

'Most of the *ton*, I should imagine. Gabe has a wide and varied circle of friends.'

'I thought you said they did not go about in society much?'

'They don't. This is the first ball I have ever been to at the Hughes family home.'

The warmth of her skin drew him closer and he pulled off his boots and jacket and joined her on the bed. With Alejandra's head against his chest and his arms about her shoulders he felt whole again, the ride home from London worrying and long.

'I wanted to be home,' he said after a moment or two. 'It seems when I leave you all I can think about is when I am coming back.'

At that she pushed herself up and faced him directly, her hands around the sides of his head and a smile on her face that held more than humour. 'I have been waiting for you, my love, and it has been a long day. Shall we shorten it?'

Her fingers went to the fall of his trousers and undid the buttons, and then the warmth of her fingers was against his flesh.

'Whatever happens out there in the world will never harm us, Alejandra. I promise you that.'

'I know,' she replied and then her full lips came down across him.

The next morning Alejandra felt a little better, though she was worried and shocked by the drawing and by such a blatant attack on their relationship. Lucien's mother and she were just starting to be civil to one another, the deathly silence that she had endured since coming to England finally punctuated by one or two warm smiles. What would an older lady think of this now? She felt for the rosary in her pocket and ran the beads through her fingers, asking for guidance.

They would have to chance on a good outcome from Gabriel and Adelaide's ball. She knew they would have to because otherwise there would always be whisperings and conjecture. After a life of such things she wanted only harmony and peace, to just fit in here without troubles and gossip.

Lucien beside her was still asleep, the dawn light across his hair marking it with gold. They had woken in the night and made love again, so the bedding was tousled and heaped about them and she felt wanton and languid.

With care she traced the line of his cheek and he woke immediately turning towards her, his pale eyes focusing into alertness as he spoke. 'For many years I have come from slumber into hardship and now... now all I have is beauty.' He reached for her hair and slid his fingers down the length of it. 'I'm glad it's no longer red.'

'I hated the colour. I hated everything about those years without you. There was only loneliness in Madrid and the flavour of grief. If anything is allowed to threaten us...here...' She could not go on.

'You have been worrying?' He stroked the lines on her forehead with one finger. 'And nothing can ever part us again, I promise you.'

'That is what I loved about you right from the beginning, Lucien. Your certainty. I felt safe and safety is an underrated commodity, I think. You realise this only when you have lived through chaos. So tell your sister, then, that she needs to fashion a dress for the Hughes ball that will make me look magnificent, like Boadicea going into battle.'

'You are sure?'

'With you beside me, Lucien, I can do anything.'

She liked it when he gathered the length of her hair in one hand and came across her. No small loving this, no fragile tryst. Throwing away problems, she savoured the warmth and the strength of him and forgot the world around them altogether.

Two weeks later Alejandra sat in the carriage and took in a deep breath as the conveyance slowed in front of the Hughes town house. They were late.

'Everyone will be there waiting for us. Don't worry.' Lucien drew back the curtain and looked out into the night.

They were to have met at the house of Daniel Wylde, but the wheel axel had been loose on the carriage on the way up from Linden Park, so they had had to wait at a tavern in Southborough until it could be fixed and made safe. By the time they had got to the Ross town house to get ready for the ball everything was a rush.

Closing her eyes against the traffic and the lights, Alejandra fingered her rosary and prayed that the evening would be a success.

'It will be fine, sweetheart.' Lucien was in black tonight, the colour of his clothing unbroken save for the snowy-white neckcloth that he had folded carefully and the paleness of his hair. 'Give them five minutes and they will love you like I do.'

But she could not be consoled by his words, she who had ridden into battle and roamed the high and dangerous passes of the Spanish mountains, she who had understood the intricacies of knife fighting and swordsmanship since she was a young girl. Alejandra Fernandez y Santo Domingo, daughter of El Vengador. No, in England the enemy was different, less seen somehow and thus more brutal. Here she could rely on neither her prowess nor her reputation. Here they could deny her and Lucien a place in society and a home in London and gossip was a vice that went on and on. For ever, if those who hated them should so wish it.

'And if they don't? If we fail...?'

'I never fail,' he returned, and the look in his light-blue eyes was exactly the one she had seen in the olive grove above the hacienda as he had walked himself almost to death to try to get fitter.

Reaching for his hand, she was glad to feel the warmth of his fingers against her freezing ones.

'Look at it like a contest, Alejandra. Two steps forward and one step back. We will never win them all over, but we just need enough.'

The chatter rose on the air as they walked to the top of the stairs, hundreds of people below in their very best attire and candles in holders along every wall and horizontal space.

'The Earl and Countess of Ross.'

The major-domo announced them, his formal tones booming across conversation, and the lull was almost instant. Every face turned their way, every eye, the silence deafening as they walked down the wide long staircase into the room proper.

If Lucien had not been beside her, she would have fallen, she was sure of it; as it was she tripped slightly and he held her still.

'Put your chin up and smile. We are married.'

And she did, simply looked the spectators directly in the eyes and smiled as if all she expected were compliments and wishes of good luck and good fortune.

Her heart still pounded in her chest and her stomach trembled with nerves, but she did not show it.

What was it her father had said once? *Attitude is all in the confidence, Alejandra. People will believe of you what you will them to.* Her mama, too, as she had brushed out her hair at night gently and lovingly. *It's not what you look like, my love. It's what's inside that counts.*

Well, inside was steel and tenacity and the will to survive. She had survived all that life had thrown at her so far and she would not allow this wonderment with Lucien to be snatched away on the flighty tail of gossip.

If they hated her, then they did. If they were harried from the society, then they were. But she had her husband at her side, close and solid and menacing.

And there were others, too, Gabriel Hughes and his wife, Adelaide, and Daniel Wylde and Amethyst. Christine was there, too, and then there was Lucien's mother walking towards her and taking her hand in her own and holding it close.

'Welcome to the family, Alejandra. An apology is too little a thing to offer in mitigation for what I have done to you, but here my name carries considerable weight and so I add it.'

'Thank you.' She held her mother-in-law's fingers and smiled.

And then it was easy, the whirl of faces, the greetings, the quiet introductions and the dancing, with Lucien always beside her, his hand on her back, guiding. When the musicians came back to their seats for another set of dances he leant down and whispered quietly, 'It is a waltz, Alejandra. Will you dance it with me?'

'I am not practised in any way,' she countered, but he stopped her.

'Let me lead and it will be simple.'

She felt his heartbeat, saw his long pale hair rest against the blackness of cloth and the small lines of laughter that ran about his eyes.

Beautiful. As beautiful as the first time she had ever met him up in the after smoke of battle by the aloe hedges. A whole history together, good and bad.

'You never doubted that this would work, did you?' she whispered as they came together, close.

He shook his head. 'After I thought about it I realised that you have the sort of beauty that draws people to them, Alejandra, and in your red dress. Well…'

He stopped for a moment before continuing.

'I used to imagine you in this, you know, even when I was sick after A Coruña. I knew in this colour that you would be unmatched. And you are.'

'Only because of you, Lucien. All of this is only because of you.'

Adelaide took her hand as they walked into supper, the quiet beauty of Gabriel's wife undeniable.

'I am so glad you were able to come, Alejandra. Gabriel was adamant that we have at least one grand ball in our life, though I am hoping that it will be the last.'

'You do not enjoy dancing?'

'Oh, indeed I do. What I don't enjoy is all the fuss of it and the necessity to be so well dressed and so very uncomfortable. Oh,' she suddenly said, digging into her small beaded reticule and bringing out a small bottle of powder. 'I have something for you. One teaspoon each morning for a week is what I give to every new wife for fertility and well-being. The power of it comes from belief,' she added, 'but I have heard that the Spanish people have a healthy love of folklore, so I am certain it shall work very well on you.'

'Thank you.'

'It is good to have you here and to see Lucien happy. He has not been, you see, for so long. Gabriel was certain that he was lonely, though I think he had plenty of chances to remedy that as the ladies here are more than forward and he is very good-looking.'

Beautiful.

Alejandra imagined him coming back to England after A Coruña, sick and hurt and sad. Such dark days for them both, caught in war and fire and death.

'I will never let him be lonely again,' she promised and meant it.

Adelaide smiled. 'Amethyst said that I would like you and I do.'

Half an hour later Alejandra walked down a small corridor to the retiring room. She needed to take a break for a moment from all the well-wishers and those asking to be acquainted with the new wife of the Earl of Ross. The evening had been such a mix of dread, nerves, wonder and elation she also needed a moment just to stop.

She was surprised to come across a man tarrying to one side of the retiring-room door.

'You may have fooled them all, but you cannot fool me, *señora*, for I know who you truly are and if it takes me a lifetime to prove it, then so be it.'

'It was you who made the picture? You are Frank Walters?'

He shook his head and began his tirade anew. 'No, I am Viscount Radford and you are a disgrace to all of womanhood if you think you can get away with such utter lies simply by appearing here on the arm of your husband this evening. You ought to be ejected summarily from society and asked never to return for you corrupt the innocence of all women...'

Such vitriol shocked her to the core, though he spoke in such rapid English Alejandra could barely make out the sense of his words.

He was close to her now, the hate in his eyes fierce and unguarded, though as he raised his arm as if to strike her the patience in Alejandra broke completely and she blocked his hand with her own, bringing his arm behind his back in one quick motion and pulling up.

He groaned and she was glad for it. With only a little push she could snap his arm in two places. It would be so very easy to do so.

'Perhaps, *señor*, is not good such hate. I can hurt you, but I think you are not worth that bother.' Jabbing her elbow into his back, she let him go.

'Stay far from me and my family. If you come near me again, my husband will kill you and I am not stop him. Do you understand?'

For the first time fear lingered where hate had been and Alejandra was pleased for it. She watched as the man almost ran in the opposite direction before leaning back against the wall.

'Did he hurt you?'

Lucien materialised from the gloom and stood there watching her.

'You heard?'

'All of it. Shall I kill him now?'

At that she smiled. 'No. I do not think he will trouble us again.'

'Good. Then are you ready to go back to the ball?'

He did not admonish her or even question her about what had just happened. He had allowed her the right to defend herself in the way she knew how and backed up her actions. If she had asked Lucien to kill Viscount Radford, she imagined he would have. Quietly. Efficiently. Without any fuss or problem whatsoever.

A man she could trust. A man who understood she was not as other women here were and yet admired her for it. He was not asking her to change in this marriage. No, he was allowing her to walk beside him equally. A partnership based on strength.

'I thought perhaps we might leave soon. It is not late, but...' The lines about his eyes creased into humour.

'I would like that.'

Threading her arm through his, they turned together to find their hosts.

Once back in their bedchamber at the Ross town house he peeled off the red gown with a careful slowness, the silk running through his fingers and pooling at her feet. Then he removed her underclothing.

'You are so very lovely,' he said when the layers of lawn and silk had finally gone, Alejandra's velvet skin burnished by candlelight. A short string of pearls at her throat caught the light and he unclasped these, too.

'I think it is the gown, Lucien. A dozen people asked me tonight who my dressmaker was. I said Mon

Soeur was the label and that I should send them the card of calling on the morrow with the name of the seamstress upon it.'

'Christine?'

'She does not wish for anyone to know she designs these dresses, so I do not quite know what to say.'

Lucien began to laugh. 'I am surrounded by women who are not as they seem.'

'That is because you are comfortable in your own skin, my love. A lesser man might be threatened by it.'

'And a lesser woman would ask incessantly for my help.'

'Your friends all admire you. Do you know that? Each one of them at different times has approached me and made certain that I know what a treasure I have been given and each one of them has intimated you were lonely. For all the years of our apartness.'

'I was.' He brought her into his arms. He had removed his own jacket and shirt and neckcloth now, though he still stood in his trousers and shoes. 'They all tried to match me up with this person and with that one, but it was only ever you...'

'Only us, Lucien. You and me.'

'Only now,' he agreed and lifted her eyes to his. 'When and where was the engraving done on the inside band of my signet ring?'

'In Vigo. I went there after Pontevedra when you did not come and paid the last of my money to a jeweller to inscribe the message. I knew I was pregnant, you see, and I thought if anything happened to

me, then our baby would need to find its way back
to you. To family.'

'Oh, God.'

'It was stolen, though, in the house in La Latina.
How on earth did you find it?'

'An English soldier had a run-in with a homeless
man in Madrid and recognised my crest. He brought
it home to London and gave it to me.'

'So you knew I was alive then, instead of gone
in the fire?'

'I hoped so, but Luis Alvarez's son confirmed it
for me.'

'You went back to the little port of Pontevedra?'

'Xavier Alvarez, Luis's son, told me you had sat
on the wharf for a long while after his father and I
left and that you had been near to crying. He then
said he saw you take the road into the hills and it
was raining.'

He stopped for a second and took in a deep breath.
'The timing would have been too tight. There was no
way you could have reached the hacienda by the time
of the fire. If it had not rained? If you had not tarried?
If you had taken the coastal road…?' His voice shook
with all the possibilities that had not come to pass.

'You think I cannot say exactly the same of you,
Lucien? If you had not come to the French prison and
helped me escape, if you had not made your appointment in the brothel under the name of Mateo, if you
had not been fighting in A Coruña in the first place.'

'But I did.'

'And we do,' she whispered, her hands across his

chest and then falling downwards. 'Only now, remember. If we live like that for all our lives, everything will be perfect. The future will take care of itself and the past is finished with. We cannot change it. All the best intentions shall not undo it.'

'Only now?'

'This moment. This second.'

He stepped out of the last of his clothes and brought her up against him hard.

'You are my world, Alejandra.'

And then they forgot to speak at all.

Afterwards they lay entwined in a tangle of sheets and quilting, close and quiet. The last of the four-hour candle had burnt down the wick, sending dark smoke into the air and strange reflections on to the ceiling.

'My mother would have liked you, Lucien. She would have been pleased with my choice.'

She felt his chest shake in humour. 'Who was she, your mother?'

'Rosalie Santo Domingo y Giminez was the daughter of one of the wealthiest landowners in Galicia. Papa and she were betrothed under the old system of marriage. He was strong and a leader of men and my mama's father admired him. Europe was being cast into war and chaos and I suppose her father thought Enrique Fernandez y Castro could protect both his daughter and them, protect their inheritance and land and cattle. As it happened my grandparents were both taken by sickness one winter soon after the marriage and everything went to my father, the new groom, and the outsider.'

'So no one was happy?'

'Well, my mother certainly was. She saw how Enrique could rally people around a cause with his logic and his menace and she understood that allies at a time of great change were more than useful. Within two years he had the pledges of thirty other landholders around us for help and loyalty and he never looked back.'

'Did Rosalie?'

'No, not really. She hated the violence and the fighting, but by then she had lost her heart to him as well as all her property. Women lose their rights under marriage, you see, and my father was a great believer in that particular concept. And so here I am as landless and moneyless as my mother was in the end, for I doubt that even if peace comes to Spain I will be able to regain possession of our lands and houses.'

'I did not marry you for your money, Alejandra, or your lack of it. I married you because I love you. Besides, my interests in manufacturing are starting to pay off and I would say by the end of the year the Ross finances will be more than healthy again.'

Relief made her breathe out heavily. 'So you were not in need of a wealthy heiress?'

'No, I was always in need of a beautiful and brave Spanish warrior.'

'Are you in need now?' She smiled and turned

towards him, her hips lifting against his side as her mouth came down across his own.

She was sick again in the morning and as she returned to the bed Lucien pulled back the sheets and took her into his warmth.

'Could you be pregnant, Alejandra?'

The shock of the words kept her still as she counted back the days since her last menses. She had never had one moment of sickness with Ross and so the thought of it had not even occurred to her.

Lifting the sheet, he traced the outline of her nipples. 'They are darker, sweetheart. Is that not a sign?'

'I don't know. I can't remember from before...'

'And you have been tired.'

'Yes, but I thought it was the listening to English and trying to understand it all the time.'

'Perhaps you might talk with Amethyst and ask her about the signs, or Adelaide.' His hand spread across her stomach now, in possession and in hope, she thought, too.

'Mama was not a woman to speak of these things and I have never had another to ask. Maria was older and forgetful and the one child she'd had was dead, so I didn't like to question her.'

'What of the other girls at the brothel? Surely there were babies born there?'

'Indeed there were, but I was their employer. It was not appropriate to ask them.' She sat up suddenly, unable to lie there any more. 'Could we go to see Amethyst or Adelaide?'

'Now?'

'Yes. Perhaps it is true. Perhaps I could be… We could be parents.' Her hands came across her mouth. 'Do you think it could be true?'

He pushed back the bedcovers and offered her his hand. 'I am a man with absolutely no idea of anything to do with pregnancy, but let's get dressed and go.'

Chapter Sixteen

All his best friends were here in the library at Linden Park—Daniel, Gabriel and Francis—waiting with him amongst the books and brandy for the birth of his and Alejandra's first child.

The doctor had been called a good hour ago and the midwife had been here most of the morning. Amethyst, Christine and Adelaide had insisted that they stay with Alejandra, too, and for that Lucien was extremely grateful.

'It's always exhausting, Luce, this waiting,' Daniel said. 'God, I remember it with the birth of Sapphire. I thought that neither my wife nor baby would live beyond the hour and that I'd be alone for ever and…' He stopped and finished the last of his brandy.

'I think Lucien would rather hear the good stories, Daniel.' Gabriel voiced his opinion now. 'The ones that speak of women having a baby one moment and getting on with their lives the next.'

'In America the Mohican women would depart

alone to a secluded grove near water to prepare for delivery.' Francis's remark was soft and Lucien looked at him in amazement.

'You think it would help my wife to be outside by herself trying to have our baby?'

'No. I am just saying that birth is often relatively painless and simple.'

'Keep away from Alejandra until she has had the baby, then. I think she might very well kill you right now if she heard you saying that.'

'Amethyst believes mankind would be doomed if males were the ones who had to give birth.' Daniel spoke again now, more careful with what he said.

Lucien simply paced from the open door to the windows and back. It had been all of three hours since he had last been allowed into the birthing room. How long did these things usually take? He screwed his fingers through his hair and closed his eyes.

If he lost Alejandra again... No, he would not even entertain such a notion.

Opening his eyes, he glanced over at Gabriel, whose small son was almost two now, but who had stayed largely silent in the discussion.

'When Adelaide had Jamie, were you afraid, Gabe?'

'More scared than I have ever been in my entire life. I think it's normal.'

'We had another child. A little boy.' The words were out before he could rethink them, falling into the silence like bullets. 'He only lived for a few minutes.'

'My God.' Daniel stood at that and joined him by the window. 'Was this in Spain, Luce?'

'After I left her in Spain. Five years ago.'

'Alejandra had him alone?'

'Yes.'

'Well, now she has us all. A whole lot of people who can help her and get her through. And get you through, too. In an hour you will be the happiest you have ever felt in your life. I promise you that.'

'What was the name of your son?'

Gabriel asked this question and Lucien was glad to bring his name here into the room as a part of a waiting family.

'He was named Ross.'

'A good name. A family name.' Francis now lifted his glass and raised it to the room. 'To Ross. May he never be forgotten.'

They each drank deep of their tipple and for some unfathomable reason Lucien could almost hear his little lost child tell him that this birth would go well, that there would be a baby who would grow up as he had not and that all would be better this time around. Lucien smiled. He had begun the arrangements already to bring the tiny body home and Alejandra had overseen the planting of olive, aloe and oak saplings in a grove by the lake at Linden Park. Familiar trees. Small whispers of Spain.

He made himself sit down and take a drink and was just about to swallow the brandy when the door opened.

'Your wife wants you, Lucien.'

It was Amethyst and the smile on her face was wide.

Alejandra was lying in the bed in a nightgown he

had brought for her a few weeks ago in London and her dark hair was streaming down over her shoulders. In her arms was a small bundle wrapped in the soft white woollen blanket his mother had crocheted all through the months of winter.

Adelaide stood to one side of the bed next to his sister, the midwife and the doctor talking quietly in the corner, though both looked up with a smile as they saw him enter.

He crossed the room and took the hand that was held out.

'We have a little son, Lucien. Well, not so little really. The doctor said he is healthy and beautiful.'

Through the swaddling clothes a tiny face peered, eyes a dark strange blue and his skin reddened.

'He was born twenty minutes ago and he is breathing all by himself.' At that she carefully placed the bundle into his arms and Lucien felt the lightness and the heaviness all at once as a great surge of love came across him.

Theirs. For ever. A son.

'We had said we would call him Ross, but when I look at him I think he is his very own person. What was your father's name?'

'Jonathon.'

'Then let us name him Jonathon Enrique. For my papa, as well. For the future and the past.'

'I like that. Do you, Jonathon?' he murmured, and one tiny hand curled around his finger, grasping hard.

Family and home had a particular feel to it that was unequalled. So did parenthood.

He brought his wife's hand to his lips and kissed her fingers.

'Thank you, Alejandra.'

'You are welcome, Lucien,' she gave back. 'Perhaps the others might come in now to meet the newest of our families.'

* * * * *

MARRIAGE MADE
IN HOPE

Chapter One

London—1815

Lady Sephora Connaught knew that she was going to die. Right then and there as the big black horse bucked on the bridge and simply threw her over the balustrade and down into the fast-running river.

Her sister screamed and so did others, the sounds blocked out by the water as she hit it, fright taking breath and leaving terror. She exhaled from pure instinct, but still the river came in, filling her mouth and throat and lungs as the cloth of her heavy skirt drew her under to the darkness and the gloom. She could not fight it, could not gain purchase or traction or leverage.

Ripping at her riding jacket, she tried to loosen the fastenings, but it was hopeless. There were too many buttons and beneath that too many stays, too much boning and layers and tightness, all clinging and covering and constricting.

This was it.

The moment of her end; already the numbness was coming, the pain in her leg from hitting the balustrade receding into acceptance, the light from above fading as she sank amongst the fish and the mud and the empty blackness. It was over. Her life. Her time. Gone before she had even lived it. Her hands closed over her mouth and nose so that she would not breathe in, but her lungs were screaming for air and she couldn't deny them further.

A movement above had her tipping her head, the disturbance of the water felt more than seen as a dark shape came towards her. A man fully dressed, his hand reaching out even as he kicked. She simply watched, trying to determine if he could be real, here in the depths of the Thames, here where the light was failing and all warmth was gone.

God, the girl had simply given up, floating there like a giant jellyfish, skirts billowing, hair streaming upwards, skin pale as moonlight and eyes wide.

Why did the gentlemen of the *ton* not teach their daughters to swim, for heaven's sake? If they had, she might have made a fist of her own salvation and tried to strike out for the surface. Anything but this dreadful final acceptance and lack of fight. His mouth came tight across her own as he gave her breath, there in the dark and cold, the last of his air before he kicked upwards, fingers anchored around her arm. At least she did not struggle, but came with him like a sodden dead weight, the emerald hue of a riding jacket the only vivid thing about her.

And then they were up into the sun and the wind and the living, bouncing like corks in the quick-cut current of the river, her legs wound about his like a vice, one hand scratching down the side of his face and drawing blood as she tried to grab him further.

'Damn it. Keep still.' His words were rasped out through shattered breath and lost in open space.

But she would not calm, the flailing panic pulling him under, her eyes wide with terror. Swearing again, he jammed her hard in against him and made for the bank whilst keeping with the current, glad when he saw others running down the pathways to reach them in the mire of sludge and slurry.

The mud from Hutton's Landing came back in memory, falling across him, pulling him down, thick as molasses, heavy as oil, and he began to shiver. Violently. It was everywhere here, too, around his legs, across the stockings on his feet, staining the full skirts of the girl, her body pinned to his own like a well-fitting glove and taking any last remaining warmth.

He needed to be gone, to be home, away from the prying eyes of others and the pity he so definitely did not want. She was retching now violently, water streaming from her mouth as oxygen took the place of the putrid contents of the Thames. She was shaking, too. Shock, he supposed, feeling his own gathering panic. He was glad when a stranger reached out to lift her from him as Gabriel Hughes and Lucien Howard joined him on the bank.

Others were there also, an older woman screaming and a younger girl telling her to be quiet. Men as well, their eyes sharply observing him as he lumbered out, the old scar no doubt in full blaze across his face.

He could not hide anything. The shaking. The anger. The hatred. He was caught only in limbo, in memory and in mud.

'Come, Francis. We will take you home.'

Gabriel's voice came through the fury, his hand slipping around the sodden sleeve of his friend's coat as he led him off. The girl was crying now, but Francis did not look back. Not even once.

She couldn't stop the sobbing or quell her fear, even as those around her shouted out orders to fetch a carriage, to find some blankets, to get a doctor and to staunch the flow of blood on her right shin.

She was alive and breathing. She was sitting on the solidness of soil and earth, perched in the thin sun of a late spring afternoon on a pathway near the Thames with all the life she thought she had lost now back in front of her.

'We will get you home, Sephora, right now. Richard has gone to find a carriage and a runner has been sent to make certain your father is informed of what has happened here.'

Her mother's voice sounded odd, strained by worry, probably, and abject fright.

Sephora closed her eyes and tried to push things back and away. She could barely contemplate what had happened and she felt removed somehow, from the people, from the river bank, even from the earth upon which she sat.

Shock, perhaps? Or some other malady that came from swallowing too much water? The horror of it all swirled in, taking away the colour of the day, and her skin felt clammy and odd. Then all she knew was darkness.

She woke during the night in the Aldford town house on Portman Square, the candle next to her bed throwing shadows across the ceiling and a fire blazing in the hearth.

Maria, her sister, sat close on a chair, eyes closed and a shawl pushed away from her nightgown because of the warmth. Asleep. Sephora smiled and stretched. She felt better, more herself. She felt warm and safe and whole. There was a bandage around the bottom of her right leg and it hurt to push against it, but apart from that… She did a quick inventory of her body and found everything else in good working order and painless.

The memory of a mouth across hers in the water came back like a punch to the stomach. Her saviour had given her air when she was without it, ten feet under in the dark, the last of his own store and precious. Her heart began to race violently and she turned, her sister coming awake at the small movement, eyes focusing as she leaned forward.

'You look better, Sephora.'

'How did I look before?' Her voice was raspy and stretched. A surprising sound, that, and she coughed.

'Half-dead.'

'The horse…?'

'He bolted on the bridge and bucked you off. A bee sting, the groom said afterwards, and a bad one. Father has sworn he'll sell the stallion for much less than he paid for it, too, as he wants nothing more to do with it.'

Privately Sephora was glad that she would never need to see the steed again.

'Do you remember anything of what happened?' Her sister's tone had a new note now, one of interest and speculation.

'I remember someone saved me?'

'Not just any someone either. It was the Earl of Douglas, Francis St Cartmail, the black sheep of the *ton*. It's been the talk of the town.'

'Where was Richard?'

'Right behind where you were on the bridge, frozen solid in fright. I don't think he can swim. Certainly he did not tear off his boots as the earl did and simply dive in.'

'St Cartmail did that?'

'With barely a backward glance. The water was fast flowing there and the bridge is high, but he most assuredly did not look in any way concerned as he vaulted on to the narrow balustrade.'

'And dived in?'

'Like a pirate.' Her sister began to smile. 'Like a pirate with his face slashed by a scar and his long dark hair loose and flowing down his back.'

Sephora remembered nothing of his countenance, only the touch of warm lips against her own, intimate and forbidden under the murky waters of the Thames.

'Was he hurt?'

'He was when he got out of the river because you had scratched his face. There were three vivid lines down his other cheek and they were running with blood.'

'But someone helped him?'

'Lords Wesley and Ross. They did not stay around, though, for by the time he had got to the pathway the Earl of Douglas looked even sicker than you did.'

Francis St Cartmail, the fifth Earl of Douglas. Sephora turned the name over in her mind. So many swirling rumours about him in the *ton*, a lord who lived on the seedier side of rightness and amongst an underworld of danger.

She had only ever seen him once and at a distance in the garden of the Creightons' ball two months prior. There he had been entwined in the arms of a woman who was known for her questionable morals and loose ways, rouged lips turned to his in supplication. Miss Amelia Bourne, standing with Sephora, had been quick to relay the gossip that surrounded the earl, her eyes full of infatuation and interest.

'Douglas is beautiful, is he not, even with that scar and though he is seen less and less frequently in social company these days, when he does appear there is always gossip. I, for one, should not listen to any such slander if a man could kiss me like that...?' Amelia let the rest slide into query as she laughed.

Sephora had returned home after that particular ball and dreamed of what it must feel like to be kissed with such complete abandon, wild beauty and open lustfulness.

Well, now she almost knew in a way.

Shaking away that heated thought, she sat up. 'Is there something to drink?'

Her sister poured her a full glass of sweetened lemonade with mint and rosemary leaves on top and helped her to sip it.

'Where is Richard?'

'He was in the library last evening with Father, trying to smooth down the gossip and contain the rumour that is rife around the *ton*.'

'Rumour?' Sephora could not quite understand what was said. Gesturing to Maria that she had had enough of the lemonade, she lay back.

'You were wrapped around Douglas like a blanket from head to toe as he came to the bank and it seemed to us as if you did not wish to let go. Richard had to pry open your fingers from St Cartmail's personage.'

'I was drowning.'

'You were wanton. The front of your jacket had been ripped open and the material on your bodice was gaping.' This summary was accompanied by a hearty laugh. 'And it suited you. You looked magnificently alive.'

Sephora ignored that nonsense completely. 'Where is Mama?'

'In bed after ingesting a stiff toddy. She should be out until the morrow so you shan't have to deal with her worry. The one thing she did keep saying over and over was that at least you and Richard Allerly had announced your betrothal so you were not entirely ruined.'

'It was hardly my fault the horse reacted so violently.'

'Mama would say drowning might have been altogether more circumspect given the intimate clutch your rescuer held you in and your dreadful state of undress.'

Sephora smiled. 'You have always exaggerated events, Maria, but thank you for staying here with me at least. It is a comfort.'

Her sister took her hand in her own, the soft warmth of her grip familiar. 'You have lost Richard's diamond ring in the incident. I do not think he knows this fact yet and will probably not be well pleased.'

'It was always too big and I saw the exact pattern in Rundell's when I was in the shop a few weeks ago so it shouldn't be too difficult to replace.'

Maria laughed. 'Just like Richard to settle for a cheap stock item, Sephora, when you plainly deserve so much more.'

'I was happy with it.'

'I doubt Francis St Cartmail would be so stingy with his newfound money were he to be wed. It is said he returned from the Americas as a wealthy man made rich from the striking of gold. He looked awfully sick after your rescue, though, almost falling over in fact with…a sort of shaking panic. I hope he is recovered.'

Sephora remembered that suddenly, the bone-deep weariness of him as he had struggled the last few yards through the mud. 'Was he hurt anywhere else?'

'Apart from your scratches to his face, you mean?' When she nodded, Maria went on.

'Not that I could see. I wondered why the earl did not stay to receive the adulation of those who had observed the rescue, though, even given his questionable reputation. It was a fine and daring thing he did and the water is deep there in the middle and cold. Richard was standing next to you, of course, with his thousand-yard stare and his implacable credentials. Perhaps that is what put Francis St Cartmail off?'

'I don't even remember Richard being there at all. I know he was on the horse beside me, I recall that, but after...'

'Douglas and his two friends were walking the other way when you screamed. They had just got to the bridge.'

Dark hair and dark clothes and the feel of knotted skin under her fingers as she had reached for him and held on.

Somehow those few moments seemed more real to Sephora than anything else in her entire life. A reaction, she supposed, to her near drowning and the fright of it, for nothing truly dreadful had ever happened to her before. Maria was watching her carefully, the beginnings of a frown across her brow.

'Do you ever think, Sephora, that incidents like this might happen for a reason?'

'A reason?'

'You have not looked happy of late and you have

seemed distracted. Ever since you agreed to become Richard's bride, come to think of it. He has all the money in the world, a beautiful house and a family who think he is stellar and that is not even taking into account his position in society, but...' She stopped.

'You never liked him, Maria. Ever since the start.'

'He is pompous and self-righteous, always congratulating himself on his next achievement and his latest triumph.'

Despite herself Sephora began to laugh. 'He does a lot of good for others...'

'And more than good for himself,' her sister countered.

'He is kind to his family...'

'And kinder to those who can aid him in his steady ascent to power within the *ton*.'

'He loves me.'

Maria nodded. 'Yes, I will give him that, but who does not adore you, Sephora? I have never yet met a soul who says a bad word of you and that includes the numerous suitors you've let down gently in their quest for your hand.'

'You give me too much praise, Maria.'

Sometimes I am not nice. Sometimes I could scream with the boredom of being exactly who it is I have become. Sometimes there is another person in me just under the surface struggling for breath and freedom.

The touch of St Cartmail's lips to her mouth, the feel of his hand across her neck, firm and forceful.

The whispered shared air that he'd given her when she had held no more herself.

Douglas had lifted her into his arms like a child, as though she weighed nothing, as though he might have carried her the length of the river and never felt it. There was a certain security in the strength of a man, she thought, a protection and a magic. Richard would barely be able to lift her with his city body and thinness.

Comparisons.

Why on earth was she making them? St Cartmail was wild and worrying and unknown. She had heard he had killed a man in the Americas and got away with it.

The following morning she felt as if she had been run over by a heavy piece of machinery, the muscles that had been sore yesterday now making themselves known in a throbbing ache of pain.

Her mother's quiet knock on the door had her turning. 'I am so thankful to see you looking well rested, my dear, as you gave us all a terrible fright yesterday. But it is late in the morning now and Richard is here, wondering if he might just have a quick word.'

Elizabeth sat on the chair beside the bed, the heavy frown across her brow very noticeable today. 'We could get you dressed and looking presentable while he talks with Father. It would be a good thing for you to be up and about for it pays to get back on the horse after such a fright...' She stopped, suddenly realising just what she had said. 'Not literally, of course, and certainly not that dreadful stallion. But normality must return and the sooner that it does the better.'

Sephora felt like simply rolling over and pulling the blankets up across herself, keeping everyone at bay. If she said she was not up to seeing Richard, would he go away or would he insist upon seeing her? He was not a man inclined to wait for anything and sometimes under the genial smile she could detect a harder irritation that concerned her.

She knew she could not stay here tucked away in the safety of her bedroom forever after such a difficulty and she also understood that to put their meeting off was only postponing the problem.

Pushing back the bedding, Sephora rose up into the morning and was glad when her maid came in to help her dress.

As Richard entered the small blue salon Sephora could see her mother hovering on the edges of her vision, just to make certain everything was proper and correct, that propriety was observed and manners obeyed.

'My dear.' His hands were warm when he took hers, the brown in his eyes deep today and worried. 'My dearest, dearest girl. I am so very sorry.'

'Sorry?' Sephora could not quite understand his meaning.

'I should have come after you, of course. I should not have hesitated, but I am a poor swimmer, you see, and the water there is very deep...' He stopped, as if realising that the more he said the less gallant he appeared. 'If I had lost you…?'

'Well, you did not, Richard, and truth be told I am largely unharmed and almost over it.'

'Your leg?'

'A small cut from where I hit the stone balustrade, but nothing more. I doubt there will even be a scar.'

'I sent a note to thank Douglas so that you should have no need for further discourse with him. I am just sorry it was not Wesley or Ross who rescued you, for they would have been much easier to thank.'

'In what way?' Disengaging his hands, she sat with hers in her lap. She felt suddenly cold.

'They are gentlemen. I doubt Douglas has much of a notion of the word at all. Did you see the way he just left without discourse or acknowledgement? A gentleman would have at least tarried to make certain you were alive. At that point you barely looked it.'

Sephora remembered vomiting again and again over Francis St Cartmail as they had waded in from the deep, seawater and tears mixed across the deep brown of his ruined jacket. He wore a ring, she thought, trying to recall the design and failing. It sat on the little finger of his left hand, a substantial gold-and-ruby cabochon.

'I took you from him at the water's edge, Sephora. My own riding jacket suffered, of course, but at least you were safe and sound. A groom found a blanket to put around you and I sent for my carriage and marshalled all those about us into some sort of an order. Quite a fracas, really, and a fair bit of organisation to see things in order on my part, but I am glad it has turned out so well in the end.'

Sephora mused over all the things Richard had done for her, all the help and good intentions, the carriage filled with warm woollen blankets, his solicitousness and his worry so very on show.

She began to cry quite suddenly, a feeling that welled from the bottom of her stomach and swelled into her throat, a pounding, horrible unladylike howl that tore at her heart and her sense and her modesty. Unstoppable. Inexplicable. Desperate.

Her mother rushed over and took her in warm arms and Richard left the room with as much haste as he could politely manage. Sephora was glad he was gone.

'Men never have an inkling of what to say in a time of crisis, my love. Richard was indeed wonderful with his orders and his arrangements and his wisdom. We could not have wished for more.'

'More?' Her one-worded question fell into silence.

He had not dived into the water after her, he had not risked his life for her. Instead he had simply watched her fall and sink, down and down into the greying dark coldness of the river without breath or hope.

Richard had done what he thought was enough and he was her betrothed. She had never met the Earl of Douglas and yet Francis St Cartmail had, without thought, jumped in to save her there amongst the frigid green depths.

She had no touchstone any more for what was true and what was not. Her life had been turned upside down by a single unselfish act into question and uncertainty and lost in the confusion of reality—these seconds, these moments, this morning with the sun coming in through wide windows and open sashes.

If Lord Douglas had not come to her, she would have been lying now instead on a cold marble slab in the family mausoleum, drowned by misadventure, the unlucky tragic Lady Sephora Connaught, twenty-two and a half and gone.

Her nails dug into the skin above her wrists, leaving whitened crescents that stung badly, and she liked the pain. It told her she was alive, but the numbness inside around her heart was spreading and there was nothing at all she could do to stop it.

Chapter Two

After the rescue at the river Francis removed his sodden jacket and lay down on the day bed in his library, closing his eyes against sickness. Everything upon him was wet, but just for this moment he needed to be still.

It always happened like this, suddenly, shockingly, placing him out of kilter with all that was around him and sending him back to other moments, other times, other places that he never wanted to remember.

Even the change of environment did not banish the panic, though it made the waiting easier here amongst his books and his throat stopped feeling quite so blocked and swollen.

'Have a drink, Francis. Then if you do happen to die on us you will at least have the rancid filthy taste of the Thames gone from your mouth.' Gabriel handed him a large glass of brandy filled to the rim as he sat up and took two generous sips before placing it down.

'This has...happened before. It's not...fatal. It's...

just damn…unpleasant.' He was still shaking and his voice reflected it, ice in his bones and shards of glass in his head. He was so very tired.

'Why?' One word from Lucien, hard and angry. 'It's the Hutton's Landing affair, isn't it? That damn blunder with Seth Greenwood and somehow his death is your problem forever.'

Francis shook his head.

'It's the…mud.'

'The mud?'

'The mud that covered us. The memory comes back sometimes…and I can't fight off the feeling.'

'God, Francis. You went to America as one man and came back as altogether a different one. Richer, I will agree, but…altered in a way that makes you brittle and you won't let us in to help you.'

Francis tried to concentrate, to sift through all of the extraneous matter and find out what was important.

'Who was…she?'

'The girl you pulled from the Thames? You don't know?' Lucien began to smile. 'That was Lady Sephora Connaught, the uncrowned "angel of the *ton*", the woman who every other female aspires to become like…and one who is engaged to Richard Allerly.'

'The Marquis of Winslow. The duke's son?'

'His only son. The golden couple. Both sets of parents are good friends. Bride and groom-to-be have known each other since childhood and the relationship has matured into more. It will be the wedding of the year.'

Gabriel on the other side of the room was less inclined to sugar-coat it. 'Allerly is an idiot and you know it, too, Luce, as well as being a damned coward.'

For the first time in an hour Francis felt his shivering lessen with this turn of topic. 'How is he a coward?'

'Winslow was there, damn it, right behind his would-be bride. He watched as that untrained horse of hers upended her over the balustrade and sent her tumbling down into the river.'

'And he did…nothing?'

'Well, he certainly didn't take a leap from a high bridge into a deep and fast-running river without thinking twice. Cowering against the stonework might be a better description of his reaction. The skin on his knuckles was white from the grip.'

Lucien looked as though he found Gabriel's description more than amusing. 'Allerly was there soon enough though when you got her to the bank, Francis, I noticed he tried not to get mud on his new boots as he all but snatched her from you.'

'Hardly snatched,' Gabriel countered. 'It did look as if the girl knew who her saviour was at least and it took the marquis a while to get her to let you go. Her bodice was ripped, too. Her beloved took a good long look at what was on offer beneath before taking off his own jacket to cover her. Sephora Connaught's mother, Lady Aldford, looked less than pleased with him.'

For the first time in hours Francis relaxed. 'It

seems as if Lady Sephora made quite an impression on you both.'

Gabriel took up the rebuttal. 'We are happily married men, Francis. It's you we hope might have noticed her obvious charms.'

'Well, I didn't. I was shaking too much.'

He leaned back against the sofa and drew a blanket across himself before finishing the rest of the strong brandy. The name was familiar and he tried to place it.

'Lady Sephora Connaught. How is it I know of her?'

'She is Anne-Marie McDowell's youngest cousin.'

Anne-Marie. He had courted her once a good many years ago, but she had died of some quick sickness before they could take the relationship to the next stage. He'd got drunk when he'd found out, so blindingly drunk he'd never made it to her funeral. Looking back, he thought his reactions had come not so much from the shock of Anne-Marie's death but from the reminder that the grim reaper took people randomly, with no thought of age or experience or character.

The family had not been pleased by his absence though and he knew now he should have handled things with more aplomb than he had.

His right cheek ached from where Sephora Connaught had scratched him, three dark lines running from eye to chin caught in the reflection of the glass that he held. He hoped they would not fester like the wound had on the other cheek as he closed his eyes.

When he had thrown himself off the bridge today part of him had hoped he might not again surface and that he would be celebrated as a hero when he failed to reappear. Such a legacy of valour might sweeten the nightly howls of the Douglas ancestors whose portraits lined the steep stairwell as he walked to his bedroom late at night and there was some comfort in imagining it such before the truth of his life was torn apart again by gossip and conjecture.

He was alone and running from a past that kept reaching out, even here in a quiet, warm room and in the company of friends. Lifting the glass of brandy to his lips, he finished the lot.

'You look like a man who needs to unload his demons, Francis.' Gabriel said this, his voice close and worried. 'Adelaide thinks you have the same appearance as I did when I first met her, swathed in secrets and regrets.'

'How did she cure you, then?'

'Oh, a good wife has her ways, believe me, and mine was never a woman to give up.'

Lucien joined in the conversation now. 'It's what you need, a woman with gumption, spirit and humour.'

'And where do you think I shall find this paragon that you describe?' The brandy was loosening his tongue and stilling the shakes and with the blanket about his shoulders he was finally feeling warmer and safe.

'Perhaps you have just done so, but do not know it yet.'

Francis frowned in sheer disbelief. 'Lady Sephora Connaught is engaged to be married to the only son of a duke. A slight impediment, would you not say, even given the fact I have not yet shared one word with her.'

'But you will. She will have to thank you for risking your life and I am certain jumping into a dangerous freezing river must have its compensations.'

'Is it the brandy that is making you both talk nonsense for I am damned sure that the so-called "angel of the *ton*" would have enough sense to keep well away from me?'

'You paint yourself too poorly, Francis. Seth Greenwood's cousin, Adam Stevenage, said that you had tried to save Seth. He said that you held him up out of the mud for all the hours of the day and it was the cold that killed him come the dusk.' Lucien said this softly, but with conviction.

'Stop.' The word came with an anger Francis could not hide and he turned away from the glances of both his friends. 'You know nothing of what happened at Hutton's Landing.'

'Then tell us. Let us help you understand it instead of beating yourself up with the consequences.'

Francis shook his head, but he could not halt the words that came. 'Stevenage is wrong. I killed Seth with my own stupidity.'

'How?'

'It was greed. He wanted to leave after the first lucky strike, but I persuaded him to stay.'

'For how long?'

'A month or more.'

'Thirty days?' Lucien stood now and walked to the window. 'Enough time for him to have changed his mind if he had wanted to. How long did you have to think about jumping into that river today?'

Francis frowned, not quite catching his drift, and Lucien went on.

'Two seconds, five seconds, ten?'

'Two, probably.' He gave the answer quietly.

'Did you think about changing your mind in those seconds?'

'No.'

'Well, Seth Greenwood had millions and millions of those same seconds, Francis, and neither did he. Would it have been our fault if you had jumped today and never resurfaced? Should we have languished in guilt forever because of your decision to try and rescue Lady Sephora Connaught? Are one man's actions another man's cross to bear for eternity if things don't quite turn out as they should?'

Gabriel began to laugh and brought the bottle of brandy over to refill their glasses.

'You should have taken to the law, Luce, and you to the ministry, Francis. Arguments and guilt have their own ways of tangling a man's mind and no doubt about it. But here's to friendship. And to all the life that's left,' he added as their glasses clicked together in the fading dimness of the library.

'Thank you.' Francis felt immeasurably better, lightened by a logic he had long since lost a hold of. He'd been mired in his guilt, it was true, stuck in the darkness like a man who had run out of hope and could not go on.

He had to move forward. He had to live again and believe that all he had lost could be found. Happiness. Joy. The energy to be true to himself.

He'd heard a voice, too, before he had jumped, from above or in his head he knew not which. A voice he knew and loved; a voice instructing him to save the girl in order to save himself and to be whole again.

God, was he going mad? Was this insanity the result of excessive introspection and guilt? Raising his glass, he drank of it deeply and thought that he had only told his friends the good half of a long and damn sordid story because the other part was too painful for anyone to ever have to listen to.

Chapter Three

Five days later his butler came into his library with a heavy frown upon his face.

'There is a gentleman to see you, Lord Douglas. From Hastings, my lord. He has given me this.'

Walsh passed over a card and Francis looked down. Mr Ignatius Wiggins, Lawyer. 'Show him in, Walsh.'

The man was small and dressed in unfashionable clothes of brown. He looked nervous as he fidgeted with a catch on the leather case that he held before him like a shield.

'I am the appointed counsel of Mr Clive Sherborne, my lord, and I have come to tell you that he has been murdered, sir, in Hastings a week ago. It was quick by all accounts, a severed throat and a knife to the kidney.

Good Lord, Francis thought. He stood to digest the brutality of such an ending and thought of the deceased. He had met him only once for he'd come to the Douglas town house with his wife, a garish but handsome-looking woman of low character and poor speech. They had come with the express purpose of informing his uncle about the birth of a baby whom they insisted was his by-blow. Wiggins had accompanied them.

Lynton St Cartmail had been furious and wanted nothing to do with such a hoax. Blackmail, he'd called it, Francis remembered, as he had ordered them summarily gone.

Clive Sherborne, however, had taken the child they had brought with them in his arms, a crying-reddened baby with dark lank hair and pale skin, even as he promised that he would instruct a lawyer to call on the fourth Earl of Douglas. His voice had been gentle and sad, a man who had not looked like the type to be murdered so heinously years later and Francis wondered what had happened in the interim to make it thus.

'Mr Sherborne had asked me to inform you of any significant events in his household, my lord, and so I am—informing you, I mean, about his death. A significant event by anyone's standards.'

'Indeed it is, Mr Wiggins.' Francis wondered briefly whether the mother, Sherborne's wife, was still alive and what had become of the girl child. He wondered why Wiggins had come back, too, given the amount of years that had passed since last being here.

'The deceased had given me a letter, sir, in better times, you understand, a missive that was to be delivered into your hands only in the circumstances of his death, for he wanted to make certain that Anna

Sherborne was…catered for. He was most adamant that I should give you this last correspondence personally, my lord, and that I should allow no other to take my stead…'

Francis remembered Wiggins distinctly, for his physical countenance looked much the same as it had. Last time he had gesticulated wildly at the screaming bundle of the unwanted newly born baby, but this time his hands were clasped tightly together, dark eyes showing an ill-disguised puzzlement mixed with fear.

'I shall not be a party to the lies any longer, Lord Douglas. Your uncle, the fourth Earl of Douglas, Lynton St Cartmail, paid me well to keep my silence about his illegitimate daughter and I have regretted it ever since.'

'He paid you?'

'From his own private funds, my lord, and they were substantial. The receipts are all here.'

The horror of the lie congealed in Francis's throat. The thought of a child, who was in effect his cousin, lost under his uncle's profligate womanising, was so shocking he felt the hair rise along his arms. Lynton had laughed off the charade of her birth as an obscene pretension by a misguided harlot to gain money from the coffers of the Douglas estate and at twenty-two Francis had had no cause to think the old earl was being anything but truthful. He could barely believe the dreadful falsehood and struggled to listen as the lawyer went on.

'This is the end of it, you understand, and I won't be held responsible for the consequences. I am elderly, my lord, and trying to make my peace with the Almighty and this deception has played heavily upon my conscience for years.'

Opening his bag, he found a thick wad of documents, which he laid down on the desk. 'This is the missive Mr Sherborne left in my care. It outlines the Douglas monies accorded to him for seeing to the child's upbringing and also any extra amounts sent. I should like to also say that although gold can buy certain things, sir, happiness is not one of them. Unfortunately, Miss Anna Sherborne is now largely at the mercy of the borough and one who has no idea of the true circumstances of her family connections and elevation.'

'Where is she now?'

'It is all there, my lord, all written down in the letter, but...'

'But?'

'The child has been brought up without proper rule of law and although Clive Sherborne was born a gentleman he most certainly did not have the actions of one. His wife, God rest her soul, was even less upstanding than her husband. To put it succinctly, the young girl is a hoyden, unbridled and angry, and she may well need a lot more from you than the promise of some sort of temporary and transitory home.'

Francis's head reeled, though he made an effort to think logically. 'Then I thank you for your confidentiality and for your service, Mr Wiggins, and sincerely hope you will bring the girl here to London in the next few days for the Douglas birthright should be her own.' He said the words quietly, the tremble of his hand the only thing belying complete and utter fury at his uncle as he paid the man off for his troubles and watched him depart.

Lynton St Cartmail's foolish and ongoing lack of responsibility had now landed firmly on his shoulders and the covering letter the lawyer had given him felt heavy as he ripped open the seal and looked down.

Anna Sherborne was almost twelve years old. He stopped, trying to remember himself at the same age. Arrogant. Cocksure. His parents had died together a few years prior in an accident so that could have been a factor in his belligerence, but Anna Sherborne's life had not been an easy one either and by the accounts of the lawyer she sounded...damaged.

The Damaged Douglas. That echo made him stand and walk to the window. What the hell was he to do with an almost-twelve-year-old girl? How did one handle a female of that particular age with any degree of success? God, no one had done so thus far in her life by all accounts and he did not wish to impair her further by his ignorance of the issues. His uncle must have known what would happen when he had turned his unsuitable lover and their offspring away with a good deal of financial support and an express intention never to see them again.

Well, she was his responsibility now. He'd need a governess, of course, some female relative with a firm and respectable hand to temper out all the knots and bumps expected in a wayward and abandoned child.

He'd need patience, too, and honesty. And luck, he added, catching his reflection in the window.

Sephora Connaught's nail-marks had settled somewhat on his right cheek, though they were still easily seen in the glass, three reddened lashes running from the corner of his eye.

On the other side the scar from the Peninsular Campaign blazed. He saw others looking at it often, of course he did, this mark that cut his face in half, but he'd made the conscious decision years ago not to let it define him. Still there were times... His finger marched along the pathway of injury and he felt the loss of who he had been and what was left now.

He was supposed to be accompanying Gabriel and Adelaide Hughes to a ball tonight given in honour of a friend's father. Part of him wished he did not have to go out and be seen after the incident by the river the other day, but the more sensible part of him reasoned that if there was speculation directed at him then so be it.

A small bit of him also hoped that Lady Sephora Connaught might also be attending the ball. He wanted to take a look at her and see if what he remembered matched the truth of her countenance.

Perhaps it was Lucien's words alluding to her as the 'angel of the *ton*' that had coloured his reminiscences, but he had begun to imagine her in a way that could only be called saintly. She'd had light hair, of that he was sure, but her face in the water had been blurred and indistinct. He did know her lips were full and shapely because he had been focused upon them as he had allowed her his breath.

An intimate thing that, he supposed, and the reason for this ridiculous but abiding interest. He had kissed a hundred woman in his life and bedded a good number, but this was the first time he had felt...what? Connected? Haunted? Aroused with such a speed it felt improper?

All of those things and none of them. Walking to his room, he turned when his valet came in to lay out his clothes for the evening and cursed his mindless and maudlin sentimentality.

Sephora Connaught was to be married forthwith to the Marquis of Winslow and he was by all terms a great and worthy catch. Still, he looked forward to seeing the elusive daughter of Lord and Lady Aldford tonight at the ball even if it was just to understand that the power of reminiscence was never as strong as the reality of a cold hard truth.

Sephora did not wish to go to the Hadleighs' ball and she told her mother of it firmly.

'Well, my dear, it is all very well to be nervous and of course after the events of the past week it is only proper that you should be, but you cannot hide forever and five days of being at home is enough. Richard will be there right beside you as will Maria, your father and I and, if anyone has the temerity to comment in any way that is derogatory, I am certain we shall be able to deal with them effectively.'

Her mother's words made perfect sense, but for

the first time in her life Sephora was not certain that anything would ever be all right again. She was either constantly in tears or as tired as she ever had been and the doctor her mother had called had told her 'it was only by rejoining the heaving mass of humanity and partaking in social intercourse that she would ever get well'.

His words had left her sister in fits of laughter and even she for the first time in days had smiled properly, but when putting on her new lemon gown this evening with its ruched sleeves and silken bodice she felt dislocated and adrift.

Her leg had healed and she hardly noticed the pain of it any more, though the doctor had been adamant that she leave the bandage on for a good few more days yet. Richard had presented her with new earrings and a matching bracelet and she had worn these tonight to try and lift her spirits.

It was not working. She felt heavy and wooden and afraid and the diamonds were like a bribe for his lack of…what?

She could not bear to have him touch her, even gently or inadvertently. She had not caught his eyes properly either lest he see in the depths of them some glint of her own accusations. A coward. An impostor. A man who could not and would not protect her.

So unfair, she knew. He was unable to swim competently, as were a great many men of the *ton*, and he had done his utmost ever since to make certain that she was healing and happy. Large bunches of roses had arrived each day, and because of it all she would associate their smell with this dreadful time forever and hate the scent of them until her dying day.

Her dying day. That was the crux of it. She had escaped death by the margin of a whisper and could not quite come to terms with the fact. Oh, granted, she was here still, breathing, eating, sleeping, walking.

And yet…she wasn't.

She was still under that water, trapped in her heavy clothes and in the darkness waiting to die.

Her skin crept with the thought and she shivered. She felt as if she might never truly be warm again even as the maid placed the final touches to her curled hair with a hot iron.

She looked presentable and calm when she glanced at herself in the mirror a few moments later. She looked as she always had done before any ball or social event of note: mannerly, gracious and composed. She had never been criticised for anything at all until this week, until she had clung to Francis St Cartmail in her torn and sodden riding clothes as though her life had depended on it.

Well, indeed it had. She smiled and the flush in her cheeks interested her. She seldom had high colour and just for a moment Sephora thought such vividness actually suited her, made her eyes bluer and her hair more golden. Usually her skin held the sheen of a statue cut from alabaster, like the one of the *Three Graces* she had seen in an art book at Lackington's in Finsbury Square. Translucent and composed. Women untouched by high emotion or great duress.

Maria's noisy entrance into her chamber had her looking away from her reflection.

'The carriage is here, Mama. Papa and the marquis are waiting downstairs.'

'Then we shall come immediately. Have you a wrap, Maria? It is cold outside and we do not want a case of the chills. Sephora, make certain you bring your warmest cloak for there is quite a wind tonight and the spring this year has a decided nip to it. After the incident at the bridge we do not wish for you to sicken, for your body's defences will be lowered by the alarm of your accident.'

And with that they were off, bundled into the carriage full of Maria's happy chatter and her mother's answering interjections.

On her side of the conveyance Sephora simply held her breath, squashed as she was between her father and Richard, and wondered how long she could keep doing so before she might faint dead away. She had got to the slow count of fifty in her room before the black spots had begun to dance in front of her eyes. She did not dare to risk the same here. But still she liked the control of it, silent and hidden. A power no one could take away from her, an unbidden and unchallenged authority.

At least the ballroom was warm, she thought half an hour later, as their party made their way through the crowded rooms, this outing so far holding none of the fear she'd imagined it might.

'You look beautiful this evening, my dearest love,'

Richard said as they took their places at the top of the room, the orchestra easily observed from where they stood. 'Lemon and silk suits you entirely.'

'Thank you.' There was a tone in her voice that was foreign and displaced.

'I hope we might have a dance together as soon as the music begins.'

Her heart began to beat a little faster, but she pushed the start of panic down. 'Of course.'

She was coping and for that she was glad. She was managing to be just the person everybody here thought she was. No one watched her too intently, no conversation had swirled to a stop as she passed a group, no whispered conjectures or raised fans behind which innuendo could be shared. No pity.

Her betrothed's first finger touched a drop of ornately fashioned white gold at her ear. 'I knew they would look well on you as soon as I saw them, my love. I was planning on keeping them as a surprise until your birthday, but you looked as if a present might be the very thing needed to cheer you up. I managed to get them at a good price from Rundell's as they have high hopes of my further ducal patronage in the future.'

'I imagine that they do.' She tried to keep sarcasm from the words, but wondered if she had been successful as he turned to look at her sharply. She had not used such a thing before, the poor man's version of humour, but tonight she could not help it. The chandelier above them gave the blurred appearance of light through water and it momentarily made her take in a deep breath.

All about her was a living, moving feast of life: five hundred people, myriad colours, the scent of fine food and the offer of expensive wine. Without thought her hand lifted to a long-stemmed crystal glass on the silver platter a footman had just presented to the party and if Richard frowned at her choice he had at least the sense not to say anything.

She seldom drank alcohol, but the orgeat lemonade tonight held no allure at all. It looked like the water of the Thames somehow, cloudy, cold and indistinct. She swallowed the wine like a person finding a waterhole in the middle of an endless desiccated African desert and reached out for another. Her mother shook her head even as Richard set his bottom teeth against his top ones and tried to smile. The glint of anger in his eyes was back.

But it was so good, this quiet escape that took the edge off a perpetual panic and made everything more bearable. Even the gaudy new bracelet twinkling in the light started to have more appeal.

The beginnings of the three-point tune of a waltz filled the air around them and when her betrothed took her arm and led her into the dance she allowed him the privilege. His closeness was not the problem it would have been ten minutes earlier and she wondered if perhaps she had been too harsh on a man who after all had always loved her and had failed to learn to swim.

The feel of him was known, his short brown hair well cut and groomed, the smell of an aftershave that held notes of bergamot and musk.

'You look very pretty, Sephora, and more like yourself.' This time his smile was genuine and she saw in him for a moment the boy whom she had grown up with and played with, though his next words burst that nostalgic bubble completely. 'I do think, though, that you should refrain from imbibing any more wine.'

'Refrain when I have barely begun to feel its effect?'

'You have had two full glasses already, my dearest heart, and you are now in some danger of flippancy.'

'Flippancy?' She rolled the word on her tongue and liked it. She had never been flippant. She had always been serious and composed and polite until she had fallen headlong into that river and discovered things about herself that she could no longer hide.

For just a second she thought she loathed her intended groom with such ferocity she might well indeed have simply hit him. But the moment passed and she was herself again, chastised by the impulse and made impotent by fright.

Who was that inside of her? What crouched below the quiet and ladylike bearing that was her more usual demeanour and appearance, the lemon silk in her gown, the curls in her hair, the dainty bejewelled slippers upon her feet?

She had a headache, she did, a searing terrible headache that made her sick and dizzy. Richard in a rare moment of empathy recognised the fact and led her over to a chair near the wall apart from the others and made her sit down.

'Stay here whilst I find your mother, Sephora. You do not look well at all.'

She could only nod and watch him go, the slight form of him disappearing amongst the crowd to be replaced by a man she recognised instantly.

'You.' Hardly mannerly, desperately said. The sound came from her in a whisper as Francis St Cartmail stood alone in front of her.

'I am glad to see you much recovered, Lady Sephora. I am sorry I did not stay to see to your welfare after...' The earl stopped.

'My drowning?' She supplied the ending for him and he smiled. It made his face softer somehow, the scar on his left cheek curled into a smaller shape and her three scratches on his right almost disappearing into a deep dimple.

'Hardly a drowning. More a case of getting wet, I think.'

Simple words that she needed. Words that took away the terror and the hugeness of all that had transpired. He was even looking at her with humour in his eyes. Sephora wanted him to keep on talking, but he didn't, though the stillness that fell between them was as distinct as any conversation.

'Thank you,' she finally managed.

'You are welcome,' he returned and then he was gone, Richard in his stead with her mother, her face creased in worry and remorse.

'I should never have let you come. I shall have a good word with the doctor after this and tell him that it was much too soon and that...'

The words rattled on, but Sephora had ceased to listen. She was safe again, she knew it.

Hardly a drowning. More a case of getting wet, I think.

She suddenly knew that Francis St Cartmail would never have let her drown, not in a million years. He would have jumped in and saved her had the depth of the water been ten feet or twenty. He would have dragged her across a current many times more dangerous or a river fifty times as wide if he had had to.

Because he could.

Because she believed that he could, this enigmatic and unusual earl with his wide shoulders and steel-strong arms.

The relief of it was so startling she could barely breathe. She smiled at the thought. Breath was the one thing she did have now here in the Hadleighs' ballroom under thirty or more elegant chandeliers and an orchestra of violinists beating out a waltz.

She was alive and well. The spark inside her had not been quenched entirely and was at this very moment bursting into a tiny flaring flame of revival.

She could not believe it.

Francis St Cartmail's smile was beautiful and the cabochon ring on his finger was exactly as she remembered it. His voice was deep and kind and his eyes were hazel, like the leaves fallen in a forest after a particularly cold autumn, all of the shades of ruin.

And people watched him, carefully, uncertainly, the wave of faces following him holding both fear and awe and another emotion, too. Wonderment, if she might name it as he stalked alone through a sea of colour and wearing only a deep swathe of unbroken black.

She hoped there was someone here he might find a shelter with, some friend who would throw off the *ton*'s interest with as much nonchalance as he did himself, but he was lost to sight and her mother and Richard observed her closely.

She did not want to go home now. She wished to stay here so that she might catch sight of the Earl of Douglas again and hope that another conversation might eventuate.

He'd smelt like soap and lemon and cleanness, the crisp odour of washed male having the effect of bringing Sephora quickly to her feet.

Her worried mother took her hand.

'Would you like some supper, my dear? Perhaps if you ate something you might feel better?'

Food was the last thing she truly wanted, but some sort of destination solved the problem of simply standing there dumbstruck, so she nodded.

After that most unusual exchange Francis went to join Gabriel Hughes leaning against a pillar on one side of the room. 'Was she what you expected?'

'You speak of Lady Sephora, I presume?'

'Cat and mouse does not suit you, Francis. I saw you talking to her. What did you think?'

'She is smaller than I remember her and paler. She is also frightened.'

'Of what?'

'I think she was sure she was going to drown and has suffered since for it. She thanked me for saving her.'

'And that's all that she said?'

'Well, there was some silence, too.'

'The stunned silence of Perseus falling in love with the drowning Andromeda?' Gabriel's tone held a good deal of humour in it that Francis ignored.

'She fell off a bridge, for God's sake. She was not chained to a rock waiting to be devoured by sea monsters.'

'Still, one must feel a certain connection when a soul is saved. I would imagine something along the lines of the life debt in honour-bound cultures, so to speak.'

'A heavy price, if that's the case? I did not see such in the eyes of Sephora Connaught, though they are surprisingly blue.'

Gabriel nodded. 'And young men have written sonnets about those orbs. The number of her suitors is legendary, though she has turned each and every one of them down.'

'For the marquis?' He didn't want to ask the question, but found himself doing so.

'Winslow fancies himself as something of an example others should be copying in both dress and manner, I think. He is said to be somewhat pompous and arrogant in his dealings with people.'

'Well, he looks fairly harmless.' Glancing across the room to where the young lord stood, Francis saw that Sephora Connaught was tucked in beside him.

'Harmless but controlling. See how he positions himself at her elbow. Adelaide said that if I were to ever constantly hover like the Marquis of Winslow does, she would simply shove me in the ribs.'

'Perhaps Lady Sephora enjoys it?'

'I think she allows it because she has never known differently.'

Sephora Connaught's profile was caught against the light—a small turned-up nose, sculptured brow and cheekbones that were high. Her pallor was almost white.

'From all accounts Winslow congratulated himself quite heartily on his organisation at the riverside, but his bride-to-be does not look quite herself tonight. Perhaps she does not concur to the same opinion. Perhaps she wishes he had thrown caution to the wind and made the more solid gesture of self-sacrifice by jumping in after her.'

'Stop teasing, Gabe.' Adelaide swiped her husband's arm. 'It was a scary and dangerous situation and I am certain everyone tried to do their best. Even the marquis for all his pedantic and fussy ways.'

But Francis was not so sure. 'No, I think Gabe has the gist of him. Winslow sent me a card the next day. While he made an art form of thanking me for my help, he also implied that further correspondence with Lady Sephora would be most unwelcome. He did not want her bothered by any maudlin recount of the incident, he stated, and hoped I had put the whole nonsense behind me because he certainly had.'

'So you are now to be an inconsequential saviour?

A man to be barely thanked?' Gabriel looked like he wanted to go over and knock Allerly's head off his shoulders.

'Winslow's father is ill so perhaps that is weighing heavily upon him.' Adelaide frowned as she added this to the conversation. 'It is, however, hard to imagine what a woman like Sephora Connaught might see in such a man.'

'She grew up with him,' Gabriel said. 'Both families are friends with strong ties and all adhere to the expectations of old tradition, so I am sure the parents are more than pleased with their daughter's choice of husband.'

As they watched, Sephora's well-endowed mother, Lady Aldford, towed her away and he observed those around giving their greetings. What was it in the young woman that intrigued him? She was the *ton*'s favourite daughter, a woman who had managed to snag one of the loftiest catches of the Season without even a hint of criticism from anybody. People admired her. She was everything that was good and true and honest and she was beautiful along with it. Cursing, Francis turned away and was pleased when a passing footman offered around a new tray of drinks.

Chapter Four

An hour later Francis was standing by one of the
tall and opened windows at the less crowded end of
the room. He wished he could have gone outside to
enjoy a cheroot, but oft-times at other balls he had
been waylaid in the gardens by women wanting to
share more than a word with him. Tonight he did not
wish to chance it.

A hand on his arm had him turning and Sephora
Connaught stood beside him, a look of pleading on
her face and her voice low.

'I am glad to have this small fortune of finding
you alone, Lord Douglas. I have written you a letter, you see, which I should have given you before
when we spoke. The marquis let me know he had
sent a card with our thanks, but I wanted the same
chance myself.'

She bent to extract a paper from her reticule and
handed it over. 'Don't read it until you are home.
Promise me.'

With that she was gone, tagging on the back of a

group of giggling women walking past, her mother to the other side of the procession.

The older lady caught his glance at that moment and held it, steely anger overlying puzzlement. Tipping his head at her, Francis turned, the letter from her daughter held tightly in his hand.

Sephora hoped she had done the right thing by giving him her missive. Please God, do not let him show it to his friends so that they might all laugh at her, she prayed, as her mother's arm came through hers and Richard joined them.

She had not been able to leave Francis St Cartmail's bravery to the ministration of Richard's thanks. She owed him some sort of personal expression of her gratitude and her relief.

The fact that she hoped he might reply, however, made her squeeze her jaw together and grimace. It was the look in his eyes, she thought, that had convinced her to approach him, that and the blazing scar upon his cheek. He'd been hurt badly and she did not wish that for him. Even the scratches she had placed there herself were still visible.

Unfortunately she knew her mother had seen her speaking with the earl, but Elizabeth would say nothing of it within Richard's hearing distance. Maria was chattering away and laughing and Sephora was so very glad for her sister's joy in life. She wondered where her own joy had gone, but did not at that particular moment wish to dissect such a notion.

Over against the pillars on the other side of the

room the number of beautiful women around Francis St Cartmail seemed to have multiplied. She recognised Alice Bailey and Cate Haysom-Browne, two of the most fêted debutantes of this Season, and both were using their fans with the practised coquetry of females who knew their worth.

'Have you enjoyed the night, Sephy?' Her father was beside them now and his pet name for her made her smile.

'I have, Papa.'

'Then it is good to see you happy after your awful fright.'

Just a fright now? She frowned at his terminology, thinking her parents had no idea of the true state of her mind.

'The marquis has decided to stay on for a while, but we thought to head for home. Richard has people to connect with, I suppose, now that his father is sick.'

'You saw the duke a few days ago. How does he fare?'

'Not so well, I am afraid. He and your Aunt Josephine are retiring to the country. I hope that he will at least get to experience the occasion of his only son's wedding in November before...'

He stopped at that and a constricting guilt of worry tightened about Sephora's throat. Uncle Jeffrey was a good man and he had only ever been kind to her, but she did not wish to shift her nuptials to Richard forward six months so that his father might live to see it. The very thought made her feel ill.

It was as if she stood on a threshold of change and to cross over it meant that she would never ever be able to come back. She was also unreasonably pleased that Richard would not be accompanying them homewards in the carriage this evening. Such a thought gave her cause to hesitate, but she could not explore the relief here in the glittering ballrooms of the *ton*.

Her mother was watching her closely and further afield she saw the wife of Lord Wesley, Adelaide Hughes, looking across at her with interest.

The cards of her life were changing, all stacked up in random piles, the joker here, the king of hearts there. A twist of fate and her hand might be completely different from the one that she had held on to so tightly and for so very many years.

The water beneath the Thames had set her free perhaps, with its sudden danger and its instant jeopardy. Always before this her life had flowed on a gentle certain course, barely a ripple, hardly a wave.

She was glad she had given Francis St Cartmail her letter, glad that she had mustered up the courage and seized the chance to do something so very out of character.

The Connaught wraps were found by the footman in the elegant entrance hall of the Hadleigh town house and moments later they were on their way home.

Francis poured himself a drink and opened the windows to one side of his library. Breathing in, he shut the door and reached for the pocket inside his jacket before sitting down behind his wide oaken desk.

The parchment was unmarked and sealed with a dab of red wax. There was no design embossed into it and no ribbons either. He brought the paper to his nose. The faint smell of some flower was there, but Sephora Connaught had not perfumed her letter in any way. It was as if the sheet of paper had simply caught the fragrance she wore and bore it to him.

He smiled at such fancy and at his deliberate slowness in opening it. Breaking the seal, he let the sheet of crisp paper unfold before him.

Francis St Cartmail...

Her written hand was small and neat, but she had made her 's' longer in the tail than was normal so that they sat in long curls of elegance upon the page.

His entire name, too, without any title. A choice between too formal and too informal, he imagined, and read on.

> *I should like to thank you most sincerely for rescuing me from the river water. It was deep and cold and my clothes were very heavy. I should have learned to swim, I think, and then I could have at least tried to rescue myself. As it was, I was trapped by fear and panic.*
>
> *This is mostly why I have written. I scratched you badly, I was told, on your cheek. My sister, Maria, made a point of relating to me the dam-*

*age I had inflicted upon your person and I am
certain the Marquis of Winslow would not have
made it his duty to apologise for such a harm.*

It is my guilt.

*I think that this rescue was not easy for you
either, for Maria said you looked most ill on
exiting the water. I hope you have recovered.
I hope it was not because I took the very last
of your breath.*

*I also hope I might meet you again to give
you this letter and that you will see in every
word my sincere and utter gratitude.*

Yours very thankfully,

Sephora Frances Connaught

Francis smiled at the inclusion of their shared
name in the signature as he laid his finger over the
word. He could not remember ever receiving a thank-
you letter from anyone before and he liked to imagine
her penning this note, each letter carefully placed on
the page. Precise and feminine.

Did she know anything at all about him? Did she
understand what others said of him with the persistent
rumours of a past he could not be proud of?

Leaning forward, he smoothed out the sheet and
read it again before folding it up and putting it back
in his pocket, careful to anchor it in with the flap of
the fabric's opening. A commotion outside the room
had him listening. It was late, past midnight and he
could not understand who might arrive at his doorstep at this hour.

When the door flew open and a dishevelled and very angry young girl stood on the other side of it he knew exactly who she was.

'Let me go.' She pulled her arm away from the aged lawyer and stood there, breathing loudly.

'Miss Anna Sherborne, I presume.'

Eyes the exact colour of his own flashed angrily, reminding Francis so forcibly of the Douglas mannerisms and temper he was speechless. Ignatius Wiggins stepped out from behind her.

'I am sorry to be calling on you so late, my lord, but our carriage threw a wheel and it took an age to have it repaired. This is my final duty to Mr Clive Sherborne, Lord Douglas. On the morrow I leave for the north of England and my own kin in York and I will not be back to London. Miss Sherborne needs a home and a hearth. I hope you shall give her one as she has been summarily tossed out from her last abode with the parish minister.'

With that he left.

Francis gestured to the child to come further into the room and as she did so the light found her. She was small and very dark. He had not expected that, for both the mother and his uncle were fair.

She did not speak. She merely watched him, anger on her thin face and something else he could not quite determine. Shock, perhaps, at being so abandoned.

'I am the Earl of Douglas.'

'I know who you are. He told me, sir.' Her voice was strangely inflected, a lilt across the last word.

Removing the signet ring from his finger, he

placed it on the table between them. 'Do you know this crest, Miss Sherborne?'

He saw her glance take in the bauble.

'It has come to my notice that you have a locket wrought in gold with the same design embellished upon it. It was sent to you after you left the house of your father as a baby according to the papers I have been given.'

Now all he saw was confusion and the want to run and with care he replaced the signet ring on his finger and took in a breath.

'You are the illegitimate daughter of the fourth Earl of Douglas, who was my uncle. Your mother was his…mistress for a brief time and you were the result.' Francis wondered if he should have been so explicit, but surely a girl brought up in the sort of household the lawyer had taken pains in describing would not be prudish. Besides, it had all been written in black and white.

'My mother did not stay around much. She had other friends and I was often just a nuisance. She never spoke of any earl.'

An arm came to rest upon a high-backed wing chair. Every nail was bitten and dirty and there was a healing injury on her middle finger.

'Well, I promise here you will be well cared for. You have my word of honour as your cousin upon it. I will never ask you to leave.'

The shock that crossed her face told him she hadn't had many moments of such faith in her young life and she was reeling hard in panic.

'A word of honour don't mean much where I come from, sir. Anyone can say anything and they do.'

'Well, Anna, in this house one's word means something. Remember that.'

When Mrs Wilson bustled into the room on his instructions a few moments later he asked that the girl be fed, bathed and put to bed, for even as he spoke he saw that Anna Sherborne was about to fall over with tiredness. If his housekeeper looked surprised by the turn of events she did not show it, merely taking the unexpected and bedraggled guest by the arm and leading her off towards the kitchens.

'Come, dearie, we will find you something to eat for you have the look of the starved about you, mark my words, and in this house we cannot have that.'

When they were gone Francis's hands moved to the tightening stock about his throat as he walked to stand beside the windows. He needed air and open spaces for already his breath was shortening.

In the matter of a few days his whole life seemed to be changing and reforming into something barely recognisable.

First, he seemed to have won the eternal gratitude of the 'angel of the *ton*' and now he was guardian to a child who gave all the impression of being 'the spawn of the devil'.

Tomorrow he would need to find out more of Anna Sherborne's story and try to piece together the truth about Clive Sherborne's death.

But for now he finished his large glass of brandy and his fingers reached into the bottom pocket to feel for his letter. Pulling it out and straightening the paper, he began to read it yet again.

Sephora knew Francis St Cartmail would not write back. It had been days since the Hadleighs' ball and she understood the difficulties in receiving a letter as an unmarried woman. Still, part of her hoped the earl might have done so clandestinely via a maid. But nothing had come.

Maria had insisted that they walk after lunch and although Sephora hadn't wanted to come this way she found herself on a path by the Thames, her sister's arm firmly entwined in her own.

'You look peaky, Sephora, and Mama is worried that you might never be right again. She has asked me to talk to you about the Earl of Douglas, for she thinks you might hold a penchant for him. She is certain that you gave him something the other night at the ball and I tried to tell her of course she is mistaken, but...'

'I did.'

Maria's words ground to a halt. 'Oh.'

'It was a letter. I wrote to him to say thank you... for saving me...for giving me breath...and to also say sorry for scratching his cheek so badly. The marks were inflamed and it was all my fault.' Stopping the babble, she simply took in a breath. 'I am glad I wrote.'

'And Douglas has replied?'

Sephora shook her head hard and hated the tears that pooled at the back of her eyes. 'No. I had been hoping he might, but, no.'

'Does Richard know about any of this?'

'That I sent a letter? Certainly not. He is…' She stopped.

'Possessive.'

'Yes.'

'How would Mama have known of it, then?'

'She saw me speaking with him at the ball.'

'You conversed with the Earl of Douglas? What did he say?'

'He implied that he would not have let me drown and that it was only a small accident. I believed him.'

'My God. He is…a hero. Like Orpheus trying to lead his beloved Eurydice back from death. The Underworld is exactly the same metaphor for the water and both rescues were completed with such risk…'

'Stop it, Maria, and anyway Orpheus failed in his quest.'

Her sister's laughter was worrying. 'When Richard holds your hand do you hear music, Sephora? Do you feel warmth or lust or desire?'

'To do what?'

'You don't?' Her whisper held a tone of sheer horror. 'And yet still you would consider marrying him? My God. You would throw your life away on nothing? Well, I shall not, Sephy. When I marry it shall be only for love. I swear it.'

Lust. Desire. Love. What pathway had Maria taken that she herself had missed? Where had her younger sister found these ideas that were so very…evocative?

'I shall marry a man who would risk his life for me, a man who is brave and good and true. Money shall be nothing to me, or reputation. I shall make up my own mind without anybody telling me otherwise.'

'There are stories about St Cartmail that are hardly salubrious, Maria.' Sephora hated the censure she could hear in her words, but made herself carry on. 'A good marriage needs a solid basis of friendship and trust. Like Mama and Papa.'

'They barely talk to each other any more. Surely you have noticed that.'

'Well, perhaps not lately, but...' She made herself stop. Further along the river three men were walking towards them, three handsome men and one taller than the rest.

Lords Douglas, Montcliffe and Wesley, Francis St Cartmail's hair jet black against the light of day. He had not seen them yet standing against the sun and she debated whether to stay or to flee.

All Sephora felt was sick, caught here between truth and falsity, skewered in the teeth of both hope and horror. She did not want this suddenness. She liked things orderly and controlled. This was all so wildly unexpected and so very worrying, but it was too late now to do anything other than brave out the encounter.

He hadn't written back. Would she see the distaste he felt for her upon his face?

'Smile, for God's sake.' Her sister's hard whisper broke through fright and she did, pinning a ludicrous grin across her grinding teeth and beating heart.

'Ladies.' It was the Earl of Wesley who spoke first, the urbane smoothness of his words propping up all the pieces that were scattering. Sephora regathered her logic and straightened.

'Lord Wesley.' Her voice. Normal. She did not look at the Earl of Douglas. Not even once, but she felt him there, strong and solid.

'It is only by good chance that we wandered this way.' Gabriel Hughes looked smug as he said this. 'Montcliffe wished to have a view of the river.'

Aunt Susan, her father's sister, had caught them up by now, arriving from a good ten yards back with her maid and a severe countenance. She gave the impression of a mother goose about to do battle, but also sensing the high standing of its opponents.

Daniel Wylde, the Earl of Montcliffe, unexpectedly took her aunt's hand into his own and led her off to the side a little. Wesley seemed most intent on asking her sister questions about the weather of late, a topic she was certain he held no abiding interest in, which left her alone with Francis St Cartmail.

'I must compliment you on your letter, Lady Sephora. I have seldom been thanked with such profuse gratitude.'

His patronage made her prickly given he had not written back. 'Well, my lord, I have never been rescued with such valour and gallantry.'

'A stellar state of affairs then for us both, such a mutual admiration.' He smiled and the mirth touched the hazel in his eyes, lightening the darkness.

At his jesting, Sephora blushed a bright red, the colour sweeping into her cheeks and down onto her neck where no doubt it clashed violently with the pastel pink of her day dress.

She had always been so certain in every social situation, so very good at small talk and mindless repartee. For the four years since her arrival in society she had been measured and polite and self-effacing. She had never uttered a wrong word or a hurtful reply to anyone before. She had been careful and godly and good. But not today. Today some other part of her long hidden surfaced.

'Are you teasing me, my lord? Because if you are I should like to say the incident for me was beyond frightening. I thought I should not survive it, you see, and although I waited and hoped for a reply you failed to send one.'

Oh, my goodness, why had she blurted that out? She could even hear a note of pleading in her tone.

'I am certain your mother would not approve of any correspondence or indeed the—'

He stopped and she imagined it was Richard's name he was about to utter, but the conversation of the others came back to encroach upon theirs. Aunt Susan was giving her goodbyes and, seeing such intent, St Cartmail did the same, walking on amongst the greenery without looking back.

'Well, I have to say that was a lovely surprise, would you not agree, girls. I knew Lord Montcliffe as a young boy, you understand, as his mother and I were good friends, God bless her soul. I thought he may not have remembered me, but...well.' She smiled. 'He certainly seemed to.'

Maria squeezed Sephora's hand and they dropped back from the company of their aunt and her maid as soon as they were able.

'St Cartmail made you blush in a spectacular way...'

'Shh. Do not say a thing to Mama about this, Maria, or about my talking to the Earl of Douglas.'

'A bit late for that I think, sister dear. Aunt Susan will probably self-combust with the news the moment we reach home.'

'But if Mama asks you...'

'I will say we met their party purely by chance and enjoyed a quick and formal greeting.' Her eyes glanced down. 'Richard has not replaced your lost ring?'

Sephora shook her head and closed her hand across the lack of it, glad that her intended had not as yet noticed it missing. Something stopped her from simply marching into Rundell's and seeking a replacement herself for she had a good deal of personal money at her own disposal. But she hadn't. She had not wanted to feel the ring there with its physical promise of forever winding about her finger. The troth of being bound to a man whose anger seemed to be rising monthly and who seemed more and more demanding of setting an earlier date for their wedding was also disturbing. The only true emotions she felt now for her big day were harried and scrambled. She was glad it was still so far away.

Richard was waiting for her when they arrived home, his smile giving Sephora more than a frisson of guilt. He looked tired today, heavy shadows beneath both eyes and the lines on each side of his mouth marked.

'I had hoped to walk with you, my angel, but was held up.' The endearment she had once liked now only sounded foolish and feeble and she had to stop herself pulling away as he took her hand in his and brought it to his lips. 'But I must say the exercise seems to have brought colour to your cheeks and you are looking even more beautiful than you usually do. I hardly deserve such fairness.'

Maria's laugh was not kind and Sephora was glad when her sister excused herself and disappeared upstairs.

Richard observed her departure. 'Maria is often morose, I fear, and I am glad you hold none of her countenance. I cannot even imagine how she will find a husband who could abide such dourness.'

The laughing, teasing truth of her sister came fully to mind as Sephora pulled away. Dour and morose were the very last words she would have used to describe Maria.

She was also aware of some dull and nagging pain that had settled in her chest, a heaviness that held her frozen. Even with a glance Francis St Cartmail could bring the blood to her skin, an energy bolt of feeling and frightening possibility that infused every piece of her body with a response. Richard had kissed her hand and all she had wished to do was to be free of him, to follow her sister upstairs and think about her meeting today with the Earl of Douglas in all its minute detail.

But the wedding preparations for their November celebration were going ahead. She even had the first fitting for her gown scheduled in at the end of the following month.

Trapped and breathless. The thought did come that she could simply run away and not have to face it. She was almost twenty-three, hardly a young girl, and wealthy in her own right, for her grandmother had bequeathed her a prosperous estate in the north as well as leaving her a generous cash settlement. The thought of just disappearing held a beguiling promise, but Richard was speaking again and she made herself listen.

'My father has asked that I bring you to visit him. He has stayed in town for a few days seeing a doctor. If it suited you, we could go now for I have a meeting in the mid-afternoon that I need to attend.'

She could hardly refuse to visit a man who had expressly asked for her company and so gesturing to her aunt that they would again be going out, she followed Richard to the waiting carriage, glad when Susan made no argument about accompanying them as chaperone.

Fifteen minutes later she sat with the Duke of Winbury in the sunny downstairs chamber of the ducal town house. He looked a little worse than last time she had seen him, more lethargic and less comfortable. There was a tinge to his skin, too, that worried

Sephora and she was glad that her aunt and Richard had repaired to the other end of the sitting room, leaving them a little time alone. She had always liked Richard's father and perhaps in truth that was a small part of why she had agreed to marry his son in the first place.

He took her hand and his skin was cold.

'You look sad, my dear, and you have been so for a while now. Is everything all right in your world?'

'It is, Uncle Jeffrey.' She had called him such ever since she could remember, her parents and Richard's the very best of friends. 'I had a walk in the early afternoon with Maria and then arrived back home to find Richard at our doorstep delivering your message.'

'He is a busy man, is he not, with his politics and his desire to make a difference? Too busy to walk with you in the sunshine, perhaps? Too busy to smell the flowers and look up into the sky?' He smiled at her surprise. 'When illness strikes and you are suddenly confronted with the notion that the years you thought you had are no longer quite so lengthy, there is a propensity to look back and wonder.'

'Wonder?'

'Wonder if you should have lived more fully, made braver choices, taken risks.'

His voice was weakening with the effort of such dialogue and he stopped for a moment to simply breathe. 'Once I used to think the right path lay in work and social endeavour, too, just as Richard does. But now I wish I had seen the Americas and sailed the oceans. I would have liked to have stood on the bow of a sailing ship, the breeze of foreign lands blowing in my face, heard other languages, eaten different foods.'

Sephora's fingers tightened around Jeffrey's. It was as if this conversation lay on two levels, the spoken edge of truth hiding beneath each particular word. She did not want to be one day wishing her life had been other than what it was and yet here already she was considering other pathways, different turnings.

Could Richard's father feel this? Was he warning her? Uncle Jeffrey had asked for a moment alone and this was something he had not done before.

'You are a good girl, Sephora, a girl of honour, a girl any man would be proud to call his daughter. But...' At this he leaned forward and she did, too. 'Make certain you get what you need in life. Goodness should not mean missing out on the passion of it all.'

A coughing fit took him then and a servant on the far side of the room hurried forward to deal with his panic. Richard also came towards them, pulling back a little as if he did not wish for the reminder of sickness or for the messiness of it. He did not venture further forward, but waited for her to rise and come to him.

'I think we should go, Sephora.' He made a point of drawing his fob watch out and looking at the time. A busy man and important.

'Of course.'

Going back to Jeffrey, she explained their need

to depart whilst Richard stayed at the doorway impatient to be gone. Her husband-to-be took her hand as she came up to him and placed her fingers firmly across his arm.

Mine.

The word came hollow and cold, an echo of uncertainty blooming even as she acquiesced and allowed him to lead her out.

Sephora dreamed that night of the water. She felt it around her face, the coldness and the dark, sinking and letting go.

In this dream, though, she did not panic. In this dream she could breathe in liquids like a fish and simply watch the beauty of the below, the colours, the shapes, the silence and the escape. Her hands did not close over her face and Francis St Cartmail did not dive in from above and give her the air of life, his tightly bound lips across her own.

No, in this dream she simply was. Dying, being, living, it was all the same. She felt the shift of caring like a scorching iron running across bare skin, changing all that was before to what it was now. And Uncle Jeffrey was there, too, beside her, sinking, smiling as he lifted his face to a breeze inside the water. Foreign lands and different shores.

Nothing made sense and yet all of it did. Permission to live did not only come from another saving your life, it also came from within, from a place that was hope and hers.

She woke with tears on her face and got out of bed

to stand by the window and watch a waning moon. Once a long time ago she had often sat observing the stars and the heavens, but that was just another thing that had fallen by the wayside.

Once she had written a lot, too, poems, stories and plays, and it was only as she got older and Richard had laughed at her paltry attempts that she had stopped. She had not only stopped, but she had thrown them all away, those early heartfelt lines, and here at this moment she felt the loss keenly.

When had life begun to frighten her? When had she become the woman she was? The one who allowed Richard to make all the decisions and bided by all his wants and needs? He was a marquis now, but his father was ill. How much worse would it be when he became the Duke of Winbury?

She wiped away the tears that fell down across her cheeks because the thought of being his duchess made her only want to cry.

She felt vulnerable with such a loss of identity and at a quandary as to how to change it. If she talked to him of her feelings, what would she say? Even to get the words making sense would be difficult and he was so very good at laughing at the insecurities of others.

She was also more frightened of him than she had ever been, frightened of his overbearingness and his lack of compassion. Even with his father today he had been distracted, impatient even, and she had seen a look of complete indifference as Jeffrey had coughed and struggled for breath.

Her touchstones were moving, becoming fragmented. She no longer believed in herself or in Richard and the thought of marrying him no longer held the sense of wonder it once had. But still, was it her near-drowning that had brought things so dreadfully into focus, the want for a perfection that was as unreal as it was impossible?

She rubbed at the bare skin on the third finger of her left hand and prayed to God for an answer.

Francis spent the next few days going through every file his uncle had kept on the Sherborne family and there were many. He'd had them brought down from the attic, the dusty tomes holding much in the way of background on both Clive Sherborne and his unfaithful wife. There was little information on the child, however, a fact that Francis found surprising.

Anna Sherborne herself was languishing against the stairwell as he walked up to instruct his men which new boxes he wanted brought down. Her hair had been cut, he noticed, bluntly and with little expertise. It hung in ill-shorn lengths about her face.

'Did Mrs Wilson cut your hair?'

'No.' The word was almost spat out. 'Why would she?'

'You did it yourself, then?' His cousin sported tresses a good twelve inches shorter than she had done yesterday and her expression was guarded.

An unprepossessing child, angry and diffident. He sat himself down on the step at her level and looked at her directly, the thought suddenly occurring to him that he might find out a lot more of Clive Sherborne's life from questioning her than he ever could from the yellowing paper in boxes.

'Was Clive a good father to you, Anna?'

Uncertainly the girl nodded and without realising it Francis let out his breath.

'Better than my mother at least. He was there often. At home, I mean, and he took me with him most places.'

'Did you have other brothers or sisters?'

'No.'

'Aunts. Uncles. Grandparents.'

'No.'

'Did Clive drink?'

She stiffened and stepped back. 'Why do you ask that?'

'Because he died in a warehouse full of brandy.'

One ripe expletive and she was gone, the thin nothingness of her disappearing around the corner of the dim corridor. But Francis had seen something of tragedy in her eyes before she could hide it, a memory he thought, a recollection so terrible it had lightened the already pale colour of her cheeks.

He took me with him most places. God, could the man have taken her there to the warehouse and to his appointment with death? Had she seen his killer? Had she seen the only man she knew as a father die? He shook his head and swore again roundly. At his uncle and at her mother. At the unfairness of the hovel Anna had been brought up in, at the loneliness and the squalor. She was angry, belligerent and difficult because in all her life it seemed no one except the hapless Clive Sherborne had taken the time to get to know her, to look after her. And now she was abandoned again into a place where she felt no belonging, no sense of safety, no security.

She'd cut her hair as a statement. *No one can love me. I am uncherished and unwanted.* His hands fisted in his lap as he swallowed away fury.

Well, he would see about that. Indeed, he would.

Chapter Five

This outing to Kew had been a mistake, Sephora thought a few days later as she walked with Richard, his second cousin Terence and his wife through the greened pathways of the gardens.

'Are you quite recovered from your dreadful accident? It was the very talk of the town.' Sally Cummings asked this in a quiet tone, her eyes full of curiosity.

'I am, thank you.' She didn't particularly want to discuss further what had happened to her at the river as she did not fully understand it yet herself and so was not at all pleased when Richard joined in the conversation.

'Sephora was left with only a small wound on her leg after all the fuss and that is quite cleared up now.' He tightened his grip on her arm. 'We were lucky it was not worse.'

She smiled tightly at this assessment of her health. Richard truly believed in the minimal effects the near drowning had left her with, but her hands still trembled when she held them unsupported and she had not slept properly for a full night since the fall.

Shaking away her irritation, she tried to look non-plussed. Richard had been most attentive on the drive here today, tucking a blanket around her legs and telling her how lovely she looked in her light blue gown. She knew this destination was not one he would have chosen on his own account and for that, too, she was grateful. It was Terence Cummings who had suggested the journey and she had assented readily because plants calmed her, the large expansive swathe of endless greens settling the air around her in a way the city never did.

Sally Cummings was usually quite a silent woman, but today she was chattier. 'You look happy here, Sephora. I heard Terence say the marquis was hoping that after your wedding in November you might venture to Scotland for a short while. The Highlands are renowned for their wonderful fauna and flora.'

'Scotland?' Sephora had not heard this mentioned before and turned to her husband-to-be. 'You thought to go there?'

Richard shrugged. 'Well, we cannot travel to Paris with all the problems in France at the moment and Italy is just too far away. I doubt I could spare so much time either, for there are things here I need to keep my fingers on, so to speak.'

'Of course.' The words were ripped from her disappointment. Just another plan that differed from what they had once discussed.

The older woman took her arm and tucked it into

hers. 'Terence changes his mind all the time, yet if I do so even once he is most unhappy with me. It is the way of all men, I suppose, their need to be in charge of a relationship and the leader in the home. My father and uncle were both the same. At least you have known Winslow forever and that must be most comforting. A shared history, so to speak.'

Sephora was not sure comforting was the correct word to use at all as the number of years they had known each other wound around inside.

Richard was two years and three days older than she was. For much of that time they had celebrated their birthdays together, their parents making a point of adding two candles on the cake after she had blown hers out, so that he could have his own special occasion. A family joke with all the small traditions observed to consolidate a union and protect the considerable property of two important families whose land marched along shared borders.

She saw the tiny scar under Richard's chin where he had fallen from a tree when he was ten and the larger one on his small finger when glass had almost cut through the tendon at sixteen as he'd run from her in a game of hide-and-seek.

Memories. Once she had cherished them. How had that changed? Now when he was with her Richard often seemed like a man who had forgotten others had opinions that were also valuable and worthy. Sometimes, she thought, he barely even bothered any more with the pretence of listening to what she had to say.

Sally's voice came again through her musings.

'You are not wearing that beautiful ring Winslow gave you, I had noticed. Is it being cleaned?'

'She lost it in the river.' Richard answered, this time surprising Sephora, for she did not think he had noticed at all. 'That actually was the worst loss of the whole fiasco at the Thames. It was an expensive ring and now the fish are swimming with it.'

He laughed at his joke and so did the others, yet all Sephora could think of were his words.

'That actually was the worst loss of the whole fiasco...'

If they had been alone she might have said something, might have tried to make him understand how hurtful a comment like that was to her. But with Terence and Sally standing next to them there was no opportunity to question him and so she left it altogether, gathering her breath and looking around at the beauty of the trees in the gardens.

Shouting from behind had them all turning and a moment later a group of men came into view.

'Isn't that the Earl of Douglas?' Terence Cummings queried. 'What the hell is he up to?'

As he said this a punch was thrown. It was so far away Sephora could not see whether it was Francis St Cartmail who threw the first punch or one of the others, but then without warning the whole situation escalated into a full-blown fight, one man being laid into by the others.

'Should you help him, do you think?' Sally Cummings asked this of both men, but Richard shook his head.

'Douglas no doubt has had a lot of practice in such things. Let's see how he does.'

Terence Cummings nodded his agreement.

Sephora could now see Francis St Cartmail more plainly and although he was one against three it didn't take long for the others to begin to fall back.

Cummings was giving some sort of a running commentary, but she did not really listen. All she could comprehend was the hard knock of fists against faces, the sound of bone against bone and the shattering of flesh. It was not a fight as she had imagined them to be, not a boxing match or a ruled combat. No, this was more ferocious and untamed, the civilised world of the *ton* slipping back into a savagery of primitive masculinity. She could never in a million years have imagined Richard letting his emotions rule him in the way these men were.

Finally after a few moments those in the larger group broke away and turned to disappear into the trees from where they had come, leaving Francis St Cartmail alone to pick up his hat and sling his jacket across his shoulders. When he turned suddenly she saw the slick darkness of blood around his lips. With his long hair loose and the white linen of his shirt straining against the sinew and muscle beneath he looked…unmatched. His stance caught at her, his stillness magnified by a gathering wind and the moving leaves behind him, a man caught in time and danger, the white clouds scudding across a cerulean sky.

And then he was gone.

'Just another one of Douglas's many fights and

disputes, I suppose,' Terence Cummings drawled. 'The man is a complete and utter disgrace to his title and seems to enjoy flaunting his skills in violence at every possible pass. He needs to be taught a lesson.'

'Well, he did save Sephora the other day—' Sally Cummings began, but Richard cut her off.

'He's a competent swimmer and it was not far to the bank side. If one is proficient at something it does not make it such a risk.'

Terence's wife caught her glance at the retort and then looked away, the undercurrent of poor sportsmanship on the Marquis Winslow's behalf evident in her frown.

But Richard had moved on now, in an opposite direction to the one St Cartmail had taken and all the talk was of the pagoda and the possibility of walking up its interesting and unusual oriental shape.

'You would not be able to manage it at all, Sally. You will need to stay at the bottom and wait for us.' Terence gave these words and his cousin nodded.

'Sephora can wait with you,' Richard said. 'She has never been one for heights.'

The anger that Sephora had felt just below the surface suddenly boiled. 'I think I could manage that.' She watched as a group of ladies and gentlemen came out of the entrance at the bottom of the structure. Many of them were years older than she.

'But Sally will have nobody to stay with her if you come.' Richard gave this in a tone of quiet reprimand, no thought or mention of Terence staying with his wife.

'Well, I do not wish to be a nuisance…' Sally's words were worried. 'It's just I have a problem with breathlessness and I shouldn't wish to get only half-way up and not be able to manage the rest of it.'

'Indeed you should not, my dear, for that would be most disconcerting for all of us.' Terence patted her hand. 'Come, Richard, we shall tackle the thing with as much speed as we can muster and be back before you know it.'

And then they left, Sally Cummings's frown the only remnant left of the altercation.

'Terence has his own worries at the moment and so it will be most beneficial for him to take this exercise. Winslow has his sadness, too, with his father's ill health, I suppose.'

The day felt cooler as they walked around the base of the pagoda and through the many scattered trees that had been planted to enhance the vistas of the place. Sephora wondered whether the Earl of Douglas had left the gardens already and looked about to see if she could find any sign of him still being there, but of course there was none.

'I am sure Francis St Cartmail is long gone.'

Sephora had hoped that her interest was not so easily read.

'You are not married just yet. Surely you are able to still look at a man who is as unforgettably fine as Douglas most assuredly is.'

Without meaning to, Sephora laughed because Sally Cummings's statement was so unlike her more usual reticent uncertainty. As if reading her mind the other woman began to explain.

'I still have thoughts and a voice even though Terence would prefer me not to have. I am sorry to stop your ascent of the pagoda, but I needed a moment to relax again. My husband is not such comfortable company these days and I find my nerves become most frayed. I am taking a pill my doctor prescribed which should allow a marked improvement to my disposition, but so far I have just felt sadder.'

Like I do.

Sephora almost said this out loud, there in the blue of the day and the green of the park, there where Francis St Cartmail had fought with his fists and with a passion largely missing now from anything at all that she did.

Sally was six years older than she was and looked twice that number. Would this be her fate, too, in that many years again, walking here in Kew and finding any excuse at all to avail herself of half-an-hour's absence from a domineering spouse?

She was trapped somehow between expectation and her own inability to understand what it was she wanted. Richard was safe and familiar and if he was also dogmatic sometimes or overbearing, then were not all relationships based on some sense of compromise? What married couple had the perfect and flawless balance?

It could not be wise to throw away all that was known and familiar for a shot at some whimsical

fantasy threaded with danger and hope. Surely such
was the way to ruin.

Smiling, she turned to Sally Cummings and com-
mented on the beauty of the gardens and was glad
when the other began to describe a plant to one side
of the small pathway upon which they walked.

Chapter Six

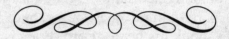

Francis visited the Wesleys the next morning with the express purpose of procuring a salve from Adelaide Hughes for his split lip, so he was glad to find both husband and wife in the front room of their town house.

'We were just speaking of you, Francis.' Gabriel made that observation as he placed *The Times* on the table before him. 'It seems as if you were in a fracas at Kew Gardens yesterday and the doyens of the *ton* are not well pleased.'

'Winslow's gossip, no doubt. I saw him there.'

'Who the hell waylaid you and why?'

'Men who felt jeopardised because I was asking questions about the illicit supply of liquor.'

'Something to do with Clive Sherborne's murder then, I am guessing?'

He nodded. He'd told Gabriel the story of Anna's guardianship and was glad that Gabriel had remembered, for it made things easier. 'His lawyer sent me a list of Clive Sherborne's enemies and it seems that they have taken up their old gripes against me. My ward is deathly frightened and I think she knows something of how Sherborne died, but is not saying.'

'My God. Are they likely to be back?'

Francis glanced across at Adelaide, who sat listening to this conversation with a heavy frown across her forehead. 'There is good money to be had in the handling of smuggled liquor. I thought I had been more than careful in my questioning, but...'

Gabriel shook his head. 'Lord, Francis, you are caught in the role of protector and getting crucified because of it and no way short of abandoning Anna to make it different. Your actions are the talk of the town and after the kerfuffle at Richmond you are becoming persona non grata to those mamas who may have thought you a good match for their daughters.'

'Thank goodness for that.' Francis took the tea that Adelaide had poured for him and smiled. He could not remember the last time he had drunk the stuff, though the taste was different from what he remembered it to be like as he took a sip.

'It's a new brew I have been experimenting with. The valerian root helps with anxiety and insomnia.'

'A medicine?'

'Tea began as that, Francis, but along the way it changed into what it is today. Anxiety comes from the absence of routine and peace in your life. You need a reason to settle down.'

He knew what they were going to say next and pushed the cup and saucer away from him as Gabriel spoke.

'We were saying that we ought to have an afternoon tea here. We thought perhaps Lady Sephora Connaught should be the first on that list.'

Francis felt the shock of her name, but stayed perfectly still. She'd been at Kew Gardens yesterday and he had seen the fright in every line of her body. He wished he had not. 'I think she is taken.'

'But not yet married.' Adelaide joined in the conversation now. 'Her lady's maid is my maid's sister and she is not at all certain the marquis is the one her mistress should be tying her hand to. She says that even before her near drowning Lady Sephora had been restless and sad. There was talk, too, of a letter in her possession with your name upon it.'

'Lady Sephora wrote to thank me. There is hardly any scandal in that.'

'Perhaps she is a lot more than just grateful.'

'What are you saying, Adelaide?'

'All the things that you are not, Francis.'

He began to laugh. 'I have spoken to her for two minutes in total and have had a short correspondence from her once.'

'You have dragged her to the side of a swollen river, skin against skin, and from what Gabe has related to me given her the kiss of life whilst beneath the cold waters of the Thames. So I want to ask her to come to take tea with us this week. Would you like to join us, too? A small and select gathering.'

Adelaide watched him carefully as she asked this. 'I shall not be inviting the Marquis of Winslow, but I will invite Lady Sephora's sister. Lady Maria Connaught is an interesting young woman in her own right. Perhaps we might see if Mr Adam Stevenage could join our party as well for he is newly back from the Americas and I always found him intriguing.'

Gabriel brought his wife's fingers to his lips. 'I think you are in your element with matchmaking, Adelaide, though Francis here looks less than enamoured with the idea. Perhaps he should humour you, though, for it is my thought that such an endeavour lies akin to your medicine. Fix the body, fix the heart.' When they looked at each other and smiled, it seemed for a second that they'd forgotten they were in company. Francis envied them for that.

'It's my lip that I've ventured here to find some salve for, Gabe, not my heart.' The ensuing laughter wasn't comforting.

'Will you come, though, Francis? Please.' Gabriel's wife had a particular way of inveigling others to do her bidding and he was not immune to such persuasion.

'I'll be there.' His promise came quickly, but he wondered even as he said it if his choice was a wise one.

When he got home again he looked at the names he had listed that could have been implicated in Clive Sherborne's murder. He knew Anna was frightened of someone from her past and he needed to understand exactly who this enemy was so that he could protect her. Mr Wiggins's documents had made mention of a smuggling ring and that was where Francis had targeted his first questions, though it seemed every family in the village outside Hastings where the Sherbornes had lived were involved to some extent with the free-trade movement, and who could blame them.

The punitive taxes imposed by successive governments were becoming more and more onerous and the contraction of jobs on the Kentish weald had probably added its bit to the growing lack of legal employment in the area.

His finger wound its way down the surnames and occupations of those Wiggins had supplied him with. The parson, the quarryman, the local squire, the boatman, the butcher, the innkeeper. The list just kept on going.

In Kew Gardens his altercation had been with a father and his two sons who'd heard of his interest in identifying those involved at the London end of the supply chain. These three had purchased cut-price brandy and spirits on the side and were firmly of the opinion that anyone threatening their lucrative livelihood with exposure was to be scared away.

Well, at least they had the measure of him now and he knew that they had played no role in the death of Clive Sherborne for they hadn't recognised that name at all when he had asked them.

Still, it was a shame Lady Sephora Connaught had been there watching on, her pale blue dress stirring in the growing wind and a look on her face of pure and utter horror.

He smiled. Well, this was who he was, too, a man who would protect his own no matter what the consequences, an outsider, a lord who had never fitted in well to the narrow and confined world of the *ton*. It was best that she knew it.

Best that he did, too, with all these foolish notions of afternoon teas and refined polite conversation. He'd have to go to the occasion of Adelaide's because he had promised her he would, but after that...

He opened his drawer and pulled out the letter Sephora Connaught had written to him yet again. When he'd made certain that Anna was safe he would leave London and go north for his manufacturing businesses were calling out for more of his time and energy. Then he would repair to the Douglas family seat in Kent. He truly wondered if he would ever be back in town.

Sephora took an age to get ready for afternoon tea at the Wesleys, which was unlike her, changing this dress for that one and this hat for another. Her maid watched her with puzzlement as she finally stood in front of the full mirror in her room.

Usually she barely glanced at herself, but this morning she did, observing her shape and form with other eyes, hazel laughing ones, the gold in them pushed to the very edges of green and brown. The fight she had observed at Kew Gardens four days ago should have made her hesitant, should have underlined all the gossip that was whispered of the dangerous Earl of Douglas. But it had had the opposite effect entirely. It made her want to understand what drove him into such frenzy.

In the mirror the blue in her eyes caught the hue

in her gown and her hair had been curled into a series of fair cascading ringlets. A hat sat atop that, a
small jaunty shape that barely covered her crown.
She had dabbed an attar of violets on her wrists and
at her throat.

Please let the Earl of Douglas be there, a small
voice entreated. She knew Lord and Lady Wesley
and Francis St Cartmail were close friends and the
hope of some sort of private meeting came to mind, a
place where she might talk to the earl and understand
what this obsession she was beginning to feel for him
was about. It concerned her that she was thinking of
him so much. She had never been compulsive about
anything before and this new side of her personality
was worrying, given her promised troth to Richard.

Maria was coming with her today, a fact that her
sister was pleased about. 'I always wanted to see inside the Wesley town house, for they say it is one of
the most beautiful in all of London. I hope that there
are others attending who are not married, though.'

'Well, I am not married, Maria.'

'You nearly are. Unfortunately.'

Sephora had to laugh and it felt good to simply
enjoy the sound. She also harboured a good deal of
guilt given that her mirth was at Richard's expense,
but she swallowed that thought down and vowed to
enjoy the day. For once she was pleased to be free of
constraint and righteousness.

She would tell him, of course, that she had been
to the Wesley function without him, but if she did so
after the occasion it would allow her the freedom to

savour it first. Squeezing her fingers together, she was glad she did not wear Richard's ring and that it had been lost and never replaced.

Lost like a part of her had been. Her heart beat with a trip of apprehension as her sister accompanied her down the stairs and they walked outside to the waiting carriage.

The Wesley town house was as magnificent as Maria had heard it to be when they were shown in to a salon twenty minutes later.

The room was huge and decorated in a colour of yellow, which lightened it and gave it an airy otherworld feel, so unlike the darker and more sombre tones Sephora was used to. There were paintings on every wall and the furniture was of a French design, ornate and gilded, cushions of flowered tapestry sitting atop a row of chairs. The curtains were of thick gold velvet and tied back with colourful braided tassels. To one end stood a group of people chatting, though all noise stopped as soon as their names were announced.

Francis St Cartmail was standing by an opened French doorway talking with Lord Montcliffe and his wife. She caught his glance as soon as she entered, quick and covert, before it moved away. Almost angry.

Lady Wesley had taken her arm as she introduced them to everybody in the room. The only person she did not recognise was a young man with long brown hair who stood slightly apart. Mr Adam Stevenage.

The name was somewhat familiar and Maria moved towards him like a magnet.

And then the Earl of Douglas was beside her, a good foot taller and much bigger in every way than Sephora remembered him to be.

'Lady Sephora.'

'Lord Douglas.'

Today his eyes in the light looked softer than they had ever before, though the brutal mark across his cheek did away with any prettiness at all and her scratches on the other side of his face were barely noticeable. She could glean no ill effects from the fight at Richmond save for puffiness on his lower lip.

'I had wondered if you would be here today. I know you to be a friend of the Wesleys, of course, so I imagined perhaps I might see you and…"

She made herself stop. Why had she blabbered that out at him and with such a dull repetitiveness?

Taking two drinks from a tray that a footman offered, he gave her one. 'Gabriel's idea of the libation at an afternoon tea is very different from his wife's, thank goodness.'

The tipple was strong and Sephora coughed slightly, thinking of Richard, who only ever wished her to drink non-alcoholic punch or lemonade.

'Wesley buys his wine from the Cognac region in France and this particular drop rarely results in any sort of a hangover. I can vouch for that.'

She smiled, liking the way the wine was warming her resolve and making their meeting easier. She was glad, too, when he stepped further out into the gardened courtyard, giving her space and distance from the others present as she followed him.

He was just so very beautiful here in the sunshine, so beautiful she imagined she could simply watch him forever. With a sudden worry she pushed her fingers against her temple where the beat of her heart was thumping.

This is where it could begin, she thought, the scandal, the gossip, the stigma, here in this little moment in the afternoon sun because she wanted to throw herself into Francis St Cartmail's arms and never let go.

A length of darkness had escaped from the leather he tied his hair with and lay in a long curl across his forehead. She could very easily understand his attraction to all those women of the *ton* who spoke of him in hushed whispers inflected with an underlying blend of avarice and fancy despite his wildness and his danger.

When his eyes settled on her own there was something in his expression that made her speak.

'How did your cheek get scarred, my lord?'

The ice in hazel glittered. 'War is dangerous.'

'And no one fixed it for you?'

'I was lost in the Cantabrians. The army of Moore had rolled on towards Corunna so I had to make my own way to Vigo and by then…' He left the rest unsaid, but he did not turn his damaged face away from the sunlight and she liked him for that.

'Well, I think it suits you.'

'Pardon?'

'The scar. People will take notice of a man who has been through such pain and lived.'

For a second she thought he flushed at her words, but then the distance returned.

'England is a soft and gentle land, Lady Sephora. It is my experience that anything reminding its people of a consuming chaos in a faraway foreign skirmish is to be avoided altogether. You are the first person ever to ask me of it directly.'

'Everybody has their secrets, Lord Douglas, and if some are more hidden than others it makes them no less painful.'

He laughed, a throaty and hearty sound that held an edge of disbelief. 'They call you the "angel of the *ton*". Do you have any idea as to what they say of me?'

Frowning, she nodded. Indeed, she had heard of all the things that were told of him. Wild. Ill disciplined. Unlawful. Barbaric. Dangerous.

'I stood trial in America for the killing of a man.'

The shock of his words was great. 'Did you? Kill him, I mean?'

'No. Not that time.' All humour was gone now and in its place was bare fury.

'Then I am glad for it.'

'Why?'

'I should not wish to be indebted to a murderer for the saving of my life.'

'And are you...indebted?'

'I am, my lord. When you came to me beneath the

waters through the cold and the dark I thought you were like a god.'

He shook his head, but she continued anyway, the need to tell him all of it and without anything held back so desperate.

'I'm to be married to a man who was also there on the bridge that day. The Marquis of Winslow. I am certain you know of him. He was the one on the riverbank who took me from you when you brought me to safety across the mud.' She waited till he nodded. 'But he did not jump in to save me. He did not risk his life for mine and I think...I think he was s-supposed to h-have.'

Horror marked her words, the truth of what she said to him out here in the blueness of the day so real and naked and terrible.

He touched her then, his hand gentle across her own, as though reassuring her. But it did none of those things because in the shock of his touch other truths surfaced, big important truths that Sephora could no longer deny.

She felt changed and heightened and alive. She felt unconstrained and sensual and womanly. It was as if in the company of the disreputable Francis St Cartmail she was someone else entirely, the person she might have been had she not let fear and propriety rule her.

I think I could fall in love with you.

My God, had she just said that out aloud? The horror of such a possibility kept her rooted to the spot waiting for his mirth. When his expression did not change she felt a relief so great she imagined she might fall down, down into a crumpled heap at his feet, clinging to his fine and well-polished boots.

The arrival of her sister, though, took the attention from such a dreadful possibility, Maria's smiling and cheerful face so opposed to all that was transpiring here. Sephora was very glad when a warm arm threaded through her own.

He was making such a hash of this, but with Sephora Connaught half a foot away from him and her blue eyes pale and kind, all the things he had thought to say to her were gone from his head and he was left…reeling. She had not mentioned seeing him at the gardens and for that he was grateful, but his time alone with her was running out like sand through a glass, each grain precious and draining away.

Mr Adam Stevenage was drinking hard and Francis watched as the young man finished his next glass and came over towards him. The sister, Maria, looked stretched and tense as she gave Sephora her greeting.

He could usually read people easily, but Sephora Connaught held so many conflicting emotions upon her face and in her eyes, that in the end he could discern only a cloudy wariness.

When he had touched her a moment ago it was as if an electrical energy had been transferred between them, a jolt of such proportion he had seen her pupils dilate. He wondered if his had done the same.

He wanted to try it again. He wanted to take her

in his arms and feel the warmth of her lips again under his…

'Pardon?' Stevenage had asked a question directly of him and he had no idea as to what had been said.

'I just enquired, Lord Douglas, what you thought of the town in Georgia called Hutton's Landing?'

'Why would you wish to know this?' Francis answered quietly, a sense of alarm growing.

'My cousin was there, you see, last year. I hoped you might give me your account of the place.'

Could Adam Stevenage's question really be this naive? Could a man with his own clear demons of drink not have heard the slander that circulated still about his time at Hutton's Landing?

'I think, sir, it is a town to be avoided altogether.' Francis hated the anger in his voice and the flat tone of memory that slithered beneath. He hated, too, that Sephora Connaught had turned to observe him and was able to see exactly what it was that he had always hidden from others.

There was tightness at his throat and the need to gulp in large breaths full of air. His hands fisted at his sides and he couldn't stop the shaking that emanated from them.

'You asked me to tell you of the flowers here in the garden, my lord.' Sephora's voice came through the growing haze and when she shepherded him across the lawn to a small grove of shrubs and perennials he followed. Away from the others she spoke quietly.

'Can I find you help? Your friends perhaps…?'

'No.'

'Then humour me whilst I try to discern the names of these plants, my lord, for whilst I am no true gardener it might at least give you a moment or two to recover your wits.'

'Thank…you.'

He listened to her voice, soft and musical, describing the scientific classifications of the shrubs. Even he knew that a lavender bush did not quite look the same as the one she insisted it was, but she was most convincing in her feigned interest and teachings. Certainly Stevenage had given up on further conversation and gone inside as had the younger Connaught sister, leaving them alone again out at the far end of the lawn.

He felt better now, more in control. He could not believe that the panic had come on so quickly for it never had done that before.

God. She would think him teetering on the edge of madness and mental incapacity for he had also been like this on the bank of the river Thames.

He wanted to be sick.

'I was buried…in mud on the side of the Flint River in Hutton's Landing. Sometimes the memory of it comes back.'

He had barely told anyone of the experience and couldn't believe he was now telling her. Still he could not seem to stop. 'I got out, but my friend didn't survive it.'

And he'd been hauled up for his murder, the rope around his throat and mud caked in his mouth, the

hatred of the crowd of people who had gathered eas-
ily discerned. 'Hang him. Hang him. Hang him.'

'Do you think Adam Stevenage knows?'

This time his smile was more real. 'Yes.'

'Could he be dangerous...to you?'

Reason flooded back and he shook his head. He did not want Sephora Connaught pulled into his shadows. Out here with the light in her golden hair she did indeed give the impression of goodness and purity. The 'angel of the *ton*'. He was beginning to realise just how aptly she was named.

'Come, let us go inside.'

He was glad when she followed him in and even more glad when her sister crossed the room to stand beside her and garner her attention.

When Gabriel offered him a drink Francis took it.

'She is very beautiful, this small and pale Lady Connaught.'

'Yes.'

'And sensible, too. Are you feeling better?'

Looking up, he caught the concern in Gabriel's eyes. Gabriel had been a spy once and managed to see all that others thought hidden. 'She was trying to protect you out in the garden and in her fragility there is also strength. She does not wear Winslow's ring. I wonder why?'

'Stop.' The word came without hope for Francis knew exactly what it was Gabriel was doing and what he himself had thought to do. But it was all too dangerous and Sephora needed to be protected. He could not stay here. It was wrong and he did not wish to hurt her.

'Will you give Sephora Connaught my goodbye? And also my thanks to your wife?'

'Of course.'

'And inform Stevenage I will see him tomorrow at my town house. At one. Tell him to make certain he is not late.'

When Sephora turned around again the Earl of Douglas was gone. Part of her wanted to simply walk out of the house and follow him, but she shook that thought away and concentrated instead on what Adelaide Hughes was saying.

'When is your wedding to be held?'

'In November, Lady Wesley. In London,' she added and hoped no more on the subject would be said. But she was to be disappointed.

'It must be hard on you, waiting so patiently for a man you love with all your heart and soul.'

Sephora could not get the next words out no matter how hard she tried to. Marriage to Richard would not be the 'all heart and soul' sort, she thought to herself. It would be far more ordinary than that. She would not see oceans or walk on different lands. She would have babies and get old beside the first man who had ever kissed her and that had been done without the passion she had imagined should have been present. It was as much as she could in all honesty hope for. The thoughts she had had of Francis St

Cartmail earlier burned underneath her conscience and she shook them away with fervour.

Francis spent the afternoon in the alehouses along the banks of the Thames, drinking and listening and asking questions.

One man had heard the name of Clive Sherborne and he dredged up more as Francis offered him a few coins to jog his memory.

'He always had a young girl with him, his daughter, I think, but he used to administer a sharp slap on her cheek every time she annoyed him and in the end she rarely spoke. He was selling cheap brandy, if I recall rightly, but I was not in the market for any of it as my wife's the one who does the books and she's a devout churchgoer. Nothing below the board, you understand, nothing that can lead to any trouble.

'I do remember, though, Sherborne held two prices for his contraband and I wondered when I heard he'd been killed if it was that which had seen him off. When I did buy on the occasion, for myself so to speak and private like, I remember it was the girl who put the coin in her pouch after counting it out.'

A picture of his cousin was beginning to form. A child dragged into the seedy underworld of contraband and men who would have no qualms in killing her for the gold that she carried. And Sherborne had struck her time and time again when she'd irritated him. No wonder she stood back and away from others. No wonder she peered out at the world with eyes that had seen too much hatred and known too little love.

If she had seen the final hours of Clive Sherborne's life, had the one who had done away with him known that she would be there, too, her father's follower, the helper who dealt with the money and counted it out? Would he be wondering right now where she was and if the girl had seen him? Could she be in as much danger as Clive had been, the next mark to ensure eternal silence?

Cold wrath began to settle inside his chest. Anna was his family, his responsibility, and as her guardian he would never let her be hurt. He was crossing off names on lawyer Wiggins's list, but he was nowhere yet near the name of the one who had killed Clive Sherborne.

'Not for long,' he whispered into the semi-darkness as he walked along the cobbled street. 'One mistake and I will have you, you bastard, and you won't even know what hit you.'

Chapter Seven

'**W**as that not just the *most* wonderful afternoon Sephora?' Maria laid her head back against the seat of their carriage and sighed. 'Mr Adam Stevenage is the *most* interesting man I have ever met, though perhaps in truth your Lord Douglas is the *most* beautiful.'

'Hardly mine.' Sephora ground the words out and her sister laughed.

'Every man you have ever met has fallen completely in love with you. Why should he be any different? You only have to forget the boring Marquis of Winslow and want him instead. You used to be braver once. You used to take risks.'

It was true, all that Maria said, but she had become more and more isolated as the years had fled by, careful of this, worried by that, cautious of a temper that Richard was having more and more trouble hiding from her.

But to just let go of everything on a whim and for a man who had not said a word that was even vaguely intimate? Oh, granted, Douglas had smiled at her and taken her hand, but he had almost certainly taken the hands of many other women in his time and more. She remembered the kiss she had observed in the garden at a long-ago ball, Francis St Cartmail's fingers wound into the hair of the well-endowed woman who had pressed herself to him.

Other worries also surfaced. What was it he had replied when she had asked if he had killed a man? *'No, not that one.'* The connotation that there had been others he had done away with hung heavily on her thoughts.

Yet Richard no longer represented safety or protection and the sum of all the other parts of him did not amount any more to enough.

Enough?

Everything had changed. Her perception of him, her trust in him, her conviction and faith in the future with a husband who would have simply let her drown.

'You think too much, Sephora.' Maria was looking at her when she turned. 'You overimagine things. I can hear your brain going around and around from here. Why don't you just…feel and follow your heart?'

'Because people depend on me. Because Richard has been a friend since as long as I can remember and he would be hurt if…' She stopped, horrified by the confession she had very nearly given.

'If you broke off the engagement and told him the truth?'

'The truth?'

'That you fell out of love with him a long time ago, but are too kind to say so.'

'His father is dying...'

'And you are, too. Inside. Mama and Papa are just so pleased that you are marrying a man who may soon be a duke they fail to see your sadness. Today at the Wesleys you looked different. Francis St Cartmail makes you look happy again and if you cannot see the honesty in that, then...'

Her voice tailed off as she leaned forward, looking out of the window. 'The Winbury carriage is outside our place. Were you expecting Richard this afternoon?'

Sephora shook her head. Five thirty. Too early for him to be calling for the evening and she had supposed him to be busy in a meeting all day with his father's lawyer.

'But what is even more odd, Sephora, is that Mama is by the window watching out for us and she looks most upset.'

Through the glass Elizabeth Connaught was using a large kerchief to dab at her face and there were other shapes behind her. A quick burst of fear tore through worry. Was her father ill? Was Uncle Jeffrey worse?

A long time later Sephora would look back on this moment and realise that none of her concern had been for Richard himself; a telling omission, that, holding the portent of all that would come next.

But for now the footman opened the door of the carriage and they walked up the steps and into a house filled with the agony of grief.

Richard came towards her in the blue salon, his brown eyes reddened. 'Papa died an hour ago, my dearest.' His hand took hers as he said this and he squeezed it. 'All I can think of, Sephora, is that I am so glad you are here with me. Together we can overcome such sadness whereas alone it is something that I might not weather.' He almost sobbed out the final words.

He had loved his father and she had, too. The duke was a good man, a true man, a man who had been kind and honest and honourable. Tears of grief formed in her own eyes and fell unstopped and Richard simply placed his arms about her and brought her into his chest while pledging his love.

'We have each other, my love. We can survive this. I promise. Papa would have wanted that.'

Her parents, usually stalwarts for propriety, had both looked away, lost in their own sorrow, whilst Maria stood there wringing her hands.

'I am sure we can, Richard.' Sephora thought her words did not contain quite the emotion her groom-to-be wanted and needed to hear, but she simply could not dredge up more.

It was all so confusing. Here, in the heart of a great emotion that should have brought them closer, she could instead feel herself spinning away, like a top on the street, the string broken and all connection lost.

She also knew she could tell them none of it, Richard, her parents, Maria, not now with the dreadful news of Uncle Jeffrey's passing and all the associated protocols that would roll out over the next few days and weeks.

A ducal funeral.

She would have to be there for Richard. They would return to the Winbury country seat, no doubt, and she would have to stand beside him and act as a suitably loving and solicitous companion.

There was no other choice.

Richard's strong musky perfume only made her head ache.

'I shall not listen to what you say. I do not have to walk like this or talk like this if I do not want to and I shall most certainly not be wearing that.'

Francis listened to the shouts in the hallway from the safety of his library an hour later. His cousin's increasingly frequent temper and tantrums sat over his house like a great dark cloud, leaving him with no true idea as to how to deal with a moody, unhappy girl. As little, anyway, as the governess he had employed, he ruminated, thinking that something would have to change and quickly.

Mrs Celia Billinghurst had come highly recommended and she had the added advantage of being his late aunt's cousin. A distant relative admittedly, but still... She had all the credentials for a credible and skilled governess and yet her small charge was simply running rings about her. He should interfere and discipline Anna, but he found himself standing still until the argument dissipated.

The day had started badly and was ending worse and all he wanted to think about was the kindness of Sephora Connaught in the garden. He shook his head and stood, remembering the touch of her hand and the shape of her lips and the pale blue eyes watching him with the same shock of connection that he himself had felt.

She was to be married. She was the product of an upbringing in the *ton*. She was far too good for him, with her honour and honesty and kindness. It was this reasoning that had made him walk away from the Wesleys' town house today.

Tonight, though, there were other arguments that were more compelling. Never once had he felt so attracted to anyone—until now with the good and pale Lady Sephora Frances Connaught.

Why had he not met her before? She wasn't newly come to the *ton* and he had been back from the Americas for a good seven months already. Granted, society had held less and less appeal to him, but he had not caught sight of her at any of the balls he'd attended, he was certain of it. Their paths had just never crossed.

When he'd thrown himself off the bridge he'd not truly seen her either, just a flash of blue and a startled scream of shock. Her hat had flown from her head and rolled in the wind, a small and pale piece of wispy felt and netting that held her stamp upon it.

But now, he could not get her visage out of his mind or the feeling of her against his skin. Hell. He opened the window above him wider. Deciding even that wasn't enough, he grabbed his jacket and hat and strode off into the evening.

Outside and walking the edginess lessened. It was getting late, he knew that, but still he did not turn for home.

* * *

White's was busy when he reached it and a stiff brandy beckoned. Inside he found Adam Stevenage drinking. Without thought he slipped into the seat opposite the lone young man and simply sat there.

'You want to know why I asked about Hutton's Landing?' Despite the liquor Stevenage had consumed, he still seemed in reasonably good shape.

'The thought did cross my mind.'

'The man who died with you, Seth Greenwood, was my cousin.'

'I see.'

'And I wanted to know exactly what happened, to be able to lay him to rest, so to speak.'

'Surely you have heard the rumours?'

'I have, but I also think there are some things left out, my lord. I knew him well, you see, and one thing I could have said of Seth was that he was not careless. I also knew Ralph Kennings.'

That name ripped across Francis's composure, but he sat still and listened.

'I went to Hutton's Landing to visit my cousin's grave. I tried to find you there, but you had left the town. Into the bush, they said, with your gun. Ralph Kennings's body was found a few weeks later thrown into one of the many canyons and he'd been shot three times, twice in each kneecap and once in the head by a marksman. Had you not served in the British army in such a capacity, my lord?'

'It's a long way to Hutton's Landing, Mr Stevenage, and a long time ago.'

'Let me understand it, then. For Seth's sake.'

Francis was amazed that this talk had not made him breathless as any mention of Hutton's Landing usually did. Perhaps it was just the sheer overtness of Stevenage's questions, his quest for the truth overcoming everything else. Or perhaps it was just that Francis's body had already been once through the rigours of memory today and did not have the reserves to do so again. Whatever it was, he sat back and was once again on the banks of the Flint River in Georgia, the cooling of winter in the air and the southern edge of the Appalachians blue in the distance.

'We'd made a claim for gold and found a rich seam, Seth and I, and then found another that needed looking into. We'd fashioned a belt to put the scrapings on, one that ran up onto the river bank and saved us a lot of back-breaking work. It was going well until Kennings turned up and wanted a piece of it.'

He could see the structure in his mind, the wood and the planks, the tailings of rocks and the glinting show of gold in the sieves after the water had sluiced the mud away. 'He knew that the venture was beginning to be lucrative and Seth was not one to stay silent about any new find.'

Stevenage shook his head. 'That sounds like my cousin. He was always an adventurer, seeking a life far from the ease of all that he had in England.'

Francis nodded. 'We were on the dredge when the whole structure collapsed and the next moment there were gunshots across the water. One of the bullets hit Seth in the shoulder and as it had rained the tide was rising. I held him up against me until he stopped breathing.'

'For most of the hours of the day, I heard.'

Francis didn't answer him.

'They told me you had paid for his gravestone, too. My family should be thanking you.'

Adam Stevenage had more than a small resemblance to Seth and Francis relaxed back into the seat as the other continued talking.

'I was glad to see you today, Douglas, at the Wesley luncheon, for I had been wanting to talk to you and you're damn hard to pin down. Lady Maria told me that her sister is to be married.'

'Indeed, she is. To the next Duke of Winbury.'

'I know that now. She just didn't have the look of a woman in love. At least not in love with Allerly.'

'I think you have probably said enough, Stevenage.'

The other lifted what was left in his glass and made a toast. 'To gold then and to the truth.'

'Gold and truth,' Francis gave back and drank. They could both of them break you into tiny shattered pieces because the shades inside each held so many different meanings. Seth's boasting. Kennings's greed. His own retribution. There was a trick to getting away from the fever before it took your soul and none of them had mastered it. But Stevenage was not finished in his confidences.

'Winslow's father died earlier this afternoon, Douglas. Had you heard? He's now the new Duke of

Winbury. The *ton* has rules for it, you see, for loving and living and dying and Lady Sephora Connaught will be caught up in it like a small leaf in a strong breeze. Hard to get away and impossible to break free.'

'You are drunk, Stevenage. Let me take you home.'

'You'd do that for me?' The younger man's dark eyes were pained, his own undisguised ghosts dancing within them.

'I would. Come on.'

'I am supposing that meeting you tonight nullifies the appointment Wesley instructed me to keep tomorrow at your town house?'

'It does.'

An hour later Francis arrived home to find a small pile of stones sitting in a careful order on the sideboard. Ordinary stones found in a garden or on any city street, each polished and arranged in size and colour. Had Anna placed them thus? He picked up the biggest one and rubbed the smoothness in his palm. He'd collected rocks, too, as a child and he wondered if he might be able to find the bags of his collections somewhere in the attics here. His cousin might enjoy them or she might well toss them back in his face.

He smiled at the thought and felt for the letter Sephora had sent him, liking it there in the warmth of his deep jacket pocket.

A surprising day of contrasts and truths. For the first time in a long while he looked forward to tomorrow, though the death of the Marquis of Winslow's father worried him more than it ought to have given Stevenage's prophecies. Would Sephora Connaught marry him out of pity? Or even duty? Outside the wind was strengthening.

A movement at the doorway had him looking up and there was Anna Sherborne, her hair tonight trimmed even shorter than he had seen it last week. She had been bathed, too, and dressed in her night attire she looked a lot younger than she usually did, although the scowl was ever present.

'I liked your stones on the hall cabinet. Did you polish them yourself?'

The girl did not come further into the room, but stood there straddling the doorway, one foot in and one foot out ready to run, he thought, ready to flee.

His eyes glanced at the clock to one side of the room. 'You are up very late?'

'I never sleep very well.' She offered this, tentatively.

'Neither do I,' he gave her back. 'Sometimes I sit and just watch the moon and I find that helps.'

He leaned forward and found a jar of toffees he kept in his drawer, taking one for himself and opening the wrapper before putting it in his mouth. 'Would you like one, too?'

He was careful in his offering, no importance at all attached to her acceptance or to her refusal. But she came forward and took a sweet, unwrapping it in exactly the same way that he had done and laying her paper down on the desk next to his.

'There is a lot more food in this house than there ever was at my old one.'

He stayed silent.

'Clive used to say that I was too expensive to keep and that if I had not been able to count well he would have put me out a long time ago.'

Francis stilled. 'What did you count for him, Anna?'

'His money. There was either a lot of it or none.'

'And he couldn't count it himself?'

'Some people can't. It doesn't mean they are dumb, it just means their brains are better at other things.'

'What was Clive better at?'

She didn't answer for a long time and then changed the topic completely.

'Clive said if you dug hard enough anyone could be buried. He said the old earl dug shallow holes.'

Blackmail, Francis thought. It came in the most unexpected ways and explained a lot about the many boxes the old earl had kept. His cousin had been the pawn in it, her whole life an extension of other people's greed and shame. But not his.

'I have my own collection of rocks, Anna.' She looked up at his use of her Christian name and he saw a look he had not seen in her dark eyes before. Hope.

'I shall find them tomorrow and you would be most welcome to have them. Some are valuable, but most are there because I like them.'

'I do that. I collect what I like, too.'

A shout from further afield had her turning and

his young cousin's maid, looking less than happy, came into view.

'I am sorry, my lord. I just saw her bed was empty and I have been looking everywhere...'

The servant looked as though she would burst into tears at any moment and his own expression was probably not helping either.

He wished he had had more moments of uninterrupted conversation with Anna. He wished she might have said more so that he could place the pieces of her life thus far with an added certainty into a pattern.

She liked counting. She enjoyed collecting rocks and he would bet his bottom dollar on the fact that she knew Clive Sherborne was being paid well to keep her. She had never once spoken of her mother and that omission in its own right was telling, too.

As the maid hurried her off Anna tipped her head at him before she turned and his heart warmed at the faint expression of acknowledgement and communication.

Francis saw Lady Sephora Connaught by chance seven days later dressed in the deepest of blacks and standing with the new Duke of Winbury and his mother next to a carriage pulled up in front of the St Pancras Parish Church in Euston Road. Perhaps it was some sort of remembrance service, he thought, for he had heard the old duke's body had been taken back to the family estate for burial, the night funerals of London deemed too dangerous.

Sephora's hand was upon Winbury's sleeve, close

and intimate, and he was leaning down slightly to speak with her, the sun in her golden hair contrasting against the hue of their clothing as their heads almost touched. Francis felt the heated stab of jealousy consume him.

A man of the church hurried out to meet them, his gestures indicating the gentle sorrow only men of God seemed so very adept at—being neither patronising nor false.

Lord, what if they were here to be married a few days after the old duke had gone to his grave and whilst still in mourning? Was that possible or even allowable? He was not certain of all the many and convoluted rules of the *ton*, but he did not imagine it could be thought of as remotely good form.

Another man had joined them and the group turned to mount the steps of the church, the older woman taking Sephora's hand on the other side and giving a perfect picture of familial harmony and solidarity.

Sephora Connaught looked small there between the larger-built Winburys as they all disappeared into the narthex of the church and then were gone.

'Hell.' He hated the fear in his voice and the feeling of hopelessness. He wanted to simply exit his own carriage and follow them up the steps to see what it was they were doing, to stop the wedding, if that was what was happening, to drag Sephora away and talk some sense into her, and say what?

Marry me instead?

Follow me into the dark corners of my life and understand my demons? He moved his head sideways and pulled on the stock at his throat. The ghost rope was there again. Too tight. He could not breathe.

Lifting his cane, he banged on the roof of the conveyance and was glad when it started to move, out into the row of traffic and away. These dreams were not for him. He had forfeited such luxury when he had shot Ralph Kennings from a distance. Three shots. All on target. The clouded eyes of death followed him even here amongst the mannered and gentle world of the *ton*, watchful and accusing.

He met Lady Sephora Connaught again the following week, this time at a small private gathering in Mayfair in Adam Stevenage's town house. The Winbury party was swathed in black though the sister, Maria Connaught, had managed to find an unusual shade of violet for her attire. A half mourning, Francis supposed, since she was not so intimately associated with the new duke.

Sephora looked the palest he had ever seen her, the whiteness of her countenance caught against the heavy dark of her clothes. Richard Allerly had his arm tied through hers and stood in his usual position at her shoulder, the newly acquired ducal title stamped into his bearing and authority.

Francis wondered why Winbury had deigned to come at all to such a small soirée, but Stevenage was wealthy and money talked, he supposed, to a man with grand and political aspirations.

Adam came over to meet him, a knowing smile on his face, and Francis's heart sank. If this was his way of getting him and Sephora Connaught together he'd done a poor job of it, his mind going over their last conversation at White's. If he had known that she was going to be here he wouldn't have come, but it was too late to simply turn tail and leave. When he'd looked at her left hand he'd seen that there was no ring at all on her third finger and a part of him had been more than relieved to find it thus.

'I hope you approve of my list of guests, Douglas. After your help the other week I thought I should return the favour.'

Francis could barely believe Stevenage to be serious, but as the host was called away from his side Richard Allerly turned to observe him. His greeting was cold.

'I had no idea you were a friend of Stevenage, Lord Douglas.'

'He is more of a recent acquaintance, Your Grace.'

Francis did not look at Sephora at all, but felt her there as her hand pulled away from Winbury's sleeve.

'If you will excuse me, Richard.' Her words were quiet and she left, threading her way across the room to stand with her sister. He was glad that she had gone.

'Lady Sephora and I are hoping to move our nuptials forward. My father's death…' Winbury stopped and for the first time Francis saw a glimpse of true emotion.

'I was sorry to hear of your loss.' It was the least he could say, this trite phrase, to fill an awkward social meeting.

'And I am sorry that we should have to cross paths like this, Douglas. I hoped I had made it clear in my letter that I did not want you anywhere near my wife-to-be ever again.'

'Well, Your Grace, if you had jumped into the damned river yourself I wouldn't have had to be closer to her in the first place.'

The gloves were off, though Francis moderated his tone given the social setting in which they stood.

'My bride's indebtedness to you is misplaced and foolish.' Now this was new. 'She does not know of the reputation you have garnered and she is a woman to whom wickedness and evil are unknown qualities.'

He almost laughed, but he didn't for the duke's tone had risen and all around people were stopping to watch. This was neither the time nor the place to instigate a conflict with the grief of a lost father so very present and with many ladies in the room.

'It has been interesting,' he replied and tipped his head before moving away. Lady Maria Connaught came to stand beside him a few seconds later as he was pouring himself a brandy.

'You probably like the duke as little as I do, my lord.'

'Pardon?' When he glanced up he saw Sephora Connaught watching them over her sister's shoulder. He also saw Winbury walking back to claim her, one arm again tucked through his as he drew her away.

'The Duke of Winbury thinks a husband should own his wife and direct her in all her actions and thoughts.'

'Unfortunate, then.'

At that the girl laughed, her dark eyes flashing. 'My sister is not happy. I think they would have parted company had the funeral not happened. As it is now Richard is using all his grief and sadness as a weapon. It is hard for Sephora to abandon such unhappiness, but I like to think she is just waiting for her chance of it.'

'Why are you telling me this?' he asked quietly, turning so that others might not come to encroach upon their conversation.

'Because you saved her once, my lord. Perhaps you might do so again?'

With that she left to rejoin her sister and when he caught the glance of Sephora Connaught upon him all he saw was fear and worry.

They had departed early, giving their apologies to Adam Stevenage and going home, Maria most upset to be leaving in such an unseemly rush.

'I would have liked to at least remain for the afternoon tea,' she grumbled as the horses wound their way into a row of heavy traffic.

'Then you should have had the good sense not to have conversed with Douglas quite so freely and you might have had that chance, Maria.'

'People are allowed to speak with whom they wish, Richard. This is England.'

Sephora's reprimand was sharp, she knew it, but the behaviour of her husband-to-be ever since sighting Francis St Cartmail had appalled and worried her. She didn't know what it was they had said to each other, but she had heard him raise his voice and knew Richard well enough to recognise his ire, an anger that continued to ferment even now, half an hour after the event.

'Douglas should be drummed out of the *ton*, for goodness sake, and would have been had he held a lesser title.'

'Mr Stevenage did imply the Earl of Douglas was almost as rich as he was. Perhaps that might be a part of the reason the *ton* does not shun him.' Maria said this calmly and Sephora took in her own breath before Richard could answer.

'It should not matter how much money he has,' she said, 'or what his title is. The Earl of Douglas saved me from certain death and for that I shall always be grateful.'

'Of course, my angel,' Richard muttered and took her hand.

'I do not particularly like that endearment, Richard,' she returned. 'It seems silly and inappropriate somehow for a woman of almost twenty-three.'

Her eyes met his, the dark anger in Richard's making her grit her teeth. She'd always humoured him and allowed him his way, but suddenly here in the carriage wending their way home she had had enough.

An ordinary Wednesday and a short and familiar journey. She could not truly understand what had just changed and broken between them, but it had, the two halves that had previously fitted together now beyond any point of reconciliation.

Smiling at the two sets of eyes turned towards her in surprise, Sephora simply stared out of the window and laid her hands in her lap, avoiding the action of wringing them together in concern.

She felt dislocated and scattered, seeing her life before her in no more than the space of seconds and minutes. Even hours seemed too far, too exhausting. She had no energy apart from the concentration needed to breathe into the next moment of her being.

She counted her breaths now often, because when things slipped out of control it gave her a small authority back, a will that was not being bent by others. Sometimes, though, she wondered if she might just slip into the space between reality and madness and never return.

Chapter Eight

Two evenings later Sephora sat and wrote another letter to the Earl of Douglas because she thought if she even left it for one more moment she would decide not to and by then it would be too late.

She asked Francis St Cartmail to meet her at Lackington's in Finsbury Square, in the back room behind the spiral staircase. That part of the Temple of the Muses was always deserted, housing most of the old and dusty treatises that were seldom lent out. Nobody would disturb them.

She set down a time and a place. The day after tomorrow at two o'clock in the afternoon. With all that had happened, she knew Mama would insist on a nap and she could use those hours to quietly escape. She had two books that needed returning and the library was one of the places she visited on a regular basis. No one would ask questions.

Of late, she had seen her mother watching her with a sort of veiled pity, the look one might give a wounded animal or a simple child. Once or twice

Mama had even enquired whether she was happy with her betrothed, the questions phrased in a way that did not require any answer as she always added some anecdote of the material gains such a marriage would entail. New gowns. A beautiful house. A place in the *ton* that was almost unequalled. A title. Sephora, the new Duchess of Winbury.

In the past she had largely ignored these sorts of comments and got on with life. But now she found she couldn't. Richard was also pressing her for a wedding date and he wanted it to be a lot sooner than she had hoped for now that his father had passed away.

Without a great array of close girlfriends and with her sister away on a short holiday with their aunt, Sephora felt isolated and alone. Her life had stalled somehow into a shadowy place, the gloom of death, the sadness of grief, the inability of Richard to extricate himself from an ever-deepening hole of grief. The colour of black consumed her.

She was constantly fidgeting and was always scared—of saying something, of not saying anything, of waiting until a good time to break off untenable promises. She had got so worried by it all that she had come out into welts of hives, all over her arms and her back, the red and swollen itchiness making her irritable and impatient.

And right there and then, in the quiet of a late evening, Sephora felt exactly as she had when she had fallen from the bridge into the river all those weeks ago, breathless and cold, her world receding into darkness.

Suffocating.

This is what it felt like to die inside and yet still live. The realisation was so dreadful she could not even cry out.

She sat that way until the dawn when the first pink light of morning came and she knew, with every single part of her being, that she would die here if she stayed silent even for another hour.

It had been so long since she felt alive, so long since she had laughed or loved or lived. Properly. When she had seen Francis St Cartmail walk into the Stevenage town house the small flicker of something she'd thought dead inside her had been surprising. Vitality. Vigour. Desire. Pushing against all that was numb and frozen and telling her she could wait no longer. Picking up her letter, she ripped the sheet into a hundred pieces and hid them under other paper in her drawer. A letter would not do it. She would go and see him herself.

When her maid finally came to her room as the hall clock struck nine in the morning, she instructed the girl to find her navy day dress and her cloak and hat. Then with her hair put up and her cheeks rubbed into colour, Sephora simply walked down the stairs and out of the house before anyone at all would miss her.

Francis was coming from his library as the butler opened the door and he wondered who on earth would be calling in on the household at such an hour.

Lady Sephora Connaught stood there in a fine blue dress and cloak, a small purse in hand and her cheeks so pale, he thought she might simply fall over before he could reach her.

'Lord Douglas,' she said and then stopped, taking a breath and beginning again. 'I need to speak with you privately, my lord, if you would be kind enough to allow me the time.'

'You are alone?' He took her arm and looked around. No one else was in sight. The sleeve of her cloak had fallen back and a large welt of redness was easily visible.

'Has somebody hurt you?' His heart began to thump as quickly as hers did, for he could feel the rapid beat of blood under his fingers.

'Pardon?'

'Your arm? Who did this to you?' When he pulled the sleeve up further there were more welts, barely a piece of skin unmarked.

She began to cry even as he looked at her, huge tears simply pooling in her pale eyes and falling down her cheeks.

'They…are…h-hives. I get…them when I am… scared.'

Swallowing down fury, Francis took her through to his library and shut the door. Just at that moment he cared nothing for propriety or the rule of manners. All he wanted to do was to take Sephora into his arms and hold her safe, but he made himself stand still. Why had she come here so early and so alone and why the hell was she so scared?

He made certain she sat in the most comfortable wing chair by the fire. It was cool this morning, the June temperatures diving after a warm spell. Bringing her a drink, he waited till she took a sip and then coughed.

'Wh-what is it?'

'Whisky. It fortifies the spirit.'

Carefully she took another sip and swallowed it. Her mouth puckered in distaste, but still she took a third.

'I need as much of…this as I can g-get, then.'

The fourth, fifth and sixth swallows had him leaning forward and taking the glass from her.

'It's usually not imbibed with such rapidity, especially if you aren't used to it, and it's a damn strong brew.'

She sat back at that, leaning her head against the leather and closing her eyes, the silence between them as perplexing as her appearance here. After a few moments though her glance caught his own and she smiled.

'You are very beautiful, Lord Douglas, but then I suppose many women tell you that. I am a woman, after all, and I am telling you that.' She hiccupped and her hand covered her mouth.

Hell. She was tiddly and fast becoming properly drunk. The whisky had been a poor idea.

'I cannot marry Richard Allerly, the Duke of Winbury. I have come here to say this. To you.'

She was well in her cups and he should not play the game that she had somehow started. He should bundle her up right here and now, ply her with strong coffee and have her taken home before things got completely out of hand. But he couldn't. The gentleman in him twisted across desire and lust. 'Why do you not wish to marry him?'

'Because...' She looked at him then with her pale eyes, a hint of light grey at their edges. 'Because... only with you do I feel...safe.'

Safe? When all he could think of doing was kissing her to feel again what he had in the water, the warmth of her and the sweetness? Safe—a sharp and innocent barb that both broke his heart and firmed his resolve. He wasn't safe, not by a long shot, but she couldn't know that yet and he wouldn't tell her.

Stepping back, he took the blanket from the sofa behind him, then wrapped it around her and brought her from the chair.

'Come, Sephora. I will take you home.'

He knew they had been observed leaving his town house, though he hoped the blanket might have obscured her identity from those who watched.

The ride back was quiet and quick, Sephora merely slumped against the seat opposite him, lost in thought. The Aldford town house had a small drive, an unusual but most useful amenity. He was glad to be free of the public gaze and yet the worst was probably to come.

A servant hurried down the stairs and opened the door and Francis helped Sephora out as she leaned on his arm, blinking her eyes as if she had trouble with her vision.

Her mother met them before they had gone three steps, the anger in her undeniable and immense and behind her the single figure of the Duke of Winbury hovered, his face as red as the welts on Sephora's arms.

'You!' There was no greeting and no explanation as he came forward, knocking Francis backward, and short of taking Sephora with him he simply let her go as he tumbled, leaving him no true time to protect himself, the hard edge of the marble steps connecting with his left temple and stunning him momentarily.

Then Winbury was kicking at his shoulder and his arm and his head. The day darkened, but he managed to get up, his own servant now between his assailant and him. Sephora's father, the Earl of Aldford, grabbed at the newly titled duke and slammed him up hard against a nearby wall.

'Stop.' Sephora's voice, from the bottom of the steps, panicked and desperate. 'Don't hurt him.'

Francis did not know whom she meant not to be hurt, but the blood from the gash at his temple was gushing down his face and he understood at that moment there was nothing to be gained by trying to explain. Not here. Not now. Not in the heat of argument and in the sharp pull of pain.

Lady Aldford was shouting, too, telling him to leave and never come back, Anne-Marie's name in the mix of her wrath. 'You have already ruined the life of my sister's daughter and I shall never allow you to despoil another.'

He felt oddly disconnected, the throb in his temple

worsening and his breath shortened. When his man took his arm he allowed him to lead him back to the waiting carriage, sitting on the seat with relief as the world spun in dizzying circles.

The last image he had of Sephora Connaught through the glass was of her turning towards the departing coach, and then falling carefully, quietly, down onto the sharp pebbled chips of the drive.

'Silly, silly girl.' Her mother's words echoed through the ache in her head and the dry pain of opening her eyes. 'Here, I have brought you hot milk.'

Lifting the beaker to her lips, Sephora was pleased for the warmth the drink provided as she scrambled for clarity. She was in her own bed and the day was darkening. Had she slept for all the hours in between? She remembered Francis St Cartmail plying her with a strong drink and him falling, his head cut and blood in his eyes. She remembered Richard kicking him, too, and her father trying to pull the duke away.

'I do not think he can forgive you for this, Sephora.'

'St Cartmail?' Her mouth felt dry and strange and her eyes could not adjust to the light.

'Not Douglas.' Decided anger now resided where worry had lingered. 'The Duke of Winbury, of course. You return from God knows where alone in the company of the dissolute and dangerous earl, drunk as any bosky in the land and expect your husband-to-be to simply shrug it off, disregard it? It is beyond the pale, Sephora, beyond any sort of reasonable excuse you could even muster. You shall be ruined. Forever.'

Her mother had begun to cry now, quietly, as she took back the drink and replaced it precisely in the middle of a cloth of folded white linen.

'You have never been a worry to us before. In all your entire life you have been a good, dutiful and sensible daughter, a girl who anyone might look at and think how very lucky we have been. Until the bridge. Until you fell off that bridge into the water below and changed completely.' Her sobs were louder now. 'Too many people saw you in St Cartmail's company and alone this morning. Richard had brought his aunt to visit us, a strident sort of woman of firm morals and unquestionable virtue. Circles, Sephora. Your behaviour is like throwing a pebble into a still pond, just a small disturbance at first and then an enormous one. We could smell whisky on your breath and you were barely coherent. I do not know how it is we will go on happily from here. In fact, I very much doubt that we can.'

'Papa?'

'Is heartbroken. He feels it is better if he does not see you just now.'

'And Richard?'

'Has gone. He sent a note to say how disappointed he was.'

Sephora turned away into her pillow, an anger surging. *Disappointed?* She knew exactly what that emotion felt like.

'I don't want to see him.'

'Well, Sephora,' her mother returned in a voice that had risen in both strength and conviction, 'I don't think that he wants to see you much either. But bear this in mind—if he does not wish to marry you, I doubt anyone else will want to either.'

Francis sat in his library with a sore head, a sore shoulder and a wrenched hand, but he sat neither alone nor at peace.

'I am telling you, Lord Douglas, the girl is a wild-cat and a hoyden and that never in all my years of being a governess have I come across the likes of this one.'

Mrs Celia Billinghurst was crying as she said this, tears leaking into the large handkerchief she held in one hand and the remains of a ripped book in the other. 'She takes no notice at all of anything I tell her. And today she...she simply disappeared from my side and did not return until a good forty minutes later. I thought she was dead.'

'Where is she now?' His jaw ached as he asked the question for the boot of Richard Allerly, the Duke of Winbury, had been remarkably accurate.

'Outside, sir. She has been told to sit and wait for me to call her.'

His heart sank. He would have to deal with the remains of another chaotic day in his household im-mediately on top of the fiasco at the Connaught town house. 'I shall see my cousin alone, Mrs Billinghurst, and let you know the outcome afterwards.'

'Certainly, sir. Though I will say that I need this job, my lord, and that I have excellent credentials as a governess and that you would be hard pushed to find another with such glowing recommendations.'

'Indeed.'

'But I do think the girl is hiding things, big things. I think she is scared of something in her past.'

'Thank you.' Francis waited until she had gone before pouring himself a stiff drink. He needed a moment before he saw his cousin and the last sight of Sephora Connaught as he had left the town house still worried him.

God, what had happened next? Had Winbury controlled his temper? Had her mother found hers? Had someone come and lifted Sephora inside to listen to her part of the story, to her concerns and worries and to understand the reason for her hives?

A small knock at the door had him turning and his cousin came through the door, her dark eyes worried and repentant.

Another girl who needed to be understood, he suddenly thought. Another young woman who had so far in her life been a pawn of all the adults surrounding her. He made himself smile as he asked her to sit.

'Mrs Billinghurst is finding your behaviour difficult, Anna.'

'I don't think she likes me much. I think she hoped I would be prettier.'

Now this was new.

'Why?'

'She said I needed different clothes and I needed to walk and talk different. She said my hair is all wrong and that my language was…dreadful.'

'And you don't wish to change?'

'Not all of that much. Perhaps a bit, but she wants it all different.'

'Should we start with your name, then? Would you like to be called Anna St Cartmail instead of Anna Sherborne from now on?'

'St Cartmail? The same name as yours, you mean?'

'As ours. You are a Douglas. It is only right that you should be called such and carry the name of the lineage you were born to.'

When she stayed silent Francis changed tack. 'Where did you go today? Mrs Billinghurst said that you were missing for forty minutes and she was worried.'

Anna coloured, but made no effort to answer him.

'Do you not like it here?'

That brought her eyes up to his. 'I do, sir. My room is nice and the food is good and I like the books.'

'But you ripped one up, I hear.'

'It was a baby book. Mrs Billinghurst said that I had to read it like a lady does.'

'A lady?'

'A lady who speaks like this.' She mouthed each vowel widely and he could not help but smile.

'What do you prefer to read?'

'Books on lands that are far from here. Stories of travel, biographies of people who have been places.'

'Such as who?'

'Jonathan Swift. Daniel Defoe. Lady Mary Wortley Montague.'

'Her letters from Turkey?'

Dark eyes sharpened. 'You have read them?'

The wife of the British ambassador had written of the Muslim Orient and Francis could not believe that this small and plain child might enjoy such a complex treatise.

'Come to my library tomorrow morning and I will show you some books I used to enjoy.'

'So I could read in my room alone?'

'Yes.'

She stood at that as if in tarrying he might change his mind.

'I would like to be known as Anna St Cartmail. I would like to be a Douglas like you.'

And with that she was gone, a slight and thin shadow against the walls, and if she had that look of the hunted at least she was starting to feel as if she might belong. He was pleased for it.

God. His day had gone from bad to worse and he did not know for once which way to turn. He wished Sephora Connaught could have been here to tell him what to do with a wayward and angry almost-twelve-year-old girl. That thought had him drinking the rest of his cognac in a quick swallow.

Everything about his life was skewered into wrongness and the 'angel of the *ton*' would hardly be interested in sharing such chaos. He was as damaged as Anna was, more so perhaps, and his household was falling to pieces around his ears.

He only hoped Sephora was safe and happy and that someone had taken her into their arms to reassure her that everything would all be right.

With a sigh he lifted his bell and asked Walsh to bring Celia Billinghurst to him. He'd need to tell the woman what had been decided for he wanted her to understand that Anna's place in his house was a right of birth and not of chance.

No cards came to ask the Connaught family to any social occasion, not the next day nor the one after that. Richard had neither called nor sent a note either and if a small part of Sephora was saddened by his actions, a much greater part of her felt only an enormous relief.

'Let's go out anyway, Sephora,' said Maria, who was now returned home. 'Let's walk for an hour or two. We don't have to speak with anybody at all.' Maria took her hand and pulled her from the seat she had been in for hours.

'I am not certain. This is all my fault and being seen with me in public will do your reputation no good. If I am to be banned from any social occasion forever, you still have the chance not to be and I think you ought to take it.'

Laughter was the only answer.

Half an hour later Sephora found herself on the pathway by the river, their ladies' maids trailing behind each of them closely.

'At least Mama has not come, Sephora, nor Aunt Susan. If there is something to be said about being a social pariah, it is that it at least allows one freedom.'

Sephora was not quite so certain as group after group passed them by without the shadow of recognition or friendliness. It was as if she did not exist any more and even people whom she might have imagined would be kind were not.

Finally they stopped and Sephora realised Maria had brought her to the exact spot where Lord Douglas had dragged her into the bank after her fall.

'Do you remember clinging on to the Earl of Douglas, Sephora? Clinging on with such a fervour Richard Allerly had to prise your fingers open to make you let go?'

'I do.'

'Do you remember, too, how Douglas shook with such ferocity his teeth chattered? A panic attack, I think, much like the one he had a few weeks ago at the Wesleys in the garden with you. He has dreadful secrets, Sephora. You can see that in his eyes even when he smiles. Adam Stevenage said that he was buried under a collapsed structure in a river once for hours in Georgia. Perhaps it was the mud here that made him remember. Did he shake in the same way out there in the deeper waters?'

He hadn't, she thought. He had held her to him with an iron grip as he kicked his way in, across the current, against the wind. But he had been steady and calm.

'Adam said that his cousin died in the same accident. St Cartmail was held at first for his murder. They nearly hanged him for it, but he was saved at the last moment.'

'By what?'

'The branch broke as he was in mid-air and the

more superstitious amongst them took it as a sign from above for clemency so he was hauled into the local courthouse instead.'

Half-hanged? Sephora's eyes filled with tears. 'My God. What happened next?'

'The magistrate determined the bullet in Douglas's arm was the same as the one in the dead man and so he was proclaimed innocent as they concluded that someone else had fired the shots.'

The horror of it all had Sephora leaning against the trunk of a tree. Francis St Cartmail had been shot along with his friend? He had not told her anything of that. 'Is this common knowledge here, amongst society, I mean?'

'I am not sure. There are certainly many dark stories about him in circulation, but perhaps not that particular one.'

Why had she not heard of the gossip? Suddenly she knew. Because her life had always been sheltered and protected and Richard had had a big hand in that. Anything difficult or sad had been strained out and discarded, half-truths or no truth at all left in their place. The falsity of it all made her feel sick, for in effect she had been pushed to the side of life to live in a vacuum, all perfectly pleasant but no true and utter joy.

She could not help the tears that came as Maria put one arm around her shoulders.

'I think I have been asleep for years, Maria, like that princess in the fairy tale.'

'So take this as a gift, Sephora, for a near-death experience has woken you up.'

Unexpectedly they both laughed.

Richard arrived at three o'clock in the afternoon the next day at her bidding and he looked as if he had not slept for a week.

'Thank you for coming. I thought you might not.' Sephora had made sure that she was dressed today not in black but in her most sombre gown, a grey-and-navy silk over which she had laid a deep grey worsted wool shawl.

'Well, unlike you, I adhere to the manners and mores of our society and its proprieties.' He did not sound at all happy.

'I know you do.' Sephora had always realised this about him, but for the first time she only felt sorry for such compliance. 'I also realise I have put you into an awful position and would like to say that I quite understand if the terms of our betrothal are now untenable to you.'

'Untenable?' For a moment she saw the boy she had fallen in love with all those years ago under the sterner face of the man he had become. 'For whom?'

Not as easy as she had hoped, then. Resolutely she took in breath.

'We have changed, Richard, both of us. Once we knew who each other was, liked who each other was, but now…?' She spread out her hands. 'Now I think we would be better to remain as friends than as anything more.'

'No.' He grabbed her hand and brought it to his lips, the kiss he placed in her palm harsh and angry. Clenching her teeth together, she tried in vain to pull away.

There was nothing there. No passion or lust or joy. No want to take it further in the hope of more, just a deadness that was astonishing and a revulsion, too, if she were honest.

'It was the river, wasn't it? You changed after that.' He wiped his mouth with the back of his hand as he let her go, standing there breathing loudly. 'I should have jumped after you, but I didn't. Is it him? Is it St Cartmail that you want? He is a murderer and a liar and worse.'

She stopped him simply by turning away. 'No, it is because of me and you, Richard, and your father.'

'My father?'

'Uncle Jeffrey told me to find my life again that day you took me to see him. He said I had looked sad for a long while and I needed to find my passion.'

'Passion?' He laughed then and the sound was not kind. 'You have always been cold physically, Sephora, cold and distant. I doubt heartily that you could discover such a thing even if you tried.'

She let the insult pass as she drew into herself. He was hurt and striking out, though in his outburst she allowed him a kernel of truth.

'Then let me go. Let me break off our betrothal and allow both of us to be free again.' She could barely believe the words had come from her, strong words and certain. It had been so very long since she had felt such.

As if he had recognised the change he simply looked at her and stepped away. 'If I do as you ask, Sephora, you shall be looked at in pity. Society will crucify you. Believe me, you will regret this.' There were tears in his eyes and he wiped at his nose with a starched kerchief dragged from his pocket, but she could not allow the weak emotion of only pity to take away her newfound power of strength. It had to be all or nothing.

Reaching across to a low table, she rang the bell and a servant came into the room immediately.

'His Grace is just leaving.' She watched as Richard gathered in his temper and departed.

Chapter Nine

Francis spent the next five days in Hastings trying to piece together as best he could the movements of Anna and Clive across his final hours. He had procured the services of a man who worked for the Bow Street Runners and the meetings he had held in both Hastings and Rye were most illuminating.

It seemed Sherborne had dealt with a London lord in many of his drops of liquor, a man who signed his name simply with an artful and sweeping 'W'.

'Find this man and you will have your killer,' Alan Wilson said over a drink in a tavern just outside Rye. 'Sherborne was funnelling off both cash and kind and rumour on the ground has it he was found out. Nobody around these parts trusted him much, but they trusted the London cove even less. Besides, Clive Sherborne was seen with his daughter just prior to his murder by a woman who was late home and she said he gave the impression of being drunk and the little girl looked scared. Those about these parts said she was a hellion, too, undisciplined and ill bought up. End up like her mother she will, they told me, with her neck broken on the backstreets and her skirt up around her thighs.'

'Her mother was killed? When?'

'Two years ago this August.'

Hell, Francis thought, this sort of place was probably the environment Anna had spent most of her time in and yet still she could read and count better than most children of her age. Who had taught her? Could it have been Clive in his more lucid moments?

'Did you find out who lived in the house with them in Hastings?'

'An old scholar boarded with them. Timothy Hawkins. He died of old age a year ago now. The girl visited the grave often and left wild flowers.'

Another loss, then, in a life full of them. If Clive or her mother or his uncle had been in front of him now Francis might simply have screwed their heads off. Instead he finished his drink and worded his next question carefully.

'Could you go to London and follow the movements of two brothers and their father? I will give you their direction. It will need to be done discreetly, for I would like to know if they meet anyone who fits the description of a London gentleman.'

On his way back to London other matters settled into a cold knot in his stomach. He did not wish to see Sephora Connaught again after the fiasco at her family town house and he most certainly did not want to see her in society hanging on the arm of the Duke of Winbury. No news had filtered through of her wedding, however, and of that at least he was glad, but he needed space and time and distance to re-evaluate his life.

The morning after his arrival back at his town house he was surprised by an early visit from Daniel Wylde.

'You damn well need to do something about Sephora Connaught, Francis. She has been ostracised completely by every strata of fine society after breaking off her engagement and Winbury has had a big hand in that by summarily dismissing her as a woman slightly deranged.'

This was the very last thing Francis had expected to hear and he remained mute in surprise.

'The Duke of Winbury is telling everybody that Lady Sephora Connaught has both an addled mind and a cold nature and that he is well shot of her. Your name was mentioned prominently as the main cause of her onset to a premature insanity.'

'Hell.' He turned towards the windows and opened them. 'I'd like to kill the bastard.'

'Well, you could do that, but a long stretch in goal will do nothing at all to help her. There are rumours swirling everywhere and one of the most persistent is that she came to visit you alone at your town house and that a number of people observed this reckless foray. It is also said that you packed her into your carriage and returned her home yourself when you knew there must be some repercussions from the unexpected visit.'

'It was the right thing to do. I thought a glass of whisky might fortify her, but she drank too much of it.'

Daniel laughed. 'Lord, Francis, you got her drunk as well? Then do the next right thing both for her and for you. She has been made an outcast. Adelaide said that she saw her and her sister out walking a few days ago and everybody gave Sephora the cut direct.'

'Hell.'

'You came home from America with the weight of the world on your shoulders and then you go right ahead and ruin the "angel of the *ton*."' Daniel breathed in heavily for a moment as though recollecting his thoughts and putting them into order. 'God knows what will happen next, but your own prospects for a satisfactory marriage have most likely just plummeted as well. A reasonable solution might be looking right at you.'

The last sentence made him ponder. Daniel had not been a man known to be overly interested in the marriage mart before and certainly had not tried to influence him on choosing a wife or a mistress if it came to that. 'Did Amethyst put you up to this?'

The slight hesitation told Francis that she had.

'My wife thinks you are lonely. She knows there are things you are not telling us and she wants to help.'

'Tell her thank you for her worry, but also tell her that I am fine.'

'You might indeed be, but Sephora Connaught is far from it. What would make her throw her more normal caution and good sense to the wind and arrive at the home of a known and disreputable bachelor unaccompanied and unmindful of who saw her?'

Safety. He almost said the word, almost simply spoke it aloud and spat it out, but Daniel would understand that sentiment as little as he himself did and so he remained quiet.

'Well, I leave it in your hands, Francis, but I never took you for a man who would forsake a woman needing help and she is most certainly one who does.'

Two hours later Francis made his way to the Connaught family town house on the north side of Portman Square. A footman showed him in, his eyes widening as he realised just who the visitor was, and led him down a long corridor to the back of the house.

'Lord Douglas, sir.'

Aldford was sitting behind his desk in a well-stocked library and he got up as soon as the introduction was made.

'Thank you, Smithson. That will be all. Please see that we are not disturbed.'

'Very well, my lord.'

When the door closed silence filled the room for the moment it took for Sephora's father to gather his ire.

'I hope you have come here to explain and apologise, St Cartmail.' Jonathon Connaught's voice shook. He was only just holding on to a temper that red-

dened his face considerably. 'After the last time...'
He stopped.

'Your daughter came to see me, Lord Aldford, and
whilst it was true I should not have given her whisky
to calm her down, I did not touch her either.'

'No, you brought her back home to ruination instead and then just left her to it.'

'I did not know that until today for I have been
away from London this past week. I thought Winbury would have seen things right.'

The name seemed to make the older man even
more furious. 'Don't talk to me about that coward,'
he shouted. 'If his father knew how he had treated
my daughter in her hour of need, he would be rolling
around in his newly dug grave, I assure you. He has
abandoned her completely.'

'I wish to marry her.'

'Pardon?'

'I have come today to ask permission for your
daughter Sephora's hand in marriage, sir.'

The older man leaned against his desk heavily and
sat down, reaching for a kerchief in an opened drawer,
then running it across his brow.

'Why?' All the fight seemed to have gone from
him.

'It is partly my fault she is in the position she now
finds herself. I need to remedy that.'

'Remedy it. She barely knows you, St Cartmail.
She probably even hates you. Her betrothal to the
Duke of Winbury has been dissolved and a great mea-

sure of the problem is down to the fiasco you created. Did you know that?'

'I did not at first, but I do now.'

'So now you have the damn nerve to just walk in here and expect my blessings or my daughter's acceptance.' The ire had returned as fast as it had waned, but Francis had known this meeting was never going to be easy. 'From memory you are also the very same man who broke my niece's heart all those years ago and you did not even come to her funeral to pay your last respects. How could we trust you to actually do the right thing this time?'

Francis stayed silent, the faults of his past mounting against him.

'I can't think why you imagine either my daughter or I would agree to this proposal, Douglas.'

'If Sephora agrees to marry me, she will no longer be ruined. I can protect her.'

'Against everyone?'

'Yes.'

'And if she does not?'

'Then I will leave. I do not want further trouble. I will also promise my confidentiality in all that has been discussed today.'

'You swear by it?'

'I give you my word of honour.'

Frowning heavily Connaught called out and the same man who had showed Francis in before opened the door.

'Yes, sir.'

'Ask one of Lady Sephora's maids to summon her to the library, Smithson. I need to see her most urgently.'

Sephora was reading by the window in her room when one of the upstairs maids came bustling in.

'Lord Aldford requires your company in his library. He says it is important.'

'Very well.' Sephora laid down the book she was reading and smoothed out the creases in her muslin day dress as she stood. Papa seldom asked her to come to his library so formally. She wondered what had happened and hoped that there was not some new and difficult problem concerning Richard Allerly.

'Is the duke with him?'

'I don't believe so, Lady Sephora.' Relief at that answer blossomed.

'But he is not alone?'

'No, Lady Sephora. Smithson said there was a visitor.'

This produced a further worry. Stopping to take up her shawl from the chair, Sephora wrapped it around herself and followed the maid downstairs.

Francis saw the instant Sephora Connaught realised it was him because she blushed a bright red and faltered as she stepped into the room.

'Sit down, please.' Her father's voice was not gentle. When she was seated he began to speak again.

'The Earl of Douglas has come here today with a marriage proposal. A protection, he calls it. He wants you to be his wife because he knows the current predicament you find yourself in is largely of his own making and he needs to remedy it, a marriage to quell the howls of an offended *ton*, so to speak. As such he is proposing a union of convenience to mend broken reputations and to lighten the gossip of a dreadful scandal that shows no sign of fading away.'

Was her father a complete fool, Francis thought as he stepped forward.

'I am hoping you will do me the honour, Lady Sephora, of becoming my wife.'

'Of course she will not, Douglas. I cannot think of anything further from my daughter's mind than accepting your—'

Sephora stood and looked at him directly. 'Why would you ask this of me, Lord Douglas?' Her eyes were wide, the blue more noticeable today in her high emotion.

'Because he has ruined you, my dear. It's the very least as a gentleman that he can do.' Her father sounded at the end of his tether.

'You could hardly want this, my lord, to be tied in marriage so...inconveniently when everyone in society knows your poor opinion on the institution itself?'

Francis was about to reply when her father strode across between them and began to speak again.

'Douglas is renowned in the *ton* for being wild and dangerous and you would do well to remember that the Duke of Winbury, for all his faults, has not been said to have killed a man. It is you who should not want this union, Sephora, you who have been held in great esteem by the *ton* all of your adult life, yet are now the subject of ridicule and pity because of the poor choices you have recently made.'

Francis had heard enough. 'I am not quite without advantage, Lord Aldford. I have returned from the Americas with a great deal of wealth for one and the Douglas title is an old and venerated one.' He saw Sephora Connaught's knuckles were white where she held them twisted together, though the hives had gone, the skin to her elbow where her dress sleeves ended now unmarked and fair.

He could not begin to imagine a more awkward wedding proposal and was about to request some time alone to explain his reasoning, when rushing feet from outside put paid to such hopes. Sephora's mother bustled in, her eyes reddened and her face furious.

'The butler said that you were here, Lord Douglas.' She was looking straight at him. 'And I could not believe that you would have the nerve to be.'

'Elizabeth…' her husband began, but she did not let him finish.

'The man standing before us is the architect of all our problems, Jonathon, the sole reason we are in this conundrum and Sephora can no longer partake in anything at all in society—'

'St Cartmail has come to ask for our daughter's hand in marriage.'

That stopped her as nothing else would have and she looked at her offspring intently. Sephora was so much smaller than her mother and deathly pale. All Francis could see was worry stamped across her brow.

'What of Richard? What of him, Sephora? What of an understanding that should at least be given some weight due to its longevity?'

'I think Winbury may have cooked his goose, Elizabeth, given his lack of any true concern for our daughter's plight. He has certainly been vocal in his criticisms of her.' Her father gave this damning summation of Winbury's character without as much emotion as before.

'He is grieving...'

'He is weak willed.'

'So you are saying...?' Sephora's mother's face had lost its flush and was now a ghostly white.

'Our duty, Elizabeth, is to see that our daughter is not ruined by gossip, and the earl, whilst the subject of much discussion, is also titled and wealthy in his own right. Believe me, it could have been far worse.'

A different silence settled now and Francis used the moment to push his own cause further.

'Might I have a moment alone with Lady Sephora?'

He thought her mother might refuse outright, but before she could speak, Sephora's father had taken his wife's hand and led her from the room. 'I will allow you two moments, Lord Douglas. Sephora, we will be right outside. If you need us, you only have to call.'

Then they were gone, with the seconds counting themselves down in the room.

Sephora spoke first. 'Thank you for asking for my hand in marriage, Lord Douglas, but of course there can be no question as to what my answer must be.'

Her words were quietly said and she blushed again even as he looked at her and gave his own answer.

'I realise we barely know each other and there are things you do not understand about me, but society can be cruel in its dismissal of a reputation and yours has definitely suffered. If I am to have any hope of protecting you successfully, we would need to be married immediately, as soon as the banns are read. On a special licence.'

He was rushing her, but the sudden and shocking thought came that if he did not she would be persuaded to refuse him, so he kept going. He did not wish to be responsible for her demise. 'I would never hurt you, Sephora. At least believe that.'

She looked at him then, directly, the shock in her face obvious. 'A marriage of convenience would hurt us both, my lord. Usually they are not happy unions.'

Her solemnly given words were stated with the sort of honesty normally only employed by the minions of the church and he liked it. Liked her. Liked the soft truth and the gentle honour and her smile that was both shy and bold at the same time.

Everything she said was true and the thought that he could not possibly be serious in such a proposal came to the fore. He barely recognised himself as he stood there, for he was being beguiled by an innocent and one who would hold no knowledge at all of the sort of man he was. Sephora Connaught was a woman oblivious of the underbelly of society with its broken lives and empty promises; a place that was by far his most known milieu.

What the hell was he doing? Why the hell was she not turning tail and running as fast as she possibly could, her near miss with Winbury a potent warning to the agony she might well suffer with him? Why wasn't he? But she was speaking again in her soft voice, trying to understand who he was, what he was.

'I do have another question, my lord. Those people at Kew Gardens, the ones you were fighting, did they hurt you in some way to make you retaliate in that manner?'

'No.' He had to be honest. 'But I thought that they might.'

'I see.' The words were almost breathed out.

'I am not perfect, Sephora.'

'Perfection is a hard thing to live up to, I have found, my lord.'

'And there are many rumours about my past that are not all false...'

'I think I have heard most of them.'

At that he laughed. My God, he couldn't remember enjoying a conversation with a woman as much as he did with her.

'Your parents are not happy with my proposal. It is also something to consider. Your cousin, Anne Marie, fancied herself in love with me, but I hardly knew her and I certainly did not encourage her feelings or return them. I didn't attend the funeral because I was drunk. Not from unrequited love either, but from the sadness of it all. The futility of a young life suddenly gone.'

'Are you trying to put me off accepting you?'

'No.' The word came without thought. 'I'm not.'

'Then yes. Yes, I will marry you, Lord Douglas.'

Her parents were back in the next second, gliding through the door and taking up the space again between them and the strange dislocation that Francis felt was multiplied.

'Your daughter has agreed to become my wife so I'll have my lawyers call upon you tomorrow, Lord Aldford.'

'Tomorrow?' Her father's word was barely audible.

'I will procure a special licence in order to be married before the week's end. My lawyers will look at an agreement tomorrow afternoon and I would like your daughter present at the discussions.'

'An unseemly haste...' her mother began, but without further conversation Francis simply tipped his head to them all and took his leave, walking out into the daylight and down the steps to his waiting carriage, the sun today warming the skin at his neck.

The Earl of Douglas had looked furious and distant in all the time he stood there asking her to be his bride. Even when she had assented in private his expression had not changed, the scar on his damaged cheek underlining all that was unknown about him.

She did not understand him and he did not know her, yet she had agreed to marry him and with none of her usual timidity.

She should have refused and that would have been the end to it. He would have gone away with the knowledge that he had done the honourable and decent thing and she would have been left to get on with her own life.

But what sort of life would it be without him? That thought had her placing her hands across her mouth in terror. Could she accept a proposal of marriage that he couldn't possibly be happy with, a union based only on propriety and public expectation? It would never work, not in a million years, and they could both only be made bitter because of it. He'd said nothing of feelings, nothing of regard, nothing of anything save for his duty to see her reputation safe.

Sitting in her bedroom watching the moon through the glass, all Sephora could think of was the wedding night. She was almost twenty-three years old and the only man who had ever kissed her had been Richard, embraces that had been few and far between and hardly satisfactory. Besides which he had called her cold.

Whereas Francis St Cartmail...

She stopped and pulled her mind away from all she had heard of the earl's sexual prowess. He would hardly be happy when he realised the true state of her knowledge of the sensual arts. Oh, granted, there were men in society who relished the chance of instructing a virgin in the matrimonial bed, but the earl did not seem to fit into that category at all. He was too raw and too carnal.

'Carnal.' She rolled the word on her tongue.

He had asked her to marry him and she had said yes and if they did not know each at all she only had to think of Richard Allerly to understand the futility

of years of congress. They had been friends forever
and yet it was such a familiarity that had torn them
apart and left them strangers.

Francis St Cartmail was unfamiliar, but he was
also kind and every time she had been with him she
felt safe and protected.

Could it be enough? Closing her eyes, Sephora
put her fingers to her temples to massage the ache
that was building there, a heavy, dull pain of confusion and anxiety.

Anna had locked herself in a cupboard when Francis returned home and Mrs Billinghurst was standing
waiting for him so that she could relay the sorry saga
of another day's chaos.

'She is impossible, my lord. We had just got out
of the carriage and suddenly she simply turned for
home and when I got here she was in the wardrobe
of her room and I have not been able to coax her out
since.' Her young son was next to her and trying his
hardest to give the distraught woman some comfort.

This was the first time Francis had seen the lad
up close and as a worried visage gazed up at him
he realised just how young he really was. Had he
been schooled, he wondered, since his father's death?
'What is your name?' he asked the boy.

'Timothy.'

'How old are you?'

'I will be twelve next year, sir.'

A different worry now formed across Celia Billinghurst's face.

'He is a good boy, my lord, and is no trouble at all to anyone.'

'Does he read?'

'He began once…' Her voice petered out as she tried to deduce the reasons behind the question, but the lad stepped forward and answered.

'I do, Lord Douglas. I taught myself and I read whenever I can.'

'What do you read?'

'Old newspapers mainly, my lord. Once I went to the library in Finsbury Square with my father…' He stopped and swallowed.

'Did you like it?'

'I certainly did, sir.'

'Good.'

A few minutes later he stood in front of the solid oaken wardrobe and knocked twice. 'Come out, Anna, I need to talk with you.'

There was the slide of wood and a click of a lock and the door opened. His small cousin held one of his books and a candle in her hand and she had been crying.

This surprised him more than anything for each time he had seen her she had been prickly, angry and distant.

'Mrs Billinghurst said that you ran away from her and came home here all by yourself. Why?'

'I don't enjoy shopping.' She lifted her chin and faced him directly.

'Then perhaps you should stay home for a time so that we will all know where you are. It is dangerous for a young lady of your age to be lost in a busy city for a great length of time.'

Relief crossed the small face. 'I can do that.'

There was something she was not telling him, he was certain of it.

'Did you see someone in town whom you were frightened of?'

She shook her head, hard, the Douglas determination stamped into her eyes and, knowing such stubbornness would be hard to budge, he changed the subject.

'I would like to hire a tutor for you, Anna, and set up a small schoolroom here as an adjunct to your governess's lessons for I think your mind is a lively one and could do with further training. Mrs Billinghurst's son, Timothy, is about your age and he enjoys reading as much as you do. How would you feel about having a fellow student in your class for two days a week?'

'I would like that.'

'Good. Then you now need to go and find Mrs Billinghurst and apologise to her. We can discuss further arrangements tomorrow when we are all feeling less emotional. Oh, and, Anna, I would prefer it if you called me Uncle Francis. We are family and it is only right.'

Much later that evening as the clock struck the hour of two Francis sat by an opened window in his library with a heavy woollen cloak about him to keep out the cold. He never slept well and tonight after all the happenings of the day he knew he would sleep even worse than usual.

He wondered what Sephora Connaught was doing. After leaving the Aldfords' town house he had gone straight into Doctors' Commons and begun the proceedings for a special licence. Could they be married the day after tomorrow with such unseemly haste and with so little pomp and circumstance?

They would need separate bedrooms, of course, with his poor sleeping habits and their lack of knowing each other at all, but he hoped in time...

What did he hope?

He hoped that she might begin to see him as he had been once before his stay in Hutton's Landing, before his life had been shaped differently, before he had killed a man in cold blood and not just under the protecting banner of war.

He'd never had a family, never had anyone who had lived with him for a very long time. His uncle and aunt had tried to be some sort of guardians to him, he would give them that, but he had been rebellious and angry after the early death of his parents and when he'd barely let them in, they had not endeavoured for a closer acquaintance.

School had fostered his friendships with Daniel and Lucien and then later Gabriel. And now Anna had come and Mrs Billinghurst and the son who looked frightened and intense and needy. A house filled with problems, but also with life. He could feel them all here around him and despite the quandary he liked the new energy.

Tipping his head, he took in air once and then twice more. He could barely believe Sephora Connaught had agreed to marry him and hoped that she would not hate him when she knew him better.

A dog barked in the distance, plaintive and sad, and the sound rolled around with that particular nuance of hopelessness he himself had often felt. A homeless animal, probably a stray. If the thing came closer, he would instruct his kitchen staff to go out and take it a bone.

Chapter Ten

Sephora fussed around and could barely settle all of the next morning because she knew Francis St Cartmail would be here in the afternoon with his lawyer. Would he have changed his mind? Would things today look very different from what they had yesterday as he realised the extent of what he had promised and regret it? Would he simply take his troths back and leave her here, the ruin of her name too daunting even for him to try to manage?

When he did finally come she thought he looked tired, the shadows beneath his eyes darker today than she had ever seen them before.

'Douglas.' Her father's greeting was cold, but when the earl's glance found her own he smiled and she forgot everything else entirely.

'Lady Sephora.' Her name slipped from his tongue. 'I hope I find you well this afternoon.'

'Indeed you do, my lord.' With Papa and both lawyers present she did not dare to address him less formally though she would have liked to, given the circumstances. It was not normal, she knew, for a woman to be present in such discussions of money and law, but as Francis St Cartmail had expressly requested her presence her father under duress had allowed it.

'I have procured a special licence,' the Earl of Douglas was saying now. 'We can be married tomorrow for my lawyer is here to set the terms.'

'Tomorrow?' Was it even possible to marry legally in so short a frame of days? She could not stop her interjection.

'If that is what you wish?' He suddenly looked more uncertain and his eyes went to the windows.

'It is, my lord.'

'You cannot mean this, Sephora.' Her father spoke now. 'You have no dress, no invitations sent, no plan for a chapel or music or the food.'

'I do not need those things, Papa.' She said this as she looked straight at Francis St Cartmail and saw the stiffness in him relax. He was trying his hardest to see her safe. The least she could do was to allay his fears of her own hope of a much larger celebration.

'Your mother will be even more horrified than she is now.'

Again the Earl of Douglas looked at her. 'If it is a grander ceremony you wish for...'

'I don't.'

His hand pushed his hair back from where the darkness had fallen over his forehead and he breathed hard. He always wore his neckcloth tied high and often pulled at it with his fingers, Sephora thought.

The 'half-hanged' explanation of Maria's came back to her and she looked away. What sort of mark would a rope leave, both inside and out?

For a moment she imagined Francis St Cartmail naked under candlelight on their wedding night; this thought so unlike anything she had ever had before she almost blushed. In all of the years she had known Richard she had not once thought of him in any sort of a sexual way and she understood with a stinging clarity why she had not.

He had not intrigued her as Francis St Cartmail did, just one glance from his hazel eyes sending her into fantasy and folly. Richard had been staid and dictatorial and set in his ways and she had gone along with every single one of his orders and protocols. For years.

'Well then, what is it you are proposing in financial terms, Lord Douglas? My lawyer is most interested to know.' Her father was a man who thought the bottom line singularly important. She waited for the earl's answer.

'All that is mine shall be my wife's on marriage, save for the entailed Douglas properties as these will be passed on directly to any heirs. Any profit from the manufacturing businesses shall also be hers.'

Heirs? A short burst of heat had her reaching for the nearby back of a chair.

'That is indeed generous, my lord.' The Connaught lawyer opened his folder and wrote down the pledge. 'You speak of your garment interests, I am supposing?'

'He does.' The Douglas lawyer brought his files forward now and her father joined them, comparing notes.

When Francis St Cartmail caught her eye and smiled, she imagined he could see the pulse in her throat leaping to his attention and turned back to her father.

'There will be a dowry, of course,' he was saying, 'Amongst other monies and properties settled upon her, my daughter owns an estate in the north that her grandmother bequeathed her and it is both fertile and in good order.'

'Lady Sephora can keep that for herself. I do not wish the gift to pass into our communal property.' The words of her husband-to-be astonished her.

'But...' his lawyer began, and the earl silenced him with only a look.

Hers. Brockton Manor was to be only hers? The hope of it made the day brighter and her mind surer. A generous husband and a fair one. Richard Allerly was wealthy, too, but she could not have imagined him passing up the offer of another estate. He liked things under his control and his say so.

Her father was looking at St Cartmail now in a way he had not been half an hour ago, the Connaught legal representative writing his concessions down as fast as he could, his professional demeanour honed in for the best of advantages.

Finally a draft of the marriage agreements was signed. The Earl of Douglas's signature was bold and he was left-handed. His middle names were Andrew and Rothurst. So many things she did not know about him. The large cabochon ruby in his ring twinkled in the light and for that familiarity she was glad.

Her father crossed the room and extracted an expensive bottle of red wine when they had finished, a tipple he rarely opened because of the cost. The butler laid out five glasses, but Sephora merely played with hers, the thoughts in her head spinning. Lord Douglas was wealthy and he was generous. He was also a force to be reckoned with in the gaining of an equitable marriage contract that was suitable to them both. All afternoon he had been certain to include her in every decision and had taken into account her opinion concerning the points she wished to comment on.

The meeting broke up then and after a quick and formal goodbye the man she would marry tomorrow at one in the afternoon at the chapel of St Mary's was gone.

Her father finished both his glass of wine and hers. 'Waste not want not, though at least St Cartmail was easier to deal with than Winbury,' he said when he had finished the second. 'In my mind Douglas is either a saint or a fool with his capitulations of money and business interests and time undoubtedly will tell us which of the two it shall be. For your sake, Sephora, I sincerely hope that it shall be the first.'

Maria arrived home just on dusk and Sephora was glad to hear footsteps running up the stairs, her door bursting open even as her sister was undoing the bows on her bonnet.

'I cannot believe so much has happened, Sephora. In the two days I have been helping Rachel Attwood with the arrival of her new baby Richard is finally gone for good and in his stead is the Earl of Douglas? Even in my wildest dreams I did not imagine such luck.'

They came together in the middle of the room, Maria cold from the short carriage ride across the city and Sephora warm from the fire, their arms wrapped about one another as if they might never let go.

'I think Francis St Cartmail offered to marry me out of guilt,' Sephora said an hour later, after the whole story had been relayed in each and every minute detail.

Her sister shook her head. 'Society has been gossiping about the earl for years now. Do you really think a man like that could be brought to heel by Richard's meanness or by Papa's anger? Have you spoken with him, privately, and asked him why he should offer you marriage?'

'I have not had the chance. He came yesterday to relate his intentions to Papa and today with his lawyers to make it official. The two moments Father did allow us to converse alone were largely taken up with him saying that he would never hurt me and with me unable to say a word that made any sense.'

'Do you love him?'

Sephora drew her nightgown up around her neck, feeling a sudden chill in the room. 'I don't know what love is. I thought I loved Richard once, but...' She trailed off before trying again. 'Francis St Cartmail makes me feel...safe.'

'Safe enough to take risks? Safe enough to be yourself? Safe enough to imagine that your opinion matters again?'

'Yes.'

Maria began to laugh heartily and fell back against the pillows at the head of Sephora's bed. 'I go away and come back to find my sister has defied all the convoluted and restrictive social mores that she has always adhered to and has absolutely no qualms or remorse for any of it. Mama is in bed with her smelling salts, Papa is counting the financial largesse of this new suitor and the *ton* is still talking of nothing else save the fall from grace of its most stellar and malleable angel. I think I should go and see my friend more often, Sephora, I really do.'

'Will you stand up with me tomorrow at the ceremony?'

'Tomorrow? My God. You cannot be getting married tomorrow?'

'By a special licence. I am wearing my blue silk, the one I had made for the Cresswell ball earlier in the Season, but did not go because I fell ill.' Her most striking dress was heavily embroidered with silver lamé and embellished with Brussels lace. Flowers and shells in the same silver threads festooned the hem, the whole thing having the effect of catching the light in a most unusual manner.

Sephora wondered how she could even think about something as unimportant as the colour and detail of her wedding gown, but unless she concentrated on the small and basic things under her control she thought indeed she might go to pieces. Would Francis St Cartmail insist on a marriage night before they had barely conversed? Or might he simply take her to his family seat in Kent and leave her there, a bride he did not want, a woman who had stumbled into her own marriage through a series of foolish mistakes? An inconvenient bride.

It was not truly his fault all this—it was hers. It was she who had gone to see the Earl of Douglas in the daylight and in an unwise lather of hope and hopelessness. He had not poured the whisky down her throat either; in fact, he had tried to stop her from drinking too much after offering it as a way to lessen the shaking in the first place.

Was he sitting there now in his town house not two miles from here rueing the day he had ever jumped from the bridge into the waters of the Thames to try to save her, and was her sister's romantic slant on the forthcoming nuptials as naive as her own imaginings of safety?

Sephora shook her head. The one thing she was very certain of at least was that she had made a lucky escape from the overbearing ways of the Duke of Winbury. For that at least she would be eternally grateful.

She was dressed in blue and silver and held a small posy of gardenias and green leaves. Her hives were back, too, he noticed, the fiery red marks crawling up the exposed skin on her lower arm and along the slender plane of her neck before dipping into the high-cut bodice at the front, a small fair figure, diminutive and pale against the other three members of her family who had accompanied her.

Lucien stood as best man, a last-minute favour when Francis's intent of doing this completely alone had wavered and he had asked for some assistance. This wasn't how Francis had imagined his wedding day might be, a hastily thrown-together affair with a bride who looked like she might simply faint away if he touched her.

'Your intended does not appear exactly happy.'

It was true. The woman who had said yes to him was now enveloped in a sort of fog of distance and a state of fear, as if just by the blink of an eye this whole charade might simply disappear, her life back to the ordained and gentle path it had been sailing along less than a week ago.

There were no other wedding guests either and the minister was observing each small separate party with a look of concern and worry. At least there was someone playing the organ in an upper-storey loft, for the music covered the awkward quietness and offered a vague tone of religious fervour.

'Do you have a ring?'

'Yes.' Francis fumbled in his pocket for the small box and handed it over. Lucien flipped the top.

'Substantial.'

His friend's surprise seemed to give some sort of signal to the minister and he called them together, the age-old words of the Anglican marriage ceremony ringing out as an echo in the emptiness of the church.

'The grace of our lord Jesus Christ, the love of God and the...'

Francis moved to position himself next to Sephora Connaught. He could smell the scent of the flowers she held and this close up he saw she shook quite badly, all her attention on the minister who had raised his hands in a welcome.

The sister was watching him closely, however, her dark eyes running across his own in a frank appraisal. Maria Connaught, unlike Sephora, did not look like a young woman who would be cowed by anything. He wondered about the difference between them. What made one sister brave and the other frightened, one woman ready to fight and another to flee?

As if on their own accord Sephora's eyes lifted to his and he saw inside the fright a further sense of resolve. Without thought he reached for her hand and her fingers curled into his own and held on. Like two people drowning together.

The oaths and promises were lengthy, but finally the rings were exchanged. His grandmother's diamond-and-ruby circle fitted Sephora perfectly, the fragile stones setting off the shape of her hand, an ancient and unusual piece that would never be repeated anywhere.

It was over just as she thought it might never be, the onerous frown of the minister, the still silence of

Francis St Cartmail, the quiet weeping of her mother and the stony face of Papa.

'You may kiss your bride now.'

But he did not. Rather the Earl of Douglas's thumb simply ran down across one cheek before he turned away, breaking any contact with her and speaking to Lucien Howard next to him.

'Will you journey down to Kent today?' The Earl of Ross asked her this question a few moments later as they moved from the church and climbed inside the waiting carriages ready to take them home to the Aldford town house in Portman Square and the prepared wedding breakfast.

'Is that where the rest of his family are, my lord?' She wondered why no one had come to stand with him. Surely there must have been some relative who would have sufficed?

The earl shook his head. 'Francis's friends have that honour, for his own parents were gone when he was ten. I should probably leave it to him to tell you his story, though, but what I will say is that he has been lonely.'

Lonely. She could see that sometimes in his eyes and in the way he watched others, a careful isolation and a remoteness that allowed few near. She wanted to make him smile, she did, even just to see the ruined dimple on his cheek crease into laughter.

As though he could read her thoughts he turned, a half-smile making him look more vulnerable and younger, his eyes an unfathomable and mixed shade of green and brown.

'It won't be long before this is all over.'

Did he wish for it to be? Had he had enough of the enforced joyousness and the false congratulations? Her mother was still weeping and had given her nothing of maternal advice at all. Maria seemed to be the only one enjoying the occasion.

'I shall be married in exactly the same manner—' her sister's voice was light and happy '—without fuss of pomp and ceremony. And afterwards I shall journey to Italy on a grand tour with my husband and stay in the hot climes for a year and a day.'

Half an hour later the party was seated in the Aldford dining room and food was being served, numerous and special plates presented with artistry and attention. But Sephora could barely eat because soon it would be just her and Francis St Cartmail, with all the corners of her shadows visible. Then Lord Douglas would discover what he did not now know.

She lacked gumption and adventure and interestingness, and for a lord who had sailed oceans and stood on foreign shores, faced danger and survived numerous threats, that might well be the most damning truth of them all.

When he stood to raise his glass and make a toast she wondered what he might say of her, a bride he'd hardly conversed with, and barely touched. The room became quiet and as he began to speak he turned towards her parents.

'First I would like to offer my gratitude to Lord and Lady Aldford for all the love they have given to their daughter. It is undoubtedly this attention that has made Sephora into the woman she is today. Thank you for allowing me her hand in marriage and I promise I shall give her the same care as you have. Always.'

Her mother had placed her kerchief down now and was tentatively smiling. Her father gave him an answering nod and finished yet another glass of wine.

'Sephora and I met unexpectedly, under the waters of the Thames, and I suppose that first encounter set the tone for our courtship. It has been a quick and breathless liaison.'

He waited till the laughter stopped and raised his glass.

'To my bride and to our marriage.'

She was glad Francis had not dredged out words of love because they would have been as false as Richard's constant proclamations of the same. Her fingernails left crescent marks in the soft skin of each opposite palm with the stress of worry and nerves.

After the toast Lucien Howard stood up as the best man.

'Francis has always made his mind up quickly. He has lived life to the full, though there are many stories of his exploits that have taken on a falsity all of their own. I have been a friend of the Earl of Douglas for a long time and he is one of the most honourable and virtuous men I know. After losing his own parents early he has become the man he is without the guidance of any family whatsoever.'

Her groom looked as if he wished Lucien Howard

might cease altogether with the compliments. But he didn't as he turned to look at her. 'He saved me once, Lady Sephora, almost in the same way as he saved you. I'd dived into the high dam at Linden Park and got caught in the weeds and it was only Douglas's quick thinking that got me up to the surface before I ran out of air completely. So here's to happiness and to a long union,' he added and raised his glass.

Virtuous and honourable. Those were the words the Earl of Ross had used and she believed him, a man who would know Francis as well as any. The wine was sweet and easy to drink and it put a buffer between this moment and the wedding night, though the hives she had woken with were becoming larger and larger red welts of itchiness.

Her mother looked somewhat happier and her sister was glowing and if her papa was drinking far more than he ought then still her family had behaved. They had got through such a charade with a sense of grace. Sephora was eminently glad for that.

An hour later she rearranged her skirt and allowed her new husband to see her into the carriage, her parents and her sister standing on the pavement waving goodbye. Then they were alone, the busy streets of London town all around them, a procession of people and carriages and noise.

Her carefully packed luggage was in the back, an array of new clothes inside, a nightgown and a peignoir made of the softest apricot silk and edged in Brussels lace. Her mother's gift that, procured yesterday from one of the most expensive French seamstresses in the city, so new it was still wrapped in the tissue it had been bought in.

'We will go back to my town house first and collect a few things, but we will need to be on the road to Kent before mid-afternoon as I don't want to be too late in arriving.'

Too late? For what? Sephora thought. For a night alone? For more whisky, but this time plied for the very purpose of softening resistance? He had let it be known that there would only be a few servants accompanying them to Colmeade House, a private affair then, with all the hours of solitude. The Earl of Douglas sat on the same side of the conveyance as she did, but he had made sure to leave a large gap between them. Nothing touching.

A stranger and one who did not try to break the silence with other talk. The beautiful ring he had given her caught at a thread on her gown and snagged it. She spent a moment trying to tease the fabric away from the pointed sharpness of ancient gold and saw that it had left a hole in the silk. Like her life, broken, no matter how hard she might try to fix it and a sign of all that might come?

'It was my grandmother's,' he said unexpectedly. 'The ring. My mother gave it to me a few months before she died.'

'How did she die?'

'A carriage accident. My father was with her. I was ten at the time.'

'So afterwards there was no one else left for you?

Today in the chapel…' She thought of the empty space on his side of the pews. 'Lucien Howard told me at the church that he and his friends were as much of a family to you as any and yet they were not there either.'

He leaned over and took her hand, his fingers as cold as her own.

'Daniel Wylde and Gabriel Hughes are out of London and I hadn't the time to wait for them to return. I'd spend a lot of weeks with them in the school holidays because it was lonely at the Douglas seat and the servants needed a break. One small child could have hardly warranted the full opening of a large house after all and I was glad to go to where there was some sense of family and laughter.'

'Who were your guardians, then?'

'My uncle and his wife, but they were dour and busy people who were not much bothered with my needs. They hadn't their own children, you see…'

'So you were alone?'

He smiled. 'I suppose that I was. I don't think I've ever told anyone as much about my upbringing as I have you and if you'd…'

He faltered suddenly, his face changing from repose to complete and utter astonishment as he looked out the window, his cane snatched up from beside him and heavily brought against the ceiling.

'Stop, right now.'

The conveyance skidded to a halt and her new husband was out of the door, a knife in hand procured from beneath the seat, its shining honed blade caught in the sunshine as he moved.

'Stay here.'

But Sephora had already left her seat and was behind him, pushing into the path of the traffic, rushing through in the small spaces left between the busyness and pulling in her skirts close so that she could indeed run to keep up.

Ahead a small girl was being dragged along by a man who had her pinned to him by one arm and she was screaming her head off whilst trying to kick back. A wicked punch across the jaw silenced her, but the rage that erupted from the earl at the action brought every face from yards around towards him.

After that things began to happen in slow motion as Francis St Cartmail slashed out with his knife and the offenders gave answering jabs with their own weapons. Two other men had joined in the fracas now, with their anger and fury. One went down, a gash across his thigh opening into red, but the gun that the third offender held was primed and ready and it discharged point blank into the shoulder of the Earl of Douglas. He fell slowly, grabbing the child and using his momentum to roll with her, the shouts of bystanders, the frightened sobbing of the girl, the whitened clammy face of her new husband as he came to a stop by her feet and lay still upon the dirty camber of the road, panting.

The man with the gun moved forward to try to extricate the child from his grasp, but Sephora simply fell on top of them both in protection, her generous silken skirts wrapped around everything as the warm seep of red blood darkened the thin fabric.

And she screamed, too, as loud as she could and as long, bringing bystanders to her aid even as she hung on to the small shaking body of the child with all the strength that she could muster and felt a hefty kick into the exposed fleshy part of her lower back as an angry retaliation for her efforts.

Then their attackers were gone, carrying the other man Francis had wounded between them and leaving a dozen or so spectators gathering about the ensuing brokenness that was left, not quite knowing what to do.

'Help. Please.' She could only mouth the words, her breath lost in the vicious last stab of pain and the horror of violence so unexpectedly meted out.

The child between them was sobbing so hard that Sephora had to gather her own will, the young girl demanding attention and some semblance of safety from the adults around her. The earl was still largely conscious at least, his hands held out before him stiff with blood and a clammy sheen of sweat across his face.

'Anna?' He looked about blindly. 'Is…she…safe?'

'Here. She is here.' Presuming Francis must mean the child, she wrapped the girl against her warmth and saw what she had not noticed before. The same hazel eyes. The same lines of beauty. The same colour of hair and grace of movement. The same stubborn line of jaw.

His daughter? His offspring? Just another secret that he had allowed her no knowledge of?

All her marriage lines fell into a dissolving welter of lies and omissions though her attention was caught by his raspy laboured breathing as he fumbled to loosen the stock at his neck.

When the white linen fell away she knew another truth as well. The deep red twisted line of where a rope had cut into his flesh was easily visible, knotted welts of skin raised one over the other, and a shocking hue of indigo beneath.

Hurt. Damaged. Left for dead. Once before and now yet again.

She lifted his head carefully, the matted dark curls falling dank across her fingers, and then she pressed her hands down hard against the welling bloodied hole in his shoulder.

'Get a doctor,' she shouted and refused to let him pass into the care of anyone else until a proper physician had come.

The first hours afterwards had been the worst.

Once home at the Douglas town house and upstairs in his chamber, Francis had begun to breathe in a strange way, blood gushing from the hole just above his shoulder blade.

'Elevate him,' the Douglas physician had instructed and with the help of a few of the servants they got him off the bed and sitting up in a large chair nearby.

Sephora was panicking, but Francis wasn't. He simply sat there gathering in his hurt and his circumstances and moderating his breathing as best he could. The bandage the doctor tightened around him finally allowed the blood to congeal, but would no doubt gush again with any movement whatsoever.

The earl's eyes were closed, the dark bruising beneath them worrying, and he was clammy. Shock, perhaps. Sephora found a heavy wool blanket at the foot of the bed and draped it across him as Mrs Wilson bustled in with a young servant and instructed her to light the fire.

'I do not think the bullet has injured any organ of great import.' The physician lifted up his bag as he said this. 'But it is a nasty wound and will need to be tended with great care in order to stop fever or inflammation from appearing. There is also a severe gunpowder burn around the site that will be painful so I will leave medicine to be administered and return on the morrow. The instructions are on the label, but the thing needed most now is a good dollop of sleep so that healing can begin to take place.'

The child, his daughter, had sat next to Sephora without speaking for all of the last hour, refusing to leave the side of the earl. Up close she looked older than Sephora had first thought her and much more unkempt. Her eyes were large orbs of pure and utter fright and her hands were freezing as Sephora brought the girl into her side, trying to warm her.

As her initial stiffness relaxed Sephora felt thin cold arms creeping about her middle.

'It is quite, quite all right, Anna,' she said softly, remembering the name the earl had used. 'The earl will recover, I am sure of it, and this terrible fright will be a thing of the past…' She stopped even as she said the words, recalling her own dislocation after her fall from the bridge. 'You are safe now. Nothing will ever happen like this again. You will always be safe.'

The shaky nod almost broke her heart, a child trying desperately to find her courage and appear brave, but when Mrs Wilson reached out and told the girl to come away Sephora could do nothing but watch her go.

'I hope she is not too hurt. The man who tried to take her on the street hit her across the mouth...'

She did not quite finish as the housekeeper nodded. 'Anna disappeared from the side of her governess earlier in the afternoon and could not be found. Mrs Billinghurst was most upset.' Her voice petered out as the physician stood to leave.

'We will put his lordship into bed now with pillows to prop him up. He needs sleep to regather his energy.' Three manservants carefully lifted him off the chair and across to the bed where the covers had been pulled back so that he could simply slip inside.

He groaned at the movements and breathed in a rough manner, but once there appeared more comfortable, the blood from a cut on his right hand staining the snowy white coverlet. So much blood, she thought, glad that the Douglas physician had not wanted to bleed him further. His pallor now was as pale as the sheets of the bed he lay in and his breath was shallow.

Another few moments of flurried activity and then everyone was gone with only silence left as Sephora shut her eyes and held her head in her hands. Today had been a revelation. Francis St Cartmail had a child, a girl child, and she looked neither much cared for nor particularly happy.

The horror of it struck her anew. What sort of man could be so lax with the needs of a daughter? Her hair stuck out in all directions, her nails were as dirty as her clothes and he had not even asked her to his own wedding?

She struggled to find some sense in the whole thing. He had gone to save the child without thought for himself and nearly died for it. Surely that must count for something and the girl had stuck like glue to his side in all of the doctoring and aftermath. Her behaviour was not exactly that of a well-raised daughter and the manner in which she had sworn roundly as they had lain in a heap on the side of the road was most surprising.

Mrs Wilson had appeared wary of the girl, as had the servants. A child who might lash out, Sephora thought, or refuse any direction? An uncivilised and worrisome child.

Her own head had begun to ache with the direction her thoughts were going in. Francis St Cartmail had wed her today without mentioning that he had been married before and had heirs already. What of the legal documents and the implications for an heir already existing? My goodness, the scandal that followed him had arrived with a hiss and a roar on her very doorstep and not two hours after they had been wed.

'I am not perfect.' She remembered his words. But

there was long distance between the lies and deceit she was suddenly confronted with and the small discrepancies she was imagining.

A marriage of convenience. A marriage forced upon him. A marriage that had not even begun before it was threatened.

She swiped at the tears that fell across her cheeks and sat up straighter. She would not cry. She was beyond even allowing such a release. She would wait for the Earl of Douglas to regain consciousness and then she would find out exactly what else he had not told her.

It was late when Francis awoke, a single candle burning on the side table in his room at the Douglas town house in London.

This was wrong.

He should be somewhere else. There was a substantial pain across his shoulder and the smell of stale sickness in the air. He wore nothing but a sheet draped over him, and he began to gingerly move pieces of his body to see what functioned still and what did not.

Sephora. The name made him take in his breath and hold it, the ache of hurt radiating downwards in a sharp and jabbing violence.

'You are awake?' Her voice was soft in the late-night silence and he looked around. His new wife sat on his other side dressed in different clothes than she had last been in, her hair tied back in a simple knot, small golden curls escaping such confinement on each side of her face. There were deep shadows under her eyes and a bruise across her cheek that had not been there before.

'What happened?'

'You were shot, do you remember?'

He nodded, the noise and the instant pain coming back.

'Anna?'

'Your daughter is safe.'

He shook his head. God. He'd not managed to safeguard either of them, but had gone down with only the barest of resistance. 'Make sure...they...don't come back.'

It was all he could do, give such a warning before the dark and pain returned and he was once again floating.

The next time he came awake there was sunlight at the windows and he was glad that it was not night. He felt better, less light-headed. He was also very thirsty.

'Is there something to drink?'

Sephora was there again, soft and competent, her hands raising his head so that he could take a sip of some lemon concoction and just as gently lowering it down again.

'How long...have I been here?'

'Two days. For the first day the doctor thought you might not live and when you took fever he was certain of it. But you pulled through and now he is pleased with your progress.'

'And Anna?'

'I have not seen her again, though I hear her, of course. Your daughter is remarkably unruly.'

'She is…not my…daughter. I am her guardian and she has only recently come…to me.'

Sephora looked away from him, her blue eyes filled with pain and a hint of relief.

'No one explained this to me.'

'She is my uncle's illegitimate child. I have brought in a governess and a tutor for her, but…'

'She is difficult?'

He nodded. 'But…getting better, I hope.' Each word was breathy with the pain he felt and he hated his exhaustion.

'She looks just like you.'

He smiled. 'I know.'

'She did not wish to leave your side when you were shot. Perhaps if she was allowed in to see you she might be more inclined to behave?'

'Was she hurt?'

'No.'

'Were you?'

She shook her head, but that was not right for he held a vague memory of someone kicking her whilst she lay across him. When she leaned forward she did so with a good deal of stiffness.

'Papa has sent over two men, one as a guard at the front of the house and the other one behind it just in case anyone should have the temerity to try to snatch her again. The place is like a fortress.'

Swallowing, Francis pulled the sheet up about his chin, a small protection of defence against the telltale marks at his throat. No doubt Sephora had seen them already, but still… His hand looked bruised, pointing to the days he had been in this netherworld of pain and semi-consciousness.

He had to regather strength and the will to decipher all that had happened. His wedding had been ruined. That thought bit into everything with a sharp truth.

'I am sorry, Sephora.'

She frowned. 'For what?'

'Your wedding day was…spoilt.'

'I hope I am not so shallow as to think that is more important than your recovery.'

He smiled, liking her honesty. 'Thank you for keeping Anna safe.'

The anger at such an attack on his family consumed him and he was glad for her solid presence. He needed to be better and to be up dealing with things. He needed to find out who had hurt them all and what this meant. When he breathed in, he could smell violets on his wife's skin and was comforted by the scent. But the blackness reached out again to claim him even as he tried to fight it.

He was asleep again and so suddenly. Sephora could see it in the even rise and fall of his chest. Such a repose needed to heal all the ravages the bullet had wrought upon him. Francis St Cartmail was not the father of Anna but her guardian and she was his cousin. The relief when he had told her that was still gathered inside her, bubbling upwards and making her smile.

His eyelashes were long and thick and sat against

his cheeks in a dark soft swathe, though the old scar held only brutality and pain.

Contrasts.

He was an earl of the *ton* who knew how to use a knife in a way few men of his station did and the whispered secrets of his past were at direct odds with the respectability and solid history imbued in his family title.

Yet in the disparity Sephora could feel something inside herself shift and grow, a strength and fortitude returning as a life balanced in jeopardy forced her to appreciate all that was still left.

His ring on her finger caught the light and she turned it so that the face of it came within her palm. When she closed her hand she felt the gold warm inside.

She'd been living in a vacuum for so long now with Richard that she had forgotten what it felt like to be so vitally aware of both the good and the bad. To feel so deeply had its barbs, but it also held excitement and purpose and possibilities. Her whole world had changed from the utter boredom and ennui of a week ago to one where the terrifying pace of her adventures left her gasping.

But alive in a way she had never felt before.

'Please, God, let Francis be better soon,' she prayed, sitting quietly as the day darkened into dusk and a chorus of birdsong was heard.

Chapter Eleven

The story of the attack on the earl on the busy London streets was all over the broadsheets and the papers. Other stories had also surfaced about his past, the affair at Hutton's Landing and a fight he had been involved in in Boston. It seemed as if every man who had once held a gripe against Francis St Cartmail was out in force making his voice heard, and Sephora could do nothing to stop the tide of growing complaints

Her parents came to see her the next morning, their faces twin countenances of worry and alarm.

'There is still time to get out of this marriage, Sephora,' her father said. 'Non-consummation of the vows are enough of a reason for the dissolution of the contracts. Any judge would see to it.'

'It is just so very awful,' her mother continued where her father left off. 'You have always been surrounded by beauty and fine living and now…now there is just base rumour and a danger from people who might attack you in the street in broad daylight.

We worry for you. We want you to come home and to be with us, to be safe, and back where you belong.'

Her parents' heartfelt litanies after nights of sleeplessness were daunting.

'Richard's mother came up to London the other day, too,' Elizabeth continued. 'Josephine says that her son thinks he has made a terrible error in his judgement and wonders if you might meet him again, to talk sensibly over all that has happened. Perhaps you could resolve your silly arguments and—'

'No.' That word was torn from absolute certainty. 'I have no wish at all to go back to what I was.'

'Then this is enough? This slander against your name. This uncertainty? It is said that it was Douglas's illegitimate daughter who was being dragged away on the street. A daughter from an affair he had with some woman of the night.'

'Well I can tell you now that is false. Anna St Cartmail is the earl's cousin. He is her guardian and has brought in a well-thought-of relative to look after her. It was not his fault that she was in danger on the streets of London and I am certain that he will see to things once he is better...'

'But will he be? I heard he had been shot at pointblank range. How does one survive that, Sephora, and live a full life afterwards?'

'With resolve, Mama.'

Her mother extracted a handkerchief from her reticule and blew into it. 'Maria said we should not be able to change your mind, but if you ever find yourself wondering what to do...'

'I shan't.'

'Do you need money, my dear, to help you through this time?' Her father's words were quiet and firm.

'No, Papa. We have more than enough.'

At that moment a filthy, huge, wet, grey dog tore around the corner of the salon, its matted mangy fur standing up against a bony spine and yellow teeth exposed. Before they could all leap out of their seats, though, the housekeeper was in the room, her clothes soaking and soap on her face.

'Miss Anna and I are giving him a bath, my lady. Lord Douglas said to bring him in and feed him, but he was just so very unclean...' She stopped as she saw Sephora's parents and swallowed, but the dog leapt past her again, its paws skidding on the shining parquet floor into the direction of the kitchen, Sephora thought, and the answering shout from Anna St Cartmail told her that the guess had been correct.

'Well, I think we have probably seen enough.' Her mother was on her feet and her father beside her. 'I can't imagine what might happen next and I hope, Sephora, if you are honest with yourself, you may not be able to either.' She sounded breathless and her words were tight, but at least she was no longer crying. Her father joined her and then they were gone, the silence of the room broken only by the howls of a dog who had obviously been dumped into a tub of water and was being cleaned spotless to within an inch of its life.

Francis was awake when Sephora looked into his room a few moments later. He was sitting on the side of his bed and had a shirt on, the thick wedge of bandage showing through the linen.

Several drawings of dogs were stacked on the bedside table. They were well executed, although the animal in pencil looked a lot more regal in bearing than the one she had just seen in the flesh.

'Anna drew them for me. She came in to see me very early and when the dog howled close by I asked her to see it was given something to eat. It is the first conversation that has been pleasant between us since she came.'

'She would be thankful you saved her, no doubt, and mindful of the fact that you nearly gave your life to do so. You seem better today?'

He gestured to a bottle of medicine. 'The doctor left me something stronger for the pain and combined with the brandy Daniel brought in, it must be working.' His humour was comforting.

'And these?' More drawings were in a pile on the coverlet, giving the impression that he had been shuffling through them.

'My ward is doing her best to convince me the animal appears more attractive than I imagine he is. I said that she could feed it a bone from the kitchen, but I gather from the noise I just heard it has made its way into the house already and Mrs Wilson has seen it.'

'It is being given a bath as we speak.'

'What sort of dog is it?'

'A large grey mangy one with yellow teeth and an old ill-healed wound right along its back.'

He smiled. 'I don't think you are convincing me to keep it.'

'Mama and Papa arrived just as it came indoors, a wet and soaking pile of smelly fur. They left as soon as they could.'

'Because of the dog or because of me?'

She could not lie. 'Stories are swirling around London about your involvement in things that are…'

'Dubious. Questionable. Suspect.'

'Yes.'

'And your parents are worrying how the "angel of the *ton*" has managed to get herself caught up in the less-than-salubrious affairs of a disreputable earl?'

Sephora smiled. 'I doubt people call me that any more and I am glad for it.'

'Glad?'

'The pressure of being always good is probably as stultifying as the one you bear of being always wicked.'

He laughed and a hand went to his injured side, his breathing rough and quick.

'There are always two sides to every story, Sephora.'

'Then who was Ralph Kennings?' She watched with a growing disquiet as a flush of anger crossed over his humour, cancelling it out.

'Who told you about him?'

'Maria. She said you were with Adam Stevenage's cousin out at Hutton's Landing and that Kennings tried to murder you.'

Hell, he had not expected Sephora to know that name and the shock of it made his heart beat so fast

Francis could feel the blood throb around the bullet hole in his shoulder.

'Ralph Kennings is a man I killed. I shot him three times, once through each knee and then a third time through the heart. He had not drawn a weapon.' Better to say it with nothing missing. Better to let her understand just how much he had lost of himself out there in the canyons above Hutton's Landing.

'Why?'

The face of Seth Greenwood came to mind, gasping his last in the mud below the ruined platform, a bullet deep inside him and his blood turning the water scarlet. But it was not that death that Francis dwelt on.

'He'd killed two children and their mother before he came upon us. He wanted gold.'

'Who were these people? These children?'

'Seth's family. He had twin boys. They were babies, for God's sake, barely walking.'

He could not tell her it all. He did not tell her what had been done to him that evening after the platform had collapsed, but the rope burn at his throat tightened about the little there was left of his breath. He could see the horror in her eyes, the brittle shocked blue even as he wondered what was reflected in his own.

This was the truth of him, the brutality and the tragedy. Thinking of Hutton's Landing negated any softness or goodness that he might have nurtured had he walked the finer line of gentility.

'Your parents want you home, no doubt? They want you safe and well away from me? Perhaps they are right.'

But she shook her head and drew in breath, holding it until she spoke again. 'Life would be different, then, in the Americas? Wilder. Savage, even.' He could hear the hope of it in her voice.

'Honour is honour, Sephora, and mine was lost there in those three easy shots. I was a marksman in the army and damn good at my job. I knew I would not miss.'

'Why are you telling me this? Why do you not defend yourself when you can only suffer from the consequences?' She stood and her hands were shaking, wound around each other in front of her, every nail bitten back to the quick.

'Because I should have told you of it before we were married. Because I am not the safe harbour you imagine me to be and your sins in the eyes of the *ton* are nowhere near as dark as the guilt I hold. I ought to have given you a choice, to have me or to not, and I didn't and for that I am sorry.'

She looked as if he had struck her.

'Richard never apologised to me once in all the years of knowing him and I didn't expect him to either because by then I'd lost whatever it was that gave me worth.'

'Worth?' He could not quite understand what she meant.

'Opinions. Beliefs. The ability to say no and to mean it. People can die by small degrees just as easily as they can by the quick slam of a bullet and sometimes justice isn't so easily measurable. Those murdered would most certainly think your honour intact given your actions and even the Bible has its verses urging an equitable vengeance.'

'An eye for an eye?'

'And a life for a life.'

Unexpectedly she leaned down and took his hand in her own, tracing the lines across the inside of his palm in a gentle touch. 'You saved mine in the water under the bridge and also perhaps out of it. Is there some sort of celestial scales, do you think, one that places human souls in arrears…or not?'

'The thought is tempting.' He liked her reasoning. He liked her smile. He liked the quiet sense she spoke and her conviction.

'If it were left to me to decide, yours would be a balanced tally sheet. And with Anna…' Dropping his hand, she pointed to the thick bandages under his shirt. 'With this I would imagine you are now ahead.'

He'd never had another person who believed in him like this, someone who would hear out his worst confessions and come up with an answer that made sense.

'Strong opinions are always valuable, Sephora, and if Richard Allerly only wanted to hear his thoughts parroted back by those around him then he is more of a fool than I took him for.'

She smiled, but he could see she was not happy. 'I believed I deserved what he gave me in the end. I think sometimes I didn't even want a different life because I wouldn't have known what to do with it.' She told this unexpected truth flatly, as though what she described had happened to someone else; a public truth rather than a private one.

'And now?'

The fierce anger was unmistakable. 'Now I am different.'

'Good for you.'

When she laughed the sound of it ran through the memory of three shots high up above the canyons near Hutton's Landing. Sometimes at night Francis imagined he had seen Kennings go for his gun, there on his hip just before he had fired, the movement against a silver dawn small but real. Today he hoped that this was true for her sake as well as for his own.

'The doctor said I would be well enough to travel down to the family seat in Kent in a few days.'

'I'd like that.'

He felt some of the tension inside him ease. His wife would come with him even knowing about Kennings? Being in the country would give him some time to work out how to protect Anna, too, and away from the gossip of the *ton* he wouldn't have to worry about what other things might reach Sephora's ears.

The tiredness that had consumed him since the accident needed to go. He wanted his energy back to look after the family he had somehow been gifted with.

The screams in the night woke her, shrill, loud, screams with desperation imbued in every one.

Coming to her feet, Sephora ran into the room

down the corridor to find Anna sitting up in bed white as a sheet and covered in sweat.

'I am fine.' The curt voice was underlined by blind fear.

'Well, you do not look it to me and when I am worried about something it is always so much easier when you have a friend beside you to share it with.'

Taking her hand, Sephora sat down beside the girl, holding on even as she tried to pull away. Anna's fingers were as freezing as they had been the last time Sephora had held them. It was as if the blood had not reached them at all in its course around her body, but left her shivering in the extremities. A child made frozen by anger.

'You are safe, Anna. There is nothing here that will hurt you. I promise.' She knew the instant the dreadful terror receded for the long and thin fingers relaxed. The girl's fear was heartbreaking, a child with demons snapping at her heels and enough fury to keep others at bay.

'If they come here to get me, you won't let them do it?'

'I won't.' Sephora was not quite sure just who Anna meant, but now was not the right time to dwell upon it, the child's heart beating so fast she could see the lawn of her nightgown going up and down. 'You belong to us now, to this family. We will never let you go.'

'No one has wanted me to stay anywhere with them before. Clive said he did, but he never meant it. Not at the end.'

Sephora had no idea who this Clive was or where the child's mother had gone, but she squeezed the thin hand and stayed quiet.

'This is the first house where I have my own room. And books,' she added. Small fingers still held on tightly. A lifeline perhaps, a raft across the deeper waters of her past?

'You helped me in the street. The man kicked you, I felt it, but you still didn't let me go.'

Tears now trickled down her face, the beauty of the Douglases stamped on her, too, but so much harder to see in the anger and under the ill-shorn lanky hair.

'If Uncle Francis had died…'

'Well, he didn't. He is making good progress and by tomorrow I think he will be up and about once again.'

'You are certain of it?' For the first time the girl made true eye contact, the dark green of the earl's own eyes looking out at her.

'Most certain. But we need to get you to sleep now so that you have some energy for that stray dog I saw you with today. He will be scared by all the change and worried you will send him away so you'll need to be calm and kind when you handle him.'

'Like you are? With me?'

Sephora blushed in pleasure. 'People come to others in different ways, Anna. Dogs, too. Sometimes in life there is no reason for things, but it just feels right.'

The girl smiled and as she tucked down under the blankets again Sephora began to hum some of the songs her mother had sung to her when she was young. A movement by the doorway had her turning and Francis St Cartmail stood there, leaning against the frame for balance, fresh blood staining the linen of his shirt where it had seeped through the bandage. He gestured to Anna, asking silently of the young girl's welfare, and when Sephora nodded he was gone.

She wondered at the pain and determination such a foray must have cost him even as she kept on singing, his Douglas stubbornness an exact copy of Anna's.

A few moments later she looked into the earl's room. He was sitting on a chair with a cloak around himself and the chamber was freezing. Every window was open.

'She's asleep?'

'Yes. I promised her that she belonged to us now and that we should never let her go. Is that something I should not have?'

'Did such a troth feel like the right one to give?'

Tipping her chin down, she looked him directly in the eyes. 'It did.'

'Then there is your answer.'

'You truly think it that simple?'

'I do.'

As she was about to speak again a movement beneath his bed by her feet made her start. 'The stray dog is in here?'

He nodded and smiled. 'Take him into Anna's room and place him on her bed. If she wakes again, he will afford her comfort.'

'Does the dog have a name?' she asked as she bent

to take hold of the new leather collar around the animal's scrawny neck.

'Hopeful,' he replied. 'I've called him that.'

Lying alone in bed a few moments later, Sephora watched the moonlight on her ceiling. She was happier here in a household filled with problems than she had been for years. There was a scrawny, abused dog lying entwined in the warm arms of an orphan child who suffered nightmares down the corridor one way and a man who held his own demons close and his past even closer down the other. Each had their secrets and their terrors. Each held the world at bay in silence and in anger. But beneath all that was difficult she felt the beginning of everything that could be easy.

Francis had called the dog Hopeful. She smiled at the name as she fell asleep and dreamed of water.

Maria and Aunt Susan came the next day and the one after that, too, and it was late on the second afternoon that her sister mentioned she had seen Richard Allerly at a small private function she'd attended with Mr Adam Stevenage.

'He had his arm entwined in that of the oldest Bingham girl and he was back to hovering. Miss Julia Bingham looked as though she was a cat who had just found the cream, though I suppose she may not be as pleased with herself in a year or two when she manages to determine the Duke of Winbury's true character and rues the loss of her own.'

'Poor girl,' Sephora returned, glad that Aunt Susan

was out of earshot over on the sofa. 'If I thought it could make a difference I might even feel the need to warn her off him. As it is I am going to just wish them the best.'

Maria turned to look at her. 'You have changed and I like it. Mama said you would not last a month in such a madhouse, but I think you will never leave the Earl of Douglas because you are happy. He makes you such even trussed up in bandages and lying in a sick room.' She began to laugh. 'I happily admit there is a strength in the man that is beguiling, and a sensuality, too. Imagine his effect on your person when he is well.'

Sephora shook such nonsense away, though part of her had been imagining the very same thing. 'Papa looked tired when I saw him?'

'He is still not speaking to Winbury at all and only a little to Aunt Josephine, which is surprising, and that is taking a toll. I think he wants to wait and see what happens here before he makes his mind up.'

'Tell them I am happy, Maria. Tell them if I had the chance to change anything at all that I would not.'

'Adam says Francis St Cartmail is a genius in his business dealings and hopes he might take him on as a partner in his manufacturing businesses up north. He also said that Douglas sent his cousin's mother money after Seth Greenwood's death, enough money to be comfortable for the rest of her life.'

Sephora was pleased to hear this. 'Richard always told everybody what he was going to do and never did it, whereas the Earl of Douglas seldom says a word and quietly sees to everything.'

'I think you love him.' It wasn't a question.

Turning away, Sephora felt a sort of hopeless longing. 'I was ruined. Surely that is enough of a reason to at least be grateful.'

'You lied to yourself every day when you were with Richard. I hope you are not still doing it.'

'Maria?'

'Yes?'

'I will miss you.'

Francis was up the next morning, dressed and eating a hearty breakfast when she came downstairs. 'Daniel Wylde is in town with his wife, Amethyst, and they have asked us to a celebration at their place in the afternoon.'

'A celebration?' She didn't feel up to the whole social gambit yet and was certain that he wasn't. They had not discussed any arrangements particular to their marriage either and when they spoke now she felt more and more as if they were strangers.

'Lucien's sister, Christine, will be there and the Wesleys, Gabriel and Adelaide Hughes. A small occasion to mark our wedding though unfortunately Lucien and his wife, Alejandra, are away in Bath on holiday.'

These people were all Francis's best friends and she was nervous of any questions that might come her way, for so far Francis and she had been circling around each other, a few truths that were surprising, and then long times of polite distance. She wondered what he might have said of her privately.

Women, too, had their ways of finding out things and although she had spoken with Adelaide Hughes and Amethyst Wylde briefly at different social events, she did not know Christine Howard at all, though she had seen her at a distance. She had never had women friends as such, Richard taking up most of her spare time.

So many thoughts made her dizzy and she helped herself to a cup of tea and sipped it slowly. 'I hope they will like me.'

Francis looked up at that and frowned. 'Why would they not?'

'Perhaps they might think...' She stopped for a second, but made herself carry on as he raised his eyebrows. 'They are strong women. I imagine that there are things about me that they cannot admire.'

'Such as?'

'Arriving at your house alone and uninvited and getting drunk on whisky. Tricking you into offering marriage to save me from a ruin of my own making.'

His laugh was rough. 'You truly think that of me? That I could be tricked into something that I did not wish to do? Something as important as marriage?'

'I don't know. I am certain you wouldn't have been interested in pursuing an acquaintance with me if I had not forced the issue, but...'

Now all humour had fled and he looked deadly serious. 'This damn bullet has so far ripped out any chance of showing you exactly what marriage should mean, Sephora, but I am recovering. Do not expect such a state of grace to last much longer.'

With that he stood, upending his cup of strong coffee before setting it down, dark eyes running across her in a way that was disturbing. He was newly shaved and his hair had just been washed and any of the illness suffered over the last week seemed to have run away with the bathwater.

A virile man with his own needs and beautiful beyond measure. Even the thought of it made her cheeks blush.

'If it's any consolation my friends were all trying their hardest to get me to see you as a suitable candidate for a bride long before you agreed to marry me.'

Then he was gone.

The afternoon began badly as the rain that had been holding off for the morning suddenly bucketed down on the small run between the carriage and the front door of the Wyldes' town house. Her hair was ruined, despite the umbrellas, of that she was sure, the curls so carefully fashioned hanging down the front of her jacket in long damp strands.

Francis St Cartmail on the other hand looked magnificent, the rain on his face and scar curled into laughter. 'God, I love England,' he said with feeling as they were shown inside. 'In America, for a good part of it, there was nothing but heat.

'Rain suits you, too,' he added as he took her cloak and passed it on to a waiting footman. 'I like your hair less…formal.'

And after that it was easy, Daniel Wylde's wife taking her hand and leading her into the room, a warm welcome on her face.

'We have been looking forward to meeting you properly, Sephora. Might I call you that? Francis has been alone for a large number of years, you see, and I always hoped that marriage would be his saving grace.'

As Lady Adelaide Wesley came forward Sephora remembered the last time they had spoken was on the subject of her marriage to the Duke of Winbury, the 'body, soul and heart' talk that had left her flustered and afraid.

Today, however, she was smiling and after searching for a moment in her reticule she lifted up a small bottle of oil.

'For fertility,' she explained. 'I give something to every new bride I know and chart which of the potions works the quickest. I have much hope in this elixir so I pray you don't disappoint me.'

The general laughter accompanying this statement meant Sephora's embarrassment went largely unnoticed.

Lucien's sister, Lady Christine Howard, was the next one to be introduced. Sephora had often seen her at a distance in society and admired her grace and beauty.

'I am so pleased to meet you, Sephora, and I do love your dress.'

Amethyst laughed. 'Christine has a business designing and making wonderful gowns though it is rather a secret.'

'Business?' Sephora had never really known a woman in business in her life. The idea of it was truly revolutionary.

'We are not quite the normal run of the women of the *ton*, Sephora. We like to fashion our own paths and woe betide the man that tries to stop us.' It was Amethyst Wylde who gave this explanation, quietly but honestly.

Goodness, Sephora thought as she digested this last confidence. She was so much more used to flighty small talk at social occasions, unimportant musings or even the more pointed gossip, and she could not believe the way this conversation was heading.

These women were...powerful, that was the word she sought, powerful in their hopes for themselves and each other, fearless in their opinions and she liked it. Maria would like them, too, she thought, and wished her sister could have been there.

At that point Gabriel Hughes lifted his glass to make a toast.

'Here's to a long and happy marriage,' he said. 'The final penniless lord and the last one to find his bride.'

'To Francis and Sephora.' Daniel Wylde spoke now and in the gaiety Sephora looked over at Francis and saw him watching her.

'To us,' he said quietly and handed her a glass. *'Ad multos annos.'*

The Latin made her smile though she wished that he might have made some mention of love.

Francis came to her room late that night, knocking on the closed door and waiting until she opened it. She was in her nightgown with a thick woollen shawl across her shoulders and some bright red slippers Maria had knitted her for her last birthday on her feet.

'I found this on the shelves of my library and I thought that you might like it,' he said and when she looked down she saw he was holding a book, bound in leather and embossed. 'It was given to me a long time ago and I remember you told me when I was sick that you wrote stories.'

When he handed it to her she saw it was a journal, each page embellished with small figures from fairy tales and beautifully executed.

She wanted to ask who had given him this, but something in his eyes stopped her. He looked lonely, his hair tonight loose so that it sat around his shoulders in long dark curls. His stock was loosened, too, and across the top of the linen she saw a small portion of the scar that traced from one side of his throat to the other.

'I am just having a hot drink. Perhaps you might join me?'

He seemed perplexed and for a fleeting second Sephora thought he might refuse, but then his reserve softened and he nodded his head. In the midst of her chamber he was hard, large and masculine and she was glad for the chairs before the fireplace to direct him to.

Pouring tea, she watched him take up the dainty china cup and smiled, for she could smell a stronger libation on his breath. Brandy, perhaps, or whisky.

'This room used to be my sister's,' he said after a moment and the shock of the information had her placing her own cup down.

'I thought there was just you in your family?'

He shook his head. 'No. I had a sister, too, who was six years older than me. Her name was Sarah. She was in London at her school on the day our parents died.'

'And you. Where were you?'

'I had been sick for a number of months with a chest infection and was recuperating at Colmeade House. After that I was never ill again. Not with that particular malady anyway.'

'Who came to tell you about what had happened?'

His eyes skirted away from her, but not before she had seen the pain in them.

'No one. They did not return that night or the next one. Finally a friend of my father's arrived to let us know.'

'Us?'

'The servants and me. The family lawyer came down the next day and I was quickly returned to school.'

'Just like that?' She was horrified and furious and she could hear the anger in her voice. 'To just send off a small grieving child like a parcel and expect him to be all right? It is archaic and dreadful and if I ever have a baby I should hope that—' She stopped when she realised what she was saying and thumbed through the pages of the journal with shaking fingers.

'It was my sister's, but she died shortly after my parents did. It's embossed with her initials, but as they are now the same as your own I thought you might like it.'

S. St C. Sarah. Sarah St Cartmail. Francis and Sarah St Cartmail.

All the little pieces of the Earl of Douglas were beginning to get filled in. Like a puzzle, this bit explaining that one and the tragedy of his past overshadowing everything.

What was it Amethyst Wylde had said today? *'Francis has been alone and I always hoped that marriage would be his saving grace.'*

He'd lost so many people and was still losing them. No wonder he had tried so hard to make sure Anna was safe when she was snatched in the street. Even his kindness to the homeless mangy dog began to have an explanation for he'd probably felt like that, too, as a child. Nowhere to go. No one to love him. She wondered how his sister had died, but did not like to ask.

'If I began to write stories again, could I read some to you?'

He looked up at that and smiled 'You'd want to?'

'Only if you did not laugh at them or tell me to stop writing.'

'Seth Greenwood used to pen tales about gold and the fever of it. He even had one published in the Hutton's Landing newspaper. He got a Draped Bust Dime for his efforts and had it mounted in a piece of old polished swamp wood with the eagle side up. I brought it home for his mother.'

'What was he like? Adam Stevenage's cousin?'

'Larger than life and full of it. I met him in New York when I first arrived in the Americas. He was working in steel, but had always dreamed of the gold and so with the last of my money and a tip he'd had from a dying priest, we headed south. We hired a wagon to make it easier for his wife and children and went down the Fall Line Road between Fredericksburg and Augusta. Three weeks later we were ready to pan on the banks of the Flint in Georgia. The same river he died in.'

Sephora was intrigued by the world described, and she was reminded of her uncle's dream of seeing foreign lands and different oceans.

'Not too many weeks ago a man on his deathbed told me that the biggest lesson in life was to find passion. It seems like at least Seth found his.'

Francis nodded and stood, the scar on his cheek caught in the light of the lamp above his head, but his eyes were soft. 'The money from the gold allowed me to invest in manufacturing and save the Douglas properties, but I'd give it all away to have Seth and his family back.'

Without thought Sephora touched him, laying her hand across his and feeling the warmth.

'I want to leave London for Colmeade House the day after tomorrow. It's time I took you home.'

* * *

The next day Sephora received a note from her mother asking her to come and see her in the afternoon, but when she walked into the blue salon of her parents' town house her heart fell.

Richard Allerly was sitting talking with Elizabeth and when he saw Sephora he got up, a smile upon his face. Her mother had also risen and was speaking quickly.

'I thought that the time had come to put all our cards on the table so to speak, my dear, and facilitate some sort of dialogue in order to clear things up between you two.'

'Clear things up?' Sephora could not quite understand what she meant, but Richard was quick to jump into the fray.

'I realise that I was rather remiss in allowing our relationship to falter and I have been hearing a number of unsettling things about your new husband which, to be honest, I could no longer keep to myself. Your mother is as worried about you as I am.'

When she did not speak he carried on.

'Douglas may have been a war hero in Spain, but he certainly seems to have made a mess of his time in the Americas. Not only was he tried in a court of law there for killing one man, but he was also rumoured to have hunted and shot another. He is a dangerous reprobate and there is no telling what he might indeed do to you, should he be inclined to.'

'Who told you of this?' She tried to keep her voice

steady, but was so furious she wondered how she could even form the question.

'It is common knowledge all across London. People are looking at you with pity in their eyes—the duped bride who has no idea of the monster to whom she is now married.'

'I see. Where is Papa?'

'He has gone to see his sister and will not be back till the day after tomorrow.' Her mother answered this question, her voice tight.

'And Maria?'

Now Elizabeth looked less certain. 'She is in Kew Gardens with Mr Stevenage and Aunt Susan.'

'Then it is a shame that they are not here, Mama, because I would have liked them all to hear what I have to tell you next.'

As she took in a shaky breath Richard crossed the room and threaded his arm through her own. 'Come, my angel. I think you need to sit down for you look flustered, pale and upset and I realise that this is all a shock, but...'

The same feeling she had had for so many years came upon her just at his words. He generated a weakness in her, a worry and a fear that was so familiar she almost felt sick. The woman she had been might well have sat and been fussed over, all her insecurities rising like butterflies off a summer tree. But she had changed and the new her was nowhere near as accommodating to perceived failings.

'Please do not touch me.' She waited until he had taken a step back before she went on.

'I shall not be commenting on the stories about the Earl of Douglas, Richard, but I will say that I know the circumstances surrounding them because my husband himself has told me.

'I will also say that for years now I have been unhappy and frightened, of you and me, of us together. You make me less, Richard, whereas all Francis St Cartmail does is make me more. I can think with him and converse. I can offer opinions and argument and ideas that are far different from his own and expect no redress or criticism. The passion for life which you said I had none of has returned and I thank you for that because without your honesty I may have never realised that my own was so lost. There is nothing you could say, Richard, ever, that would tempt me to be the girl again who I was with you. That girl has gone. She has grown up and become this woman and I like her strength so very much more.'

Her mother had simply sat down on the sofa and Richard looked as if he might strike out, but Sephora smiled through the undercurrents and held herself together.

'I am leaving London for Colmeade House in Kent tomorrow, Mama, and I have no idea when I shall be back, but I hope we will be gone for a while. Maria, no doubt, shall be down to visit and you and Papa are welcome when you can understand that the Earl of Douglas is the man I have willingly chosen to be my husband forever and I have absolutely no regrets about my decision.'

With that she simply turned around and took her

leave, a few strides to the front door where she collected her cloak and hat and then down the steps and into the waiting Douglas carriage.

Once there she took in a breath and brought her shaking hands up in front of her, her marriage ring glinting in the light.

She had done it, she was free, the cloying possessiveness of Richard Allerly behind her once and for all. Every word she had uttered held a truth that was astonishing and illuminating and wonderful. Francis gave her strength and power and the ability to be herself.

Dragging her journal from her bag, she found a pencil and began to write of how it felt to be alive and young and free. To know the passions that her uncle had spoken of on his deathbed, the gifts of life and hope and happiness.

'I'll live life for you, too, Sarah,' she promised, the pad of her finger tracing the embossed initials in the leather of the cover as the whole of her world opened up into new possibility.

Chapter Twelve

Colmeade House came into view finally. She knew Francis had found the journey uncomfortable for she could see a sheen of sweat across his upper lip, although he only smiled at her when she mentioned her concern. Anna on her other side had been turning and squirming for the whole trip just to catch a glance of the carriage behind theirs, the one that was carrying Mrs Billinghurst, her son, Timothy, and the dog.

'Hopeful does not like travelling. He was sick the other day when Timothy took him across London and Mrs Billinghurst said that it is his stomach and that some dogs are born that way.'

'Well, he has another minute or two to last at the most for here is the estate now.' They all looked out of the window at this, the vista of a Palladian-style home greeting them, the stone tinged almost pink in the afternoon sun.

'But it's so beautiful,' Sephora found herself saying, the edge of slight ruin taking nothing from its grandeur.

'My great-grandfather built it, but ever since it's been left to stand against the elements and with the help of passing time and little capital invested in it this is the result. My own father hardly touched it.'

'There is plenty of room for Hopeful to run around in it anyway,' Anna said quietly as the carriage came to a halt. 'Will it be safe for him?'

'It is safe for the dog and safe for you, too, Anna. There is nobody and nothing here to hurt you, I promise it.' Francis said this in a tone that did not brook argument and when Anna smiled at him Sephora could see a softness there that made her look beautiful. Breathing in, she looked away and swallowed back the tears.

The park went as far as the eye could see, falling to a lake in the foreground and a round loggia of sorts far in the distance, the tall trees that bordered the open spaces planted with the idea of creating a pattern of space and grandeur. The heritage of the Douglases was as unexpected as it was beautiful. She'd imagined a smaller estate and one in better condition. This would need much in the way of time and energy to see it functioning properly.

She remembered then what the earl had told her about his not coming home as a child because it was too much of a nuisance to open the house for one small boy. The boy who would inherit everything. The child who had been an orphan just as Anna was one. What must this place have represented to a son who had just lost his parents? The missing tiles on the roof, the aged patina in the stone, the flaking paint on every window sill observable? Beautiful, but beaten somehow, rich in its lines of architecture, but poor in its maintenance.

Timothy had joined them now with the dog and his mother, Mrs Billinghurst, behind them. Some of the Douglas servants from town had come down to Kent two days prior to get everything ready. Sephora was glad Francis had hired a number of men to make certain the property was secure.

In front of the wide stairwell those serving the house had lined up, the aprons the women all wore white and shining in the sun.

'Come, I will introduce you, Sephora. Many of these people have served my family for generations. Mrs Billinghurst will take the children inside for luncheon.'

She wished she might have simply followed them up the wide steps into the house, but came behind Francis to meet his staff. The earl was charming to each of them though she could see the distance he also maintained. A smile here and a question there and then they, too, were on the way up the steps and into the house proper.

He took her into a salon to his immediate left and shut the door behind him, leaning against it and closing his eyes. It had been weeks since the attack in the streets of London and each day he had got better and better, but the long trip had exhausted him. She could see it in the grey tinge on his skin.

Crossing to a cabinet she opened the door and pulled out two glasses and the first bottle that came to hand. 'Drink this. You look as if you need some fortifying.'

Francis smiled when he tasted the tipple. He was sitting now on a wide sofa near the door. 'Whisky?' he asked. 'Seems appropriate somehow. At least if I get drunk you won't have to take me home and as we are already married Winbury will no longer be a problem.'

Their glances met across the small distance and something inside her moved. The wound had stopped him coming to her room in London as he had tried to recuperate, but here…already she could see an expression on his face akin to intimacy.

'I do wish for this marriage of ours to be a proper one, Sephora.'

'Proper, my lord?' She used the words carefully.

'I would want you to sleep with me, every night. It won't be a sham.' He glanced up at her then without any hint of question and she swallowed because suddenly Richard's words were back in her ears echoing around the chambers creating uncertainty.

'You are cold and unfeeling in this way, Sephora. You always have been.'

Was he right? Already her heart was beating faster in worry and she stared at him mutely, unable to formulate any answer at all to explain it away.

The colour had gone from her face, Francis thought, simply drained like water in a sink at his words. She looked horrified and frightened, not the normal worry of a wife who went to her marital bed for the first time but something else.

'Did Richard Allerly ever…?' He stopped there because she was shaking her head madly. Placing his drink on a table he stood as she answered his question.

'No. He was not like that and I was glad for it.'

'Not like what?' Lord, this conversation was getting away from him and why would she be glad?

'Did he kiss you?'

'Yes.'

'And you liked it?'

'No.' Now her eyes were like wide saucers of pure shock.

'But you loved him?'

'At first I did. A long time ago. After that I was trapped. Everyone just expected us to be together. Like you expect seasons to change or Christmas to come or the organ to be playing in a church on Sundays. No thought in it really just…'

'Presumptions?'

'Exactly. And at the end I hated him.'

This was said so softly he could barely hear her.

'He said… Richard said…I was cold and passionless and had always been that way and I think it is the truth.' Her fingers were clamped into shaking fists, every knuckle stretched into white. 'Once I overheard Papa saying the same thing to my mother. Perhaps it is the sort of weakness that runs through a family and blights it, a fatal flaw like Hamlet with his pre-

varications or Achilles with his ego. And if so then
I am not...'

He reached out for her, simply taking her lips, hard
and honest and without hesitation; and if he felt her
tremble he ignored it, opening her mouth under his
and coming within. To plunder, to taste, to know what
it was that lay between them in the shock of their contact, to feel the red hot want of lust and roiling waves
of desire that raced inside. To show his unusual new
wife that she was not frigid or damaged at all.

And then he broke away.

'Passionless? I do not think you are that.'

But she stood there dazed, with her mouth open
and her breasts heaving and when he registered the
voices of Anna and Timothy coming down to them
along the hallway he leaned forward and whispered.

'Tonight, Sephora, tonight I promise to show you
just what burning feels like.'

It was happening all over again just as it did at the
river; one action that changed her perception of the
world, one kiss that had made everything different.

And his promise of tonight? The loosening of
something inside her made her light-headed and light-
hearted and transformed her from the woman she was
before to the one she was now. She had felt everything the stories talked of when he had kissed her,
the breathlessness, the possibilities, the wonder. The
wooden Sephora Connaught had simply melted into
a living flame, wanting him, wanting more, and un-

derstanding so terribly all that she had missed with a man who had only ever made her feel less.

The dog brushed up against her, his wet nose leaving a trail of darkness on the silk of her skirt. Francis was laughing at something Anna had said and Timothy was chatting to him as if the Earl of Douglas were the masculine embodiment of everything wonderful.

This was a whole full life given to her when she had least expected it and risen from the ruin of her mistakes. She decided that she would drink whisky with her husband for the rest of her years and smiled. She was glad that he had given her the time to recover by distracting the others though when his gaze came across hers she remembered again his heated promise.

Tonight. Her eyes went to the clock above the mantel, only a matter of hours until it came, and he winked as he saw her interest there.

'Can we walk to the top floor of the house and see the view?' Anna asked this of Francis.

'Are you scared of heights?'

'No.' Anna's voice was becoming more and more certain and today her ill-cut hair was held back by a hairband. It suited her. So did the smile that came as Francis held out his hand and she reached for it.

The two of them ate that night at a table set for a king. There were lilies on the sideboard, from London Sephora supposed, their scent heavy and compelling. The silver was well polished and the plates were Sèvres, bordered in gold and aqua and monogrammed in the middle—the letter 'D' hung with greenery and colourful tiny flight-filled birds.

The Earl of Douglas was almost as decorated as his plates, his jacket of green velvet and his waistcoat of a burgundy-and-saffron-embroidered silk. She had never seen Francis St Cartmail in anything other than dark and sombre hues before and though he looked well in those the bright and striking colours of tonight's garb were breathtaking. The cabochon ruby on his little finger shone against the candles. As if he recognised what she was thinking he lifted his glass in a toast.

"'A wife of noble character who can find? She is worth more than rubies.'"

'I would say a man wrote that line, my lord.'

He laughed and paraphrased quickly. 'My wife of noble character is worth more than rubies and I have found her.'

They both sipped at the red wine after that, a short distraction while they garnered their wits, Sephora thought, and was glad the footman hovering at her shoulder had gone. Hovering as Richard always had. She pushed the thought away and reached for a new question.

'How old are you, my lord?'

'Thirty-four.'

'And you had not thought to marry before?'

'No.' Simply said. The dimple on his undamaged cheek was shadowed in the candlelight and there was humour in his eyes.

'I saw you once before I met you properly. You

were in a garden kissing a woman and not all that politely for she looked more than amorous. It was a ball, if I remember correctly, and I had stepped outside for a brief moment to gather air.'

'It is the plight of a bachelor, Lady Douglas, being pounced on like that. But you have rescued me from such folly forever and I thank you for it. I never saw you at all in society. Perhaps it was because I tried to attend as few events as I could justifiably manage.'

This was how flirting worked, Sephora suddenly thought. This cut and thrust of pleasure and coquetry. If she had had a fan she might have flicked it across her face in the practised way she had noticed others manage. A small diversion. A studied amusement.

She felt more beautiful than she ever had before.

'I'm certain I shall have to do so again, Lord Douglas. Rescue you, I mean, for I have heard your name whispered by many hopeful females after all.'

He finished his glass of wine and set it down. 'When I make a promise, I always keep it.'

'That is indeed a comfort, my lord.' She could not quite interpret what he meant by that. The promise of tonight? The promise of forever? The troths were all getting mixed around in her head and in the pit of her stomach another more languid feeling was growing.

She pushed back the lacy golden shawl from her shoulders and saw his eyes flare. This dress had been carefully chosen to be within the barest whisper of modesty. At the time she had sworn she should never have the courage to wear it, but now...

Now she rounded her shoulders and leaned forward, the ample flesh of her breasts pressing against the thinness of fabric. Francis St Cartmail's reaction almost made her smile, but she shook away mirth and concentrated on something far more dangerous.

'Richard Allerly told me he loved me constantly. The words are easy to say, you see, and when I failed to eventually believe in his sentiments I thought I should never ever wish to hear them again. Not like that. Not worthless and without value. Not parroted without any meaning whatsoever.'

'You wish to know in other ways?' His voice was silky and rough, and if they had been sitting closer she might have reached out then and touched him, to hold his fingers tightly in her own.

But distance had its own appeal, too. A suspended moment. A deferred intimacy.

She took another sip of her wine and watched him.

God, his timid innocent wife was turning into a practised siren, in her golden almost nothing sheath of a gown and with her surprising confessions. She knew how she was affecting him and that was the worst of it. He had been chased down by women ever since he could remember, but none who set his blood to boil like this one could, the words of her disclosure on love spilling into disbelief.

She did not wish for him to give her the troth? She wanted to feel it instead, the breathless pull, the intimacy, the scent of desire.

Go slowly, he commanded himself as the betrayal of his body filled unhearing flesh and the shock of connection drew his skin into goosebumps. There was still the whole dinner to get through, the second course only just coming from the kitchens in the capable arms of a handful of footmen bearing platters.

Sephora pulled her lacy shawl upwards at the intrusion and smiled, the fabric settling across fine breasts and hiding the swell beneath gossamer silk. But he had seen. He knew what had been there, was there still. The sweat on his upper lip prickled with heat and he used the starched linen napkin to wipe it away.

He had lost his appetite for everything save her, but she was thanking his man for the portion of meats just served, and he could do nothing but watch.

'It is a wondrous feast,' she said and looked up, the pale blue of her eyes in the candlelight almost see-through.

'It is,' he answered and knew he did not speak of the food.

'Like artistry?'

'Exactly like it.'

When she picked up her eating utensils the light from the chandelier above caught on a tine of the fork, sending beams of colour into her hair.

An angel. His angel.

The thoughts of ravishment dimmed a little under this realisation and settled into a place that was more manageable. He was pleased his serving staff had withdrawn into the kitchen as he had asked them to do.

'I want heirs.'

He knew he had shocked her, but two could play at this game and he'd had far more years of practice.

'How many, my lord?'

Hell, at that moment Sephora Connaught reminded him so much of a seasoned courtesan that he laughed. A surprising twist. He could barely keep pace with the reactions of his traitorous body and he was struggling with the changeover, whereas she seemed to be relishing them.

'Would four suit you, my lady?'

'Two girls and two boys? A considered choice? Prescriptive. Accounted for.' The smile was in her eyes now, too. She was teasing him, provoking him, taking his words and turning them around into something else entirely. It was so seldom that anyone else had ever managed to do that, that he was speechless.

Shifting back in his seat he took account of what he had learned tonight about his unusual wife. She was beautiful, of course. However the beauty lay not only in her outside appearance, but inside in kindness, humour and honesty. She was also clever, ruthlessly so, a woman who might turn a conversation completely on its head and smile through his confusion.

The third thing worried him the most. She was so damned sexy he felt like taking her then and there on the rug in the dining room in front of a burning fire, just to see how the flame glowed on the white of her skin and the sheen of her breasts and the pale gold in her hair.

'So, you wish for a fruitful marriage without any mention of love? The act but not the words?'

'The truth rather than the falsity.' She was quick with her reply.

'When I see Winbury next time I think I am going to knock that damn head off of his shoulders.'

She laughed, but quietly, as if in his troth she found a certain solace.

'I would hope that you do not. He is a man whom I have left behind, a weak man I think, and half a lifetime is too many years to regret. If I could ask you for anything it would be for honesty.'

He smiled. 'Honesty can have its bite, too, Sephora. What would you say if I told you I want to take you to my bed right now and show you the true beauty of what can be between a man and his wife?'

She stood then, taking the linen serviette from her lap and placing her fork and knife carefully on her plate.

'I would say, my lord, that I am finished with dinner.'

The Earl of Douglas made her brave and different. He did not hide behind words but said them to her face in a way that she could not fail to understand the meaning. He wanted her and she wanted him, but the wants were not coated in falsity or childishness or arrogance.

She did not shiver or shake or cower either. Perhaps it was the wine or the fire or her meeting with Richard Allerly yesterday. Most certainly it was the look in Francis St Cartmail's eyes and the way he smiled, without any hint of deceit, a man who knew his wants and needs and let her know it too.

He did not move up beside her to thread his arm through her own but waited for her to come to him. Her choice. His acceptance. The superfine of his jacket sleeve beneath her fingers was soft and they went up the stairs without speaking into his bedchamber.

His was a big room; the double-hung French doors leading to a balcony that looked out over the countryside and the lake. But it was not this vista her eyes went to. The four poster bed was hung with tapestries curled onto mahogany rods and plaited with multicoloured ties. The coverlet was of embossed blue velvet to match the shade of the walls. Eight-hour scented candles burned quietly on each side table next to it.

A Lord's bed, an earl's lair, for the whisper of history was imbued in the oil portraits on the walls and in the intricacy of the old wooden carvings.

But he did not rush her. Rather he crossed to a small cabinet and poured out two glasses of wine before drawing her over to an alcove before a fire.

'Here is to you, my beautiful Lady Douglas. May we grow old together in lust.'

She liked his toast, the truth of what he said in his eyes, just as she liked the taste of the wine and the feel of the fire. Draping her shawl across a nearby chair she turned to face him. Perhaps it was her turn now to talk of the truth. She drained her glass and placed it down.

'I have not ever...' Her glance went to the bed.

'Then we will go slowly.'

'And I worry...'

He stopped those words with a finger full drawn against her lips. 'Shh. There are no rules.'

The same finger began to trace a different path, across her top lip and around one cheek before falling to her chin and neck and then lower. She shivered, but it was not from the cold. All she knew was burning heat and closing her eyes against the intensity of him she simply felt. No rules he had said, neither right nor wrong.

The pad of his finger rose across the swell of her breast and then the flimsy silk was parted and he found the heavy weight of flesh and measured it in his palm. Relentlessly, quietly, his fingers now around her nipple, playing with the nub so that a thousand other feelings burst inside her and she pressed closer.

'Let me have you, Sephora. Let me love you.' These words were breathed against her skin, whispered and desperate, the shock of them crawling up her spine before bursting open.

'Yes.' She found her reply and gave it, her want the echo of his own and naked with hope.

His teeth came down over one breast, taking exactly what he willed. A considered vanquish, a well-thought-out triumph. It was not anxiety that consumed her now but bliss and her fingers came through the length of his hair, the tie gone as it fell down around his shoulders in a thick and midnight black.

Her husband. Her lover soon. Every thought melded

into one until there was no logic left as he lifted her in his arms and placed her down upon the bed.

She was small and he was large. He was dark and she was fair and in her pale eyes he could see both acceptance and fear in equal measure. But she lay there still, looking up at him, her bodice falling about her waist, her breasts exposed to the candlelight and the firelight and the moon.

He wanted to see her when they came together. He did. He had never liked the darkness and she was far too beautiful to hide in it.

Pulling the skirt of the golden gown upwards his hand spilled under silk, past gossamer stockings of white, past the satin ribbons at her thigh. Up into the very warmth of her, a single lace barrier that he disposed of quickly before he came in.

She gasped and began to ride him, head thrown back and her bottom rising, no longer fearful only questing, her breath louder, the veins at her neck stretched. He laid his other fingers splayed upon her stomach and pressed down, feeling himself beneath in the flesh of her, detecting movement. Harder. Quicker. Deeper.

She came like a flame burst, all heat and light and burning, the muscles inside tightening as she took what he gave her without reserve, low groans of pleasure breaking over the final stillness. The wet of her ran through his fingers and there were tears on her cheeks and astonishment in her eyes when she opened them.

'Now you are ready for me.'

'There is more?'

He laughed, but the sound held more lust than mirth. 'Ah, Sephora, love, but we have only just begun.'

She watched as he undressed himself, too languid to help. The jacket and shirt came first and then the neckcloth, the snowy unwound whiteness revealing the dark crimson scars beneath.

'From a rope,' he said as he saw she watched him. No more details. No more emotion. Just the plain fact as to what had happened across the terrible truth of the result.

She wanted to reach up and touch him there, to re-assure him, to comfort him, but he had moved now to the fall of his trousers and the tug of his shiny black boots. And then he was naked, his skin golden in the firelight, muscle defined and sinew rising. Other old injuries, too, showed up on his body; a slice of wound beneath the reddened injury from the bullet and two more parallel scars at the top of his arm.

A warrior's body, beautiful, strong and defined.

But when her eyes dropped lower she forgot to think at all, the full and aroused masculinity won-drous and terrifying. She knew what a naked man looked like because Maria had found an old broad-sheet folded into a book with a lewd drawing upon it. The illustration on the page, however, had not quite explained the truth of flesh and desire in a man like Francis St Cartmail.

Her fingers of their own accord reached out and touched him, the rock-hard warmth of smoothness less worrying within her palm, fitting there as though it was meant. When he groaned and stretched she knew she was doing to him as he had done to her and her fingers explored further. The light touch of knowledge drawing a picture for her, understanding his secrets.

And then his hand came across her own and he drew her up against him, the golden sheath of her gown falling as liquid to the floorboards, a small puddle of the last veil between them, the final revealing. She could see it in his eyes that he thought her beautiful, but it was his hands that traced her outline, down the side of her breast and on to the curve of her waist and then lower into the warmth between her legs.

This time he simply sat and lifted her onto the hardness of him, slowly slipping in, one inch and then two, until resistance loosened and he was buried far inside.

She cried out as the pain stung, but he did not release her. Rather he moved slowly and by degrees, allowing her the familiarity and the fullness, the feel of him stretched across her flesh until she thought she might simply break open like a peach falling from the fruit tree in the late summer.

Split with ripeness.

He moved again and another feeling warred with the first. Not as sore now, not as hot, and he always returned to that first final deepness.

'Feel me there, Sephora. Feel me wanting you.'

Whispered words, against the heavy beat of her heart and the shallow pulls of breath, the quiet ease of gentling against the sharp edge of triumph.

His other hand grasped her bottom as he began to

move, with force, with strength, no soothing movements now but the full measure of lust.

And instead of pain came ecstasy, thin and quiet
at first before crouching to spring fully formed into
every part of her body, tearing away restraint as she
cried out loudly.

But still he did not allow her rest.

'Come with me, sweetheart, come with me now.'

And the light filled her, like honey and sunshine,
shimmering through the heat, taking will and purpose and preference, the urgency from him at odds
with all that was languid inside of her as he pressed
in one last time and stiffened, breath gone and eyes
closed against the light, the beaching waves of release
covering each of them, pulling them home.

Neither of them moved, still coupled together, a
new union rising from the separate.

'Sephora,' he breathed out when he could finally
talk. 'I think that you just took me to Heaven.'

And she laughed at that and felt him leave her, a
residue of wetness that had her reaching down though
his own hand fell to cover hers.

'No. Take me in. Take me inside when you sleep.'

And so with only a gentle push of a different fullness and a slight shift of her body, she did.

When Sephora awoke, Francis was no longer there
and the light from the opened curtains told her it was
well past her usual time of waking.

The realisation of why had her turning into the pillow. She had been wanton and shameless, the ache in her lower body underlining her thoughts.

In the night, when the stars were still high in the sky, she had reached out for him and drawn him in yet again, startling him into wakefulness as she had played with sleeping flesh until new purpose had formed.

She had sat above him pushing back the covers so their skin was limned in moonlight, the long lines of flesh and bone made unreal somehow by the dimness. He'd kissed her afterwards, his tongue finding hers and they had shared breath and warmth and safety.

Her fingers drew a line across her lips now. She wanted him again here on the ancient bed, here as the clocks ticked on towards the noontime and the outside world lazed in the season's sun.

'Francis.' She said his name out loud, liking the music in it and the softness; the name of one of the angels in the Bible. She smiled thinking of his darkness and the scar emblazoned as a brand across his cheek. She wondered how he had got the mark and made a note to ask him. He had said something of the war in Spain if she remembered correctly and being lost in the mountains outside Corunna. The same war where his primary job had been that of a marksman, shooting the enemy when backs were turned or when they had thought themselves safe.

A dangerous solitary occupation she imagined, cut off from others, left to the elements. She had read the stories of the Peninsular Campaign and seen the pictures. She wished he was here next her so that she might turn and take him in her arms to keep him safe or to feel him inside her making her want things she had never thought possible.

A little later the door opened and he was there fully dressed, back today in unbroken black.

'I wondered when you would wake. You have been sleeping like the dead.'

His eyes were soft, licked in warmth and his hair was back in its severe tie, dragged back off his face.

Reaching up she took his hand and laid it across one breast. The change in temperature between them was startling and arousing.

'I want you.' Her words. Uncensored. Shocking in the daylight. She did not even blink as he watched her but moved up against his hand and pushed all the covers away.

The tangle of her hair and the ruin of the sheets. A fallen angel, shattered by passion.

When he sat and lifted her onto his lap she had no recall of him unfastening his fall as his manhood came within her, no warning, no caution. The ache of it made her arch back, but he did not break his motion, intent on his lesson, his mouth against the column of her throat and biting down.

And this morning he taught her that loving need not always be soft or gentle. The other side of the same coin of passion had its paybacks though and when she bit into his shoulder he came, the hot rush of completion running over the cold shiver of truth. Only with each other were they whole.

Then he laid her back and pulled the covers across her. 'Sleep now, Sephora, until I come again. No one will disturb you.'

And he did come again once in the afternoon and then in the evening to take her in the way he wanted, slow and quiet. It was a netherworld she lived in waiting for him, only breathing until he was there again, the strength of his hands against the sheltered softness of her body.

He rarely spoke and she did not either. She had not asked for the words and he obeyed her. A taken wife used with care until every part of her body became accustomed to his touch.

And when the stars rose amongst the darkness he had food brought to the chamber and he bathed her in a warm and soapy bath and dressed her in a nightgown of fine lawn. The bed was made up too, crisp and new and as he tucked her within it, he kissed her on the forehead and left.

She woke again in the early hours after midnight, refreshed from so much sleep and he was not there. Taking a heavy blanket from the bed she draped it about herself and left the room with a candle to light her way, reasoning that her husband would be downstairs in the library she had seen yesterday.

He sat on a wide leather chair with his feet up on the windowsill and the room was freezing. When he saw her he smiled but didn't move at all. 'I don't sleep well.'

'And you like the cold?'

Each window was full open, and the cloth from

around his neck was discarded on the floor, the vivid scars on his throat easily seen in the moonlight.

'Maria told me the story of what happened.' She gestured with her hands. 'Adam Stevenage relayed it to her. I hope you do not mind?'

'It's only a story,' he said suddenly. 'Just words.'

'Can you give me the truth of them, then? I would like to hear it from you.'

Shrugging his shoulders he leaned back, the brutal marks dark in the soft fold of his skin.

'It was near Christmas and it was cold. I remember looking up in the early dawn and seeing a shooting star and wishing on it. Gold, I asked. I wanted gold to come home and live on and to save the Douglas inheritance as well as to show others here that I was not feckless and reckless and dissolute. I wanted enough to start a family with and to know my neighbours; all the things others so effortlessly seemed to manage but which were lost somehow to me.'

His words were made slower with drink. Whisky, she determined, by the little that was left in his glass.

'My partner Seth Greenwood came down in the morning and I was tired. He'd risen warm from the bed of his wife and I envied him that. I could hear his babies crying even at that distance and see the flame of the fire against the glass. A home.' He looked at her then. 'There is a certain appeal in the word, I always thought. More so perhaps because I never had one.'

Leaning forward, he half filled his glass again and she did not try to stop him. Let him lose himself in the arms of drink she thought as she had lost herself in the embrace of passion.

'Kennings came after the day broke, quietly on a down-wind track. I saw him come and thought he was there to talk. The dogs didn't bark though and I should have taken that as a warning. They didn't bark because he had already been to the house and done his business.

'I think he'd cut through the tethering of the platform against the bank, maybe when we were away the afternoon before registering our claim. Kennings did not know that then. It was only later he'd have realised that it had all been for nothing.'

His eyes met hers. 'And that is the final irony of what did happen. The nothingness. The futility. The empty void of oblivion that held no payback for anyone.

'He shot at us as the rig collapsed. I felt the bullets rifling through the water, five or six perhaps and loaded quickly, but then I hardly think he'd shoot slow with the stakes so high.

'The first two ripped across my arm and the third went into Seth's shoulder. When the water ran red and there was only silence Kennings probably thought he'd done his job and all that was left was to make certain that the claim was his.

'I couldn't lift Seth up out of the water so I stayed there with him. Hours later he slipped away into the river and I was hauled up into the teeth of a furious lynch mob wanting revenge and retribution. Seth's wife had been found by then, you see, and the babies, and Kennings had spread the word that I had done it. Jealousy was the motive, he said, and greed.

'Seth's body was gone with the river somewhere, Kennings bullet in him and I was so freezing I could barely talk enough to give my side of the tale.

'They hanged me from a cottonwood with its bare winter branches and its ragged bark, but they picked the wrong bough and the branch broke. When the lightning came a second later there were those in the group who felt strongly about signs from God and his omnipotent displeasure and so I was brought instead into town, the rope still around my neck and my throat swelling.' He smiled, but there was no humour there. 'If the damn hanging did not kill me then its effects nearly did. And after,' he stopped and swallowed. 'Afterwards breathing at night was always harder and I could not lie down for a long, long while.'

'Even now?'

He nodded. 'Especially now when there are so many more to keep safe.'

Suddenly she understood why there was a gun next to him and another on the flat of the sofa. 'It's Anna? You know who tried to kidnap her?'

'Only a list of suspects, but I am narrowing it down.'

Panic made her stand. 'It is dangerous, Francis. These people have already shown what they are capable of.'

'Clive Sherborne was running his own sort of books and because of that Anna is in danger from those who knew about it.'

'How do you know this?' She was simply horrified by what he had said. 'Who are they?'

'I've had people investigating Sherborne's murder since it happened. Anna's guardian, Clive Sherborne, had been providing the finance for a number of years to bring spirits in illegally from France, but he got too cocky with the merchandise. He onsold some of the brandy to London pubs at a rate that was more than what it should have been and pocketed the difference. The man who killed him found this out.'

Her mind whirled into a hundred directions and then they all converged into one. She knew the moment he saw the conclusion she had reached as eyes bruised in anger, fell away from her own.

'Anna was there.'

'I think Sherborne was in it deeper than his lawyer realised and it was easier to involve a child in the transactions than another adult who might betray him.'

'My God. The nightmares...?'

'She thinks she is next.'

This explained why she had wanted all the reassurances of never being sent away from them and why she seldom liked to go outside. But it also threw up other worries.

He reached for her then, opening the cocoon of his blanket, his sleeve pulled back in the moonlight and his jacket gone. Positioning her own wrap over them both she came in tight against him in her thin nightgown and felt his utter warmth and safety.

'It's like that time in London,' she whispered and

he tilted his head, still watching the landscape before the house.

'What is?'

'You will save her just as you did me.'

The hoot of an owl from a line of trees to one side of the driveway had the edges of his mouth turning upwards. 'It is said that when you hear a bird calling from the west, good luck will follow.'

'Is that west?' she asked and was pleased when he nodded. 'How many would come here if they had the mind to?'

'Only a few. The Free Trade is a communal business, you understand, and there are many in it who wouldn't be there were the government less greedy. Good men, honest men, men who just want to feed their families. Still, every endeavour has those who are less inclined to follow the law and take it into their own hands. Especially with the lure of gold.' He breathed out and looked at her directly. 'I had a letter today.'

The words made her stiffen. 'Unsigned, of course?'

'The missive threatens further retribution to my family should I continue to hunt for the one who hurt Anna.'

'So we shall not be safe until he is caught?'

'Daniel will be here on the morrow. Luce is in Hastings listening to what is being said and Gabe is making a list of the pubs Sherborne supplied in London. We will find them.'

'That is why you were in that fight at Kew, wasn't it? For Anna's sake?'

'Yes.'

'And everyone called you reckless and dissolute.'

'I was never a person to worry about what anybody else thought.'

'But if you are hurt or…' She could not even finish.

'I won't be. There are only a few hours of darkness left until the morning and no one will come when it's light.'

He kissed her then quickly, the warmth of his lips across hers demanding and rough as one hand cupped the swell of her breast. Like a promise. She felt him draw in breath as he let her go, watching again and vigilant.

Outside through the windows the gardens of Colmeade House looked magical, mystical and quiet.

'It is beautiful,' she whispered, snuggling in, the blanket warm but his body warmer.

'It is a fortress,' he returned, 'and none will harm us here. I swear it, on my life.'

'I believe you.'

She wondered where the frightened woman of a few weeks ago had disappeared to, for if anyone was to come and hurt Francis or Anna she would kill them with her own bare hands. She swore to the heavens that she would.

And so they sat there until the morning, sometimes speaking, oft-times not, and the old stray joined them just before the dawn, like a guard dog, his ears pinned back as he listened in wariness.

She smiled to herself as the sun rose across the hills bathing the land in pink and yellow. She would never have seen the birth of a new day as the wife of a duke. She would never have lain in the arms of half slumber as she was doing now, the blankets warm and Francis's body strong around her own.

She loved him. She had known that for a long while now, but if she had instructed him not to give her the words then she could hardly whisper them herself. But she did inside, as an aria and a melody, her fingers threaded through his and the breath he took mingling with her own.

This was life as it was supposed to have been lived, fearless, brave and uncompromised. The diamonds in her wedding ring winked in the light of the morning and she liked the promise of warmth in the air.

Chapter Thirteen

Sephora watched Anna the next morning as the girl came down the stairs, the dog Hopeful back on her heels and Timothy not far behind.

She was thin and the lines of worry still marked her brow, but she seemed happier nonetheless, more childlike as she giggled watching Timothy attempt a cartwheel and failing. Here at Colmeade House Francis had insisted the son of Mrs Billinghurst be given a position of companion for his ward. The idea had seemed to be working well and the two of them were becoming good friends.

'What had you planned to do today, Anna?' she asked from her place at the table. Francis had not come down to breakfast yet and she imagined he would be trying to catch up on at least a few hours of sleep before their visitors turned up.

'We are building a fort in the attic with all the old furniture left there. Uncle Francis said that we may,' she continued, 'as long as we do our lessons in the afternoon.'

Another day indoors then, Sephora thought. The child never ventured outside either, unless they were with her, and she started each time she heard the noise of a horse arriving at the house. Mrs Billinghurst had also made it known that Anna wet her bed frequently and that she still enjoyed reading in a wardrobe with the doors closed.

Complications and complexities.

Timothy Billinghurst was watching her intently and she smiled, the boy blushing so that the skin on his skull showed red under the fairness of his hair; another child who needed careful handling, lost between the death of his father and the brittle poverty of a genteel mother who had been left with very little on the death of her husband.

'The earl's friends Lord and Lady Montcliffe will be coming today. Perhaps they would be interested in seeing the fort you construct when it is finished. I know I'd like to.'

A little smile from Anna was her reward, but Sephora had started to treasure these tiny gifts, her heart warming in response.

'There is some silk in my room you might like to use for the windows. If you want to come and get it after breakfast I would be happy to lend it to you.'

'Mrs Wilson already found some velvet,' Timothy replied, 'so we can use that for the walls.'

'A communal endeavour, then.'

Sephora only wished that she might spend the morning tucked up with her husband, in the safe warmth of his arms.

* * *

Daniel and Amethyst Wylde arrived after lunch, but the smiling Earl of Montcliffe whom she had met at the wedding looked a lot more serious now and went almost immediately off with Francis to his library, leaving her alone with Amethyst.

'Would you like to walk in the garden with me?' Lady Montcliffe asked, giving Sephora the distinct impression that Amethyst Wylde wanted a place to talk where they could not be overheard or listened upon.

A few moments later out on the pathways Daniel's wife halted in her observation of the formal gardens and turned to face her.

'I hope you don't mind my asking, but are you aware that the Duke of Winbury has named the date of his wedding to Miss Julia Bingham?'

Surprise was the only emotion Sephora felt at the news. And relief perhaps too, that Richard might have found a woman whom he could love in her stead.

'I didn't know that, but I am happy for him.'

Amethyst stooped to pick a sprig of lavender, twirling it in her fingers so that the scent wafted in the air between them. 'My father used to say that the world is like a pack of cards. Take one away and the rest fall into new patterns. Perhaps this is exactly what is happening here.'

'He sounds wise.'

'Papa passed away a year ago, but at least he saw my children born and he loved them.'

'You did not bring them today?'

'No. We left them with their grandmother because…' She stopped.

'Because they are safer there?'

'Then you know?'

'About Anna and the smuggling ring? Yes.'

'Did you also know that Francis received a medal in the Peninsular Campaign under Moore for his skills in shooting? He kept a whole regiment from being wiped out by allowing them safe access across a dangerous pass whilst he gave them cover. I should imagine these men will be child's play for him. Besides he has Daniel, Gabriel and Lucien to help him now. He is not alone.'

'Thank you.'

'And you are not alone either, Sephora. If you ever need advice or help you only need ask.'

'I think in the last few weeks I have become a different person to be honest. I used to think I was less than I am now and that it was normal for a man to tell a woman what to do. Richard did that to me and I accepted it, but Francis doesn't and yet…' She stopped.

'Yet?'

'The stakes are so much higher because of it and if I lost him I think I might simply fall to pieces. I am sick to my stomach with the fear of it.'

She had not meant to say as much, but under the gaze of kind dark eyes she found herself pouring out her heart and with little censure.

But Amethyst Wylde only smiled. 'Every wife who loves her husband feels the same, Sephora. In great love there also resides great loss and who cannot dismiss that.'

'You feel this with your husband?'

'I do, but these men of ours are warriors, and to clip the wings of a hawk is to destroy it. Better to fly alongside them, I always thought, for in knowledge there is less worry.'

'And that is why you came today?'

'It was a part of it although Adelaide also sent me to deliver a stone.' Rummaging in her bag she came out with a sphere of shining crystal. 'She said I was to give it to you for Anna. It is black tourmaline and used to calm fear in a child. She said to tell the girl its protective property will reflect all the bad thoughts of others away from her, like a magical mirror, and that it is the most powerful of the protectors. She also said that the one who owns it must lay the tourmaline in the sunshine every month to ensure its properties stay full and perfect and it is at its most fierce when placed under the user's pillow at night.'

For a moment Sephora could almost hear the unusual Adelaide Wesley saying this, her words blowing on the wind in an echo, and although she had never truly believed in the dark arts she was suddenly touched by the power and the beauty of a gift delivered just when she was most in need of it.

'Can you thank her? Can you tell her I will always be grateful for her thoughtfulness?'

Amethyst smiled. 'I shall make certain to give her your message, but she also sent one for you alone. I was to tell you that the oil she gifted you for fertility was proving a most excellent success and that there had been a record number of twins born in the surrounds of the Wesley estate this year.'

Sephora laughed at this confidence and beneath the walls of Colmeade amongst the scented walkways of an ancient garden she felt a peace that she never had before. This was her home and she was happy.

'I am so glad Francis found you, Sephora. Has he shown you the view here from the parapets yet? No. Well it is more than wonderful although he has never come back here enough.'

'He said as a child he felt a nuisance. Perhaps that is the reason?'

'His sister died at Colmeade House. Did you know that?'

She hadn't because he'd never told her, and Sephora thought with a heavy heart that everything she had found out about Francis St Cartmail was from someone else relating another awful past tragedy. She wanted to hear the truth from him, what he had felt, how he had managed. She wanted to hold him safe and tell him that she would always be there for him, by his side, and that he was her world and her anchor. All the words she had forbade him to use were sitting on her tongue as she looked towards the house in the hope that she might see him at the window of his library.

The Montcliffes stayed for an early dinner and then they left. Francis looked more relaxed than he had all day and Sephora reasoned he must be making progress with the matter of the smugglers.

Mindful of Amethyst's description of the view from the parapets she asked him to take her up there and a quarter of an hour later they were standing behind a low-slung wall on the very roof of the place, looking over a view that went on forever.

'My father used to come here for hours,' Francis said after a moment or two of watching Sephora at his side take in the majesty. 'He said this vista gave him the space to think and he would bring all his major problems up here to solve them.'

'Did your sister like it here, too?'

'Sarah?' The familiar anger at her loss welled from nowhere and he shook his head. 'No. She didn't like heights. My mother was the same.'

'Amethyst spoke to me of her today. How did she die?'

Her question was quiet but direct and instead of turning the personal away he loosened the stock at his throat and pointed to a thin line of grey a good mile away. 'See that river. It was winter and she had come home for a weekend with my aunt. After the rains the banks around it were swollen and she fell into it…'

He heard her take in a breath, and saw the grief and anguish in her eyes as she spoke.

'Like me? But no one saved her?'

'She was alone. Some people…believe she jumped.'

A small hand threaded through his, holding on tight. 'I don't believe that. If it helps at all I don't think Sarah would have thrown her life away. After all she was your sister, with the blood of the Douglases running through her. Strong blood. Unafraid and brave.'

He smiled at her fervent reply and took in a breath.

'I hope that was the case. I hope the soil just gave way as she was walking. I hope hers was a quick death.' He could imagine her alongside the river, watching the water and thinking. She'd have picked up small bits of flowering plants and old pieces of wood because he could long remember her doing so each time she had taken him with her. 'Perhaps girls need their mothers more, too. Like Anna. Without a guiding hand they might feel...'

'No. You were there and there was still Colmeade House. If she came here it meant that she loved it and perhaps a part of that was that she loved the outdoors. I think it was an accident and there was no one there to save her. Is her death the reason you dived in after me?'

He smiled and looked down at her, her blue eyes tearful and a worry in them that broke his heart.

'I jumped because I knew I had to, Sephora.' He saw her frown, but he knew suddenly that what he said was true. His father had come here to solve his problems all those years before and here he was trying to understand his own.

She believed in him even though many others didn't. She took his fears and put an interpretation on them that was believable and honest, words that made his heart whole piece by piece until his breath came easier. He could talk with her as he had never talked with anyone before.

Bringing her into him he turned her to the view and as the sun went down across the far hills they watched the majesty of it together in silence.

A little while later he spoke again. 'Today I have whittled those involved in the smuggling ring down to only two names. Tomorrow I will leave for London to confront them both.'

'It sounds dangerous?'

He laughed. 'Men of this ilk are always cowards and I have enough skill with a pistol and my hands to easily overcome them if they offer resistance. Besides, I want the chance at vengeance, for what he did to Anna and to us.'

He bent to her neck and kissed the soft sensitive parts with his lips and tongue. She tasted of freshness, soap and violets and when she tried to speak again he simply placed a finger across her lips.

'Make love to me here, Sephora, on the top of the world under the night sky. Just us. Without any other worries. Please.'

'Yes.' Her whisper was firm and he lifted her skirts and came in from behind, the warmth of her enveloping him, taking him in.

The cries were there again, not piercing screams as they had been once before but softer. From his chair by the window in his bedchamber Francis could see Sephora stir, but as he was awake he pulled on some clothes and walked down to Anna's room.

Her chamber was full of light when he came into

it, three candles glowing on her bedside table. His cousin was not in bed but sitting on the very end of it.

'I heard you crying.'

Her face was puffy and red as she looked up at him. 'I...am sorry if I woke you up.'

'You didn't. I never sleep well.' He felt at a loss as to what to say next, but Anna helped him.

'Sephora said that you lost your parents when you were young. Did you ever feel afraid because of it?'

'Not afraid exactly. More angry, I suppose.'

'But you loved them?' She waited till he nodded before going on. 'My mother was hardly ever home, but Clive...was nice sometimes.' Tears ran down her cheeks and she wiped at them with the edge of her nightgown. 'I see things.' This was said very quietly, each word enunciated with an exaggerated slowness.

'What sort of things?'

'I saw Clive when he was killed. He had the money in a bag and he had taken it. A man wanted it back.'

'Where were you when this was happening?' Francis tried to keep the tone of his voice soft, but the fear he could see on her face and hear in her words was worrying.

'Hiding under the hay. Clive told me to stay there and not come out, no matter what.'

'Did you see him? Did you see the man who killed Clive?'

'Just for a moment. He was tall. Clive thought he was a friend, I think, and they talked for a while, but so quietly I couldn't hear what they said.'

'And after?'

'The man left and I stayed hidden for a long time. When it was dark I came out and there was blood… everywhere…and I ran home. The gold was gone and I think he might try to take me away again. I think he wants to kill me, too.'

'I will never let him. I promise you, Anna. You are safe here. To get to you he will have to go through me first and now I know exactly who he is I can find him.'

Her chin began to wobble and she threw herself into his arms, a wet and soft little girl clinging as though her life depended on it.

He'd never been so close to a child before save for Seth's twins, but they were babies and the sobs racking through her made him grit his teeth. Her father had disowned her, her mother had seldom been around and Clive had used her foolishly in order to gain his financial rewards. No adult around her in all her life had been stable and good and true. But he would be. He and Sephora. His arm came around her back and he let her cry until she was finished, the front of his shirt soaked.

Across the room the old dog was yawning and stretching. 'I think Hopeful is tired and wants to go to sleep. Do you think you can now?'

Anna nodded. 'I like it here. I like my room and I like the books and the wardrobe and the attic at the top of the house. I like my name too. Anna St Cartmail. It means I belong.'

'Good, because this will always be your home.'

'And the man who tried to get me in the city…'

'Will never be able to try again.' As he said this Francis thought there would be a lot more at stake than just the words, but the explanation seemed to give Anna comfort because she scrambled back into bed.

Tucking the sheet up about her chin he bent to kiss her on the forehead. Like his mother used to do to him, he thought, though it had been a long time since he had remembered that.

'Can I blow out the candles now?' He asked her before he left and was pleased when she nodded.

A moment later he was back in his own bedroom. Sephora was sitting on the chair he had been using.

'I heard some of what Anna said. No wonder she is so very frightened.'

'Clive Sherborne knew the man who killed him and Anna said that he was tall. There are two names left on my list and one of them has a disease that has stunted his growth.'

'And the other?'

'A lesser lord of the *ton*, but not for much longer.'

'Would I know him?'

He held his smile and shook his head because he knew that the man was a cousin to the Duke of Winbury and Sephora would know him well.

Terence Cummings. The name hammered under each breath he took. *I will have you tomorrow and you will likely not know what hit you, you bastard.*

Sephora felt a jolt of some worry inside her as Francis turned away, a distant scattered recollection that had her reaching for the sense of it.

'You think this lord is high up in the smuggling chain.'

'I do. He'd have sent those who attacked me at Kew and he was probably there somewhere too, watching and hoping they might have hurt me a lot more than they did. People like that dwell in the shadows and attack in a way that holds no sense of justice and they like to see the results of their handiwork.'

He pulled her up from where she sat and she felt the heat on his skin despite his being out of bed in the middle of the night.

'But come, Sephora, let's warm each other. You are freezing.'

'And will you stay there beside me? All night?'

'I shall.'

He never seemed to feel the cold. Even now with his bare feet and light shirt and trousers he felt as hot as a furnace. She saw he had loosely tied his neck-cloth around his throat and smiled. A further protection for Anna. When he shed his clothes to sleep naked she thought again how very beautiful he was.

'What will you do when you find this man?' The blankets were back across them now and she lay in his arms, moonlight falling across the bed.

'I'll teach him a lesson in how not to treat a child and then I will bring him along to Bow Street.'

'Good,' she said and pushed herself up across him to take his lips beneath her own. 'Make sure your lesson is one he remembers.'

Sephora awoke an hour later into full consciousness, her eyes opening and her heart thumping. A lord of the *ton* he had said, and tall. A man who knew his liquor and would travel often. A man who was down on his luck in funds and had dreams of a lifestyle far more grand than his title allowed. A man who felt entitled and hard done by. A man who had been there in the gardens of Kew and would be interested in watching the fight between the Earl of Douglas and the others.

Francis was lying with his head on the pillow beside her, staring up at the ceiling, his feet moving up and down as if in deep contemplation.

'You haven't slept?'

He did not answer.

'What is the name of the lord you suspect, Francis?'

At that he turned, his eyes hard. For a moment she thought he might not tell her anything, as was Richard's way, but then the words came.

'Terence Cummings.'

The truth of the name had her scrambling up into sitting. 'He is a cousin of Winbury's and he was there at Kew. It was him who had led us down that particular pathway in order to come across you, in order to slander your name. He was there in the street in London, as well. I remember that now because I tried to call out to him but he did not come forward. Anna would have recognised him and he knew it.'

Francis took her hand in his own, his forefinger running across the ring he had given her on her wedding day. 'I don't want you involved in this, Sephora.

If you were to be hurt…' He stopped and swallowed, but she was not to be silenced.

'Richard did that to me, Francis. He made me less than I could be by his protections and in the end there was nothing left of respect in either of us.'

'What are you saying?'

'I know this man and I know his wife. Cummings's father, Richard's father's cousin, was the second son of a Viscount so he did not inherit much. He needed to work for it.'

'Or kill for it?'

'Can we prove that, do you think? The fact that he murdered Clive Sherborne for the gold and that he was the one who tried to take Anna?'

'I can goad him into thinking I have the proof until I do, for we are close to finding the paperwork trail he left. But to do so I will have to return to London.'

'Then take me with you to help.'

She hated the way her voice shook with fury and desperation, but she stuck to her intent and stared her husband directly in the eyes.

'Could I stop you?' There was the slightest humour in his tone.

'No.'

'Then let us try to have some sleep and we will leave in the morning. Anna can go to the Wyldes for a time until it is safe for I don't want her anywhere near the man and Montcliffe is impregnable. Celia and Timothy will accompany her. Confronting Cummings will however probably mean another dive in my already lowly standing in society if you are up to handling that.'

She smiled. 'I shall be right there beside you, Francis, and our reputations are the last thing to be worrying about. It's Anna we need to protect. But I remember something else Sally Cummings told me. She said that she and her husband would be leaving for an extended tour of Italy at the end of the month and that they might not be coming back to England for a long time.'

'That's the effect of a stolen fortune in gold because, believe me, someone will know that he has it and will want a share too. It also means we have to move quickly though or otherwise he will be gone.'

Sephora smiled. 'I used to be so scared of life I barely had an opinion, but now...'

'Now you are beside me identifying murderers and exposing them. I am not certain if that is such a good thing.'

She stopped him by bringing one finger to his lips. 'It is my salvation.'

Chapter Fourteen

They arrived in London late in the morning after seeing everyone safe at Montcliffe and letting Daniel and Amethyst Wylde know what it was that they were doing.

Anna clung on to them both as they left.

'When will you come back?'

'As soon as we have dealt with the man who tried to hurt you,' Francis stated. 'After that we can all live in complete safety.'

Maria was waiting for them with her maid in attendance at the Douglas town house as they arrived and she wanted to know every single thing that had happened since they had last been together. She also had surprising news of her own.

'Adam Stevenage has asked for my hand in marriage, but Papa is not pleased with the match and refuses to give his blessing. He thinks that if you did not marry a duke then I shall be able to. I am going to give him a month to get used to the idea and if he has not then I shall simply run away to Italy with Adam. It's a place I have always longed to go.'

Sephora watched Francis as he stood over by the window. Within a second of being in the house the problems of her family seemed to have landed upon him. But instead of being irritated as Richard would have been, he looked amused.

'Go to Venice and to Rome and then travel south to Naples to see Herculaneum and Pompeii.'

'You have been there?' Her sister looked astonished, but before he could answer the first question she had asked him another. 'You think I should go, then?'

'It sounds as if you have already made up your mind.'

'Mama and Papa and Josephine Allerly decry any place that is not England.'

'So our parents are talking with the Winburys again?' Sephora asked this because last she had heard they were not on speaking terms.

'Indeed they are. Josephine is at our house every second day because she is not happy with Richard's choice of bride-to-be and rues your loss.'

'His loss and my gain.' Francis came to stand next to Sephora and took her hand in his. Unexpectedly Maria blushed and began to mention the ball that was to be held the following evening.

'Richard and his newly betrothed will attend. Mama and Papa are going too.'

Sephora's heart sank at that information, but perhaps a ball might afford another opportunity.

'Are Richard's cousin Terence Cummings and his wife likely to be there?'

Maria laughed. 'I suppose if Richard is there then they will be too. I never liked him much and I thought Sally Cummings always seemed browbeaten. Perhaps being domineering and arrogant is a Winbury family trait? Why do you ask?'

'Cummings was there on the day Anna was snatched and I wanted to enquire if he saw anything we'd missed.' Not quite a lie, but not the truth either.

'You ought to be careful with him for I don't trust him at all and Adam almost came to fisticuffs with the man a week or so ago.'

'Why?' Francis asked this and Maria grimaced.

'He said something derogatory about you and Adam took umbrage. Cummings actually tried to get Adam to come into a business he'd invested in, something with liquor, I think, and he said he was doing very well in it. Their heated words put an end to that.'

When Maria was gone on the promise of seeing them tomorrow at the Clarkes' ball, Francis pulled Sephora over to the window and brought his arms about her. His embrace felt warm and comforting.

'Everything that's said of Cummings draws the noose tighter in about him. Daniel let me know that he was seen in Hastings on the night that Clive Sherborne died.'

'But it will be safe? You will be safe?'

'I will be and in public it might be easier to get to him. He won't have the opportunity of refusal to see me, though with your parents in attendance I'll understand if you want to wait...'

'No.' Her answer was certain. 'I want this finished with and Anna safe.'

He tipped her chin up and covered her lips with his own, a quiet languid kiss that turned suddenly into more. The quick streak of want made her breathless.

'If anything were to happen to you because of this...'

'It won't.'

Her finger drew a line down the edge of his cheek and settled on the scar. 'Amethyst said that you were decorated for bravery? Where are your medals?'

'In a drawer somewhere. There were a lot of other braver men who died doing the same thing as I did.'

'What was it you did to receive such an honour?'

He brought her closer so that she could feel the breath of him across her hair as he spoke.

'Our regiment was used to cover the movements of Moore's retreating army and to do that we were engaged in all the rearguard clashes. Between Lugos and Betanzos we lost more troops over a week than we did in the whole of the expedition altogether. It was the snow and the freezing rain—the mountain passes were slippery with ice and by that time discipline in the rank and file had broken down completely.'

'So it was every man for himself?'

'Well, it was and it wasn't. The French were close behind, you see, and the action at the back was causing as many deaths as the freezing temperatures fur-

ther up. So I positioned myself on a hill overlooking
the valley and picked the French off as I saw them,
and little by little our troops got through.'

'And your cheek?'

'You can't stay unseen forever, or protected, as
gunshot is easily traceable. A group of men came
at me from behind and a sabre caught my face. If I
hadn't turned when I did though it would have sliced
off my head and I saved myself by falling down the
ravine behind me, grabbing at rocks as I went to slow
my descent.'

'Then you followed the others towards Corunna.'

'No. By then I'd lost a lot of blood and so I made
for the closer port of Vigo. I travelled north-west at
night mostly and found a ship home. The transports
had left by the time I made it there, but a Spanish sea
captain took pity on me and transported me to England. His wife fixed my face.'

'She sewed it up?'

'She couldn't do that because by then it was too
inflamed. She poured hot water over the wound and
made a poultice of bread and milk. Whatever paste
she concocted to draw out the badness worked. The
scar just reminds me of how lucky I was to survive.'

'But you don't value your medals?'

'War makes you realise heroism is a changing
thing. One moment this and the next one that. I took
my orders and did my duty like a hundred other officers in the continent and a lot of them died without recognition or praise.' He raised his hands up
in front of him and looked down. 'Before that war I

was a different man. I thought less about death and more of life.'

Sephora closed her own fingers about his. 'I was the same. When I fell into the water from that bridge there was a part of me that thought it might have been easier if it just ended then. But I've changed now…'

'…and we are both made whole.' He finished the sentiment for her.

Different words from the ones Richard had constantly bombarded her with. Not *I love you*, but much, much more. The truth had her reaching for him.

'Love me, Francis,' she said as he nuzzled into her throat.

'I will.'

She dressed carefully for the Clarkes' ball in a gown that she had always thought looked well upon her. It was made of heavy silk with a woven pattern of blue leaves in flossed satin around the bodice and hem. The light had a trick of catching the silk and satin in a way that made the fabric almost live. Teamed with long gloves and a velvet pelisse mirroring the shades of the dress she felt…braver. She smiled at the thought, but it was true.

If she was going into battle she needed to be looking her best. She'd not had one outbreak of hives since becoming Francis's wife.

Francis wore his usual black, stark and sombre, the cloth and cut of breeches and jacket a classical one. He'd queued his hair tonight in a way that was not as severe as he usually wore it, and it suited him. His one nod to the more decorative came in the wearing of his ruby ring. Sephora thought he had never looked more beautiful or more dangerous.

'If Cummings attacks, you need to leave immediately. Do you promise me this, Sephora? Should I have to worry about you, too, I will be distracted and if you were to be hurt…' He stopped and swallowed.

'What if Terence is armed?'

He lifted the left opening of his jacket and she saw the heft of a knife beneath and was glad for it.

'But could there be others with him, do you think? Others in the *ton*?'

'Anything is possible, I suppose, but I have a feeling he acts alone. Anna saw only him in the warehouse and you said he was leaving the country with his wife at the end of the month, so he is probably not the sort to want to share his spoils. Ralph Kennings was the same.'

'He was a loner?'

'He was a man who wanted to have it all and he did not care whom he trampled on to make it happen. I'd known him in the Continent before I left for the Americas.'

This was new. He'd never offered information like this unbidden before. She stayed quiet hoping he might say more.

'We were in Spain together. On the hills above the pass where I had dug in to try to help the soldiers from the regiment below and I saw Kennings turn and shoot a British officer. Later I found out it was his wife's brother he had killed and later still I discovered the woman herself had disappeared. Putting two and two together I think he got rid of them both because she was a wealthy heiress and he wanted the money. How wealthy is Sally Cummings?'

Sephora simply stared at him. 'Very. Her father protected her assets in a document that said she would not inherit anything until she had been married for ten years. He never liked Cummings, you see, but apart from limiting the access to her funds there was not much more he could do about it.'

'And how long has she been married now?'

'It must almost be that number. You think he would murder her?'

'Killing is easy after you have done it once.' The hard tone he used made Sephora frown. 'I barely blinked an eye when I shot Kennings. It was only afterwards that...'

He stopped.

'That you regretted it?'

'Yes.' This time the hazel in his eyes was glazed in pain and torment.

'I love you, Francis.' The words came without thought, and they came from her heart, body and soul. 'I have loved you from the first moment you gave me your breath beneath the water and every second since.'

Unexpectedly he laughed. 'I take you to my bed and love you in every way I have ever learnt with care and attention and fortitude and you do not say anything. Then when I confess that I have killed a murderer in cold blood and am sorry for it, you tell me this. Is there some law of logic that exists only in women, some way of tangling a man's thoughts until they do not have a mind of their own, until there is no certainty of anything any more? Save that of knowing I love you too.'

'You do?' She could barely utter the words with the thickness in her throat.

'When you fell off that bridge with your riding habit a living emerald in the sunshine and your tiny hat spiralling through the air behind, I thought... I thought if I could not find you beneath the water then I should die with the trying before I gave you up.'

Sephora smiled at such a truth. 'Was it preordained do you think, a bee sting at that exact moment and a horse that would react so violentl? One moment later and it would not have happened as it did or a moment sooner and you may have missed me altogether.'

'Love can be a powerful thing,' he whispered and reached for her hand. '*"Doubt truth to be a liar; But never doubt I love."* With me it will be always and forever, Sephora.'

She felt the tears pool in her eyes. 'When this is over I want you to take me home, Francis, and I want for us to have babies. Lots of them, as many as we can fill Colmeade House with for I am done with the *ton* and London town. All I need is you.'

The large ballroom at the Clarkes' town house was full and busy when they arrived and found their places with Gabriel and Adelaide Hughes, Daniel and

Amethyst Wylde and Lucien, Alejandra and Christine Howard.

Sephora was glad Francis would not be alone in this quest and glad, too, that her parents were nowhere at all in sight. Despite the fighting words of a half an hour ago she felt nervous and worried though her elation with the proclamations that they had given each other also lingered.

She'd known she loved Francis for a long time and had felt the same regard back from him, but the words she had once censored were now valued and dear, no longer the oft repeated worthless and unimportant sentiments that they had been with Richard.

When a waltz struck up he leaned over and asked her to partner him. 'It will give us a better view of the room and those within it,' he said quietly as they took their place on the floor.

With his arms about her and the chandeliers above, Sephora simply leaned into his chest and felt, this moment, this second, with a husband who was good and strong and true. And beautiful, she added. So beautiful she could see a myriad women watching them, watching him. Her fingers tightened about his.

'Winbury is at the far end of the room, Sephora, but I can see no sign of Terence Cummings.'

She smiled, her musings so different from his alert watchfulness. Gabriel and Adelaide danced nearby and the Earl of Wesley's eyes scanned the room with the same purpose as Francis did.

Then Sally Cummings came into view, standing alone beside one of the large windows and looking upset. A sense of foreboding filled Sephora. How easily she could have been a woman exactly like her in ten years or so if she had married Richard, for the uncertain nervous expression was familiar; she had seen it so many times on her own face in the mirror.

When the waltz finished Francis led her from the floor towards her parents, who had now arrived and were standing on one side waiting for them.

'I hope you are well.' This greeting was given by her mother with some coldness though her father was a little more effusive.

'It is good to see you again, Sephora. I have missed you, but you look happy.'

'Is Maria here tonight?' She glanced around for her sister.

'Not yet. I think she will no doubt make an appearance a little later. Aunt Susan is with her.'

Her father turned then to Francis. 'I hope your ward is recovered after her fright in London, St Cartmail, and if there is anything I can do to help you find the culprits please do ask.'

'Thank you, Lord Aldford, but it is all in hand and the man responsible for the kidnapping should soon be facing the law.' Francis was polite but distant and Sephora thought at this rate the two men should never know each other well enough to be friends. She was glad when Lucien Howard greeted Francis from behind and her parents moved on.

'Cummings is here. He was in the card room, but he has gone outside now for some air. He's been drinking heavily so you might want to be careful. I'll give you a few moments to sound him out.'

Thanking Lucien, Francis took her arm.

'I would ask you to go and stand with your parents, Sephora, but I can see it in your eyes that you will not go.'

Despite the situation his voice sounded relaxed, but then he had been in difficulties many times in his life before by all accounts and was probably well able to disguise any misgivings. Her own heartbeat pounded in her ears.

Francis scanned the space around them as they walked through the wide French doors. Two men at the far end of the terrace were engaged in conversation and at the other end a couple lingered.

Winbury's cousin was drinking, for two empty glasses sat on a marbled table near him and he held another one. A dash of anger crossed his face as they joined him.

'I did not think you were back in London, Lady Sephora. All my sources said that you were ensconced most happily at the Douglas family estate in the middle of Kent.'

'Indeed we were until this morning, but business has called us to the city.'

There was a look in Cummings's eyes that began to worry Francis and turning to Sephora he spoke quietly. 'Could you go inside and get me a drink? I find I am suddenly thirsty.'

He wanted his wife away from here and from undercurrents he could not quite understand for there was some wrongness in this situation that played about the edge of his caution. Sephora did not turn away though and as the two from further along the terrace moved closer he saw their faces for the first time. It was the men who had tried to take Anna in London though they were dressed far differently today. Cummings had known them after all, just as Sephora had said he did.

Pushing Sephora behind him he did not wait for them to attack. His first punch brought down the heavier man and he lay there motionless though the younger man had brought out a knife and was circling him with it.

Without hesitation Francis took his own blade from the strap at his breast and crouched, a flash of steel against the darkness as he moderated his breathing, slowing it down and steadying it before moving forward.

His opponent was good but Francis was better and within a few moments he was able to strike the weapon from the other's fist and bring his blade down into the soft flesh of the man's arm. He couldn't kill him, not here a few yards from a ball in progress and a room containing a hundred women who would be horrified by such violence.

Using the heavy handle he slammed down hard across the other man's head as the fellow ran at him and he too, fell to the floor.

Then things took an unexpected turn as Cummings lunged for Sephora and his grip was tight around her neck.

'Drop the knife, Douglas, or I will kill her.' The words were snarled and furious as Francis raised his hands. Sephora's face was deathly pale and her eyes were wide. As Cummings's fingers pressed deeper, Francis did exactly what he asked, laying the knife to one side of him and speaking quietly.

'It is over, Cummings. I know what you have done. You can only make it worse for yourself by harming an innocent.'

He moved sideways slowly as he spoke, the anger in him blood red and boiling. One second was all it would take to get to Cummings, but it had to be the right second. A neck could be broken easily with enough pressure and Sephora's was slender and small. He could do nothing at this moment but wait. The first man at his feet was recovering and he saw Cummings's eye flicker at the movement.

'Clive Sherborne was a colleague of yours, was he not?' Francis asked the question because in an impasse of this sort it was good to engage the participants in dialogue in order to buy time. He knew from experience that the longer these standoffs went on for the less likely someone would be hurt.

The man was arrogant enough to think he could still get away with murder, but Francis could see Lucien's outline against the doors.

'Clive Sherborne was an impediment. But why hurt Anna? What had the child done to harm you?'

'She was never a child, don't you see. She was his snitch, the one with the eyes and the brain. Without her that coward and thief would have never risen as he did through the ranks of the smugglers. Without her he'd have been dead long before he was.'

'My cousin saw you kill her father. She was hiding under the straw in the corner of the warehouse. She can identify you, Cummings, and she has.'

The older of the two men Francis had knocked down now sat up, a quiet movement that took Cummings's attention, and he loosened his grip.

It was enough.

Francis flung himself at Winbury's cousin knocking both him and Sephora over, coming up across Cummings quickly and punching him hard as his wife scrambled away. With his free foot he kicked the recovering miscreant in the head, pleased at the cracking sound of a skull hitting stone.

'Run, Sephora,' he ordered, wanting her out of the reach of any more violence, but instead she stayed where she was and spoke with feeling.

'You were there, Terence, there on the street when the man tried to kidnap Anna. I called to you for help, but you disappeared. You didn't want anyone to see you let alone a small girl who recognised you as the one who had murdered her father.'

'Prove it, Douglas.' Terence Cummings was so wrathful now he could barely get the words out, blood pouring down his face from a broken nose. 'Who'd believe you anyway, with your more-than-questionable reputation and the marks of a criminal around your throat?'

His shout drew others from the main ballroom out onto the terrace and Lucien came to stand beside him. Sally Cummings was there too, but she made no move to stand beside her husband, her face ashen and her eyes sunken.

Then Richard Allerly pushed through to kneel down to his bleeding cousin.

'If you have killed him, Douglas, I will have you hanged properly this time and a good job, too, you bastard.'

The hushed anger of the gathering crowd was familiar and Francis tried to take in breath to answer, but his throat felt tight. Sephora's parents stood ten yards away behind him, the horror on their faces reflecting all that they imagined their daughter's life to have become.

A whole group of people who hated him and would not spare the time to even find out the truth. All of a sudden he could not even be bothered refuting the accusation. His eye ached, his hand and back, too, and one of the damned miscreants had managed to land a punch right on the wound of his healing shoulder.

A voice then rang out across all the others. It was Sephora and she was no longer anything like the girl he had first met. Now she was a furious avenging angel who faced the crowd with all the anger of the wrongfully damned and looked them all straight in the eyes.

* * *

These people thought the Earl of Douglas was the one at fault here, so easily and seamlessly, so without thought, explanation or reason. It was how the *ton* worked after all. Anyone who did not quite fit within its narrow confines was to be ostracised and excluded, cast out into the role of wrongdoer and disreputable.

Francis looked battered and defeated, the cut across his eyes sending blood onto his damaged cheek and he was holding his right-hand side and breathing harshly.

Well, she would fight every person on this terrace if necessary and then more besides to protect him. The anger pummelled through her like a living bolt of fire, untrammelled and vehement. He had been accused wrongly in the Hutton's Landing by a crowd baying for his blood and she would never let anything like that happen again here.

'Terence Cummings is the murderer… You all have it wrong. He was the one who killed Clive Sherborne and tried to kidnap a young child. He is a smuggler who makes money out of others' misfortunes and it was him who paid men to attack the Earl of Douglas on this terrace and in Kew Gardens. I swear this is true on the hope of my soul in Heaven.'

Lucien Howard and Gabriel Wesley had the men in hand and their presence added to her truths. Sally Cummings was crying profusely but in a softer tone now and she made no effort to refute the accusation.

'We'll take him to Bow Street.' Lucien said this

and a murmur ran through the onlookers. She saw a quick communication go between him and Francis.

For so many years her husband had fought alone, managed alone, lived alone. Well, no longer. She would make certain he was seen by others in exactly the same way she saw him. Honourable and solid.

Without thought she faced the Duke of Winbury. 'Perhaps, Your Grace, you should be more careful about whom you associate with in the future. Your cousin appears to be everything you say he is not and we have the witnesses to prove it. He is a murderer, a kidnapper and a thief.' Her words were easily heard and she did not falter as she caught the face of her mother. Elizabeth looked shocked and pale. 'My husband and I will wait to receive your apology, Richard. I hope it will be forthcoming.'

With that she simply stepped back and threaded her arm through Francis' and without a backward glance they made their way from the terrace, through the colourful crowded ballroom, past the silent watchful musicians and out into the night. Hailing the waiting Douglas carriage, they quickly got in.

'It is over, Francis.' Sephora saw that he shook and the pallor of his skin was white.

'God' was his only reply and she laughed then, a way to relieve the tension she was to think later, a way to find a pathway through everything that had happened. He had given her breath beneath the bridge all those weeks ago and she was giving him some back right now. A space. A time to regather.

The small and utter truth of love.

This came without reflection or thought. It was the wholeness of them together, two halves that were perfectly melded and undeniably linked.

This was what marriage should be like. A formidable team who would fight everyone who tried to harm them and would be balanced and equal and honest. No one side dominant, no other side weakened. She would never let him down as certainly as she knew he would not disappoint her either.

'I love you, Francis,' she said and meant it. 'You are my heart.'

When he smiled back she placed her hand across his and watched as his bloodied and shaking fingers wound about her own.

Gabriel Hughes, Daniel Wylde and Lucien Howard came to the town house an hour and a half after they had arrived home and they were jubilant.

'Those who Cummings had employed to rough you up, Francis, were only too pleased to tell the truth of their part in the proceedings in order to escape heavier penalties. Sally Cummings herself provided the rest of the proof by promising to produce papers implicating her husband in the sale of illicit liquor across many outlets in the city. She said he needed to be locked up for good as he was a threat to each and every one of the upstanding citizens of London town.'

'Comprehensive, I'd say.' Francis was astonished. 'Why did she do it, do you think?'

'Oh, she told us that and in a voice that most of the *ton* would have been party to. She'd been bullied by him for far too long, she said. Her father had warned her of the nature of the man, but she had not listened. The Duke of Winbury looked nothing but furious at such aspersions towards his family.'

'Miss Julia Bingham made short shrift of the night I noticed.' Lucien Howard said this as he helped himself to a glass of Francis's best brandy. 'Your parents too, Sephora, were less than impressed by Winbury's defence of a man who was so patently lying. Your mother was crying, but this time I think it was at the realisation of her own foolishness in believing in the lies about your husband and the dispersing crowd itself felt much the same, Francis. I think you have been exonerated.'

'Out of great evil comes a goodness.' Gabriel Hughes muttered this and they all laughed, the relief of the evening's tension unfolding in a way they could never have truly predicted.

Sephora took her husband's hand in her own. If she ever lost him... She stopped herself. Once she had worried about things from dawn to dusk, but now with Francis at her side anything and everything was possible. She could breathe again, easily.

Chapter Fifteen

Two days later they were finally at Colmeade House and everything was back in place. Anna had been overjoyed at being home again and, after sitting down and reassuring her that all her worries were over, had easily settled to sleep that night.

'Mrs Billinghurst looked the prettiest I have ever seen her appear,' Sephora said softly as Francis and she lay in bed later that night, the curtains pulled back and the wide summer sky about them.

'Her husband died a long while ago and left her largely penniless. She is probably as relieved to have a home as Anna is. Timothy seemed well too, and Hopeful looks fatter than when we left him.'

'Mrs Wilson feeds him the best scraps from the kitchen. I've seen her do it. You are beset by a houseful of strays, Francis, who are all thriving here. Myself included.'

He laughed at that, the lines at the sides of his eyes creasing into humour. 'A houseful of family,' he amended, 'and I should never wish to change it.'

'What will happen to Terence Cummings do you think? And Sally?'

'Cummings will stand trial for the murder of Clive Sherborne and his wife will undoubtedly return to her family with a much better understanding of what she needs in a husband. She is still young and wealthy. Let's hope she chooses a man next time who is honourable.'

'My parents sent a note to ask if they might come down to visit when we are settled in again. It arrived today.'

'I'd like that.'

She sat up and looked at him directly. 'Would you? Even after all that has happened with them?'

'They were trying to protect you from difficulty and who is to say that I won't act the same when Anna brings home a suitor and he is not everything I'd hoped for her.'

'I wish I had known your parents and your sister. I wish they were here too, with us.'

'Perhaps they are. If I ever lost you, Sephora, I know that you would sit here right next to my heart. You would never be gone from inside me. I swear it.'

'You see that is why I love you, Francis. You do not parrot the words that mean nothing. You only ever give me a truth and after all the lies I am so thankful for it.'

'The truth?' His voice was hesitant, a tone in it so unlike the certainty she usually heard she felt a shift of worry. 'Can I tell you something, Sephora? Something that sounds…strange?'

He sat up now too, and leaned against the head-board, bringing her in beside him and tucking her there close.

'When you fell into the water I heard my sister's voice as clear as day, and as certain as I hear yours now beside me.'

'What did she say?'

'She said, *"Save her, Francis, and save yourself."* I heard her plainly and that has never happened to me before or since. And she was right.'

'Right?'

'We saved each other.'

She nodded. 'I've been writing poems in the book you gave to me. Can I read one to you?'

When he said he would like that she leaned over to the bedside table and opened the small top drawer, extracting her diary from it.

'It's not very good and you might think...'

He placed a finger over the words. 'Go on.'

Clearing her throat she began, though she felt as nervous as she had ever been before.

'"*You brought me from the darkness; And the cold of below; Up into the light of laughter and love; And breath that was mine to live in...*"'

'Breath,' he whispered when she had finished the next few verses and took her hand into his own. 'We gave each other breath, and what more from life could you want than that?'

'I love you, Francis, with all my heart.'

As his hands threaded through her hair he sealed

her lips with his, pushing forward to find all that it was he offered.

He was her heart just as she was his. They had both been lost and were now found, the loneliness and uncertainty swept away in a wave of truth.

She had crossed a threshold and everything she had known was changed for finally she was home.

* * * * *

MILLS & BOON MODERN IS
HAVING A MAKEOVER!

The same great stories you love,
a stylish new look!

Look out for our brand new look
COMING JUNE 2024

MILLS & BOON

afterglow BOOKS

From showing up to glowing up, Afterglow Books features authentic and relatable stories, characters you can't help but fall in love with and plenty of spice!

OUT NOW

To discover more visit:
Afterglowbooks.co.uk

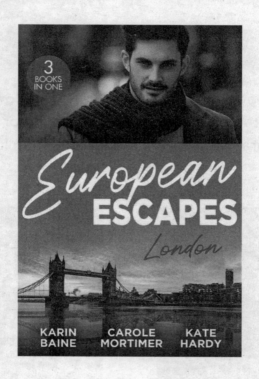

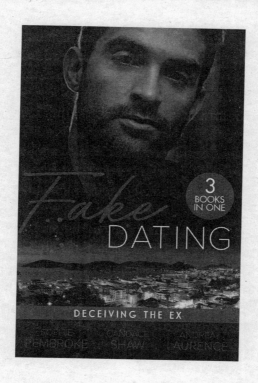

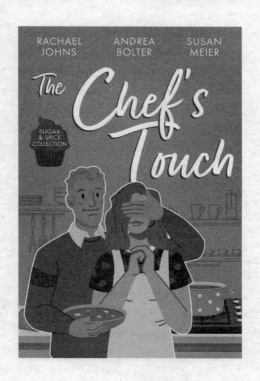

LET'S TALK
Romance

For exclusive extracts, competitions and special offers, find us online:

- **f** MillsandBoon
- **X** @MillsandBoon
- **⊙** @MillsandBoonUK
- **♪** @MillsandBoonUK

Get in touch on 01413 063 232

MILLS & BOON

THE HEART OF ROMANCE

A ROMANCE FOR EVERY READER

MODERN

Prepare to be swept off your feet by sophisticated, sexy and seductive heroes, in some of the world's most glamourous and romantic locations, where power and passion collide.

HISTORICAL

Escape with historical heroes from time gone by. Whether your passion is for wicked Regency Rakes, muscled Vikings or rugged Highlanders, awaken the romance of the past.

MEDICAL

Set your pulse racing with dedicated, delectable doctors in the high-pressure world of medicine, where emotions run high and passion, comfort and love are the best medicine.

True Love

Celebrate true love with tender stories of heartfelt romance, from the rush of falling in love to the joy a new baby can bring, and a focus on the emotional heart of a relationship.

HEROES

The excitement of a gripping thriller, with intense romance at its heart. Resourceful, true-to-life women and strong, fearless men face danger and desire - a killer combination!

From showing up to glowing up, these characters are on the path to leading their best lives and finding romance along the way – with plenty of sizzling spice!

To see which titles are coming soon, please visit

millsandboon.co.uk/nextmonth

MILLS & BOON
HEROES
At Your Service

Experience all the excitement of a gripping thriller, with an intense romance at its heart. Resourceful, true-to-life women and strong, fearless men face danger and desire – a killer combination!